# THE LIONESS

GIGI GRIFFIS

This is a work of fiction. Though inspired by a true story, the details of characters, setting, events, etc. are products of the author's imagination. Any resemblance to persons living or dead is purely coincidental.

For content warnings, visit gigigriffis.com.

Text copyright © by Gigi Griffis
Cover designed by MiblArt

All rights reserved.

*This one's for the villains.*

# 1343

# CHAPTER I
# CLISSON, FRANCE

The end began with the cat.

Black as the depths of the sea—seeming less like a cat and more like a cat-shaped hole in the world—the cat arrived at Castle Clisson just as the sun lit up the courtyard with its morning hues of pink and gold.

Jeanne watched from an upper window with a half-smile as the panicked servant girls tried to shoo it out, screaming and skittering away any time it turned toward them. Black cats were bad omens. The familiars of witches. Dark portents. Messengers of the devil himself.

The servants crossed themselves and squealed and brandished rags and sticks. Even serious Sandrine—usually the least easily ruffled of Jeanne's attendants—stood back from the animal, not screaming, but not making a move to help either.

Jeanne rolled her eyes and turned from the window to make her way down to remove the offending creature herself. She didn't believe in omens or the familiars of witches or that the devil had enough interest in the affairs of men to send his servants disguised as animals to torment them.

But she did believe in fleas.

Cats had no place in her castle, so down the stairs she went. But as she rounded the last corner and stepped into the courtyard, the cat no longer mattered at all. Because a sweaty, sharp-smelling, panting young soldier stood flanked by her gate guards, holding a letter with the king's seal.

Her heart tripped over itself and picked up speed.

It was about Olivier—she knew before she opened it. Her warrior husband, love of her life, father of her youngest children, had been captured by the British months ago, and Jeanne had spent every day since trying to get him home. She'd written letter after letter to every damn fool at the French court. She'd ridden across the countryside to beg Charles de Blois, the Duke of Brittany, a good friend and a relative of King Philip's, to petition the king for her.

She'd wanted to ride straight to Paris and demand an audience with Philip herself, but Charles had talked her out of it. "The king needs a light touch," he'd said. And he was right, Jeanne knew, even if it made her body hum with impatience. She was all sharp edges, no patience for the diplomatic nonsense of court. She'd been like that even as a child. Wild and fierce and usually fighting mad, never patiently explaining her side of things. Unless kicking someone's shins instead of punching them in the throat counted as patience.

Her mother had tried to teach her. Noble couples ruled together because the world believed it brought balance— the man a symbol of unflinching justice, the woman one of mercy and diplomacy. The two united were more powerful than either one could be alone.

"You stand for mercy, Jeanne," she'd said.

It never stuck.

And, so, at Castle Clisson, noble justice was a double-edged sword. Diplomacy was Olivier's domain. Jeanne's version of mercy was a quick death.

But now, patience or no, sharp edges or diplomatic ones, someone had finally sent news. Was Olivier dead? Alive? Had the king arranged a prisoner trade like Jeanne had been begging for? She ripped the letter from the messenger's hands and started reading before he could even explain himself.

It took her three reads to comprehend the words, but eventually the letter's meaning became clear. Olivier was safe.

*Safe.* The word she'd been starving for.

She closed her eyes to keep from crying, silently thanking every god and saint she could think of. When she opened her eyes again, she saw the cat and thanked it too. Probably blasphemy. But who knew which god, saint, holy relic, or even messenger of the devil was responsible for bringing Olivier safely home. Jeanne believed in hedging her bets.

She read the letter a fourth time—every word a relief. The British had agreed to a prisoner trade and a truce. Her husband and four other noblemen had been sent on their way, shipped across the English Channel, seen by the king's best doctors, and declared in good health.

Jeanne cleared her throat and steadied herself, then looked up at the messenger. "Is there anything else?"

"Yes, m'lady. On the Duke of Brittany's request, your husband is a special guest of the king, and a tournament has been scheduled to honor him and the other returning war heroes and to celebrate the truce."

Jeanne's mischievous smile returned to her lips. Finally, the world had righted itself. Her husband was back. A truce was set. And a tournament in his honor—it was more than she could have hoped for.

She nodded to the messenger and the guards, then strode back into the castle. The cat followed, servants crossing themselves and jumping out of its way. Jeanne ignored it, no longer thinking about fleas.

She went straight to the nurseries, dropped to the ground and wrapped wild little six-year-old Oli in her arms. He squirmed to get away, always more of a fighter than a snuggler, but Jeanne held on tight, kissing his face as he scowled and squirmed and whined, "*Maman*, stop!"

Four-year-old Guillaume, the most tenderhearted of Jeanne's babies and never one to miss a snuggle, threw himself on top of his maman and squirming brother. And little Jeanne—two years old and always terrified of missing out—launched herself clumsily into the melee as well, knocking grown-up Jeanne onto her side, where she burst into a simultaneous fit of tears and laughter as she tried to wrap all three in her arms at once. Her family—her bright, wildly alive, breathtaking family—was secure again.

The children's nurses stood back, smiling at the exchange as Oli—who'd succeeded in squirming away—picked up a toy sword. "I challenge you to a duel, Maman!"

"A duel?" Jeanne sat up, eyes dancing, tears still streaming, trying to force her face into a look of solemnity. "Good knight, I shall take up your challenge!"

She sat forward on her knees and reached for one of the small wooden swords as Oli launched forward with a rebel yell and clacked his sword against hers, his tongue poking from the side of his mouth in intense concentration. He didn't have any training yet, so he did as children do:

aiming sword at sword, never actually trying to hit Jeanne, to get around her defenses.

A fierce pride built in Jeanne's chest. One Olivier was a war hero, the other was practicing for a day when he might be the same. Guillaume and little Jeanne, watching from the sidelines, could grow up to be anything.

She let Oli get another few good clacks in, then ducked to the left and wrapped her arms around his waist, disarming him with her left hand and lifting him squealing into the air.

"Maman, you cheated!" he bellowed with all the offense his six-year-old voice could muster. "I was beating you!"

"Yes, little man. You were a true knight," she said, placing him on the floor and kissing his forehead as he squirmed away and aimed his sword at her again. "But Maman has some important things to do now."

"What important things?" he asked, straightening and clasping his hands behind his back in a perfect imitation of his father.

Before she could answer, there was a tug on her skirts and a startled gasp from one of the nurses at the side of the room.

Jeanne turned to find sweet Guillaume holding the black cat in one arm—its legs hanging almost to the floor— and tugging on her with the other. "Maman, is she for us? Can we keep her?"

The nurses crossed themselves. Little Jeanne realized what Guillaume was holding and squealed with delight, rushing toward him. Oli leaned slightly to the left to peek around Jeanne's skirts.

She looked at each child in turn, her heart softening. Their father had been in a dungeon for months upon months. Their mother was about to leave them with their nurses for weeks. They didn't understand any of it, and she wasn't going to deny them the cat. Fleas be damned.

"Yes, but she'll have to be washed," she said, looking at the nervous nursemaids so that they understood that the task would fall on them.

The two youngest squealed and hugged and petted the cat, who took it all in stride, but Oli wasn't one to get distracted.

"Maman." He stomped a foot as she turned back to face him. "*What important things?*"

"Little warrior," she answered, kneeling again to be eye-to-eye with her son, "I'm bringing your papa home."

## CHAPTER 2

# PARIS, FRANCE

Jeanne's skin was flush with excitement and impatience as she wandered the tournament grounds searching for Olivier. It had taken too long to ride to Paris. She'd gotten in too late, arrived at his rooms just after he'd left, and now finding him among the thousands streaming onto the grounds was near impossible.

She'd seen Duke Charles—her friend who'd petitioned the king on her behalf—in the corridor on her way out and now she cursed herself for not going after him. She should have asked if he knew where on these godforsaken grounds Olivier was preparing for his fight. But he'd seemed busy, giving her a small wave before walking briskly away, and she'd been too impatient to do anything but go straight to the tournament grounds. She sighed at herself. By the age of forty-three, you'd think she'd have learned that impatience only made things take longer.

Now, she weaved her way across the familiar scene. The metallic ring of swords colliding echoed across the fields, occasionally drowned out by the cheers and jeers from the surrounding crowd, already betting on the training fights. Soldiers and knights danced deftly toward and away from each other in the circular dueling arena. A step to the right here. A lunge to the left there. A straightforward attack from a bigger, stronger opponent. A quick bit of footwork from a slender young noble. A clever series of feints from the king's current champion.

Jeanne passed the duels and training fights and wandered to the jousting arena, a set of straight wooden poles running across its center, marking each jouster's side. Bulky armored men charged toward each other with heavy poles and curved shields. Larger men used their weight to unseat smaller men. Smaller men used their agility to unseat larger.

Excitement sparked across Jeanne's skin. She loved everything about tournaments. The dust. The fights. The bloodied noses. The screaming, frenzied crowd. And Olivier, somewhere nearby, strong and tall, fastened into boiled leather and gleaming steel, testing the balance of his sword.

The first time she met Olivier was at one of the bigger, more colorful events she'd attended—right there in Paris. He'd been cocky then. Handsome, widowed, and hiding his grief by whispering sweet nothings to any woman he came across. When he was fool enough to try that with Jeanne— cornering her in a dim hallway at the opening day's feast, telling her she was the most beautiful woman he'd ever seen, and going straight in for a kiss before she'd even answered—she punched him in the nose.

She smiled a little at the memory of his shocked expression, the way he'd staggered backward and brought his hands to his face. After a few stunned moments, he burst into laughter, and Jeanne, still outraged, had turned on her toes and marched imperiously back to the main hall.

It wasn't until she saw him fight a few days later—powerful, strong, and agile with a sword in hand—that she accepted his fervent apologies and stopped ignoring his advances.

Fourteen years later, she still loved to watch him fight. They called him a wood-waster. The kind of man who destroyed poles and shields beyond recognition every time he took the field.

By the time Jeanne found Olivier at the hand-to-hand combat field, it was too late to do anything but watch him spar. The crowd was already screaming its approval at both the tall, dark-featured noble who'd returned a hero from British captivity and his light-haired, light-complexioned Flemish opponent, come down from the north to prove his mettle. Jeanne elbowed her way to the front and leaned forward on a rail to watch.

The two circled once, twice, and then Olivier attacked—feinting right and swinging left. The northern knight danced away with a booming, pleased laugh.

So began an exceptional fight. Two seasoned warriors feinting, fighting, attacking, defending. Olivier took a blow to his sword arm and returned one to the northern knight's upper thigh, knocking him off balance. The crowd screamed its approval and threw cabbage, rocks, and handfuls of dirt into the arena in a frenzy. Around Jeanne, men took bets, women cheered support, and children darted through the legs of the adults, playing out their own duels with sticks and practice swords.

Olivier kept coming, raining blows on the northerner from every side. The northman lost his laugh, his focus now on defense.

Jeanne smiled. Watching Olivier fight was almost as good as doing it herself. Her muscles felt pleasantly tight, and she found herself shifting on her feet with each strike. It reminded her of her own most recent fight—against a traveler who'd seen her riding alone on a road near home and thought she was an easy target. She'd broken his nose before tying him behind her horse, dragging him back to the castle, and challenging him to trial by combat.

They'd thrown the man in a two-foot-wide pit up to his navel in the middle of one of her husband's fields, given him his choice of weapons, and unleashed Jeanne to the fight. She would have preferred to fight him face to face with none of this pit-up-to-the-navel nonsense. But such was the law—a woman was given the advantage in trial by combat.

They said it was because women were weaker. They said it was because women were untrained. They said it was fair because women were more likely to be merciful. *They* didn't know Jeanne.

But the law was the law. She respected the crown, and if that meant taking an advantage in combat, well, the man had brought it on himself when he'd wrapped his meaty hand around her ankle and tried to pull her from her horse.

Even with its irritating unevenness, the fight had been exhilarating. And, of course, Jeanne had won.

She imagined Olivier was feeling that same exhilaration now as he lunged left, dodged right, swung his sword in a perfect arc. And then, out of nowhere, his opponent dodged under Olivier's elbow and swung his own sword hard against Olivier's side. The crowd gasped as Olivier lost balance and the northman lifted his weapon to deliver a winning blow. Jeanne sucked a breath through her teeth.

But it was a feint.

A trick.

And when Olivier's sword came up, it not only caught

the northman's but tilted just enough to the right to throw the man off balance. Just long enough for Olivier to bring his own sword back around and stop it a hair's breadth away from his opponent's neck. After a stunned, unmoving moment, the northman's shoulders slumped and he dropped his sword.

*Defeated.* Just as Jeanne had defeated her attacker in trial by combat. Just as they both had defeated their enemies over and over again. Just as they both would defeat their enemies in the years to come.

The crowd roared. A whole rotten cabbage arced through the arena and caught the northman on the shoulder. Jeanne thought she heard Olivier's gorgeous, wild, roaring laugh cut through the cheering.

He glanced up and she winked at him from the sidelines, wishing that their babies were there to see their father triumph and then wishing that her two oldest children—from her first marriage—had made it to the tournament. They were grown, their own father long dead, and Jeanne could never understand why they wouldn't let Olivier step into the gap. If they could only see how strong he was. How clever. If only they'd come watch him fight.

It was mid-afternoon that same day when the king called the noblemen—all captured by the British in the siege of Vannes and so recently returned—to the field. Each had traded his armor for his finest clothes. None wore a sword. It was an unusual choice for men being honored for their feats at war, Jeanne thought, but she supposed fine clothes looked better than boiled leather and armor, and swords felt more out of place with fine clothes.

All day, Olivier had been shuffled from fight to fight, obligation to obligation, with barely a moment in between to wink at her across a field, reach across a railing and squeeze her hand. But after this, the day would finally be theirs. Jeanne could wrap her arm through his and they'd slip away to be alone. *Finally alone.* After so many months apart and now so many hours of watching him fight without being able to throw herself into his embrace.

How she longed for that moment.

As the men lined up in the dusty arena under the brilliant summer sun to be honored, recognized, showered in praise and gratitude and favors, Jeanne shivered with a thrill of anticipation and pride. She sat with the courtiers and nobles in one of the boxes, built to shade the upper classes from the sun or rain, a few rows away from the king's box, where the most powerful people in the kingdom, including her friend Duke Charles, enjoyed the best view in the arena.

She caught the young duke's eye and he inclined his head toward her. She passed him so quickly earlier that she hadn't had a chance to thank him. For listening that day she'd ridden to his castle and pleaded for his help bringing Olivier home. For petitioning his uncle, King Philip, to make the trade that had set Olivier free. Now she mouthed the word. "Merci." And he inclined his head again, mouth twitching with the perpetual smirk he was known for, the one that told everyone he believed he was the smartest person in the room.

Suddenly, the voice of the king's champion boomed across the field, ordering silence. The Parisian peasants quieted. The nobles sat straighter in their seats. It was time for the ceremony. Time to recognize these great men.

King Philip stood and motioned to an advisor Jeanne didn't know. A spokesman.

She frowned. These men had risked their lives for the crown. The least the king could do was address them himself. Why choose a lesser man? She'd heard the king had gotten stranger in recent years—moody, impulsive, secretive, untrusting to a fault, no longer the friendly young man who'd knighted Olivier so many years ago—but still, he should have been king enough to address those who'd fought for him, were captured for him, nearly died for him.

But he wasn't king enough, apparently. So the spokesman cleared his throat, unrolled an official-looking paper, and read aloud in a steady voice. "Great noble houses, Parisian citizens, noble Frenchmen—in this, the year of our Grace one thousand, three hundred and forty-three, His Grace, the King of France, defender of his people, hereby declares each of these men present—Olivier, Lord of Clisson; Geoffroi, Lord of Malestroit; Jean, Lord of Montauban; Alain, Lord of Quédillac; Denis, Lord of Plessis —to be traitors to the crown."

There was a collective gasp from the sidelines. Jeanne's breath caught in her chest, sharp. Did he just say...? Had she heard right? Was he calling Olivier a *traitor*? She stood, raising her hands in front of her as if fending off a blow.

The speaker continued. "Together, these men conspired to hand Vannes over to the king of Britain. They made alliances with King Edward and are enemies of the true king, King Philip, and his kingdom of France. They have thus been sentenced to death by beheading, to be carried out immediately."

The arena hissed with a thousand gasps. And then, all was chaos.

Nobles stood, shocked. Someone behind Jeanne

collapsed. Someone else started screaming. Stones zipped through the air into the field—aimed at who, Jeanne didn't know.

She stood, frozen at first, unbelieving, her body gone cold, her teeth chattering despite the hot sun. She *couldn't* have just heard what she heard. Her husband was a war hero. This was a tournament in his honor. Not even a king known for his secrets and dark moods would do this— disarm his own men and order their execution without a public trial. It simply wasn't done. It couldn't be true.

But it was. On the field, the king's soldiers rushed in and forced the noblemen to their knees. Blocks were pushed in front of them, their heads held down on the blood-stained wood. Some struggled; others were frozen in shock. The man to Olivier's left punched a guard in the jaw. Jeanne thought she heard her name.

She jumped out of the box and tried to barrel her way through the crowd, but it was too thick, too panicked. People were screaming, launching whatever they could get their hands on over the onlookers and toward the action, booing the supposed traitors, throwing punches at anyone who jostled them for space.

Jeanne took an elbow to the head and returned the favor, but it didn't move her any closer to the men on the field. The crowd was a wall, a fortress, a heaving ocean, throwing her backward, pushing her down. If she didn't get out, she'd be trampled. So she climbed back into the box, where she could see what was happening.

The executioner was walking—slow, purposeful— toward the men, his axe sparking like flint in the sunlight. Five steps away. Four. Three.

Time slowed and Jeanne's vision narrowed. She stared at Olivier's head—that dark hair she'd run her hands through a thousand times, the ears she'd whispered all her secrets into. She wished she could see his eyes.

The executioner raised his axe.

Jeanne whispered Olivier's name one last time, the noise choked from her closing throat, barely audible.

And then the axe came down.

## CHAPTER 3
# PARIS, FRANCE

It took less than two minutes for all five noblemen to die. Less than two minutes for Jeanne's joy to turn to ashes in her mouth. For Olivier—just returned to her —to be stolen away.

Forever.

She felt herself moving forward again, climbing over people this time. Reaching into her boot for the dagger tucked tight against her ankle. She had no plan, no thoughts. Just shock shuddering through her. Just movement. Just the finely-honed instincts of a trained fighter—a woman who'd spent her life throwing herself into the fray. Instincts that pushed her toward the violence instead of away.

Someone grabbed her by the arm. She whipped around ready to strike, until she realized it was Pieter—her right-hand man and Olivier's closest friend, an imposing broad-shouldered man with unusually short black hair, scarred charcoal skin, and a thick beard that hid his expressions and gave him a reputation for stoicism.

"We should go," he whispered, eyes darting as the

crowd fled, screamed, cheered, and cried around them. "You're not safe here."

She tried to pull away, but Pieter gripped her arm tighter.

"If you go down there, it's suicide. Think of the children."

She turned to look back at the arena, to the king's box, and caught the Duke of Brittany's eye. His face was inscrutable. Did he know? Did he know what King Philip had planned? Did he know why? He was one of the king's most trusted advisors, but he was also one of Olivier's closest allies. Whose side was he on now?

"The children," Pieter said again, firmly.

He was right. They needed her.

She sucked in her breath and followed him into the crowd, keeping her dagger pressed to her side. Pieter had one hand on her arm and the other at the hilt of his sword. Some people were jumping out the front of the nobility's elevated boxes, others attempted to rush down the ladders at the back, others stood agape in the crowd, still others nodding—in firm and unquestioning agreement with any declarations the king made.

It took every ounce of strength Jeanne had not to claw their eyes out.

Instead, she let Pieter wind her through the crowd, out into the city streets, and through a narrow doorway into a dim room. They stopped just inside, both panting.

"Where are we?" she asked, clutching her dagger tighter.

"A brothel. No one will look for you here. We can hide you until we know if you're in danger too."

Jeanne stared at him. A brothel? How did Pieter even

know where to find one? Oh. No. She didn't want to think about that.

She didn't want to think about anything.

The brothel. Pieter. The tournament. Olivier. Olivier tall and proud. Olivier triumphant. Olivier dead in the dust.

*Dead*. He was dead.

Her children were fatherless.

And she was hiding in a brothel.

She barely noticed that Pieter had taken her arm again, this time leading her deeper into the candlelit hall, where he whispered with a woman Jeanne's age—likely the establishment's proprietor—handed her some coins, and swept Jeanne up a staircase and into a small room with a distinct musty odor.

Her stomach turned. God, she was going to be sick. She rushed to the window and threw it open, letting the warm air rush in, gulping it, coughing, trying to swallow down the sticky spit that coated her mouth.

What had just happened? One moment Olivier was a conquering hero. He'd risked his life for the crown. He'd stood for the king. And the next moment, the king had killed him.

Jeanne wrapped her hands around the window frame and squeezed, biting down so hard that her jaw throbbed, stifling a scream. How could this happen? How *dare* they? *Cowards*—the king and every single man in his employ. She was going to kill them. Every single one of them with her bare hands. The king. His executioner. Whoever accused her husband of treachery.

She'd rake her fingernails down their faces. She'd kick out their teeth. She'd kill them slowly, let them feel every inch of her blade go through them. Then she'd cut off their heads—just like they did to Olivier. Could you kill someone by beheading and driving a knife through their heart at the same time? Because she was going to try.

They were cowards. They were thieves. They were wolves dressed as noblemen, ready to tear out the hearts of anyone who wandered too close. She bit her tongue and tasted blood. She was going to destroy them.

Didn't they know the danger of a woman wronged? Had they never heard of Sybil of Anjou, who came under attack during her pregnancy and then torched the attacker's lands and forced his submission? Or Empress Matilda, the rightful heir to the English throne, who took it back by force when her cousin tried to steal it? Or Isabella de Aquitaine—the She-Wolf of France, Jeanne's personal hero—who, just a few years ago, overcame her husband to put her son on the English throne?

She was going to destroy them like Isabella destroyed the English king. Like Sybil destroyed the count who attacked her. Like Joanna la Flamme—the fire-starter who'd encouraged the women of Hennebont to tear their skirts and throw themselves into battle when the duke laid siege to her city—had destroyed her enemies' camps.

"Jeanne? M'lady?" Pieter's voice was a strange whisper a few feet behind her. Jeanne could barely hear him through the rage building in her gut like a fire.

She didn't answer.

"M'lady, I need to go back out into the city. To find out what happened. To find out if you're safe. To find out if our men are still for us. Will you be alright here alone?"

She turned, then, lips pressed together in a line, chest heaving. "Yes. Go. Find out who did this. Find our men. Find out what just happened. And bring me my damn sword."

With that, he was gone. Jeanne was alone.

Alone. Alone. More alone than she'd ever been before. Her head throbbed where she'd taken that elbow to the temple, and it was like she was back in the crowd, unable to fight her way through. Unable to get to Olivier.

That had never happened to her before. Fighting had always been what saved her, what saved the people she loved. The first time she'd killed a man, he was after Louise, her oldest daughter from her first marriage. She'd taken Louise to the forest. A treat, since they both loved the coolness of the trees, the sound of birds singing, drunk on the slow warming of spring. And when a mercenary came into the clearing and attempted to drag Louise away, Jeanne had put her dagger through his ribs.

Fighting was her answer, had always been her answer. There was nothing in the world she couldn't solve with a fight.

Except this.

This time, she'd been too far away. She'd been too at ease. She should have known that nothing was ever safe. She should have stayed closer to Olivier. Should have fought harder. Should have killed her way through the roiling crowd. Killed the soldiers. Killed the executioner. She should have made the whole world go quiet until all she could hear was the sound of her own heart beating— and his.

But she hadn't. She'd *failed* him. Jeanne wanted to scream, to rage. She still wanted to kill every single person who supported the damn king. The room was spinning. She couldn't stop shivering. Couldn't swallow. Couldn't breathe. Tomorrow, she would burn them all to ashes. But for now, in a brothel, with no one watching, she curled in a corner and cried like a lost child.

## CHAPTER 4
# CLISSON, FRANCE

They rode hard and fast through the night with a small company of Olivier's loyal soldiers at their backs. Pieter led the way, with Jeanne a half-length behind, thinking the whole time of the children, praying frantically to everything and anything that the king hadn't punished them for their father's so-called crime.

Twice, when they stopped to water the horses, would-be knights tried to challenge Pieter to duels, fancying themselves the white knights of legend and him the literal Black Knight from the stories. Pieter took it all in stride. Jeanne was less patient and kicked more than one of the challengers in the face from her horse, which sometimes stopped them in their tracks and other times started the very fight she was trying to avoid. The fools were always defeated in moments—by Jeanne, by Pieter, by their men—but even the five minutes it took to disarm a man or break his nose or send him running for the tree line was an unacceptable delay.

The king's soldiers were combing the capital for her

even as they rode. She was wanted for questioning, they said. Wanted for consorting with a traitor.

She gripped the reins harder, sucked the frigid night air through her nose, reveling in the pain of it raw on her throat. The pain meant she was alive. It meant she had gotten away. It meant her children still had a mother, and she would live another day to kill the damn king.

The man was everything she hated: a coward who thought himself a powerful predator, a man who blamed others for his own failings, a man with no concept of justice. She should have listened when she heard the rumors about how secretive and paranoid he'd become. She should have listened when they said the king promised safe passage to John de Montfort after the battle at Nantes, only to go back on his word and take poor John to prison. John was her enemy then, so she hadn't cared. Worse, she'd *laughed*. But now she knew: a king who goes back on his word with enemies is a king who betrays his friends too.

They didn't stop to eat. They barely stopped to sleep and water the horses. It was a wonder no one dropped dead. But, ultimately, they all made it—exhausted, some nearly falling off their horses, but everyone alive as Castle Clisson came into view and Jeanne urged her horse ahead, speeding across the fields, over the bridge, and into the courtyard almost before the gate guards could even sound the alarm.

She flung herself from her horse and yelled for someone to water him as she tripped and ran past the cat standing quiet sentry in the courtyard, through the stone halls, and into the nursery.

"Maman!" squealed Little Jeanne—the first to see her, as both boys were engrossed in some sort of miniature tournament game involving clay figurines.

*Safe.* They were safe.

Grown-up Jeanne had them all in her arms in seconds, kissing their giggling faces, holding them to her chest.

"*Maman*, you're squishing me!" whined an indignant Oli.

"Yes," Jeanne murmured. "Yes, I am."

She didn't move as Oli squirmed out of the hug, rushing to the corner to retrieve his play sword.

A moment later, Pieter was in the doorway, blocking the whole thing. He stared at Jeanne and the squirming, squealing children and let out a long, loud sigh.

"They're unharmed," he said, the relief in his voice palpable.

Jeanne nodded, shaking a little as she pushed her face into Guillaume's hair, feeling the warm aliveness of his scalp on her cheek.

"Where's papa?" Oli demanded, raising his play sword.

Jeanne's heart wrenched; she didn't know how she was going to tell them. "Later, baby."

"What are you going to do?" Pieter asked after a beat.

Jeanne glanced at the nurses, both obviously curious but staying out of her way. "Leave us," she said.

Pieter stepped aside as the women slipped into the hall and disappeared around the corner. The cat zipped in and wrapped itself, purring, around his legs. Jeanne stayed where she was as Guillaume and Little Jeanne both settled into her lap. Oli stood just out of reach, watching Pieter with a hint of hero-worship in his eyes. It was rare that he got to be around his father's soldiers, and he was usually speechless with wonder at them when he did.

On the frantic ride south, Jeanne had tried to understand what happened, to make sense of it, to know what to do next. She'd imagined every scenario for their return—

the children safe, the children gone, the children dead. If they were gone, she would have killed the damn horse riding hard back to Paris going after them. If they were dead, she...well, she wouldn't let herself think about that too long. She couldn't imagine a plan for that scenario. It had been hard to convince herself they were safe with the first two scenarios choking her with fear. But now she knew they were fine, she also knew what she had to do.

Her husband was dead, and her remaining family was in danger. She wouldn't let that stand. She was a noble— the warrior class. She was born to defend castles and rule lands, lead armies and fight for her honor. It's what the nobility did. It's what they'd always done. She already had a fighting force at her disposal, as all nobles did. Men loyal to Olivier; men loyal to her. She had allies. She had wealth.

She sat straighter. "We have to avenge him."

"Avenge who, maman?" Oli pointed his sword at her again.

"Later, darling. I'll explain later." Jeanne held out a hand, but Oli batted it away.

Pieter pursed his lips and furrowed his brow. "Avenge him how, m'lady? This is the king you're talking about, not some peasant or even a nobleman with a small army. We'll never get to him."

"I'll find a way," she said. "But I need more men. Sir Sanders came into an unexpected inheritance last year and has been begging to buy the tapestries in the hall. We have to get to him and neighbors like him before they hear anything—sell anything we can, raise a bigger army."

She paused, running her hands through Little Jeanne's soft brown hair, breathing in the smell of her, then went on. "We'll need a ship. Maybe two. The sea will be the best place for us. On land, they have numbers. On the sea, we have fog. We can take the king's ships by surprise, ruin his war efforts and trade affairs."

Pieter touched two fingers to his lips, thinking. "You won't kill the king at sea, m'lady. Once he knows you're there, he won't come anywhere near it."

Jeanne narrowed her eyes. "I don't want to kill him, Pieter. I want to *destroy* him. I want to take everything he cares about and burn it to the ground. I want him to suffer before he dies." She paused. "They say the Genoese are the best ship-makers in the world. Pick any soldiers you want —your best negotiators, the smartest men in the castle, the most loyal—and send a contingent to Genoa to get us a ship and a crew. We'll meet them in Vannes in two months. That should be long enough to accommodate the journey."

Pieter squatted to get closer to eye level. Oli inched toward the big man, reaching a small hand out to touch the sword in its sheath, then going wide-eyed and stepping backward in wonder. Pieter offered him a small smile.

"You could run," Pieter said, his voice a whisper. "You still have your wealth and your children. We could get a ship and you could disappear. Go somewhere the king wouldn't find you. Olivier would want you to be safe."

Jeanne didn't answer. How could he even suggest that? Running was giving up—on Olivier, on justice, on everything she believed in. It wasn't an option. It wasn't *her*.

"I'm not a coward, Pieter."

"I didn't say you were."

"And yet you think I should let murder go unanswered." Jeanne's voice was sharp-edged.

Pieter answered carefully. "No. I'm trying to keep everything he cared about safe. That means you and the children. I promised him."

"If you promised to keep us safe, then ride with me," she said. "Help me honor him by destroying his enemies."

Pieter let a long breath and nodded slightly—not in agreement, perhaps, but in a way that let her know he would support her. Then he spoke again, quieter as he glanced at wide-eyed Oli and the two now half-asleep children in her lap and then back at Jeanne.

"You'll need more than armies for this. You'll need allies. We need to get word to your friends, to your grown children, to the families of the other men he killed."

Jeanne nodded. He was right. Olivier had always talked about Pieter's sound advice, and now Jeanne was glad to have it too.

"And the children?" he asked.

"I'm going to hide them." Jeanne kissed the top of Little Jeanne's head. "I'm going to hide them where he'll never find them."

# MEANWHILE...

## PARIS, FRANCE

QUEEN JOAN WAS TOO OLD FOR THIS SHIT.

Why was it that men never seemed to grow up, to tire of toddler-style tantrums and teenage drama? She'd spent fifty years hearing men talk about how emotional women were. Well, she had something to say about that.

It wasn't *her* wailing and tearing her own hair out when Vannes was lost. It wasn't her bloodying her knuckles on stone castle walls when the British king declared that he had changed his mind and wanted the French throne after all. And it wasn't her now marching around the plushly decorated sitting room—all rich red fabrics threaded through with gold, and hearty stable oak carved to perfection—with her chest puffed out like some absurd bird, crowing about the success of killing "the traitors."

No, that was the king of France. *Protector of the Realm.* The man on whom everything hinged, including Joan's power and position. Her very life, really, because even that may not be spared if the British king were to take the French throne. She was bound up with Philip, and he was bound up with her. Tantrums and all.

She tamped down her irritation, adjusted herself on the gold-patterned settee, and watched as he paced the thick red rug, ordering a harried serving girl to pour more wine. "I have secured France, Joan! I've really done it now. The backstabbers are gone, and everyone knows what will happen if someone else tries it!"

He smiled and Joan returned the expression, making sure the mirth appeared to reach her eyes. "I'm glad you're feeling confident, dear. But if I may urge some caution: you have killed those men, yes. But you still need to assure the loyalty of their allies. Their wives."

"Wives." He let out a small dismissive noise that made Joan's lips purse unintentionally. He was so inconsistent, this man—one moment telling her she was the most trusted advisor in his life, the *only one* he'd fully confide in; the next, reducing all wives to a huff of breath.

"One wife in particular."

"If you are about to lecture me about that bitch trying to take the Breton duchy again..."

"No, not Joanna. We'll deal with Joanna." Joan took the goblet of wine the serving girl handed her and arched a single eyebrow. "I'm talking about Jeanne d'Belleville."

Philip stopped pacing and took a seat across from her in an elaborately carved chair, letting his energy settle. "Which one was that again? I don't remember ordering the execution of a Belleville."

Joan sighed. Her husband might only remember Jeanne via her connection to Olivier, but Joan knew who Jeanne was before that. The little wolfhound, her mother called her. The woman who tamed Olivier when he was womanizing his way through the palace. Joan had met her many times since then, and every time her impression was that this was not a woman to trifle with. Jeanne was as bound up with the affairs of Clisson as Olivier.

"You may remember her as Jeanne d'Clisson. She's originally from Belleville."

"Ah yes, Olivier's wife. The one who doesn't smile."

"Much like you, my love." Joan couldn't help herself.

Philip laughed at that. "Touché, wife. I am a serious man living in serious times." He lifted his goblet with too much force, sloshing red wine over the rim.

"My point, husband, is that we would do well to pay attention to her and the other wives. You've sent soldiers to bring everyone for questioning and we've cleared the others of involvement with their husbands' plans, but Jeanne has disappeared. It doesn't bode well."

"My dear Joan, thoughtful as always. But I assure you, this woman won't be a problem for us. I'm sending soldiers down to Clisson as we speak. She'll fall in line, as they all have, especially if we tell her she has to defend herself against accusations of her own treason. Fear will make her work even harder to get into our good graces. Women are pliant like that, especially because I plan to make it abundantly clear that any treachery toward the crown will be met with not only death, but something worse."

"Something worse?"

"I'm not just after the lives of these traitors; I'm after their immortal souls."

A beat. A breath. Joan opened her mouth to protest, but Philip stood and held up a hand.

"That's enough for now, love. Let me celebrate my triumph."

Joan's stomach tightened, a hard walnut-shaped thing at her center. Her husband could only mean one thing when he said he was after immortal souls. He meant that he was going to deface the bodies, make it impossible for them to rise in the resurrection at the end of days. *Deny them heaven.*

It was a dangerous strategy. An aggressive one. A man's strategy. No nuance. No mercy.

She pressed her thumb along the smooth contours of her cane, resting lightly beside her chair, an action that usually comforted her. Usually reminded her that she always had something to lean on, stability she could count on. But now that comfort couldn't overshadow the unease building across her skin.

Her husband had killed noblemen without warning, without trial. He would desecrate their bodies. And he thought it all a triumph. He thought it the most dire kind of warning against treachery. But if things were reversed—if Joan was the one receiving word of the desecrated corpse of a family member—she'd see it as only one thing:

An act of war.

If Jeanne d'Belleville saw it the same way, more bloodshed lay ahead.

## CHAPTER 5
# CLISSON, FRANCE

J eanne was pacing in her sitting room, scheming, when Pieter knocked three times and let himself in at her command. He was a little early for their daily war council, but Jeanne was ready. She'd been thinking about the children and wanted to make plans to get them away as soon as possible. She opened her mouth to tell him, then stopped herself.

Something was wrong. Pieter's normally relaxed face was tight and somber, his forehead deeply lined.

Jeanne took a deep breath. "What is it?"

He looked down and away and took a deep breath of his own. "I don't know any way to soften the blow, m'lady, so I'm just going to tell you. We've had a messenger from Nantes. They've sent Lord Olivier's head down from Paris and displayed it on the city wall."

Jeanne pressed her fingers into her scalp and ran her hands down to the sides of her face, holding them at her cheeks. His head. Dear god, what was *wrong* with the king? You didn't kill noblemen without a trial, without evidence —and you damn sure didn't humiliate them like this.

Displays were for enemy soldiers, commoners who betrayed the crown, deposed kings. Not noblemen.

According to the Church, destroying a body meant destroying the soul's chances of resurrection. It meant the king hadn't just killed Olivier, he'd damned him to hell. And Nantes—Nantes was Duke Charles' city. Did the duke protest or was he supporting the king? Had he known all along what awaited them at that tournament? Could the man she'd gone to for help be her enemy?

Jeanne's mouth tasted sour, and her throat tightened. She thought back to that day in the castle—the duke waving at her before hurrying away. Had he known then? Had Jeanne missed a sign? Could she have saved Olivier if she'd been paying attention? The guilt rolled through her like a gut punch, and she couldn't catch her breath.

"M'lady?" Pieter murmured. "Jeanne?"

"God, Pieter. Philip took everything from him."

Pieter's expression of pain must've mirrored her own. "I'm sorry. I'm so sorry. Your husband was a good man. The best I knew."

His voice broke a little at the end, and Jeanne blinked back tears. Sometimes she forgot that Pieter loved him too. They'd been friends and sparring buddies. They'd fought side by side, time and time again. Pieter wasn't just with her for the money—or even for the honor. He was with her for Olivier. Olivier had been the one who'd pushed for Pieter's knighthood. Pieter had saved Olivier's life in two different battles. Pieter missed him, she realized, maybe as much as she missed him. They'd been like brothers.

She reached out, placing a hand lightly on his forearm. "I never asked him how you met," she whispered.

Pieter's face relaxed into a small smile. "When I was nine, my papa brought me to Clisson. He was a blacksmith, always assumed I'd also be one. But I wanted to be a knight. A big dream for a small boy."

Jeanne laughed. "I can't imagine you small." "Oh, but I was. And scrawny too. But all I wanted in the world was to be a knight. I was like your Little Oli. Always challenging cats and horses to trial by combat. Nicking practice swords to practice on my own."

A lump rose in Jeanne's throat. Would Little Oli someday be like Pieter—honorable, loyal, a knight worthy of the name? A man willing to face the most powerful man in the kingdom to do right by his friend?

Pieter went on. "One day, I was practicing in the fields when I saw some older boys in the distance. They were shouting, so I went to see what was going on. It was Olivier. They'd found a cave, and he'd crawled in and gotten stuck. The other boys were bigger and couldn't get in to help him, but I could."

He smiled, his eyes crinkling and shining. "I helped him get unstuck and then I pulled him backward out of the cave. He was...well, you know Olivier. He kept saying he was fine and that he could've gotten out by himself and that he hadn't been scared one bit. I just stood there nodding because those boys were all older and I was a little scared of them, a little in awe. And then somehow we were all laughing and they clapped me on the back and asked my name. And we were friends from there forward. Olivier would come see me in town, and I'd come to the fields to practice with them."

Jeanne's throat burned with tears. God, she missed him. It was the first time someone had talked about him—not his head, not his death, but *him*—since she lost him. She felt herself softening, breaking, tears dripping down her face as she listened.

"When I turned twelve, Olivier asked his father if he'd take me as a ward. We were so far below them, I never thought he'd say yes. I don't know what Olivier said or did, but his father agreed and I moved to the castle. I trained with Olivier. I fought with him. We have—had—been friends for over thirty years."

Jeanne closed her eyes, letting the tears wash down her face. Normally, she'd be angry to be crying, but in that moment, it felt so right. So just. Her tears were a gift to Olivier, and to Pieter—the man standing beside her to help make things right.

When she opened her eyes, Pieter was crying, too. Something she'd never seen before. Something that made her love him fiercely.

She took a step toward him, lifted herself onto her toes, pulled him toward her, and kissed his tear-damp cheek. "We'll make the king regret the day he started this, Pieter. We'll make him regret what he took from us. We'll make him regret the damn day he was born."

With those words, something roared to life inside Jeanne. A spark she'd nurtured since childhood, struck into flame by Olivier's death, and now taking shape, building speed. Jeanne had always been a threat, simmering, dangerous, but now she was an inferno. And her rage was going to reduce France to ashes.

LATER THAT AFTERNOON, the king's soldiers arrived.

There were four of them, which Jeanne considered an insultingly low number. The king clearly didn't see her as a real danger. This was just a show of power, a subtle threat, an attempt to make her believe her husband was a traitor.

"What should we do, m'lady?" Pieter asked from across the lofty stone hall.

Jeanne wondered what the king knew and didn't know. He couldn't know she'd been selling off her possessions and recruiting mercenaries, could he? He couldn't know—though he would soon from his four soldiers—that she had called in her fighting force from the surrounding countryside, that some hundred men were already setting up tents around Castle Clisson. He couldn't know she'd sent messengers to her allies, asking for support. That she planned to visit the families of the other executed men and ask for their support too. If he did, wouldn't he have sent more than four?

"Tell them I'll see them here in the hall." Her lips pursed. "But before you let them in, send me a guard of twelve. I'll hear what they have to say"—she paused—" and if I don't like it, we'll send them back in pieces."

Pieter took a deep breath. "Are you sure, m'lady? If you kill the king's men, you make yourself his enemy. There's no turning back."

"We're already enemies, Pieter," she answered, her voice sharp. "The king made that choice himself."

IN THE GRAND HALL, Jeanne faced the soldiers, her expression unreadable. The space was strangely empty with all the grand tapestries and the old hardwood table gifted to them by Olivier's parents gone. It made her feel somehow smaller and larger at the same time. Like there was too much space around her, like there was nothing for them to focus on but Jeanne herself.

On either side of her, her two best archers stood at the

ready for a close-range shot. Alexi, a man whose inappropriate humor irritated Jeanne but who she begrudgingly admitted was the best archer in her force, and Roland—furious, wild, passionate Roland who looked a boulder and fought like a devil. He was good with a bow, good with a sword, best with his thick fists.

"M'lady," one of the king's soldiers said, grimacing at the archers, "there's no need for that. We're here on official business. We're not routiers."

Jeanne almost wanted to laugh. *Routiers.* Military men who turned to crime in truce times, when the king cut off their military pay—pillaging the countryside, robbing the peasants, laying siege to castles they'd protected just months before. The man thought her cold reception was because she'd misjudged him, not because she knew exactly what he—and his king—were.

She stared coldly down at him and didn't dignify his comments with answer. They'd come here with threats. They'd be answered with threats.

After an uncomfortable moment of silence, another of the king's soldiers cleared his throat and read the charges from an official letter. "Jeanne de Clisson, you are hereby charged to appear in Paris before the crown to defend yourself on the charges of treason against the crown."

Well, this was new. Now Jeanne was a traitor too? Not an accomplice, but a traitor herself. So either the king thought she and Olivier had plotted against him together, or he knew she was plotting against him now. The latter thought gave her some satisfaction. The king should know that Olivier was no traitor. But he should also know that Jeanne was going to destroy him.

He looked up from the parchment and cleared his

throat again. "You will accompany us to Paris. We will act as your guard."

Jeanne laughed, a dry derisive sound that echoed through the hall. "Sir, your king has just beheaded my innocent husband without a trial. Do you think I'm going to just ride into Paris and let him do the same to me?"

The soldier's eyebrows drew together. "M'lady, he is the king. He must have had information we don't have."

"And is that how it works now? No trials for nobles who've spilled our own blood and the blood of our armies defending the king? We don't even get to defend ourselves because your king"—Jeanne lowered her voice—"*has information we don't have.*"

The man opened his mouth. Closed it.

"No, your king had no such information, sir. I know my husband. He was the most loyal man in this wretched country. More loyal than your king could ever hope to be. We defended the king every time he called on us. We fought his enemies, the duke's enemies. The king knighted Olivier himself. And now some sort of rumor—with no proof! If he had proof he would have given Olivier a trial!—some damn foolish rumor turned him against his own allies."

A flush rose across Jeanne's skin, anger building from spark to fire, her voice the dangerous calm before a storm. "So you can see why I don't trust your damn king to get it right. I won't be coming with you to Paris. In fact..." Jeanne motioned to her guard. "You won't be going back to Paris either."

The soldier's eyebrows flew upward in surprise, and he drew his weapon as Roland and Alexi let loose their arrows and the rest of Jeanne's guard closed in. With twelve against four, it only took seconds for them to dispatch the king's men from this world.

*You stand for mercy, Jeanne.* Her mother's words echoed in her head. Jeanne answered the thought with a burning heart.

"Burn them," she commanded, her eyes hard as her men dragged the bodies from the hall.

The Bible said an eye for an eye, tooth for a tooth. That was justice, not mercy. If the king desecrated Olivier's body, denied him his eternity...well, Jeanne would make sure all that was left of his men was ashes. They'd come to escort her to Paris for questioning, so she had them escorted into the void.

## CHAPTER 6
# BRITTANY, FRANCE

Five days after the king's guard arrived at her castle, Jeanne, Pieter, the children, Alexi, and Roland approached a small dark-stone building perched at the edge of a cliff overlooking the English Channel.

The coast was wind-swept and frothy white with waves beating against shards of scattered rock. Stars shone bright above, illuminating the scene almost as brightly as the sun. And the simple stone structure stood stark against it all, a shadow along the cliff.

Jeanne's heart fluttered. Was hiding the children away the right thing to do, or would they be safer with her? She knew the answer. It was what had brought her here in the first place. Of course they were safer without her—she was about to take on the king of France. And yet leaving them behind didn't *feel* safer. Jeanne was exposed and uncomfortable and uncertain, three things she rarely experienced.

She dismounted her horse and reached into the traveling wagon for Little Jeanne, displacing the cat—now named Monster by Oli's decree—who gave her an accusing look, stretched, yawned, and then hopped over the other two sleeping children and onto the muddy ground. Little Jeanne stirred as her mother draped her over one shoulder. Pieter lifted out Oli, and Alexi lifted Guillaume, pretending to stagger under the tiny boy's weight, then grinning at his own foolish joke.

Jeanne rolled her eyes and started for the shadowed building. It was a nunnery she'd visited many years ago—the most hidden place she'd been able to think of. It was so quiet, so still. *Please, saints, don't let them be gone.* She knocked on the thick hardwood door.

Shortly, there was a stirring inside—the sound of footsteps and an internal door opening and closing. And then an elderly nun stood before Jeanne holding a candle and narrowing her eyes.

Jeanne thought she might collapse from the relief. The nuns were still here.

"Yes?"

"May we come in?" Jeanne asked, shifting Little Jeanne on her shoulder, her arm burning from the weight. "These children are in danger."

The nun's eyes went wide as she stepped aside and motioned the company into the small entry room. Several other nuns—younger, curious—stood inside.

"Miriam, light some candles," said the older one. "Aalis, make up a bed for the little ones." She motioned to Jeanne. "You, come in here."

She led them into a small, clean kitchen and motioned for them to sit at the long hardwood table. And she sat as well—heavily, Jeanne noticed. Was she injured or ill in some way or was it age? Hesitation rose in Jeanne's body, tensing her muscles. Could these women protect them? Could she actually leave her children behind here?

Then again, what other choice did she have? Any day

now—the moment he realized his soldiers hadn't returned —the king could send an army to her doorstep. Especially if he discovered the men she was amassing, the plans she was making, the quiet support she'd found throughout the nobility, the way she fell asleep every night imagining what it would feel like to kill him with her own bare hands.

No, this was right. Her children weren't safe with her. Even if she could accept their father's death—which she couldn't, wouldn't, would never accept 'til the day she died —the king could still come for them all at any moment.

The children had to stay. They had to hide. They had to have the protection of the Church. The king wouldn't find them here and wouldn't attack a nunnery.

"Explain yourselves." The old nun stared at Jeanne, expressionless.

So she did, in a low voice to keep from waking the children. She told the nun who she was, told her about her god-fearing husband who'd been struck down without a trial, his body desecrated by the king's men. She told her how she feared for her children's lives—the little lambs, precious in the eyes of god, yes?

Then she mentioned the most important part: the gold she'd provide for their safety. Nuns might be swayed by god's will and soft-hearted stories, but in Jeanne's experience, the real foundation of loyalty, even in the Church, was the heft of one's coins.

"Will you keep them here?" She searched the nun's face for any sign of agreement. "If you do, I assure you, you'll never want for anything again. My purse is yours. My loyalty too."

The old nun's nod was sharp and definitive. "Whatever number you're thinking of, double it. We don't invite trouble with the king without adequate compensation."

Jeanne tossed a pouch full of coins onto the table between them, and the older nun nodded approvingly. She stayed seated but ushered the younger women toward the children. "My sisters will help you get the children into bed," she said to Jeanne. "But I'm sorry, your men can't come any deeper into the building."

The younger nuns helped Jeanne and her soldiers rouse Guillaume and Oli with murmured assurances and gentle hands. Oli woke cranky and wrinkled his nose at them, swinging a fist at nothing in particular, whispering something about villains and knights. Guillaume toddled along behind him, eyes half-closed, thumb in his mouth.

Jeanne followed the nuns deeper into the building with Little Jeanne on her hip, led by a single candle's flickering light. After passing a few closed doors, they turned left into a small room. Two straw mattresses had been pushed together under a small window, its shutters closed. The first nun pressed her candle into a holder by the door, then guided Guillaume to the bed where he fell right back asleep. Oli climbed in beside him and turned defiantly toward the wall.

Jeanne placed her daughter beside the boys and lifted a blanket over all three. Her hands trembled. Every few minutes the reality of what she was doing hit her like a training sword to the gut. She was actually doing this. She'd already lost one part of her family, and now she was leaving the rest behind. Alone. Helpless. With no one to fight for them.

When they woke and she was gone, would they hate her? Would they be frightened? Would they understand that she'd left them behind not because she wanted to but because she had to? The questions made her want to scream and hit something.

She reached out again, touching the two nearest heads: Guillaume and Jeanne. Warm, sleepy. Innocent. Guillaume who fed field rabbits and slept with Monster curled beside him every night. Little Jeanne who followed her big brothers around in awe like they were her own personal gods. Oli who would one day fight monsters like the king himself.

They didn't deserve such a broken world. Such an unjust world.

They would understand. They *had to* understand.

She kissed each sleeping head, like she could press the message into their very minds.

It took hours for Jeanne to force herself up and out of the room. Hours of watching their breathing, soft and steady. Hours of missing them even as she was still with them.

But as the sky started to pink, she forced herself to her feet, through the cold hall, to the kitchen for a last conversation with the elderly nun, and out to the horses. Pieter was there, standing watch. Roland was asleep on his bedroll beside the horses, snoring like a storm, while Alexi was using some dried meat to coax Monster to curl up beside his superstitious friend's face.

Jeanne quirked a half smile at the devil-cat, then mounted her horse. "Wake up," she hissed over her shoulder, watching as Roland opened his eyes, swore, and scrambled away from Monster, promising to gut Alexi if he ever tried that again.

"What are you blaming me for?" Alexi said, hands up in mock offense. "Maybe the cat just likes you." At Roland's scowl, he grinned and added, "They say devils like fools," before darting out of reach out Roland's meaty fists.

Jeanne let out a snort at the exchange. And then the cat —who she'd expected to stay, terrorize the nuns, and find a way into her children's bed at night—leaped onto her lap. Monster stared up at Jeanne a moment, made a brief catty noise, and batted a paw at the half-empty leather saddlebag. First with surprise, then with amusement, Jeanne realized the damn devil-cat wanted in. She wondered if she should force the cat to stay with the children. She'd be a comfort to them, if the nuns didn't chase her off—which they probably would. But, then, Jeanne was herself oddly comforted by the thought of a cat in her saddlebag. A warm presence. A constant reminder of the children. A creature that chose to stay by her side. A friend, even.

If she could call a cat a friend.

She lifted the top flap and the cat curled into the space, the saddle bag all hers.

## CHAPTER 7

# BRITTANY, FRANCE

It had been four days since Jeanne left her babies at the cliffside nunnery, and she couldn't stand still. She was ready to march, ready to move on the king. Ready to rip his head off. But Pieter—thoughtful, diplomatic Pieter—had suggested they wait.

It would take a while for Philip to realize his messengers hadn't returned, even longer to figure out why, and longer still to gather a fighting force to come after her. Her friends were sending soldiers to her cause. There were already over two hundred, and every day, more arrived, rolling out bedrolls in the fields below the castle and beside the river, lighting campfires, filling the air with the shriek of steel and the constant low hum of male voices.

"Build up your army before we march. The ships won't be ready yet anyway," Pieter said, and she knew he was right, even as she couldn't stop whatever it was inside her screaming to *move.*

If she couldn't march, then she needed to hit something. It had been weeks since she'd trained. Since she'd stretched her legs and tensed the muscles in her back and danced around the training yard, knocking Olivier's men on their asses. They were preparing to go to war with Philip, so it was time to get back into the arena. This was how she'd move while standing still.

Jeanne had always trained for battle—ever since she was eight and ran screaming into the practice yard shouting that it was unfair to train the boys and not her. That day, she'd grabbed a wooden training sword and knocked both the sparring eight-year-old boys over in three blows. Her Lord Uncle—Lord of the castle since her father's death five years before—laughed until his face turned red and tears ran down his stubbled cheeks. Her mother—an incredible hunter and falconer, fierce in her own right—winked down at her. And ever since then, she'd trained.

She'd trained with the boys, trained with the men, trained with her husband, which—more often than not—turned into a whole different kind of wrestling match.

Now, she went back to training with the men—offering them payment for knocking her down—and training harder than she ever had before. Pieter was not only her best strategist but also her best fighter, and imposing as well. The men called him Mont Pieter—part man, part mountain. And so she called on him most often.

At first, he'd gone easy on her. But as soon as she noticed, she'd gone at him twice as hard, bloodying his nose and bruising him in the gaps between his armor until he stopped worrying about hurting the lady of the castle and started defending himself in earnest.

It was a deepening of their friendship. Her bruising his ribs, him knocking her down. Both, she knew, fiercely missing Olivier.

Now, she swept into the training yard like a storm, dragging Pieter behind her. Two young soldiers were scuffling hand to hand at one side, while two older knights who'd been sent by her allies watched and shouted instructions from the other. Other men stood around talking, laughing, sharpening weapons, and placing half-hearted bets on the scuffle.

Jeanne ignored them, stepped back, and channeled all her fury into a screaming attack. She loved to attack first. It was the last thing anyone expected.

Of course, Pieter knew her and was ready. Their practice swords collided. Then again. And again. Pieter swung at her left side and she dodged right just in time, sweeping her own sword toward his knees. He brought his sword around in an instant to catch hers.

As predicted, the thoughts in her head quieted as she danced, light on her feet, dodging thrusts and swinging her blade into any opening Pieter gave her—as well as some he did not. She was wholly, single-mindedly focused on the movement of her body. The tensing of muscles in her back, her legs, her shoulders. The balance of her body and her sword. The movement of Pieter's muscled arms, his heavy, blunted practice sword.

Her breathing settled into a familiar rhythm. Her body hummed with purpose.

She was vaguely aware that more men were gathering on the sidelines, Alexi shouting odds and taking bets, Roland calling him a hedge-born bastard, other voices murmuring all around her. Normally, the bet-taking would annoy her. But not now. Not with every bit of her focus on Pieter's movements.

She was going to win. She could feel it in her marrow.

His neck was unprotected, his sword flashing downward as she hopped out of reach. She lifted her sword for the winning blow...and then Pieter caught her across the stomach and knocked her onto her back, air rushing from her lungs with an ugly cough.

The field went silent. Pieter stood over her and offered a hand.

"Never fight angry, m'lady." His voice was even.

*Oh yeah?* she thought. And with that, Jeanne let out another enraged scream and swept her practice sword into the backs of his knees, knocking him to the ground beside her.

The silence erupted into sound—laughter sweeping through the field, followed by cheers. Jeanne sat up, surprised. When they started, they'd had half a dozen men watching. Now, there were dozens. Maybe a hundred. And they were roaring—laughing, stomping their feet, smashing closed fists against boiled-leather breastplates.

"Pay up!" Alexi demanded, poking Roland in the chest.

Roland scowled at him and then Jeanne.

"To the lady of Clisson!" a voice boomed across the chaos.

"To the lady of Clisson!" a hundred voices answered.

Pieter was laughing heartily too, tears forming in the corners of his eyes and then streaming down his cheeks in mirth. Jeanne glared at him from her seated position, a slight satisfied smile creeping onto her face as she stood and dusted herself off.

"*Always* fight angry, Pieter."

THAT WAS the day Jeanne's army became *Jeanne's army*.

Before, they were other people's men. Olivier's. Her allies'. Some knew her and were loyal to her. But now, they all tilted their heads as she walked by. They stomped in unison and called her the wildcat. The saw her for what she was—a spark, a flame, a raging inferno.

As her army doubled in the next few days, the new men were greeted with stories of Jeanne fighting mad. Jeanne winning trials by combat. Jeanne, who'd knock you down the moment you thought you'd won.

And now, as she walked through the fields with Pieter, surveying her army, between tents and past fires surrounded by men on their bedrolls, she knew it was time. Time to march. Time to get answers about what had turned the king against them. And then time to destroy him.

"Whose idea was it to put that damn greedy bastard on the throne anyway?" a seasoned soldier with a silver-white beard croaked at his fellows across a fire.

Jeanne stopped to listen, Pieter pausing beside her. Most of the men around the fire were new to her, but Alexi and Roland were there, warming their hands and listening, breathing in the scent of roasting meat. The others didn't notice her, but her two archers both caught her eye and inclined their heads.

"Not mine," another soldier said. "You heard of the new taxes? Hearth tax. Salt tax. All conveniently started just as the king stops paying his soldiers because of a damn truce."

A third soldier grunted. "That's always how it works with a fella like that, though, isn't it? Everyone who's been in battle with him says he's a coward. A fool! Men like that don't value what we do. He'll just throw us aside, refuse to pay us, then demand we pay the crown. Never mind that he'll need us again in two years when the truce expires."

"I think he'll need protection sooner than that." Alexi winked at Jeanne and pretended to string an arrow into his bow.

Laughter traveled around the fire. "Just when he thinks

he can sit back and take our money, here comes the world's fiercest woman to eat him alive."

"I think she'll capture him and torture him until he goes insane."

"Good. He deserves it."

"As long as *she* doesn't declare a damn truce too—lord help us."

Jeanne smiled to herself, then stepped out of the shadows. "I don't believe in truces." She took in their faces as several men stood and a chorus of "m'lady" danced through the group. "So you're ready to wreck the king's pretty little truce?"

"Aye!"

"You're ready to show a coward for what he is?"

More men gathered to her, drawn by the shouting. "Aye!"

"Do you think that bastard needs to learn he can't just use people and throw them away?"

Still more men pressed in. "Aye!"

"Then it's time we take our complaints straight to him —at the end of our swords."

"AYE! AYE! AYE!"

The volume built until Jeanne thought Philip must be able to hear it from Paris. She wondered if he was quaking in his boots yet. Wondered if he'd wet the bed like a child. Wondered if he had nightmares about the fire that would consume him.

She looked at each of her men in turn and nodded. "We march tomorrow."

And for the first time since they'd returned to Castle Clisson, Pieter agreed, echoing her words in his steady, low voice behind her.

"We march tomorrow."

## CHAPTER 8

# BRITTANY, FRANCE

Jeanne marched north to a garrison formerly defended by her husband at Château-Thébaud with forty soldiers at her back. The fields around the castle were the rich brown of a countryside creeping toward winter, the forest at their backs a riot of autumn colors.

She wore black—black dress, black veil, black cap—just as they'd expect. She was a widow grieving her lost husband, come to kiss the flagstones of a castle he'd defended, come to pay homage to the men he'd fought with, come to collect any belongings left behind.

She thought of Olivier, standing tall in his finest clothes, waiting for a reward that would turn out to be treachery. Then she thought of him months before that fateful day, on one of the many days they'd taken the children to the riverbanks to play. He'd spent a cool morning with Little Jeanne balanced on his shoulders squealing in delight while he showed Oli fighting stances. Guillaume had stood in the shallows trying to make friends with the fish, gurgling at them and giggling until he tired of the game and joined Olivier's stance lessons.

Jeanne had stepped to the side to watch, to soak them all in, her heart bursting with so much love she thought she might overflow. The moment was perfect. Olivier was perfect. The kind of father every child deserved but most didn't get. Oh, *merde*. Thinking about him made her want to laugh and scream and stab someone all at the same time.

When Jeanne's host arrived at the castle's heavy wood gates to meet them, she rode out ahead and called to the guardsman, her voice ringing through the cold mid-morning air.

"I am Jeanne de Clisson, widow of Olivier de Clisson, Lord of Clisson, knight of France, who fought in this very garrison for the freedom of its people. I come to pay homage to your lord."

Her voice trembled a little and Jeanne hated herself for it. Never show weakness. Never give away your intentions. Never let them see—or hear—your fear.

*As a woman, they'll let you fight, but you'll have to fight twice as hard.* Her mother told her that when she was eight and first started training for battle. The day she'd run into the practice yard shouting that it was unfair to train the boys and not her. She'd have to be better than everyone, her mother said. Smarter, too. She'd have to turn herself to stone—strong, untouchable, immovable.

Still, so many years of training later, so close to the garrison Olivier had patrolled, she couldn't control the falter in her voice.

To her relief, the guardsman didn't seem to notice. All he saw was a grieving widow, a friend, a woman whose husband had once fought nobly alongside his lord. For such a woman, it only made sense to throw wide the gate.

And so they did—slowly raising the defenses as Jeanne sat straight and kept her expression neutral, channeling her mother's lessons and her hero Isabella's strength and cunning. Isabella de Aquitaine who had successfully assassinated a king. Isabella who'd put her son on the throne. If she could succeed against all odds, so could Jeanne.

As her men piled into the courtyard, smiling friendly faced and non-threatening at the castle's guardsmen, Jeanne glanced at Alexi, carefully positioned to her right. She gave a slight nod. In an instant, the archer had nocked, drawn, and released—his arrow catching the gateman in the eye.

He was dead before he even knew he'd been hit.

Dead before he could close the gate.

Dead before he realized a horn had sounded, and hundreds of Jeanne's men were rushing from the nearby woods and up the hill. The trembling, black-clad, grieving widow was here to take the castle.

THE BATTLE WAS over before it began.

Fifty young soldiers had been left to guard a castle the king hadn't imagined would come under attack, and Jeanne's company of four hundred took them easily. It had been brazen—marching toward the king, toward Duke Charles whose loyalties were still so uncertain in her mind, toward a castle that Olivier had defended. Only an insane person would ride north with such a tiny host to wage war on a well-defended king. No traitor would march straight into the executioner's land.

But it had worked.

Men always believed she'd behave in the way they expected. And that belief was their downfall.

Jeanne's soldiers ringed the courtyard, holding twenty

or so captured men, waiting for her orders. She sat atop her black stallion like a quiet statuesque wraith, waiting for the lord of the castle to be brought before her—a lord who was a close confidant of the duke and an advisor to the king. The man who would know *why* Philip had taken her husband from her, who else was involved, the reason Jeanne had come to this godforsaken fort.

Pieter dropped the lord at her horse's hooves. He was a short man, though strong and muscled, with light eyes and lighter hair. His face was flushed red, and his arms and hands were bleeding from defensive wounds.

"What is this? What are you doing?" he sputtered, pushing himself up from the dust, his nostrils flaring.

Jeanne gripped the reins tighter, but her voice was calm, the tremor gone. "Tell me, m'lord, what do you know of my husband?"

"Nothing, m'lady! He was a fighter here before. That's all I know!"

Fool. Did he think she'd marched in here just to take him at his word? "No, sir, it *isn't* all you know, and I don't have time for this. Tell me now or I'll cut off your hands."

The man was quiet, breathing hard. He glanced around the courtyard at the still, stone-faced soldiers. Jeanne wondered if he thought she wouldn't do it. If he thought her weak. The idea was infuriating. If he refused to answer, she would make him. If he thought there was any way out but to tell her the truth, she'd dismount her horse and rip off his fingers herself.

"Very well." She didn't break eye contact with the bleeding lord. "Pieter, start with a finger."

As Pieter moved forward, hand on his dagger, the man shied away. His face changed from calculating to a nervous, jittery, lip-biting fear. "Wait. Wait. I...What is it you want to know? Your husband fought here. He fought in Vannes. He was captured and returned. He was killed by the king in Paris. But surely you know all this already. What else do you think I know?"

Jeanne was steady now, strong. In control. "Who accused him?"

"The people in this garrison are not responsible for your husband's death, m'lady." He licked his lips. "If I tell you, you'll let us go, yes? You'll have mercy?"

Foolish question. As much as Jeanne wanted to jump down and put her knife to his neck, she kept her voice calm. "Of course."

The man nodded, his face twitching with nerves. A beat passed, then another. And then finally, he spoke. "It was Charles, m'lady—the Duke of Brittany."

A murmur rippled through the gathered soldiers. The reins dug into Jeanne's palms as she clenched her fists.

The duke.

Her *friend*.

The man she'd gone to for help, who'd told her not to ride for Paris and plead with the king for Olivier's freedom. He'd started this. He'd ended it. But the question was *why*. Did he actually think Olivier was a traitor or was there something else? Had he hated them all along—even as they'd fought and sweated and bled in his battles to take his dukeship back from the traitor John de Montfort such a short time ago, even as they'd laughed together and feasted together for so many years?

She'd wondered about the duke, of course, but she hadn't truly believed he was involved. At worst, she'd imagined he'd gone along with the king's plans. Unforgivable—but nowhere near as unforgivable as being the one who'd caused this whole mess.

The lord's eyes searched Jeanne's face for a reaction, his tone apologetic. "Charles de Blois suggested to the king that the loss of Vannes was impossible without an inside man, and that the English gave Olivier back for too low a sum. That he was clearly in league with them. A spy sent back to our shores to undermine us."

A long cold silence followed before the man went on, discomfort pinching his words. "It seemed obvious, m'lady. Charles' argument was a sound one—why would the British hand him over for so little? If it weren't your husband, you'd agree..." He trailed off at the end, then attempted to rescue himself. "I mean, obviously the king overreacted. No trial...well, that's...But you know King Philip, m'lady. He's prone to fits, and he's suspicious to a fault. There wasn't anything any advisor could do to change his mind. Once Charles presented his theory, there was no stopping any of this."

So that's why the duke had asked all those questions about Vannes. Jeanne released the reins, painfully opened her hands, and looked down at them. Could no one be trusted? Did no one care about doing right? When she'd gone to Charles for help, he kept asking her what happened at the siege even though she hadn't been there. Kept asking her about British tactics and what went wrong. At the time, she'd thought he was just trying to puzzle it out, but now it made sense. It's why he was so insistent that she go home, so adamant that she wasn't a good enough diplomat to approach the king. He believed Olivier a traitor, and he didn't want her to interfere.

She'd gone to Charles for help, and he'd killed her husband.

Jeanne held back a scream—held herself still, the only sound her breath hissing out through her teeth.

The lord bowed as well as he could while kneeling, his voice nervous. "M'lady...I'm sorry for your loss, but your quarrel is with the king. If you would please leave us..."

"Leave you?" Jeanne's voice echoed across the courtyard, punctuated by an incredulous laugh, rage coursing through her like a physical force. "Sir, you could have stopped this madness, and *you did nothing*."

The man glanced around him and wrung his hands. "That's not fair..."

She silenced him with a shake of her head. "No. I've heard enough. You did nothing, so I will likewise do nothing while you are killed just like my husband was killed."

He opened his mouth but did not speak.

"Behead him," she ordered. "Kill every person in this garrison. Take anything of value." She paused, taking in the towers rising into the gray sky above her and turned herself to stone just like her mother taught her. "Burn it down." She spat the words like venom. "Burn it to the damn ground."

## CHAPTER 9
# BRITTANY, FRANCE

Next time, she would leave one man alive.

The garrison at Château-Thébaud still smoked in the distance, but with no one left to tell them who was burning down their castles, how would the king know it was her? How would the duke know who to fear?

More than anything, Jeanne wanted them to know. To know they'd misjudged her. To know what would happen when they chose dishonor and cowardice over fair trials and friendship and loyalty and all that was right. To know she was coming for them—coming for everything they held dear, everything they'd fought for.

Her men marched behind her, steady, reliable. Pieter rode a little ahead, alert for danger, taking reports from scouts sent along the road. Jeanne reached into her saddlebag, where Monster now took up residence every time the company rode. She laid a hand on the warm sleepy ball, calming a little at the consistency of the cat's breath, the rhythmic rise and fall of her ribcage—strange, likeable little creature. Messenger of the devil indeed. The cat felt more like good luck than anything else. Did that mean Jeanne was in league with the devil? She quirked a smile at the thought. Let the bastards fear her even more.

She urged her horse forward. They were heading for the castle of Galois de la Heuse—one of the duke's most loyal officers. It might be too much to hope that her grieving widow guise would work a second time, but Jeanne was feeling reckless and restless. Wild. Imagining how Charles' smirk would die on his lips at news of Galois' fall. If she couldn't punch it off his face herself, she'd peel it off ally by ally.

The first fortress she'd taken had been for information. The second would be a message. *I know. I know what you did. And I hope you know that I know.*

She drove the men on faster than she normally would, and they reached the gates by nightfall. They were tired, but Jeanne wanted the element of surprise more than she wanted the company refreshed. She rode ahead, skirts whipping in the cold evening winds like something possessed and repeated her performance from Château-Thébaud—this time without the tremble in her voice. Where she'd been nervous, now she found a strong, certain rightness. She was a soldier. She was a wildfire. She was god's wrath come down on the heads of these greedy cowards and self-centered fools.

To Jeanne's disappointment, Galois wasn't there to grant her an audience, but this garrison, too, threw its doors wide for the widow Clisson and her troops. The man left in charge would be an ally of Galois and Charles, as well, so Jeanne could still make her point. Her men swept in, weapons drawn, battle cries on their lips. They rounded up the soldiers, brought them to Jeanne in the cobblestoned courtyard, and forced them to their knees.

The man in charge—a military leader whose name Jeanne didn't know or care to know—knelt among them, his dark eyes trained on Jeanne, arms held behind him by hard-faced Roland.

She dismounted her horse and struck him across the cheek with the back of her hand. "Do you know why you're here?"

He righted himself and stared at her, chin jutting forward, eyes unyielding.

She struck him again. "You're here because your friend Charles de Blois had an innocent man killed. You're here because the king and his men think justice can be bent to suit their own needs." She pulled her sword from its scabbard and pointed it at him. "Any last words?"

His lip curled upward, and he spat at her feet. Jeanne looked down at the spit, then back at the man. He was the worst kind of fool—defiant in the face of justice when he should be begging her for mercy. She turned to the men surrounding her. Her own soldiers alert. Her enemies kneeling, some wide-eyed in terror, others with faces pinched in anger, the youngest boy, perhaps sixteen, silently crying. No one had yet told him that wars had losers, she thought. They weren't all glory and triumph.

No one expected to lose. Poor child.

Having wriggled free of her saddlebag, Monster now sat on the back of Jeanne's horse, watching. Tail twitching. Bearing witness. Reminding Jeanne of her own sweet, innocent children—children who deserved justice for their father.

She spoke loud and clear. "I am Jeanne de Clisson. My husband was betrayed by his king and his friends. *I* was betrayed by my king and my friends. Let it be known that I have vowed vengeance." Her breath came hard and strong as she turned back to the kneeling nobleman. "That I will fight the king and *anyone* who stands with him until the last breath leaves my body."

Then she raised her sword above her head, tilted her face upward to scream into the sky, and brought the blade down hard and fast.

Her first beheading wasn't clean, but the man was just as dead as he would have been had she hit his neck at the right spot.

She'd seen many men die in her life—in battles and sieges, beheaded and hanged in the squares—but he was the second she'd killed herself and the first she'd killed so intentionally. The first had been different, a split-second decision in defense of Louise. This time, something shifted inside her, the crossing of an invisible line. It was strange—and strangely satisfying. She'd trained her whole life for battle and now she was in it, fighting for justice with her own two hands.

Galois' followers cried out. Screamed. Several tried to run away and were skewered by Jeanne's men. Roland, in particular, was in his element, single-handedly catching two of the runners. Who knew a man shaped like a boulder could move so fast?

Only a few soldiers remained, alive and quiet. Waiting to see what Jeanne would do next. It was for them that Jeanne had made her speech, taken the trouble of announcing her intentions instead of simply razing the fortress. One of them would be her messenger. The man to tell the king and the duke what happened. The man to give them nightmares.

Jeanne studied their faces. One was older, bearded, his wind-pinked face resigned. One was the crying boy, with hair like a raven's wing, so black it almost looked blue. And the third was some indeterminate age in between with a straw-colored face that matched his straw-colored hair.

She motioned to the two older men. "Kill these two"—her hand fluttered toward the younger—"but leave this one alive. Tie him to a stake outside the castle, just far enough away to live. Take the valuables, and burn this stinking rat hole to the ground."

Leaning down, her face inches from the boy's, she whispered, "You tell the king what happened. Tell him that Jeanne de Clisson is going to take *everything* away from him. Tell him he'll never be safe."

# MEANWHILE...

## PARIS, FRANCE

FEAR DESCENDED ON THE THRONE ROOM. It reminded Aria of a cold plunge into a mountain lake, taking her breath away, freezing her lungs.

She'd been scrubbing that stubborn rust off the stones in the corner, stealing glances at a life-sized painting of Queen Joan, whose dress was a riot of lace and leather fastenings. The painting was new, and it put the rest of the hall to shame with its glamour. Aria had been happy, even through the backbreaking, monotonous scrubbing, daydreaming about what it would feel like to have that lace against her own skin. It was the most glamorous thing she'd ever seen.

But then a boy about her age—sixteen—had been ushered into the hall. His hair was black as a night sky, his pale skin mottled with a flush the same color as the rust Aria struggled to scrub out. And when he'd told the king he came from the castle of Galois de la Heuse, that a woman named Jeanne de Clisson had burned it to ash, that's when the fear had dropped frozen over the hall.

Because this wasn't the kind of thing you said to the

65

king, especially not with Duke Charles there. Something about him emboldened the already too-bold monarch. Aria had seen the king order deaths as easily as he ordered a meal. Lives meant nothing to him. Winning was everything. Especially winning in front of someone whose respect he craved.

Staying on hands and knees, Aria moved slowly backward toward the door as the boy finished his tale. Every nerve ending in her body was screaming at her to run. But a servant couldn't run. A servant must be invisible. So she backed up quietly, slowly. Inch by painstaking inch.

Silence crystallized into ice in the wake of the boy's story before the king broke it, his voice as tightly coiled as a snake. "Where is she going?"

The boy bowed lower. "She didn't say, Your Grace."

Duke Charles' tone was measured. "Why did she leave you alive if everyone else was put to the sword?"

"She said to tell you she's coming for you. She said you'll never be safe."

God's nails, did this boy have no sense? Didn't he realize that repeating threats made you complicit in the king's eyes? Aria rose and continued her steady retreat toward the exit.

She wasn't fast enough.

The king's anger boiled over, his volume rising. "Kill him. I will have no threats in this hall."

The boy stepped back in alarm and turned as if to run, but he was run through instead, ended on a soldier's sword. As he died, he seemed to grow younger, his expression tiny, hopeless, terrified. He was sixteen, fifteen, twelve, nine. His eyes were alive, afraid, empty, dead. Aria couldn't look away.

On the raised steps behind the boy, the king's face was

purpling with rage, his fists tight at his sides. The boy twitched one last time and then stilled, the pool of blood spreading, seeping into thin cracks in the floor.

Aria would be the one to clean it later. She'd be back on her hands and knees, scrubbing the boy out of the floor like a rust stain. Without taking her gaze off the most powerful men in the kingdom, she moved her hands along the rough wood of the door to the hall, searching for the latch.

"What will you do, Your Grace?" The duke's voice was somehow still even. Emotionless.

Rather than answer directly, the king said to his guards, "Raise a fighting force, immediately. Reroute anyone you need. Send word to our spies. We need to know where she is. We'll take her and whoever dares join her."

The duke nodded, and the king growled his next words. "She'll be dead within a month."

Aria's left hand finally found the latch. Before the king decided to kill more innocents in place of this dangerous woman, she slipped through the archway and out into the hall, bright with tapestries.

With no one there to see her or report her for behavior unbecoming of a servant, she ran.

## CHAPTER 10
# BRITTANY, FRANCE

Compared to the empty castle Jeanne had left behind, this grand house was bursting with color. She'd gotten so used to gray stone and echoing halls as she sold off her belongings, it was almost a shock that every wall of this dining hall was all tapestries, art, sculpture. Deep blue, rich green, passionate red.

A servant had drawn thick curtains across the windows, but in a better light, the hangings would be glorious: unicorns leading knights through the forest, lions holding the king's flag while marching into battle with odd little dogs at their heels, knights battling giant snails that were meant to represent a cleverly disguised enemy, slimy, underestimated. Meant as a reminder of the inevitability of death. It was a stark backdrop to the grieving widow sitting across from Jeanne on a peacock-colored settee, all black fabric and downturned lips. Herself a reminder of the inevitability of death.

"I'm sorry for your loss."

Jeanne's words felt so hollow, so inadequate, but what else could be said? She didn't know how else to open the conversation, to communicate to this family that she had come in peace and that she understood what they'd been going through since the king killed their beloved father, brother, son, husband right next to her own.

The widow, Amélie, shifted in her seat and slowly closed her eyes. The man to her right—an uncle or cousin, Jeanne couldn't remember—put a hand on her shoulder. It reminded Jeanne of her own childhood: her father gone too early, her mother and uncle bound together by grief, managing the castle and its men.

"I've come because I'm righting this wrong," Jeanne said.

By Amélie's obvious surprise, she mustn't have heard the rumors already circling the countryside about Jeanne's personal war against the king. She must have thought this was just any other visit. A woman come to express condolences.

Hope lit in the other woman's eyes. The man beside her stroked his auburn beard.

Jeanne sat straighter and tried to channel her diplomatic mother. "We deserve a better king. Philip killed our men without even the courtesy of a trial. He took brave, loyal men and called them traitors. He desecrated their bodies." She could feel the heat of anger rising on her skin as she spoke, her tone urgent. "I don't know about you, but he came after me too. His guards came to drag me to Paris for questioning."

Amélie gasped at this and spoke for the first time. "He hasn't sent anyone here yet." A wry smile twisted her face, and her next words cut like a dagger. "Maybe he doesn't think I'm a threat."

There was a fire in her eyes, and Jeanne knew this woman's loss was felt as acutely as her own.

On Pieter's advice, she'd had several conversations like this as they marched for the coast. The families of the other lost men hadn't been her allies before, so she hadn't asked them to send troops when she was initially building her army. But now that she could come in person, look them in the eyes, see for herself whether they were ready to turn their loss into a weapon.

There were so many families in mourning. So many lost men. Not only Olivier and his fellows from the tournament, but dozens of others who'd been named traitors and snuffed out like candles in the weeks since. Philip and Charles had been busy indeed.

France's surface seemed as it always was, but behind the feast days and the soldiers training and the children playing in the castle courtyards, a storm was brewing. Behind their curtseys and m'lords and courtly smiles, the families of the wronged were furious.

There was always a turning point in these talks, a moment when the person across the table saw Jeanne's fury and dropped their own mask. For Amélie, this was that moment—the moment when the king added insult to injury by not seeing her as a threat.

"Our children are only two," she said. "Twins. The king left them fatherless, and he won't even show me the evidence of this so-called treason. I've asked. I've sent a messenger every week. And every week, they're ignored." She stood, fists clenched around her black skirts, lips pressed together so tight they almost disappeared. "We should have supported Edward's claim to the throne when we could."

The statement was a sort of breathless blasphemy. Edward, the English king, had a legitimate claim to the French throne—better than Philip's in many ways, his lineage through his mother, Jeanne's hero Isabella, more direct—but the nobles had been too nervous. Ruling France *and* England had seemed too much power for one man. They'd feared the meshing of cultures. They'd feared losing themselves.

And so they'd forced Edward to back down. They'd chosen Philip, backed Philip. Paranoid, proud, war-hungry Philip who hid behind a handful of advisors and cared nothing for justice. The two countries had been at war ever since.

Amélie went on. "We should have taken Joanna de Montfort's side when she joined the English and fought the duke at Hennebont."

A shiver traveled up Jeanne's spine. Joanna de Montfort. Joanna la Flamme. Who'd told the women of her city to rip their skirts and take up arms. Who'd somehow ridden out of a city under siege and burned the duke's supplies. Turned him into a fool. She'd been Jeanne's enemy then, before Jeanne knew what the duke was. But Amélie was right—Joanna had known all along what the rest of them had only now realized: the French king and Breton duke couldn't be trusted.

Jeanne unclenched her jaw, stood, and took Amélie's hand. "Let's stop him then. We can't undo what's been done, but we can fight."

Amélie held Jeanne's eyes, her voice steady. "Tell me what you need."

"The two things no woman can wage war without," Jeanne answered without hesitation. "Funds and spies."

## CHAPTER II
# BRITTANY, FRANCE

A few days later, Jeanne stood in the great hall at Châteaubriant, watching her grown daughter, Louise, pace. At twenty-nine, Louise was dark-eyed, full-figured, and every inch as beautiful and intense as Jeanne remembered. Geoffrey, equally intense but much quieter than his sister, frowned at them both as he leaned against the table and tracked Louise's anxious movements.

Behind them, a newly commissioned stained-glass window cast blues and yellows across the floor. The scene was religious and triumphant: a risen Jesus emerging from the tomb. It was beautiful—and strange. Jeanne's oldest children had never cared much for religion. They went to Mass, of course. Everyone did. But commissioning religious art for the great hall was new, and Jeanne felt a strange sense of loss at the sight. There was no telling how your children would stretch and grow without you.

"You know they're calling you a traitor, right?" Louise faced Jeanne, hands on hips. "We received messengers just yesterday. They're talking about confiscating your lands—*our* lands. They said you ignored a summons, and that the king's messengers never returned. Is it true? Have you turned on him?"

Louise had been like this since she was a child—full of questions, trusting nothing. It was always *Maman, who is Titivillus?* "He's a typo demon, darling." *What's a typo demon?* "A demon who tricks the monks into making mistakes on their manuscripts and collects their mistakes into bags." *Why?* "To show those mistakes to God and keep the monks out of heaven." *Why?* "That's his job." *Why?* "The devil gave it to him." *Why?* "I don't know, darling." *Why?* "Ah, *merde.*"

All of her children had done that to some extent, but Louise did it until Jeanne wanted to smash her own head against the castle walls to make it stop. She kept going even after Jeanne had stopped answering. Was that how it was going to be now? Louise's badgering was mostly irritating, but also a kind of comfort. Despite the hints of change in the hall, Louise was still her Louise. Still so very much herself.

"Louise, love," Jeanne said, trying for a moderate tone, "the king turned on *me*. I didn't start this."

"But you could end it."

"You think it's that easy? The king killed an innocent man in front of thousands, chopped his body into pieces, and hung his head on a wall. You think he's reasonable?"

Louise paused. "So, Olivier was innocent then?"

Jeanne's eyebrows flew upward. It was true that Louise and Geoff had never gotten close to Olivier—she'd always assumed it was some sort of misplaced loyalty to their own father, who'd passed fifteen years ago—but to question his loyalty? To think so low of him? The question stabbed at her, an assassin she hadn't expected.

"How could you even ask that?"

"I didn't know him." Louise's tone was even. She wasn't backing down. "It's a reasonable question."

"Olivier was loyal to a fault, Louise. If you asked me if I believed he could lose his temper on one of his men, yes, I could. If you asked me if he could be irritatingly arrogant, yes, he could. He certainly had his flaws. Sometimes, he was over-sure of himself, and he wasn't careful with his wealth. But that man never—not once in his entire life—broke a promise. He was loyal to the king and loyal to Duke Charles, and *they* are the ones who turned on him."

"You're sure you're not just blinded by love, Maman?"

A low anger built like coals disturbed. Was this what people thought? That the king was right, and Jeanne was a fool? "You know me better than that. I'm not a blind supporter of *anyone*. When Olivier mismanaged my dowry after we married, *I sued him*—and I won. When he refused to pay those peasants over the land we confiscated, I told him he was wrong in public court." Her voice steadied, wrapped itself in steel. "Do you think I'm some sort of weak-willed follower? We were equals, Louise. Partners. And I've never been afraid to see what he is and stand up to him."

Jeanne stepped forward and wrapped Louise's hands in her own, pressing her warmth, her sincerity into them. "I wouldn't lie. I wouldn't support treachery. I'm telling you that he was innocent. I did not start this. You asked if I'm going against the king—and yes, I am. Just like I would fight anybody who hurt either of you."

She looked from Louise to Geoff and back again. "If you think going along with the king will keep you safe, remember that Olivier spilled his own blood for Philip, spent months in a dungeon in Britain, was probably tortured for him. And that man *still* declared him a traitor and killed him without a trial." Jeanne's anger was full force now. "For your own sakes, please do not trust him."

Looking pensive, Geoff finally spoke up. "What do you want us to do, Maman?"

"I want you to stay on your guard. I want you to never ever trust the king or the duke. I want to know if you'll stand by me while I fight those who betrayed us." She took a breath. "And I want you to pretend to denounce me publicly, but help me stay informed about my enemy's movements."

*Merde*, she'd thought this would be easier. Jeanne felt her own rightness through every part of her body, but she wasn't sure it was enough. Everything hung in the balance now. Her first two children—grown and gorgeous and still so naïve—were either with her or against her.

And she didn't know what she'd do if it was the latter.

Louise and Geoff exchanged a look. Jeanne knew it was part of the easy way they communicated, always seeming to know what the other was thinking. They'd always been close—a rather funny pairing with Louise so bursting with opinions and questions and Geoff so quiet that sometimes it seemed he'd forgotten how to speak.

"We'll have to think about it," Louise said, arms tight across her chest. "You can't expect us to betray France with only a moment's consideration."

WHEN JEANNE RETURNED to her men outside the castle walls, the camp was roaring with laughter—the wrong backdrop for her dark mood. She pressed her way through the crowd, looking for someone to scold or fight.

Roland was in the middle of a circle of laughing

soldiers, trying to get away from an eager pack of dogs. Every time he turned to shoo one away, another would come up behind him and try to hump his leg. He'd shake that dog off only for another to latch onto his other leg.

"What in god's nails..." Jeanne said, her irritation giving way to amusement.

The man next to her answered between laughs. "He called Alexi a bitch earlier, and Alexi said, 'We'll see who's a bitch,' and then he did some sort of black magic." He bent over, overcome with mirth. "Now every dog in the castle thinks Roland's the bitch."

Normally Jeanne would roll her eyes at these kinds of antics, but there was something impressive about turning fierce Roland into the bitch of Châteaubriant. For once, she could see why the soldiers thought a joke was a breathtaking riot.

"Who's the bitch now?" called a voice from the circle, unmistakably Alexi, undeniably smug.

Roland roared and charged in his direction, tripping over dogs. "You hedge-born bastard, what did you do? Come out and fight me like a man!"

"But you're not a man, didn't you hear? You're a bitch!"

As the crowd screamed with laughter all over again, Jeanne left to find Pieter. "Just don't kill each other," she called over her shoulder. "Save it for the king."

IN THE HALL the next morning, Jeanne's body was tight with the possibility that her oldest children might not stand with her—a thought that hadn't even crossed her mind before she'd arrived. She studied Louise's face, tense and drawn, and wondered what it meant. Without their support, she couldn't protect them. If they stood with the king, they stood in danger. Jeanne didn't care about their support for her own sake, but if they didn't see the king as a threat, he might destroy them.

It was like being on the tournament grounds all over again, her body cold, her throat closed, waiting for a disaster outside her control. Watching the axe drop.

Louise spoke first. "We need more time, Maman."

"And you need to leave," Geoff said. "If the king suspects you're here, if word gets to him...we can't risk that exposure. You said it yourself—if we're to be your spies, then we need to publicly denounce you. And if we decide to do that, it can't look like we let you stay here."

It made sense. Jeanne's children were trying to be practical, a trait they had no doubt inherited from their father's side. Careful consideration instead of flailing fists. But still, Jeanne wanted them to be more like her. Certain. Immediate. Decisive. That's what love felt like. This felt like betrayal.

"Maman, don't just stand there," Geoff said. "Say something."

"We'll be gone today." Each word was a spiderweb crack in Jeanne's heart.

By comparison, Louise's voice was all practicality. "We'll send word after you. Where are you marching?"

Jeanne hesitated. If they weren't with her, was it safe to tell them? The shame of the question sliced at her—these were her *children*. Of course she would trust them. Of course she would give them the time they asked for. And of course they'd come around. They had to.

"Vannes," she answered. "We'll set sail from the city where Olivier defended France."

## CHAPTER 12
# BRITTANY, FRANCE

J eanne visited three more castles before they arrived at the coast. Three more noble families who hadn't previously been her allies but now were. Three more families ready to avenge the men they'd lost, their hopelessness replaced by fury and fire.

Her spy network grew full and far-reaching, a web spun by a clever spider, unseen by the king. The only missing thread was Louise and Geoff, whose silence lodged like a pebble in Jeanne's boot—a small and constant worry, impossible to ignore.

A half-day's march from Vannes, where Jeanne would meet her ship, she stopped her company for the night. Pieter joined her in the tent for their daily war council, candles flickering around them, cold black mud beneath their boots. A flimsy cot in the corner was the only place to sit, which was why they always stood. Monster melted out of the shadows to wrap herself around Pieter's legs.

"M'lady, the company are ready to march on Rennes, as you asked."

Jeanne nodded. With only one ship, she couldn't

THE LIONESS

accommodate four hundred men, so she'd handpicked the best of her force to stay with her while the rest would act as a decoy. Pieter had paid them a generous severance to keep marching north, drawing as much attention to themselves as possible before returning to her allies. She didn't need to give the king any advantages—he'd know where she was soon enough. With any luck, he'd think she was marching with the larger host, going on to take Rennes. With even more luck, he'd panic.

Her heart thrilled at the thought. There was something incredible about the movements of war. It was a fight like Jeanne had always fought, but on a larger scale. You thrust and parried, dodged and shielded, twisted and feinted, ground your opponent into dust.

And grind the king into dust she would.

All her plans were falling into place. Her scouts had already confirmed that her ship was waiting in Vannes. Her decoy men would march on Rennes come morning. And just yesterday, she'd received another report from the noble spy network she'd woven together in the last couple months.

The news wasn't anything unexpected—the king had confiscated what was left of the Clisson lands and declared her an official traitor against France. He was gathering a force to meet hers. According to one Parisian noble, he'd thrown a tantrum about how her behavior meant he'd been right about Olivier being a traitor, and treachery was like a disease: everyone around you caught it. *Do you think she'll ride on Paris?* King Philip had then asked, his voice smaller.

It was what she'd expected, but it was satisfying to hear it all from someone else. To hear how much her movements had enraged her husband's killer. To hear he was *afraid*. She wondered if this was how Isabella felt when she realized

79

she could take the British throne. By all accounts, she'd been a master strategist. Had it been this thrilling for her or had it just felt necessary?

Pieter was speaking again, softer now, searching her face. "Do you think about him all the time?"

All thoughts of Isabella vanished, and Jeanne's chest tightened—a stab of shame for momentarily forgetting *why* she was doing what she was doing. The truth was that she tried not to think about Olivier. Or rather, she tried to think of him in abstract terms. She was going to avenge him. She was going to make him proud. She was going to protect his children.

But think about *him*—about his smile, his laugh, their history? It was too much. It made her weak when she needed to be strong. It made her uncertain when she needed to be decisive.

If she thought about him—riding in tall and strong from the fields with a saddlebag full of flowers he'd picked for her, chasing the children through the courtyard in a game of dragons and knights as they squealed in delight, running two fingers along the back of her neck in his tender way—she wasn't sure she'd make it. She wasn't sure she wouldn't shatter into a thousand pieces or throw herself into the steel-gray sea they were marching toward.

She shook her head, stifling the memories as they rushed in. "No, I—I try not to."

The answer felt inadequate, but explaining meant thinking more about it. She wished she could go back a few minutes and get lost again in thoughts of Isabella, of triumph instead of loss.

Pieter whispered, barely audible, "I lost my greatest love...loves, too. My wife, our child. At first I couldn't think about them either."

Jeanne turned to him in surprise. Pieter had been *married?*

He smiled a little at her response and let out a breath. "I wasn't sure if Olivier had told you. I lost them both in childbirth, one after the other, just minutes apart." He lifted a hand, fingers pressed together, and then opened them as if releasing something invisible into the sky. "Gone."

Jeanne's throat was tight, and her eyes burned—she hadn't ever thought to ask what Pieter had lost in his lifetime, other than Olivier. But they'd all lost so much, hadn't they? She'd lost her first husband, Geoffrey, when she was in her twenties. Then her first son with Olivier, Maurice, born three years before Oli and with her for a year. One sweet, short year. And now, at forty-three, she'd lost both Olivier—the one man who'd seen her and loved her for the wildcat she was—and her children, alive but out of reach.

She watched Pieter's face as he went on.

"At first, I thought I would die. I was going to...I was going to do it myself. Fall on my sword. But Olivier guessed what I was planning. He caught me and talked me out of it. 'What would one more death accomplish?' he said. He told me he needed me to stay, that the world needed me to stay. I think..." Pieter met Jeanne's eyes then. "I think somehow maybe he knew. Maybe he knew he'd be gone, and you'd be left behind. Maybe he knew that...we'd be here."

He paused, staring at the shadows on the tent's waxed canvas. "He made me promise that if anything happened to him, I'd keep you and the children safe. I don't know if he was trying to give me purpose, to remind me that we were brothers—if not by blood, then by battle—or if he knew that someday he would...be gone."

Jeanne reached across the space between them and

placed her small hand gently on Pieter's enormous one. "I'm sorry," she whispered.

For a few quiet moments, she let her heart break first for Pieter and then for herself. She let the full range of emotions sweep through her—fondness for Olivier, rage that he'd been stolen from her, sadness for her loss, and a deep throbbing loneliness she hadn't previously let herself notice. Beside her, Pieter watched the candlelight flicker on canvas, lost in his own thoughts.

## CHAPTER 13
# VANNES, FRANCE

*Dearest Maman,*

*Geoff and I have conferred, and we are with you. I know you prefer instant answers, but you know I'm not one for rashness. Geoff says to tell you that we believe you that Olivier was not a traitor. Personally, I thought you would assume as much since we have agreed to help, but he says we should make it clear.*

*As for news, I'm told Duke Charles is on his way to visit us, presumably to ask about you. We will attempt to get him to reveal something instead. Geoff sends his love, etc. etc.*

*Your Louise.*

The letter was the most beautiful thing Jeanne had ever seen. It was so very Louise—her style, her frankness. And Geoff's softening at the edges. Well, his attempts at softening.

The relief uncoiled across her skin. After she'd finished reading and followed Pieter to the docks, she couldn't tell if her love for the new ship was born of its own breathtaking wonder or if her soul was simply primed to love the next thing that came into view.

Either way, the ship was magnificent. The best craftsmanship on the sea, they said. Faster, lighter, and more maneuverable than any other model. *And more beautiful,* she thought, with its three oak masts rising stark into the sky, the triple sails for agility and flexibility, the planks laid smoothly for a sleek look and faster movement. Carvel built, they called it.

It would be easy to outrun the French military, which was fortunate—according to her scouts, the king's forces were searching for her as they spoke. Jeanne smiled. Let him come. The king was slow, just like his diminished navy of clunky single-masted ships. Jeanne was agile. Always had been. Always would be.

She watched her men load the cargo, the seasoned captain she'd hired to serve as her first mate shouting orders. Barrels, crates, and cages of live lobsters, eels, crabs, salted fish, fruit, spices, almonds, ale, and wine. Clay ovens for the cook. Spare timber for repairs at sea. Hanging lamps for the cabins. A cow for fresh milk. And, of course, weapons.

Swords. Bows. Arrows. An axe sharp enough to split hairs.

Jeanne boarded, running her hand over its heavy wood and leaning against the rail to look back at Vannes—the ironically beautiful port her husband had defended from the British, where he'd been captured and this disaster had begun. And now, the place where Jeanne would take her battle to the seas. She thought it was fitting that in the future, thoughts of Vannes would sting the king as much as they stung her.

THE LIONESS

Pieter joined her on deck, where Alexi and Roland were already preparing to set sail, and she reached out to squeeze his hand. Ever since he'd told her about his lost wife and child, she'd felt the same fierce protectiveness she had for her own children. Pieter had lost his family, and Jeanne had lost some of hers. He was someone she'd fight to the death for. They were each other's family now. Lost in thought, Jeanne didn't notice anything amiss until Pieter's normally even voice shifted uncertainly. "What *is* that?"

The answer was dozens of ravens, moving along the docks. Flapping black wings and beady eyes, sharp beaks and ominous caws followed a slight-figured man as he picked his way toward them, eyes locked on the ship. A single man was little threat, but Jeanne was unsettled. She rested a hand on her dagger's hilt.

The man was closer now, and he was beautiful, Jeanne thought, with his warm-brown skin, high cheekbones, and long eyelashes. Those big brown eyes. He caught hers, grinned, and gave a small bow. To Jeanne's surprise, Monster darted down the boarding plank to rub herself around the man's ankles in a frantic slalom, purring loudly and sending ravens scattering in every direction.

"You are Jeanne de Clisson?" The man's voice was higher than she expected. Perhaps he was a eunuch, with his young unbearded face, that unusual voice.

"I am," she said. "And you are?"

"They call me Arley." He bowed again, and a raven hopped onto his shoulder. "I'm here to join your crew."

Ah, so that's what this was about. The man hoped for a commission, some gold.

"You've come too late," Jeanne said. "The crew is already set."

"You haven't heard what I can offer, m'lady. May I come

aboard and speak with you instead of shouting across the water?"

Although Jeanne had intended to say no, she was intrigued despite herself. She nodded. Pieter raised his eyebrows at her, which she took to mean he agreed that this strange man would be worth hearing out.

Monster mewed impatiently, and the raven on Arley's shoulder took flight as he lifted the cat into his arms and boarded Jeanne's ship. "I'm an accomplished astrologer and herbalist," he said. "I can heal your men. I can read the stars."

Jeanne wasn't sure what she'd expected, but it wasn't that. Superstitious nonsense. There was limited space on her ship, and she wasn't going to replace a seasoned fighter with a star-gazing eunuch. Her amusement was gone as fast as it had come. "I have no need of herbalists and star-readers."

Pieter spoke up. "We *could* use a healer. Men on ships get sick. You've heard the stories; you know it's a difficult life. We could—"

Jeanne waved her hand dismissively but laughed when she saw Monster had now taken up residence on Arley's shoulder and was staring at her imperiously. "The cat likes you, but I've yet to see herbs heal any truly impressive battle wounds."

"And how accomplished could you be?" Roland piped up from where he'd been securing some ropes. "Can't even grow a beard. You look like a little girl. I could snap you in half with two fingers."

Jeanne didn't disagree with the last part, but she didn't need Roland's interruption, so she narrowed her eyes at him until he went back to his task.

"I can help in other ways." Arley was persistent, she'd

give him that. "I know how to light men on fire and how to make people see what we want them to see."

"We all know how to light men on fire." Jeanne laughed again. "Use a torch."

The young man opened his mouth to argue, then closed it again. "I see you'll need a demonstration." He placed Monster lightly on the deck. "I'll be back tomorrow."

As he turned to leave, Jeanne said, "Don't bother." But the ravens took flight, cawing like mad, drowning out her words.

## CHAPTER 14
# VANNES, FRANCE

As promised, Arley was back on deck the next day, unsettling ravens perched all around him on rails and masts and boxes. Monster prowled the rails, sending birds looping overhead before they landed again farther away from her.

"Why do you want to join us so badly?" Jeanne thought she already knew the answer—it was sure to be gold or fame or a misplaced sense of adventure.

Instead, Arley cocked a cheeky eyebrow and held out his hands, palms up, displaying an impressive collection of scars. So perhaps not as soft as Jeanne thought. "The enemy of my enemy is my friend. I hear you're planning to kill the Duke of Brittany, and I'd like to help."

Now *that* was a surprise. She wondered what Charles had done to him. She wondered how many others the duke had wronged and how she could find them, use them. She still had no use for the leech-bleeding and herbal medicine Arley was offering, but he was right that any enemy of Charles was a friend of hers.

"We're already a full crew." Jeanne tried for a softer

tone than usual, to keep the man on-side. "I'll send you to my allies, but we don't need star charts on a warship."

"Even though all your enemies do?"

"Even though those fools do."

"Jeanne—" Pieter started, then stopped when she shook her head sharply. He'd made a case for having a healer on board after Arley left yesterday, but while she agreed that his advice had always been sound before, the idea of trading a trained fighter for a skinny doe-eyed stargazer seemed so beyond foolish that even considering it made her anger rise.

Arley watched the exchange, then nodded, bowed, and pulled a candle from his tunic. Jeanne cocked her head. Was it some sort of good luck charm? *Merde.* She was glad she'd told him no—she was already tired of this.

Which was why she wasn't ready when Arley lit the candle, raised his hand to his mouth, and blew fire across the arm's length between them, setting Pieter ablaze.

Jeanne's breath caught in her chest. Pieter. Oh god. *Pieter.* Her one friend left in the world was going to die because she'd let down her guard. Arley, the skinny nothing she'd dismissed as a superstitious child, was an assassin. Shock, fear, fury—a dozen terrible emotions pierced her like arrows. She had to kill him.

Jeanne reached for her dagger, but Arley threw something into the air, turning the ship into a chaos of wings and screaming caws as the ravens took flight, blocking her view. Jeanne turned back to Pieter, ready to grab him and throw him into the sea—the only thing she could think of that would stop the fire. But by the time she turned, the flames had vanished. Pieter was fine, standing there in shock, patting his face with unbelieving hands.

Jeanne grabbed her dagger to put it through the

damned astrologer's heart. But the boy was gone, disappeared in the chaos of the flapping, shrieking birds.

"He has to join us now."

Jeanne had never seen Pieter so energized. He practically bounced around the deck, nearly taking out the men carrying cages of chickens on board. The last of the stores were being loaded all around them, the men trickling in from the taverns and brothels where they'd spent their last hours onshore.

"He tried to burn you alive," she answered, her tone somewhere between wonder and irritation.

"No! *No*—if he'd wanted to do that, he would have. He only wanted to show us what he could do. He's a genius."

"Or an assassin. A poor one."

"Nobody's that bad of an assassin. The fire didn't burn a single hair off my beard. It was a trick. It was *magic*."

*Merde*. Pieter was right. Again. Arley said he could light men on fire—and then he'd proved it. Jeanne didn't need people pretending to kill those she loved, but even she could see the value in the kind of trickery this young man seemed to have up his sleeve.

She relented. "Alright. He comes. But only if you can find him before we set sail. I'm not waiting for the damn herbalist."

Pieter grinned, gave another very un-Pieter-like bounce, and left the ship.

Two hours later, they were ready to sail.

Pieter was back with Arley in tow—no ravens in sight this time. The man had enough sense to look repentant instead of triumphant, and despite herself, Jeanne found she was glad he was here.

Everything was loaded. The crew—including Alexi, now sporting an impressive black eye, she assumed compliments of Roland after some practical joke or other—waited at attention. Monster, who'd been prowling the decks since sunrise, sat beside Arley, tail twitching, stare unblinking, watching Jeanne with the rest of them.

The seasoned sailors smiled at the cat in a way soldiers on foot never had. To Jeanne's amusement, she'd earlier learned that black cats were *good* omens at sea. They kept sailors safe. They boded well for the voyage. It was strange and somehow comforting how different an omen the same animal could be with a simple change of location. Messenger of the devil on land; beacon of hope at sea.

Jeanne took a deep breath and stood a little straighter as she faced her men. "What are you waiting for? To the sea we go! Take any vessel flying a French flag." She then spoke to her first mate. "Come get me if you see a ship on the horizon."

With that, she retreated below deck to her cabin, Monster the good-luck devil-cat trotting at her heels.

## CHAPTER 15
# THE ENGLISH CHANNEL

Someone was knocking on Jeanne's cabin door.

"Come in," she said brusquely, assuming it was Pieter or her first mate.

Instead, in came Arley. There was something about him that made her think of her children. Maybe those big eyes, the baby face. A pang of longing shot through her. She wondered what they were doing now—hoped the nuns played games with them, took them to the beaches. Hoped Oli still fancied himself a knight. That Jeanne still worshipped her brothers. That someone gave Guillaume all the snuggles he could handle.

"M'lady," Arley cleared his throat and closed the door behind him. "I've come to tell you something—something I'd like to keep between us."

Jeanne forced herself to focus. Was he here to tell her how he set men on fire or coaxed ravens to do his bidding? Perhaps why he hated the duke. Jeanne was intrigued and waited for him to go on.

"Pieter was just explaining the, ehh...seats of ease." Arley wrinkled his nose, and Jeanne stifled a laugh.

Ah, yes, the seats of ease—the boards jutting out from the front of the ship so that her men could do their business and the wind would blow it away. As a noble and the lady of the ship, Jeanne had a chamber pot in her cabin, but for men crammed together in a shared cabin, the seats of ease it was. Luckily, they all seemed to think it a very good joke. She'd already heard Alexi teasing Roland about how he was going to fall off in the night and then nobody would remember him as a warrior but as the "shit who died taking a shit."

Jeanne quirked a small smile and tilted her head. "Yes, what about it?"

"I—I can't use them."

Oh *merde*, did the young man beg his way onto her ship only to request special treatment? "I suppose you'll just have to burst then."

"No, you don't understand. I *can't*. I'm...I'm not who you think I am." Arley rushed on before Jeanne could ask what he meant. "I'm not a man, and I don't want the crew to know."

Jeanne paused, trying to untangle the words. "Are you telling me you're a eunuch?"

Arley barked a surprised laugh. "I'm telling you I'm a woman."

"No, you're not."

"Yes, I am."

Jeanne snorted. "Where's your figure?"

"Bound up with cloth. It's not hard to hide, especially since I've never had much *to* hide, if you know what I mean."

"Why?" Jeanne asked. "Why are you dressed as a man?"

He—she—shrugged. "It's safer."

And Jeanne supposed it must be. What would it be like

for everyone to think you were a man? To never try to touch you, to kiss you at the strangest moments. To never question whether you should train with the boys. To assume you belonged anywhere you wanted. The idea was breathtaking.

"I'd like to use your chamber pot from time to time, to keep my secret."

"What's your name? Is it really Arley?"

"Amée." The word came out a whisper, the barest breath.

Amée. A pretty name for a mystery of a woman. Jeanne suddenly wanted to laugh—her life was so strange now. Devil-cats and ravens, women dressed as men lighting her fiercest soldier on fire without burning a single hair off his head. How had Amée become what she was? How had Jeanne?

"You can use my chamber pot," Jeanne said. "But in exchange, you have to tell me what Charles did to make you want him dead."

"I WAS THIRTEEN WHEN GISELLE, my mentor, found me," Amée began, her words slow and measured. "She pulled me off the streets, taught me herbs and stars, how to heal people and comfort them."

The two women had settled into chairs in Jeanne's dim cabin, facing each other. A candle flickered from beside the bed, another from the desk. Jeanne leaned forward, elbows on her knees, listening.

"She was the town's astrologer. She visited nobles to read their charts, worked with the local doctor to determine the most fortuitous times for treatments, even consulted with the duke himself. She was proud of that. He'd send for her before important battles and say, 'Read what God's written in the stars for me.'" Now Amée's voice was bitter, mocking. "He had this reputation for generosity. He'd double Giselle's fees, and he once stopped to have his men help us fix our cart when a wheel came off. He was kind to us—that's the worst part."

Jeanne knew what Amée meant. It was bad enough to be wronged by a powerful man. Worse when everyone else thought he was a saint.

"There was a priest in town who *hated* Giselle. Hated us. He'd preach in the squares about how astrologers were devil-worshipers—no matter how many times she told him that the church sanctions astrology. The king uses astrologers, the *pope* uses them. But this one priest, he thought Giselle was a heretic—" Amée stopped and took a deep breath, her face pinching in on itself.

"They stormed in and took her while I was out gathering herbs in the forest. It took me two days to find out they'd thrown her in a dungeon. No trial. I went to the duke to petition for her release, and you know what he told me?" She clenched her fists, pressed them into her knees. "He said he'd help. And then the next day, they *executed* her."

Jeanne felt the familiar heat of rage flush across her skin. It was the same story. Charles pretending to be your friend before cutting you off at the knees. Had he always been this person and she'd just never seen it? Did he take pleasure in offering up hope and then snatching it away, that permanent smirk of his mocking you as he destroyed whatever you loved most?

Amée went on. "When I went back to ask him what had happened, he told me he *was* helping. He was helping her never deceive anybody again. He was helping me to live a godly life free from heretical influence."

Monster hopped off the bed and into Amée's lap, curling into a ball, purring, eyes shining in the candlelight. Amée ran her hands along the cat's back, her voice soft now, but strong. "I tried to kill him myself. Got a job in his kitchens to poison the food, but when they sent me to take it up to him, I saw—" A look of disgust flitted across her face. "Did you know that he hurts himself?"

Jeanne startled. "What do you mean?"

"I went in with the food, and he was shirtless, his chest red and scratched, infection seeping out. He wears these tiny ropes around his chest, tied so tight that they fuse into his skin. He puts sharp rocks in his shoes so that when he walks, he suffers."

Jeanne's stomach turned, and she raised a hand to cover her mouth. She knew, of course, that Charles was pious. The duke was known for his views on suffering—that it was everyone's Christian duty, that the only true offering god would accept was one's pain. Someone at a party had once even told Jeanne about the rocks in his shoes, beaming as if it wasn't the most foolish thing she'd ever heard. As if life didn't make them all suffer enough without putting rocks in their own damned shoes.

But this—the ropes, the infection? *This* was something else.

In her mind, Charles had stepped across the line from fool to fanatic. From Amée's disgusted expression, it was clear she felt the same.

"I dropped the tray. They made me get another, but I didn't have more herbs to poison it, so I waited and tried again a few days later. But I wasn't careful enough. They caught me, and I had to run." Amée's hands were back in fists, held up in an involuntary declaration of war. Jeanne's heart clenched along with them.

"In the end, I failed her," Amée said, tears pooling in her eyes. "They took my only friend in the world, and there was nothing I could do about it. I couldn't even punish him."

She lifted her eyes to meet Jeanne's. The calm and confident mask she'd been hiding behind dropped away, and Jeanne saw that she was haunted. Lost. And that fierce protectiveness—the one Jeanne felt for her children, the one she felt for Pieter—rose through her, pushing her to her feet. She was going to kill Charles with his own damned ropes, shove his shoe-rocks down his throat until he choked.

"You didn't fail her. You just needed a little more time— and a few more allies."

Amée smiled, then. A pretty thing.

And Jeanne smiled back as she added, "If Charles' dearest desire is to be a martyr, let's make him one."

## CHAPTER 16
# THE ENGLISH CHANNEL

It was late on their fifth night at sea when Jeanne spotted the first ship on the horizon.

At first, it was too far to see what flag they were flying. Too far to tell whether they were friend or foe. Alexi and Pieter were tasked with the night watch, and Amée was walking with them because she loved the night, the stars, and because—as far as Jeanne could tell—she and Pieter had become fast friends. They'd played cards almost every day since setting sail, talking about magic shows and astrological predictions.

Jeanne waved them over to the rail where she was standing at the ship's bow. "Alexi, come get me when you identify the flag. If it's French, we take them. If it's British, we'll fade back into the fog. Pieter, keep scanning the horizon—if more ships appear, come get me *immediately*."

Both men turned to their tasks while Jeanne headed below-deck. It was a dank, ripe place—full of unshaven, unwashed men snoring in elevated bunks, food that had somehow already spoiled, and unidentifiable fluids sloshed into the corners. Jeanne wrinkled her nose and forced herself onward. She was used to the sharp tang of men sweat-drenched after a battle, but so many of them in an enclosed space was hard to take. It was a relief that the stench didn't reach her own private cabin or the wind-swept deck.

Jeanne moved into the dim room, ready to wake her men—if the ship on the horizon turned out to be French, she wanted them all alert, weapons in hand. At the first elevated bunk, she opened her mouth to speak...and it stayed open in outrage.

The nearest man was naked. Spread-eagled, snoring softly, and bare as the day he was born. Jeanne looked at the next bunk, then the next. She moved through the rows. Naked. Naked. Naked. Almost every man aboard her ship was sleeping without a scrap of clothes.

She exhaled in a hiss. Were men actually this thoughtless? Did they think an attack couldn't happen at any moment, that the extra twenty seconds spent tucking in their bits didn't matter? Did they genuinely believe themselves safe?

Sybil of Anjou wouldn't have slept naked during a war. Isabella wouldn't have slept naked when her assassins were on their way to the king. Jeanne touched her own chest, fully clothed and fully armored with boiled leather and metal plates. She was ready for battle—and her men were sleeping fool-faced and unprepared. She wanted to scream.

Instead, she lit a candle, drew her dagger, and tucked it up next to the first man's exposed groin. It was Roland. "Wake up, you reckless fool," she hissed.

The boulder-faced archer started.

"Don't move, or you'll regret it."

Roland stilled, his eyes wide and white, his mouth pressed into a firm, angry line.

"Every man in this room," Jeanne shouted, "listen up!"

The men stirred and murmured. All around, they sat up, stood from their bunks, and looked around, still half-drunk on sleep.

"There's a ship on the horizon," Jeanne said, cold, clear, and loud. "I came down to ready you, but *this* is what I find." She motioned toward Roland with her chin. "All of you naked, splayed across your bunks, and not a single one of you ready for battle! What do you think this is? What do you think you're here for?" Jeanne was shouting again now, nearly shaking with rage.

"From this night forward, no man will sleep naked on my ship. You'll be ready for battle *at all times*. We won't always have a chance to dress. And, as I'm demonstrating" —Jeanne twisted her knife so it gleamed in the candlelight and the man under it tensed—"you are more vulnerable when you aren't wearing breeches." She withdrew her blade, purposefully nicking Roland's thigh. "Now get dressed, and ready yourselves for battle."

With that, she whirled around and marched back up onto the deck, stopping briefly on the way to berate her first mate for letting the men sleep naked and vulnerable.

He frowned. "M'lady, how else would they sleep? That's how it's done."

"Not on my ship," she snapped. "They'll sleep ready for battle, or they'll sleep in the depths of the sea."

His head shake let her know that he was irritated but would pass along her message, that he'd keep the men in line from now on. Satisfied, she nodded curtly and started up the ladder.

Alexi was at the top, on his way to get her.

"It's a merchant ship, m'lady. Flying the French flag."

# THE LIONESS

THE MERCHANT SHIP saw them coming, but it didn't matter. Jeanne's Genoese warship was sleeker, faster, and ten times as agile as the heavy dark-wood ship on its way south with cargo bound for Aquitaine or Castile. They rammed the oars and stopped the vessel in its tracks before its crew even knew what was happening.

Her crew dropped planks and grapples to board the enemy's ship in droves—Pieter strong and fierce in the lead; Alexi and the other archers picking off men with their arrows from the deck; the frightened naked Roland of an hour ago trying to redeem himself by fighting like a bear who'd lost her cubs, taking out almost half of them by himself. Jeanne threw herself into the fray, light on her feet, focused, cutting down the opposing crew as they tried to push her back.

There was a single nobleman on board—stocky, blonde, arrayed in finer clothes and with a well-made sword singing through the air. By the time Jeanne launched herself at him, he'd already felled two of her men.

For Jeanne, the real fight had begun.

The man was strong and well trained, his eyes narrowed in concentration, his swordplay tight and swift. Jeanne danced and dodged, swinging at his neck, his knees, his underarm. He caught each blow easily and then, too quick to block, his own sword flew left and caught her in the shoulder. Jeanne hissed in pain.

Somewhere behind her, there was a gasp.

But Jeanne's armor held—it would be a bruise, not a cut. Rage rose in her chest, and she flung herself at the nobleman, bringing her blade down at his head with all the force she could muster. He blocked the strike with his own sword, and then, with a look of surprise and horror, he dropped it.

Jeanne had driven her dagger into his side. It wasn't just her own men who foolishly thought themselves safe—not expecting a fight, the nobleman wasn't wearing chain mail under his garments. Pieter rushed forward to disarm him, forcing him to his knees.

Hair flew wild around Jeanne's face in the cool wind, her braids having come half-undone during the battle. Her shoulder throbbed in time with her heart, but the bruise was nothing. Less than nothing. She had taken her first merchant ship—and nothing could dampen that victory.

"Take the stores and the valuables," she called to her men. "Bring me anyone left alive."

Minutes later, a collection of ragged enemy sailors were arrayed on deck—a wizened captain, five young crewmembers, a skinny, scowling first mate, and the bleeding nobleman Jeanne had taken down herself. Something sinister and satisfying swelled in her chest.

The nobleman's tone was disgusted, his face a sneer. "Disgraceful," he hissed. "Just look at you—a highborn woman attacking her own countrymen."

Jeanne slipped her sword back into its scabbard, her knife already hidden away in the folds of her dress. "Oh, you're my countryman then? Because it's your king who killed my innocent husband. That's not very countryman-like, is it?"

"And you're avenging him, are you?" He bared his teeth. "A little woman with her hair down in public like a common whore."

Jeanne leaned in until her face was mere inches from his, and she smiled. "This little woman just destroyed you on the battlefield."

So he didn't like her hair down? Well, perhaps that was how she'd kill him. A little woman with her hair loose like a common whore. Standing tall again, she pulled the pins out and threw them along the deck, imagining each as a dagger straight at the king. None of his allies would tell her what to do.

She shook her hair out, wild and wavy from the braids, like a mane. A feral animal—a wildcat going in for the kill. "Now, where were we?"

The man scowled.

"Oh yes, I remember. You called me a whore, and I was about to behead you like the king beheaded my husband." Jeanne glanced over her shoulder at Roland. "Bring me my axe."

The angry noble's face paled, and his brows drew upward in surprise.

"Oh," said Jeanne, "did you think I would spare you? Why? Because you're a noble I can ransom and you think I'm a common pirate? Or perhaps because I'm a woman, and you think I'll have mercy on your worthless life?"

Roland pushed the axe into her hand.

"Whatever your reasons," she said, "they were wrong. This is war. There is no mercy. The king killed the merciful Clisson." She lifted the weapon. "All that's left is justice."

Jeanne's second beheading was cleaner than the first. A single strike got the job done. And then, still angry, still righteous, she stepped to the nearest sail and wiped the blood off her hands.

There was something satisfying about the two long red handprints. She was finally doing what she'd set out to do

—picking off the king and duke's allies one by one. Sacking their merchant ships. Ruining their plans. And the blood on the sails was a message, a flag flown high, a reminder that Jeanne was the kind of threat who did what she promised to do. Like the rocks in the duke's shoes, she would never stop needling. Sharp when they least expected her. A pain they couldn't escape.

She left three sailors alive to tell the tale, setting them adrift and burning their ship. As they rowed away, a whisper flew back to Jeanne on the wind.

"Lioness," they said. "The Lioness of Brittany."

# MEANWHILE...

## BLOIS, FRANCE

Juliet de Penthièvre, the Duchess of Brittany, watched as her husband removed the tightly wound ropes around his torso, pink with dried blood. With each new wound revealed, her heart contracted, as if by removing his ropes, he was binding her with ropes of her own.

His were real, chosen. Hers were fear.

Fear of what would happen if he killed himself with this pain obsession—if the next time a fever racked him, it would tempt him all the way to heaven, leaving her behind to defend a duchy under siege. Fear of who he was becoming—a man whose avid prayers and sweet devotion had slid into more extreme forms every year. The pebbles in his shoes came first; the ropes were a later addition. On the last saint day, she'd walked in on him self-flagellating with a leather whip.

He asked if she could see Jesus' face in the wounds.

The pope had received him with open arms. The churches nearly worshiped him as their own saint. And Juliet should be happy, proud. She should thank god each day for a devout husband. She knew that.

Yet she couldn't stop the churning in her gut, the unsettled, sharp-edged fear that lived in her skin and her shoulders and her headaches.

"They're calling her the Lioness." Charles' voice was calm as he dropped the final rope, allowing his physician to examine the wounds.

He was speaking to Juliet, not the doctor, but Juliet already knew about the lady Clisson's new name—she'd read the letter before hand-delivering it to Charles, as she always did. The king must have been in a fit while dictating it. His language had been harsh and chaotic, telling them that the lady Clisson had taken at least two merchant ships, disrupting important trade routes. Her men had killed many at Rennes, though that much Juliet had known before the letter, since Rennes was their own doorstep. Past battles had decimated the king's fleet, so he was scrambling to build more ships, to go after the Lioness on the Channel.

Charles had scoffed upon reading that the lady Clisson was said to dye her sails in the blood of the slain, but Juliet believed it. She'd seen what her husband was capable of; why would the lady Clisson *not* be capable of dying sails in blood? They lived in a brutal world.

"Are you listening, my love?" Charles looked over his shoulder, his eyes serious.

She'd loved those eyes once. She'd been proud to be with someone with such pretty eyes. Their unfathomable depths had been a source of intrigue, a mystery for her to unravel.

Now, she only wanted to unknow his mysteries.

"Yes, sorry," she said. "Does her new moniker worry you?"

It wasn't where he wanted the conversation to go. She

could tell because he redirected it, as was his habit. "I've been praying about it, and I'm sorry to say that we're going to have to do something drastic."

Juliet's bound-up heart squeezed tighter, but she didn't answer. Didn't ask what he meant. She had learned the hard way that she would always regret asking that question. But as the doctor tended his wounds and Juliet stood with her hands folded demurely across an ice-blue skirt, he answered the unasked anyway. And it was just as terrible as she had imagined.

"We need to know where her children are. Much like god sent the bears after the children who teased his prophet, the ends here will justify the means."

## CHAPTER 17
# THE ENGLISH CHANNEL

Her hero Isabella was known as the She-Wolf, and now Jeanne was the Lioness.

As she lay in bed in her cabin, staring into the darkness, the name shivered through her—a thrill every time she thought about it. She wondered what news had reached the king. Did he know she'd taken his castles? Did he know she'd taken those first ships? Was her name even now flitting across France from ear to ear, spoken in hushed tones? *Lioness. Fire-starter.* She who has no mercy.

They would remember her. They would remember Olivier. She wondered if the news would reach the children. She wondered if they'd be proud.

She ran her hands over the rough woolen blankets and found Monster, curled in a soft warm ball to her left. For the first time since setting off, she let herself daydream about Olivier. About his hands, rough and calloused and gentle on her skin. About his laugh, never quiet, always a sudden crash. Sometimes it would startle Little Jeanne. They'd be playing and—boom—laughter, and Little Jeanne would

108

topple onto her rear, eyes wide. Then her brothers would laugh, and she'd laugh too. Guillaume would try to pick his little sister up like the sweetheart he was, even though he wasn't big enough. And Olivier would laugh again and sweep the little angel into his arms.

Jeanne missed them all.

She wondered again what the children's lives looked like now. Were the nuns forcing them to sit up straight and learn their letters? Did they get enough sunshine? Had they forgiven her for leaving? The thought made her heart ache, and she breathed deep and slow to keep from crying. Crying wasn't an option. Not here. Not on her ship. Not with her men so close. Not when she could be called back into battle at any moment.

She focused on the ship's noises—the loud groan of timbers grinding together, the smack of waves. And something else. A soft noise, scraping along the floor.

Jeanne froze, listening as it slithered closer. Was someone in her room? Had her ship been boarded without her knowledge? It seemed impossible, yet something, *someone*, was moving toward her in the pitch black.

She slid her hand along the side of the feather mattress to where she'd affixed her dagger, wondering if she could slide off the bed without being heard. Which side would this phantom attack from? A trained fighter would opt for the side where his dominant hand gave him the advantage, so Jeanne took a risk. As quietly as she could, she rolled to her left—the intruder's right—landing lightly on her feet. Monster had moved, and her path was clear. But the noises had stopped. Had the intruder heard her? She crouched, waiting for another movement, dagger in hand.

And then it came.

The man leaped onto the bed with an audible thump.

There were no ripping noises of a knife plunged where her neck had been. *It's not an assassin*, she realized. This was one of her crew, come not to take her life, but her *dignity*. Outrage beat through her like a second heart as the man discovered she wasn't in the bed. He cursed. And then Monster was back—screeching as only a cat can—and she must have scratched him, because the intruder cried out in pain. Jeanne felt a rush of love for the little devil.

She could hear the man now, sense the shape of him scrambling on her bed, so when she transferred her dagger to her left hand and channeled her anger into a punch aimed at his head with her right, she connected. His grunt was somewhere between surprise and pain. Jeanne didn't wait for him to process the blow—she tossed her dagger back into her right hand and hurled herself into him, sending them both crashing to the rough wooden floor. Something flew from his hand and skittered across the room.

She found his shoulder and twisted hard, forcing a scream out of him. "Don't even twitch, you damn traitor," she hissed, pressing her dagger to his neck. Louder, she called, "Pieter! Alexi!"

There was a shuffling outside the door, then a tentative unfamiliar voice asked, "M'lady, did you call out?"

"Yes. Bring a light, quick!"

The door opened, and a young sailor whose name she didn't yet know entered with a candle in hand. When he saw the scene on the floor, he froze. "M'lady! What happened?"

She twisted her attacker's shoulder tighter as she answered through gritted teeth. "This man attacked me. Bring me the light. *Show me his face.*"

By now, more men were crowding in her doorway.

THE LIONESS

Pieter pushed through them and into the room, his lips pressing into a thin, repulsed line. Amée slipped in behind him, eyes wide, hand fluttering to her heart. Alexi was there too, but his usual jokes were nowhere to be found.

The young crewman brought the light closer.

*Roland.*

Jeanne's stomach sank. She'd thought that Roland was one of her most loyal men. He'd come with them to hide the children. She'd trusted that he was better than the rest. Was she a fool? Or...was it because she'd threatened him to prove her point about sleeping nude? Had he turned, so quickly, to a man with a grudge? Was this how it would always go—she'd chastise her men, and they'd respond with rebellion?

If she were a man, he would have fallen into line, she thought darkly. Everything had consequences. If she didn't chastise the men, they'd think her weak. Since she had, one of the men she'd thought most loyal had decided to punish her. She released Roland's shoulder, stood, and stepped back. He groaned and lifted himself with his good arm.

"Explain yourself." Pieter's voice was a low threat, his own dagger drawn.

Roland just stared, his face pale, belt undone—a testament to his intentions.

Jeanne couldn't keep a man like that on her ship. There were rules at sea. If a man killed another, you tied him to the corpse and threw the pair overboard together. If one punched another, you tied him up and dunked him in the sea three times. But what was the penalty for this? For attempting to teach your captain a lesson with rape. For the attempted theft of dignity.The penalty for mutiny was death. And this was a sort of mutiny.

Yet she felt the rage draining out of her. She was tired of

111

fighting men without honor, of being the only one who seemed to care about what was right, of looking on in horror as men she'd trusted—the duke and now Roland— took what they wanted and stabbed her in the back. Could she do this? Could she spend her life chasing justice when no one else cared?

She sighed and shook her head at the pale, quiet man awaiting his fate. She should kill him herself, run her sword through his heart. But she was so tired. Better to let the sea do the job for her. Let Roland fight until the cold stole the fight from him and pushed him into the depths.

"Jacques," she said, turning to her first mate, "throw him into the sea."

# 1344

CHAPTER 18

# THE ENGLISH CHANNEL

*Dearest Maman,*

*The king is attempting to confiscate our lands. He's already taken Clisson, but he'll have Châteaubriant and Belleville over my dead body. I've taken the matter to the courts.*

*The duke's visit did not yield any important information, but I believe he is satisfied that we are not in contact with you. Please be careful with any messages. If the king finds out we're on speaking terms, it will undermine my case.*

*Geoff says I should also tell you to try not to get yourself killed because you matter more than our lands, but you know what I meant.*

*Your Louise.*

THE LIONESS

Jeanne clutched the message in her fist as the storm built around her and the ship swayed ever wilder on the raging ocean. For once, she wasn't the most furious thing on the English Channel—now, it was the storm.

As the ship rocked and rain drenched them all and the men below deck heaved in misery, she reread the message she'd received two days ago. She tucked it into her bodice, relieved all over again that Charles had gone away convinced and that her two oldest children were safe. Nothing else in the note was news. Of course the king would try to take any lands Jeanne had claim to. Of course Louise would fight him tooth and nail.

Jeanne pressed a hand against her bodice, as if touching the note could let her reach across the miles to her daughter. Something about it had left her homesick for all of her children. Especially with the storm building upon itself, lightning cracking open the sky.

The ship dipped again, this time deeper, and Jeanne stumbled into the mast, smacking her forehead against the slick wood.

Jacques appeared at her elbow. "M'lady, the storm is too bad, and the boat is too heavy. We need to lighten our load."

Jeanne shook her head, water flying off her in every direction. "We need everything we have."

"We won't need nothing if we're all dead."

Thunder cracked, and lightning lit the clouds like fire, and Jacques motioned toward the sky as if it had made his point for him, then crossed himself. Jeanne frowned. She'd chosen him because they said he knew the Channel better than anyone. If he said they were in danger, it must be true.

"Do it. Tell the men to lose everything we can afford to lose." Jeanne was shouting now, to be heard over the roar of the storm. "The ovens, the food, my desk—everything but the weapons. Do you think we can save the mast?"

She hoped it wasn't that bad, but what did she know about sailing? In the months she'd been at sea, this was the first frightening storm they'd faced. She knew that the reason they kept an axe onboard was for storms like this, storms that got bad enough that the only way to keep a ship afloat was to cut down the mast and hope they could float to shore without it.

She almost laughed at the absurdity. She'd escaped the clutches of the king, burned his allies' castles to the ground, turned half the country against him. And now she might have to destroy her own ship and hope god saw fit to drift them to a port that wasn't full of enemy soldiers out for their blood.

"It's not quite so dire yet, m'lady," Jacques shouted. "We'll lighten the load to keep her steady and pray that the storm doesn't get worse."

And then he was gone, yelling at the crew about jettisoning supplies, his exact words stolen by the howling wind. Lightning ripped the sky in half over and over. Wind tossed Jeanne's ship like it was nothing. The rails dipped down again and again to touch the sea, waves crashing across the deck. Thunder raged.

Jeanne turned her face skyward and took a deep breath. She knew she should be afraid, knew that this was bad, knew they might all die. But she felt strangely calm. Focused. As if the storm wasn't an enemy, but the world finally seeing her rage and embracing it as its own.

THE STORM *WAS AN ENEMY*. Jeanne had been a fool to think otherwise.

She stood on deck, a rope around her waist, the other end tied to the ladder leading into the dark terror-quieted belly of the ship where men crossed themselves, held onto whatever they could, and heaved in time with the waves.

The wind whipped Jeanne's ship back and forth, and in turn, the ship whipped her. Swinging to the left, her shoulder smashed into the rail, and she almost lost her grip. The icy rain dulled the pain—if it didn't feel so awful, she'd say the cold wet numbness was a gift.

Only a few crewmembers were with her to drop and raise the sails as needed, hold the ship steady, point it into the waves. They were all similarly secured with ropes to keep them from flying into the sea. Jacques had ordered everyone else below, including Jeanne, who'd stared him down until he threw a rope at her and yelled, "Then tie ye self up unless you want to drown."

She was glad for the rope now. She'd already lost her grip on the rail a dozen times, crashing into and slipping along the wave-drenched deck. Without the ropes, every person on deck would have gone over.

The ship pointed precariously upward, climbing a massive wave, and Jeanne's stomach swooped as she dug her hands harder into the rail. The prow was the sturdiest part of the vessel, the safest place to take the waves' unending blows, but as this one crashed down, sending Jeanne to her knees, she wondered if it could withstand this kind of beating.

*Damn this storm.* She'd thought they'd had an understanding. Just hours ago, the sky's rage had been beautiful. Now, it was going to kill her.

It wasn't that Jeanne was afraid of death. But what a pointless way to go. Dead on the whims of the ocean. Dead against something she couldn't fight with swords and daggers. Dead without first destroying Philip and Charles.

*No.* A familiar rage rose wild in her chest. She wouldn't die before she killed the king. She'd raise herself from the damn grave before letting that happen. Those bastards wouldn't get away with what they'd done.

Another wave—and Jeanne flew backward, barely keeping hold. The ship cracked ominously beneath her.

"Jeanne." Pieter appeared, clinging to the ladder's rungs, then emerged, slow and shaky. She wondered whether he was strong enough to hold himself steady, and immediately got her answer when a wave sent him crashing face-first onto the deck.

"You shouldn't be up here," she said.

"You're bleeding," he answered.

Jeanne shrugged, but the effect was lost as the ship hit another wave and she stumbled forward. She knew she was bleeding. Could feel the raw scrapes across her palms, another warm across the side of her face. Another sudden jerk and Jeanne slammed into Pieter, who was lifting himself to his feet. Her shoulder smacked his ribcage, and he made a strangled sound that reminded her of a stepped-on cat.

"You should go to your cabin," he shouted.

"And be skewered by flying daggers?" she shouted back. "I'll take my chances out here."

Jeanne didn't really care about the daggers. The storm was terrifying, yes, but the idea of being below deck, helpless in the dark, awaiting an unknown fate—that was worse. At least up here she could scream at fate as it tried to fling her from her ship.

THE LIONESS

"It's safer there. Out here..." Pieter's voice dropped off as they both watched a crewman go flying across the deck, jerking so hard at the end of his rope that Jeanne was convinced he'd broken his back. But the man curled into a ball—alive, capable of movement—and stayed there for a few moments before pushing himself to his knees and scrambling back toward Jacques, who was scaling the mast, adjusting the sail.

Lightning again tore across the clouds overhead, and Jeanne's vision pulsed white. Where before she'd felt determined, angry at the storm, now her rage had cooled into a deep unease. She was helpless here. So much more helpless than she'd ever been. Men she could fight, but this—this was something else altogether. She couldn't reason with the storm. Couldn't fight it. Couldn't magic it away with Amée's tricks. They were at its mercy, and Pieter wasn't even wearing a damn rope.

She let go of the rail and untied the rope at her waist.

"What are you doing?" Pieter shouted as she pulled it tight around him.

"Saving your damned life."

She tugged the rope again to loop it around herself, but before she got it re-tied, a wave crashed over them, this time from the side. The ship tilted farther than Jeanne thought it could tilt, and she wrapped herself fiercely around Pieter as both were tossed through the air, slamming into the ship's railing, a tangled mess of bruises and blood. She pushed to her knees, coiled the end of the rope around her middle, and tied the tightest knot she could manage with shaking hands.

"Jeanne." Pieter's voice was softer now, barely audible over the screaming storm. He lifted her to her feet and moved toward the ladder. "We need to get below, or we're not going to make it."

She smiled without humor. "We probably won't make it even if we do."

## CHAPTER 19
# THE ENGLISH CHANNEL

They survived the storm.

The ship was battered and waterlogged, the men tinged green with seasickness, Jeanne scratched and scraped from her ill-advised time on deck. The supplies were gone, but they were alive, and when the sun rose bleary through the storm's leftover haze, the ship was intact.

Louise's letter wasn't. When Jeanne pulled it from her bodice, she found it soaked through, the ink bled beyond recognition. Jeanne wanted to cry. Such a small thing, that letter, but it had meant so much. The storm had spared Jeanne, but not her comfort.

"Land ahead." Pieter's voice rang across the deck as he pointed through the haze to an English fishing village in the distance.

Jeanne, Alexi, and Amée joined him at the rail, watching the village inch closer. It was smaller than Jeanne would have liked—a tiny cluster of buildings in a small cove—but it looked big enough to buy some basic supplies. Food. A new clay oven. Most of the chickens had made it through the storm, but Jeanne wouldn't mind having a few more.

Pieter turned to Alexi, who was uncharacteristically silent. "I'm sorry about Roland," he said. "I know he was your friend."

Jeanne startled. Why was Pieter bringing that up now? She glanced at him, but he was focused on Alexi who, she suddenly realized, she hadn't seen laughing since they'd watched Roland fade into the distance, a struggling speck in the cold gray channel. *Merde*, she hadn't even noticed Alexi was sad. Hadn't thought that anyone might miss the man who'd tried to hurt her.

"Eh, he was a crooked-nosed knave." Alexi waved away the concern, but his voice was flat.

Amée caught Pieter's eye and offered Alexi a half-smile. "They tell me you're the best practical joker on the ship."

Alexi shrugged.

"Come on now, tell him a joke!" Pieter chided. "Tell Arley about the time you put fish in Roland's bedroll."

Jeanne joined in. "Or how you managed to get a castle full of dogs to follow him around and make love to his ankles."

At that, Alexi grinned. "It was a great joke."

"What about the time you put itching powder in his armor?" Jeanne said.

Pieter punched the other man playfully on the shoulder. "Or when you paid all the men to scream every time he walked by for a whole day?"

"I didn't know what he was then," Alexi said, glancing at Jeanne, his voice heavy with feeling.

She shrugged, uncomfortable with the raw emotion. "None of us did. None of us knew what he'd become."

Alexi let out an audible breath. "I think I'll go help with the inventory. Figure out what we need."

Jeanne watched him go, then turned back to the rail. They were closer to the village now, and her heart dropped —what had looked from afar like a healthy trading port, all timbered houses and strong wooden piers, cobbled streets and rich green gardens, was a wreck. The storm had ripped the little village apart. Collapsed roofs jutted up from houses and side yards like broken bones. A mudslide weaved through part of the town, burying carts and gardens. Boats had shattered against the rocks where they'd been tethered for safekeeping. One was inexplicably lodged in the branches of a tree.

If Jeanne had expected to find shelter and comfort and replenishments, she knew now that they'd be lucky to find enough for a single meal for her men. Still, they disembarked at the village and wandered through the wreckage, asking about supplies.

One woman scowled as she dragged her fingernails through the thick mud at her door. "You nobles, you think money solves everything. Have a problem? Throw some coin at it! Well, your money's no good here. Look around, fool—we can't sell ye what we don't have."

The same sentiment—if less colorfully presented—was there at every turn. The gardens were under mud. The chickens killed or run off into the storm. If people had anything left, they weren't telling.

"What do we do now?" Amée asked, as she, Pieter, and Jeanne climbed into the rowboat to make their way back to the ship, anchored just outside the cove. "We could follow the coast," Pieter suggested. "Find another fishing village."

Jeanne swept her hand toward the thick, soupy fog and the sky still dark and heavy with threat. "And what if it storms again? No, we'll just have to go without until the fog clears and the danger is over."

Amée looked thoughtful. "We've weathered it once. We could make it again." Her voice grew more certain. "I heard them call you the Lioness. A lioness doesn't hide in her cave because there might be other predators in the fields. She hunts. Your enemies can hide in coves and starve to death after storms, but we're pirates. You *are* the storm. And that" —she motioned toward the Channel—"is where the supplies are. On well-stocked merchant ships and in French port towns. What if the storm isn't something to avoid, but rather something to embrace?"

The tempest had been terrible, and it had left Jeanne tentative, cautious. But there was something exciting about the thought of attacking from the fog, from the storm. Amée was right. They could spend their time wandering and resting and regrouping, or they could do the thing their enemies would least expect—attack when they had nothing left.

Pieter grinned from the back of the rowboat as he pulled the oars through the steel-gray water. "Aren't you glad I told you to bring him along?"

Jeanne tried to scowl at him but couldn't keep a smirk at bay.

"Time to find ourselves another merchant ship."

CHAPTER 20

# THE ENGLISH CHANNEL

Jeanne's ship sliced through the fog like butter as the crew of the stranded merchant vessel scrambled—some rushing for weapons, others choosing to abandon ship and take their chances in the water. Their mast was gone, a casualty of the same storm that had taken Jeanne's supplies. Yet the merchants hadn't jettisoned their own supplies, preferring to lose their means of navigation to their livelihood.

Too bad they'd now be losing both.

Jeanne grinned like a villain as her men flew across the gap between the ships with the practiced ease of seasoned pirates. They dispatched the crew efficiently, tossing one man into a wind-beaten rowboat to live and tell his tale.

So soon their fortunes had turned. Jeanne's ship was bursting with everything they needed—livestock and chickens, a new oven, replacement desk, candles, spices, food, and wool garments from Flanders. Her men whooped at the victory and stripped down on deck to change into the fine Flemish clothes. Jeanne was in such a good mood, she didn't even care that they were romping around half-naked.

Amée had been right. They were *pirates*. She was a *lioness*. They shouldn't behave like cautious merchants and honor-bound warships. Unpredictability was their sword and shield, facing storms and threats head-on their greatest weapon.

"Tonight"—Jeanne's voice rang out across the deck—"we feast!"

"Aye!" her men roared.

And feast they did.

The crew spread across the deck, dipping into salted beef-stew thick with beans, crunching hard flat sea biscuits, passing bottles of wine back and forth. Alexi, grinning for the first time in weeks, slipped some pickled fish into Jacques' stew, leading Jacques to shout the younger man down. Pieter watched on, delighted, as Amée disappeared and reappeared dried beans.

Everywhere Jeanne looked, her crew was spirited. Half a day ago, she'd thought they were all going to die, and now she felt a wild sense of triumph. They'd lived through the worst that she could imagine. Nothing could stop her now.

"How did you become an illusionist?"

It was late. Jeanne had retired to her cabin, but she was still jittery from the storm and their victory and hadn't wanted to be alone, so she'd sent for Amée. She didn't even know what she wanted to talk about, just that she wanted to be herself—not the Lioness, not a leader of men, just Jeanne—with another person. Another woman. For just a little while.

"Is that how you think of me?" Amée tilted her head. "As an illusionist?"

"It's what Pieter calls you." Jeanne settled on one side of her bed and motioned for Amée to sit as well. Monster slipped out of the shadows and curled in Jeanne's lap, the rumble of her purr like a steadying force. "You came to me as an herbalist, a healer, and an astrologer. But I've seen you disappearing beans and guessing at cards. You used ravens to disappear yourself that first day. Not to mention the fire. I doubt you read all those tricks in the stars."

Amée laughed and settled in beside Jeanne. "You're right. Astrologer is the safest word. Herbalist, too. They're terms the Church likes. *Science*, not magic. But the rest of what I do...some would call it magic or heresy. It's the kind of thing you have to be careful with.

"The world loves their illusions—traveling magicians, metal lions that move across the stage on their own, eggs that dance away from you when you try to grab them, men who catch on fire without catching on fire. But people are also afraid of them. Afraid that we can really set men on fire or disappear their fortunes or even take down kings and countries."

She stared at Jeanne as if measuring her up and carefully weighed her next words. "And, of course, I'm even more dangerous. Because outside the cities, they think I'm a foreigner, a Moor. They believe I cannot possibly be a Christian, a Frenchman, like them. In the cities, it's easier. They've seen brown skin before, and the Church teaches them about how Philip the evangelist converted a black eunuch on the road, so while they still think I'm foreign, they accept that I can also be a Christian. Not a devil. Not a witch. Not a...danger. Unless, that is, they think I'm dabbling in magic."

Jeanne listened, rapt, irritation fluttering at all the people who looked at Amée and saw a threat for no reason but her skin. It was the opposite of Jeanne's experience of the world, where she was reduced to a non-threat because of her sex. Jeanne had spent her whole life proving she *was* a threat. It sounded like Amée had spent hers proving she wasn't.

"Damn fools," Jeanne cursed.

Amée smiled and, after a thoughtful pause, went on. "You asked how I became what I am. I started with astrology and herbs, reading and writing, because that's what Giselle did, and so that's what she taught me. Mint to aid digestion. Hemlock mixed with fennel to cure the bite of a mad dog. Belladonna to poison or heal, depending on the application. Star charts to determine the best times for surgery, proposals, or war. The more I studied, the more I loved it." Her voice was higher now, excited. "I especially loved learning about King Arthur's Merlin. Without him, Arthur was nothing. He changed everything; his magic is what created the king. And I always wondered"—Amée blushed then—"if maybe Merlin was a woman."

Jeanne laughed. "Wouldn't people have known? They say he had a beard down to his knees."

"Did *you* know?" Amée raised an eyebrow. "Does the crew? They think I'm a baby-faced boy. Nobody's even wagered a guess that if they kicked me in the balls, I'd just smile at them, unharmed. And if you don't think women can grow beards, you haven't met the old women of my village."

Jeanne laughed again. *Merde*, Amée was strange—and wonderful. Nobody saw the world this way. No wonder she had everyone fooled.

"They also say he fell in love with the Lady of the Lake," Jeanne offered, curious to hear the next rebuttal.

"And a woman can't fall in love with a woman?"

*Damn.* When Jeanne was growing up, the British king had very clearly preferred men to women, so of course the reverse might also be true. With her bone-deep devotion to powerful women like Isabella the She-Wolf, it wasn't hard to imagine someone stepping beyond admiration and into love.

"You're right," she acquiesced. "Merlin could have been a woman." And then a thought occurred to her. She needed to check in with her spy networks soon—to send someone she trusted to gather information, collect more funds to pay her men, visit Louise and Geoff and then her smallest children at the nunnery without being detected. Who better than her very own Merlin?

"Merlin," she said, her tone teasing, and Amée's look of surprise and delight was deeply gratifying. Jeanne reached out, wrapped her hands around Amée's smaller ones, and squeezed. "I think you'd make a rather excellent spy. What do you say we put ashore and find out what Charles and Philip have been doing in our absence?"

Amée's smile matched Jeanne's own. "I say yes."

## CHAPTER 21
# THE ENGLISH CHANNEL

Three weeks after Jeanne sent Amée ashore for information and funds, an oar-controlled warship appeared on the horizon.

Her body hummed with nerves and anticipation as she gripped the rail, half-listening to the men preparing for battle behind her. They'd been at sea for a year now, and it had been a triumphant one. They'd taken merchant ships, sent burning French flags flying through the air and into the Channel, and lost fewer than a dozen of her own men in the process—unless she counted Roland, dead not in battle but through betrayal.

With every merchant vessel they took, new rumors reached her, and each one sent shivers of delight through her body. She was the Lioness of Brittany, they said. She dyed her sails in the blood of her victims, they said. She wore her hair down and cut through men like air. She was a ghost, a wraith, the devil's wife made flesh.

On the mainland, they feared her. They worshipped her. They whispered her name in hushed tones. She hoped with every fiber of her being that the king and the duke felt the full force of that fear.

But in a whole year of sweeping out of the fog to pillage and plunder, Jeanne had never faced a warship. Now one was on her horizon, straight-lined and heavy. If the king wasn't afraid of her yet...he was about to be.

As they'd done so many times before, Jeanne and her men approached the less agile enemy ship, bows taut and arrows in place.

"Loose," she cried, and the arrows flew.

"Nock," she cried, and the archers pulled another round tight.

But even as Jeanne's arrows flew, the warship's archers returned fire. As Jeanne's men swung aboard the warship, swords raised, the warship's men were boarding Jeanne's, bringing the fight to her. Unlike their battles with merchant ships, this ship was prepared.

There had never been a fight on Jeanne's deck, and she was caught off balance when a thick-necked, copper-skinned man flung himself onto the planks right in front of her and attempted to cut her down. Her own sword blocked his, and the fight exploded. The man was strong, but Jeanne was fast. She caught his strikes—each sending a bone-jarring wave of pain through her arms and shoulders—and then dodged to the side, leaving him to swing at empty air. He roared.

Out of the corner of her eye, she saw Pieter take down two French soldiers with a single blow. The man was a wonder with a sword—every inch his nickname, Mont Pieter. She'd have to ask him to teach her the move. But for now, she brought her sword up to block another attack, then another. Her arms burned with the effort as she waited for an opening.

And then it arrived.

A soldier stumbled into her opponent's back, and the blow he'd been preparing to deliver was knocked off course, falling heavy and harmless to Jeanne's right. She darted left and forward and swung her own sword at the man's exposed neck. He was dead even before he fell.

Jean kicked his sword away and turned on her toes, scanning for danger, for enemies that still needed dispatching. Instead, she found the battle nearly over. Pieter had two disarmed soldiers on their knees. Alexi had taken an arrow to the shoulder and was being tended to by a fresh-faced mercenary of Jeanne's.

"At least it's not my romantic arm," he joked, "if you know what I mean."

Most of the enemy soldiers were already dead, but a few lay face-down on the deck with her men poised above them, swords in hand.

And then, like an unexpected gift, one called, "M'lady Clisson! We have another nobleman."

By now, they knew Jeanne felt strongly about fighting her own fights. Any nobles who still served the duke and king were dead to her, and she'd cause their literal deaths herself. Her man brought the noble—young, black-haired and beige-skinned, with a grim expression and a long nose —and forced him to his knees before her.

"Last words?" the Lioness asked, raising her sword.

The man pressed his lips together and then, unexpectedly, broke into an eerie smile. "Yes," he whispered. "The king has your children."

## CHAPTER 22

# BRITTANY, FRANCE

Jeanne's face tingled with shock, and her vision blurred. Could it be true? Could the king have found Oli, Guillaume, and Little Jeanne?

The whole deck of soldiers—French crowned and mercenary alike—held its collective breath.

"He found your damn nunnery and burned it to the blessed ground," the nobleman hissed.

*Nunnery.*

He knew about the nunnery.

*Oh god*, it must be true.

The man smiled, enjoying the look on her face. "I didn't approve at first, but now that I've seen you...now that I see you are the devil himself, I can't help but think he did the runts a favor when he burned them alive."

Jeanne lowered her sword, her breath stuck in her chest. Her mind couldn't settle on any one thought. The faces around her blurred together, and her whole body throbbed with longing and fear and desperate disbelief. Questions she couldn't fully form rose and fell.

And then, without even knowing she was doing it, she raised her axe and silenced the man who'd told her—the man who'd supported the king's decision to burn her innocent, perfect babies, the one thing in the world Jeanne had left.

THE FIVE LONGEST days of Jeanne's life were those between that man's words and reaching the nunnery. This time, she took only Pieter, leaving Alexi and Jacques in charge of the ship and its crew. They raced along the coast by horseback, with Monster tucked into her saddlebag ignoring the jarring pace.

Until she saw it for herself, Jeanne was dedicated to not believing it true. If she rode fast enough, she assured herself, she'd get to the nunnery in time to save them. She'd get there in time to find them all alive. She refused to entertain any other possibility.

Then they reached it.

Jeanne nearly fell off her horse as a wave of grief hit her —it had been burned, just like the nobleman said. The sun was setting, turning everything orange, as if it was still on fire, but all that remained was blackened stone walls and scorched earth. Ash-smeared bones.

Jeanne jumped from her horse and circled the perimeter, as if the children might be hiding there, as if there were any place left to hide. She turned in a full circle, scanning the trees, stopping only when she spotted Pieter. His hand was pressed to his mouth, tears streaming heavy down his cheeks. Grief raw and sharp in his eyes.

They were *gone*.

They were really, truly gone. The world tipped over and Jeanne fell to her knees, sobbing, digging her fingers into the gray, ashy dirt.

# MEANWHILE...

## PARIS, FRANCE

THE KING HUMMED WITH GIDDY EXCITEMENT as he reached for Nicole and she danced away, teasing. That was how he liked things. A little game of cat and mouse: her pulling away, him drawing her in. Her surrendering slowly, unlacing her corset inch by inch. Him triumphant.

She'd been his mistress for two years, and she knew his moods well. Today, he was already feeling jubilant. He'd won an important battle, wooed an important ally. Something like that. Today, he wouldn't want to play long. He had already won some bigger game.

And he'd want to talk about it.

She pushed him gently onto the bed—all red velvet and blue silk—and slid in beside him. "Pray tell, what makes my king's eyes dance like that? Not another woman?" Her tone was mock offense. She wasn't really worried, didn't care if she stayed the king's mistress or was shuffled into obscurity. What she cared about was wealth—the wealth she had now, as he lavished it upon her; the wealth she'd have when he tired of her, the expected severance payment of a mistress dismissed.

He laughed at her question, kissed along her collarbone. "In a way, but not the way you mean."

She ran a finger along his ear exactly how she knew he liked.

"Jeanne de Clisson. I've finally defeated her. Finally found her weakness."

"And what weakness is that, my king?" she teased, an eyebrow arched as he traced a gentle finger down her throat.

"Her children."

It wasn't what she was expecting, and her normally carefully-crafted expression shifted with confusion, uncertainty, fear. She repeated his words, as if that might make sense of them.

"Her children?"

"Yes!" He sat up beside her, bouncing, gleeful, having either not noticed or not cared about her reaction. "I found them! I found the little brats! My men burned their nunnery to the ground. They're dust now. Ashes. She won't go on. She won't be able to go on!"

Nicole went cold as understanding dawned, sickening and jittery across her body. *Children?* Was he talking about burning *children* alive? Was he really laughing, giddy, over this? Her throat constricted, stomach boiling, as she tried not to react. Tried not to let the horror jump back from heart to face.

*She won't be able to go on.* This was what her king thought triumph was. Not beating someone in battle, not defeating them with ideas, might, superior skill. Triumph to this man was the murder of children.

Nicole thought of her own child—the king's bastard daughter. Could he really feel that way about children even when he had so many of his own? Ash. He'd called them ash. She couldn't breathe. He leaned in to kiss her, but she only gasped into his mouth.

"Come now, lover. Celebrate with me."

He kissed her again, and she tried to kiss him back, tried to shut down the part of her that was screaming its terror across her skin.

He pressed her onto her back and straddled her. "Let's try something different tonight."

She didn't—couldn't—respond. Frozen, too stunned, too sick, to know how to react. Then his hands were around her throat. And she really couldn't breathe at all.

## CHAPTER 23
# BRITTANY, FRANCE

Amée arrived quiet as a whisper and somber as a shadow.

One moment, Jeanne was alone in the ashes, her cheek pressed hard against the cold ground, her body quaking. The next moment, Amée was there, her arms around Jeanne's shoulders, surprisingly strong.

"I rode as hard as I could when I heard," she whispered. "Oh, Jeanne."

And then Pieter was there too, lowering himself to the ground with them. Jeanne looked up, unreasonably hoping that somehow she'd misunderstood. That they were at the wrong place. That the children were safe.

She knew it wasn't true, but her heart couldn't accept that this was it. Perhaps, she thought wildly, she'd wake up and Pieter wouldn't be crying, and Amée would tell her it was a nightmare. Instead, Pieter's face was pinched in grief, Amée's eyes a well of terrible understanding.

Jeanne clutched at the ashes, sharp and gritty in her hands. And then she heard Monster, kicking and screeching, battling to get out of the saddlebag. Did cats feel grief? Did she know what was going on?

The thought of Monster grieving was a strange comfort, and Jeanne's heart quieted ever so slightly as Pieter went to unlace the bag. The cat flew out like a hunted fox. She stopped next to Jeanne to sniff her, sniffed the ashes, then hissed long and loud, her fur standing on end and her tail thrust skyward.

The ache in Jeanne's heart grew deeper, spreading and tensing as if to break her apart. The cat knew, and she missed them too. It was like the cat was confirming her worst fears and somehow paying tribute to her loss at the same time.

Without warning, Monster turned tail and zipped along the cliff and into the brush. Jeanne lowered her head into her hands, leaning into Amée as sobs overtook her again. Until something rapped hard on the top of her head.

When Jeanne reopened her eyes, Monster was back in front of her, tail to the sky, fur bristled, staring. And then, she once more streaked into the brush. Jeanne watched her go.

Was Monster...could she be...trying to tell them something? Could the devil-cat possibly be asking Jeanne to... follow?

No, that was madness. Mad to think and madder to say. But Jeanne spoke it out loud anyway. "What if they escaped?"

Amée's eyes told Jeanne she thought it an impossibility. And it was. She knew it was. It *was* an impossibility.

And yet...

What if?

Jeanne stood and shook her head to shove away the wildly irrational thoughts. It was denial, nothing more. But

THE LIONESS

then Monster was back again—tail and fur erect, butting into Jeanne's shin since she could no longer reach her head. Pieter was on the ground, head in his hands, too absorbed in his grief to see. But Amée's eyebrows rose as she gave Jeanne a long probing look, and with a shuddering breath, Jeanne followed the cat into the blue-tinted evening.

Although it was madness, although it was impossible, she *had to* follow. If she didn't make sure, she'd always wonder. What if she overlooked Little Jeanne stranded on a cliff's edge or Guillaume whimpering in the brush? So she'd search every cliff, every cluster of bushes, every hollow in every tree before she left. The farther she went, the more certain she grew. She had to search every hollow. Every tree. Every cliff edge and beach cove. Then and only then would she truly believe that her babies—her precious, innocent babies—were gone.

Branches tore at her skirts and mud sucked at her boots as she struggled through the brush, following Monster over some invisible path. Pieter and Amée caught up and he whispered something about securing the horses, but she didn't care. Nothing mattered except forward motion and a straight-tailed, agitated cat.

They wound through harsh low bushes and over uneven stony ground, along a blade-thin path winding sharply down the cliffs and to a stretch of beach in a cove guarded by imposing rocks just a few yards out to sea. Was there still hope, or was Monster simply following an animal trail, leading Jeanne to nothing? She choked on the thought.

Tears streamed down her face the whole way to a small fisherman's shack with a tiled hole in the roof leaking gray smoke into the sky. Monster turned to look at Jeanne—her candle-like eyes so intelligent. *God, please*—please *let her be*

141

*taking me to them.* Jeanne hated herself for clinging to a chance so slim, yet simultaneously felt an impossible pressure of hope building in her chest.

Uncharacteristically timid, knowing that the spell would soon be broken, that she'd have confirmation the cat had led her on a wild goose chase, that her hope had been for nothing, Jeanne steeled herself and knocked. There was a bustling inside, and the sound of children—*children!*—and then a short plump woman with a no-nonsense expression opened the door.

"Yes, what do you want?" she asked, hands on her hips.

Jeanne opened her mouth to speak but coughed instead, trying to force the unreasonable words out through her sand-dry throat.

Pieter's hand came down warm and gentle on her shoulder. "Madame," he said, his voice hoarse, "this is Jeanne de Clisson. Her children were housed in the nunnery. We were wondering..." He paused. "We were wondering if you know what happened to them."

The woman eyed them with suspicion. "You've wasted your time, sir. I haven't seen any children."

But she had. There were children here. Jeanne *knew* there were—she'd heard them just moments ago. Unless it was all in her head.

Finally, she found her voice. "Oli! Guillaume! Jeanne! If you're here, come out. It's Maman! Come out. Please, please, come out."

There was a long pause, and Jeanne's legs gave out beneath her. She fell to the sand, darkness eating at the edges of her vision. She was such a fool. The cat had been following the scent of fish, the trail of an animal, the—

A squeal of delight rang through the air. Little Jeanne— hair flying unruly behind her, arms flung out like a starfish,

THE LIONESS

taller and rounder but unmistakably herself—burst through the door.

"Maman, Maman! You came back!" she screamed, throwing herself into her maman's shaking, unbelieving arms.

Four more small pale faces appeared from behind the door: two girls who must have been the fisherwoman's daughters, and two faces she knew even better than her own.

Guillaume and Oli.

They were alive.

They were safe.

The curious, strange, wonderful devil-cat had led Jeanne to her children.

## CHAPTER 24
# BRITTANY, FRANCE

T he king would pay for what he'd done. An eye for a damn eye. A burned-down fortress for a burned-down nunnery.

*You stand for mercy, Jeanne.*

No, she damn well did not.

Pieter tried to talk her out of it, begged her to whisk the children away from the coast and straight to the ship where they could safely make plans.

"They'll be safe with you," she answered. "Protect my babies. Arley and I won't be more than a day."

"Or maybe you won't come back at all." His voice was sharp, a pinprick to a mother's guilty conscience.

Yes, two women taking down an entire fortress was dangerous. Yes, Jeanne might not return. But that's what love was—you fought for your family, punished the men who hurt them. Love was a fire, and fire didn't stop raging just to save itself.

Before Pieter could protest further, Jeanne and Amée were gone. First, they visited the nearest town to buy clothes appropriate for a pair of kitchen workers—the same

144

THE LIONESS

disguise Amée had used for her attempt on the duke's life. From there, they kept to the coast, through the shadowy forest on their horses, and toward King Philip's nearest military fortress.

They stopped only once, to rest the horses. Jeanne used the time to unfold Louise's latest letter, returned with Amée.

*Dearest Maman,*

*We have heard little of the king's movements lately. He is happy about some victory or other, but no one knows what it is. Something to do with the Church, I believe, since he just gave them a handsome sum of money and invited the Pope to some grand event. We are not invited, which is a slight I cannot help but think traces back to his feelings about you.*

*Not to worry. I don't think he suspects us of anything, only that he means to slight us after your piracy and us managing to keep our lands. It really is inconvenient to be disliked by him. I am starting to feel truly annoyed.*

*Your Louise.*

JEANNE'S HEART followed the shape of the words, rising in rage at the insinuation that Philip had triumphed—knowing it was because he'd burned the nunnery—and then settling into something like fondness by the end. Because yet again, the letter was so very Louise. Jeanne missed her. Geoff too.

After a short rest and a drink at the stream, Jeanne and Amée remounted their horses.

"Tell me everything," Jeanne said as they picked their

way through the trees. It was the first moment she'd had to ask Amée about her spy mission.

"Amélie sends regards—and funds. I left them with Pieter. You've already read Louise's letter. Not much there, but her and your son are well. Everyone says Philip seems to be honoring the truce with Britain. He's been rather quiet, holed up and charging everyone those new taxes they hate so much."

Jeanne snorted. "Of course, they do. He bleeds the country dry at war, then charges the peasantry to fund the next round."

"They say Queen Joan is urging him to break the truce just to get him out of the castle. They're calling her evil again, saying she's marked by the devil and that they should have known she'd run France into the ground."

Irritation skittered across Jeanne's skin. Philip was the problem—weak-willed, paranoid, by all accounts a terrible soldier. He'd killed dozens of nobles in the purge after Olivier. And yet, the peasantry blamed his wife. Perhaps Joan was urging Philip to do things, but he didn't have to listen. Whatever he did, it was on him. Philip was *king*.

"The duke is well," Amée continued, her previously calm tone taking on an edge. "His rival for the Breton dukeship has fled to Britain, and Charles is attending Mass twice a day to celebrate. He's been 'purging the land of evil'."

"What does that mean?"

They reached the edge of the forest. Both women dismounted, led the horses back a bit, and tied them in a thick patch of trees. Fortress torches, newly lit in the twilight, flickered in the distance. "It means when people saw me riding the roads near Nantes, they called me a Moor and a devil and told me I'd better run if I knew what was good for me. It means Charles is holding heresy trials—

killing people again in the name of his god." Amée's movements were sharp as she pulled the clothes from her saddlebag to get changed.

"I hate him."

Amée nodded. "I hope the infection from those ropes kills him."

"No," Jeanne said. "That's too easy." She pulled the new dress over her head and tugged it into place. "I want him to die with my knife in his chest, knowing that his betrayal cost him everything."

It was all that was left to say. Jeanne looked at Amée and knew she felt the same. They were going to kill Charles or die trying. Both women stuffed their usual clothes into the saddlebags, straightened their disguises—Jeanne's a kitchen maid, Amée's a kitchen boy—and shuffled toward the fortress, heads down like servants.

At the gate, Jeanne ducked reverently and batted her eyes at the guards who mindlessly waved them through—servants below their notice. It was almost too easy, she thought as they walked through the courtyard and then the fortress' interior. Men were so ridiculously confident, so sure that a servant girl, stable boy, or kitchen wench couldn't possibly do them harm. Arrogant, overconfident fools. Jeanne and Amée would be in and out before they knew what hit them. She'd teach them to underestimate her again. She'd teach them to underestimate any woman. And she'd teach them the cost of hurting little babies.

Rage coursed through her at the thought—a wildfire catching in the dry brush—and she pressed her lips together to keep from screaming. She wanted to hit something. Someone. Any of the king's men she could get her hands on.

But no. Starting a fight would get them caught, get

GIGI GRIFFIS

them killed, and then who'd fight for her family? She'd stick to the plan. She'd do the king more damage by channeling her rage into something quieter and more deadly.

A few steps into the fortress, Amée split off to find the servants' quarters. Jeanne mentally mapped the lower level —kitchen to the right surrounded by food storage, great hall to the left, servants' quarters up that staircase, soldiers' quarters across the courtyard—and then she began her work, making her way from the back of the fortress to the entrance.

She started the first fire in a food storage room, knocking the flint together, blowing the sparks into small flames that licked at the dry sackcloth and wooden crates. When she was sure it had caught, she stepped into the hall and marched onward.

Her second fire was in the stables—trickier because when she arrived, a young man was tending the horses. *Merde*, she hadn't been planning on killing anyone outright. A fight would make noise and draw attention. Attention would bring reinforcements. Reinforcements meant capture. Perhaps she could knock him out instead, but with what? She didn't have anything heavy on her.

Unless...

"Bonjour," she whispered, ducking her head and batting her eyelashes.

The man looked up. "I haven't seen you around before."

"I'm new," she said breathily. "And I'm lost, you see." She spread her hands out helplessly. "I was wondering if you could show me?"

"Of course." Grinning, he strode toward her. "Where are you trying to go?"

When he was only inches away, she took his hand and led him into a corner, pressing her back against the wall.

Delighted, he leaned in for a kiss. Jeanne quirked a smile, reached for the back of his neck, and slammed his forehead into the wall.

*Fool.* She stepped over the unconscious body and lit her fires. They caught even faster here, surrounded by dry hay and heavy timber.

When she left the stables, she moved briskly. She could already see a tendril of smoke from where Amée had lit her first fire in the servants' quarters, and it wouldn't be long before others started to notice the spreading flames. Soon there would be alarms singing out all across the fortress.

Her last stop was the soldiers' quarters. It was early evening, and no one was in, just as Jeanne had hoped. She worked quickly, each straw mattress catching fire faster than the one before. She coughed from the smoke and burned herself twice, but still she kept going. The king had tried to kill her children, so she would make damn sure he lost this fortress. And then, with mattresses blazing behind her, she scurried out of the room—and crashed straight into a barrel-chested soldier rushing in.

*Merde.* She stepped back and searched his face. He was startled and confused, looking first at her and then at the smoke now billowing through the windows. In the distance, people were shouting.

Jeanne pushed down her rage and threw herself into the man's arms. "I'm so glad you're here, sir! I saw smoke and went inside to see what was happening—and there's fire everywhere!"

She wished she could fake cry, but Jeanne had never been good at pretending. The only reason the young man in the stables hadn't seen straight through her was that he wanted it to be true. Would this one recognize her lies? She readied herself to pull the dagger from her hip, but the man was too distracted by the smoke. He moved her aside and rushed into the burning quarters, shouting behind him, "Go get help!"

"Yes, sir." Jeanne suppressed a sneer, lifted her skirts, and ran. When she reached the gate, she screamed, "Fire! Fire, m'lords! There's fire in the quarters!"

The three guards turned and saw the smoke. The man in charge ordered one man to stay behind while he and the other took off toward the growing inferno. Distracted, the remaining guard watched them go as Jeanne slipped behind him, drew her dagger, and drew it across his neck without hesitation.

Amée materialized out of the darkness, nodding, and Jeanne knew that meant three other fires were burning across the fortress. Too many for the men to put out in time. *How do you like it, Philip?* she thought. *How do you like the ashes and the bones?*

With no one to stop her, Jeanne lit the timber structure around the gate. After one last glance at the multiple smoke trails rising into the sky, she fled, Amée quick and quiet at her side like a ghost—the perfect accomplice. They mounted their horses and were off through the night.

Satisfaction coursed through Jeanne. She'd done it. The king had burned her sanctuary to the ground, and she'd burned one of his. But as she rode, the satisfaction dulled and faded, and her rage once again grew until she thought she must be the one burning.

"What are you thinking?" Amée's voice broke through the night.

"It's not enough."

How could a single fortress pay for what he'd done to her? He'd taken her husband without reason, but to take her children? Children so young they couldn't possibly defend themselves? And to not only try to kill them, but to burn them, denying them the Church's resurrection?

"The king is a monster—and it's not enough." Jeanne's voice was breathless now. "They're babies. He didn't take them hostage. He didn't threaten them. *He tried to burn them alive.*"

She suddenly wanted to be back there, watching the fortress burn. She wanted to run in and stab every one of Philip's men to death herself. She wanted to feel her hands around his throat. She felt like she was going to burst out of her skin, a screaming, violent ghost too full of fury to be held together by a body.

Amée's tone was hard. "My question is...how did he know?"

"What do you mean?"

"How did he know where to find your children?"

Jeanne startled. How *had* he known? Her stomach knotted at the thought—how could he have known where the children were? "The only people who knew were Pieter, Roland, Alexi, you, the nuns, and myself," she said. "Pieter and Alexi have been with me the whole time."

"And I don't believe either would betray you," Amée added. "Honor is the most important thing to Pieter. He promised Olivier he'd take care of you, and he'd die before he broke that oath."

Jeanne was strangely cheered knowing that Pieter had shared so much with Amée. Their regular card games apparently covered deeper ground than most of her men's conversations, which seemed to circle around women and bodily functions.

"Obviously *I* didn't tell the king," Jeanne said, "and I don't believe you did either." God, what a terrible thought.

Amée—her Merlin, her friend—stabbing her in the back like Charles and Roland.

"So that leaves the nuns, the Church," Amée said bitterly.

The words from Louise's letter rose up to haunt Jeanne —she'd said it was something about the king rewarding the Church. Jeanne clenched her fists tighter around the reins and urged her horse on. *The Church.* God's nails, she hadn't even considered the possibility. The Church had betrayed her. One of the nuns had told the king. Or one of the nuns had told someone else in the Church, and that person had told the king.

The fact that she might never know who it was made her even more furious. Had they died in the fire? She hoped so. She hoped they'd suffered. She hoped they'd felt the full agony of the fire intended for her children.

She wished the king could feel it.

Amée's voice broke through her thoughts again, soft this time, anger burned down into sadness, her whisper barely audible over the crunch of leaves under the horses' hooves. "The Church can't be trusted, Jeanne. Giselle saved my life, took me in when I had nowhere else to go. She taught me to read the stars, to tame the ravens, to make pine needle tea. She taught me how to feel safe. She was the best person I ever met, and they took her. Innocent like your children, and they took her."

Jeanne's fury burned even brighter and she imagined herself riding through the countryside razing churches to the ground. This time she wouldn't leave her usual man alive—let their god tell them who had done it.

Amée spoke again, her voice so pained that Jeanne wanted to reach for her hand across the dim forest path. "They took her, and now I can't remember what her voice sounded like, what the house smelled like after rain, how it felt to be safe like that. It's like they took part of me and no matter what I do, I can't get it back."

She paused. "I thought burning down that fortress would make me feel better—stronger, righteous. I imagined Charles' horror at finding out; I could picture his anger and his fear. But a man like that...does he even care? Does one fortress even matter to him? I'm starting to think he'll always win. They'll always win."

Amée was crying now, and Jeanne's protective heart raged. How did they end up with such an unjust world? How did so many women end up battered and broken against these sharp, careless men? She wished she could break *them* like that—watch them shatter with grief and the unfairness.

And with that wish came frustration, because Amée was right. They'd been wearing down the king's forces for a year. They'd taken his ships. Jeanne had killed his supporters with her own two hands. Yet at best, she was a splinter in a finger, a pebble in a shoe. The king was still living his life. Charles was still living his life.

Jeanne glanced over at Amée, silhouetted against the trees, her eyes shining in the moonlight, and she felt an understanding pass between them. Philip and Charles were the ones they wanted—and they remained out of reach. They were too well protected. *That* was the riddle to solve. Destroying their ships was satisfying in the moment, but what she really wanted was them. Not their allies. Not their fortresses. *Them.*

When they reached the fishing cottage, Jeanne dropped heavily from her horse. Why was this so damn hard? Would there ever come a day when she could get close enough to take their lives? She stood in the sand and breathed deep, willing her heart to calm and her rage to soften—she didn't want to storm in and wake the children. Amée took her hand, and Jeanne squeezed, grateful.

*Someday*, she promised herself. Someday she would find a way to get to them. Until then, she'd continue to strike at them in the dark with ships and fire and lies.

## CHAPTER 25
# BRITTANY, FRANCE

As Jeanne reboarded her ship, relief hit her like a wave. Little Jeanne was on her hip, face buried in her neck, and with her free hand, Jeanne was trying to wrangle both boys, touching one shaggy head, then the other. They were safe. They were alright. And she couldn't stop touching them—ruffling their hair, hugging them to her chest, placing her hands on their cheeks—to make sure she wasn't imagining things. To make sure they were real, they were here, they were alive and well.

The fisherwoman hadn't been much for explanations, but from what Jeanne could tell, when the soldiers broke in through the front of the nunnery, Oli had pulled his siblings out a rear window. He'd led them down the cliffs where they sometimes played with the fisherwoman's girls on the shore. Pride and horror battled for Jeanne's attention at the thought of Oli so brave, so knightly, so young, and so very alone.

But alone was something he wouldn't be again.

It was clear now, as perhaps it should have been from the start, that they were safest with her. No one could be trusted—not the nuns, not the Church. From now on, they'd stay in the one place the king couldn't reach them—with their mother.

She ushered the children below deck, instructing Jacques to set sail as she passed. Perhaps getting far away from the coast and out into the Channel would let her push the smoke-stained nunnery from her mind. In her cabin, she set Little Jeanne down on the elevated featherbed with its woolen blankets and colorful bedspread, and the now-four-year-old started playing with the enclosure curtains.

"You can't see me," she squealed, pulling them in front of herself and giggling madly.

Jeanne smiled and squatted before the boys. "You've gotten so big."

Oli pursed his lips and looked away. He'd been giving her the silent treatment ever since she'd found them, insisting on riding back to the ship with Pieter, shying away from her hugs. Jeanne's heart twisted in her chest. He didn't understand why she'd left. Would he forgive her? The question made her sick.

Guillaume was less angry, but it had been so long since she'd seen him, he ducked his head and glanced at his brother as she spoke. He still worshipped Oli—and at least they had that. At least they'd been together.

"Oli," she said, gently turning his face with her hand, "you know I left to keep you safe, right? You know I didn't *want* to leave you?"

He crossed his arms, and it was like he'd punched her in the gut. She should have tried to explain before she left, but they'd been so young...what could she have told them? Oli would have wanted to come with her, thinking himself a great knight, and Guillaume and Jeanne would have simply been too little to comprehend.

156

"Talk to me, darling." Her voice was soft. "Tell Maman what you're thinking. It's okay if you didn't understand why I left. We can talk about it now."

"I don't want to talk." Oli marched to the bed and flung himself behind the curtain with the still-giggling Little Jeanne.

Jeanne turned to Guillaume, her heart frantic in a way it had never been before. "And you, little love, will you talk to your Maman?"

Her voice broke at the end. She needed Guillaume—whose own heart had always been so big, whose love had extended to everything from Jeanne herself to bugs he found in the yard—she needed him at least to forgive her. If he forgave her, maybe Oli also could in time. Maybe she hadn't ruined everything by hiding them away.

Guillaume smiled shyly, dropping his gaze to the floor and swiveling his toes, and then he stepped forward to wrap his arms around her neck. For the second time in a few days, Jeanne sobbed as her heart broke—this time from hope. Hope that she could repair whatever damage she'd done. Hope that now, with her, they'd be safe. Hope that somehow everything would be okay.

"Oli," she whispered.

Behind the bed curtains, nothing moved and no one spoke. If he wouldn't forgive her outright, maybe he would for a bribe.

"You're old enough now for training," she said. "I can have Pieter start you with the sword and Alexi on a bow. Would you like that?"

She waited a long moment, still holding onto Guillaume, who was now playing with a loose thread on the back of her dress. And then, just as she thought he wouldn't answer, Oli poked his head out from behind the curtain, searched her face, and nodded. He hadn't changed that much. He was still his warrior father's—and his warrior mother's—son.

"Where will you take them—the children?"

Jeanne and Pieter stood at the rail, staring out at a sea that shimmered with starlight. It was late. The children were asleep in Jeanne's cabin, guarded by Alexi, who'd been instructed twice that waking them up would not be a funny joke. Amée sat alone across the deck with her back to the mast, watching the stars, while two men patrolled, watching for enemy ships.

"Nowhere," Jeanne answered. "The safest place for them is here with us. I can't protect them anywhere else."

"You can't be serious." Pieter's voice was deep and disapproving.

Jeanne's hackles rose. "I'm always serious."

"King Philip is a madman—he's not going to leave them alone. And how could you think they're safe here? We're raiding ships, for god's sake."

"And not a single damn one of those ships has cost us more than two men. The children will be in my cabin, Pieter, safer than they were in the damned nunnery. We've been sailing for over a year now, and we're good at it. We fight and we win. Yes, there will be more battles, more merchant ships to take, but I can keep my children safe. I *will* keep them safe. And I don't have to give up on Olivier to do it."

Pieter shook his head, balled his fists. "You're really going to do this?"

"What else would I do?" He'd never talked to her like

this before, and Jeanne wanted to hit him. She spoke through clenched teeth. "It's not like you've given me another suggestion."

"Run! Hide. After everything that happened, I thought you'd take them away from all this. Defect to the British and retire to the countryside. Take your money, take your children, and go."

"I can't abandon Olivier's honor!"

"He wanted you to be safe!"

They were shouting now, and Amée was staring at them from across the deck, her eyes wide and mouth hanging open.

"Justice matters more than my safety!"

"And the safety of Oli, Guillaume, and Little Jeanne?"

Jeanne snarled. "How dare you accuse me of putting them in danger. I'm taking them *out* of danger!"

Pieter paused, closed his eyes, and took a deep breath. His face was still pinched with anger, but he leaned back and lowered his voice. "It's my fault. I should have pushed you to run with them sooner. I thought we were doing the right thing—hiding them, getting justice for him—but this isn't what he would have wanted."

"Don't tell me what the love of my life would have wanted, Pieter. I knew him better than you did."

Pieter pursed his lips as if holding something back, then he forced his voice into its usual even tone. "Just tell me you'll think about it. Please. I promised I'd keep you all safe, and I almost lost them. I can't..." He trailed off, his eyes brimming with tears.

Anger and protectiveness warred for Jeanne's attention. Did she want to yell at him some more or hug him for loving her children so fiercely that he was willing to fight even her?

Her anger deflated, but her resolve stood strong. "No, they're safest here, and they deserve their father avenged. I'm not giving up just because the king is a depraved lunatic. I won't."

Before she'd even finished speaking, Pieter turned, stomped across the deck, and disappeared below. Jeanne's anger flared again as she watched him retreat. He'd never walked away from her. They'd never fought like that—not with words, not outside a sparring ring.

Jeanne wanted to charge after him and scream until he saw reason. Olivier was his best friend. How could Pieter give up on justice for him so easily? She looked around, ready to pick a fight with the nearest crewmember, but everyone had made themselves scarce. She settled for punching the railing three times in quick succession.

She wouldn't give up on Olivier, she sent a promise into the sky. No matter what. She'd keep their children safe, and she would never—*ever*—give up.

# 1345

## CHAPTER 26
# THE ENGLISH CHANNEL

Jeanne was right—the children were safest with her. For months, she kept seizing merchant ships, punishing the king's men, and she did it all with her babies at her side.

Oli, now nine, was the fierce little fighter he'd promised to be, practicing his stances and movements on deck any time the skies and horizon were clear. Pieter was training him, if begrudgingly and with plenty of subtle and not-so-subtle hints about how they should sail for Britain and retire where they could train in the countryside.

Guillaume mostly stayed below deck, with Monster trotting along at his heels like a cat-shaped shadow. He sometimes trained with his brother but had no enthusiasm for it. Instead, he devoted himself to anything Amée wanted to teach him—herbs and letters and how to disappear beans. Jeanne wondered if he was more suited to scholarship than war, and the thought gave her a strange relief. At least one child was likely to survive this cruel world.

And then there was Little Jeanne—her mother's most

constant companion. When Jeanne sparred with Pieter, Little Jeanne watched from the deck. When Jeanne kept watch, Little Jeanne followed along, fist wrapped tight around her mother's skirts. When Jeanne went ashore to meet Amélie's spies and left her behind, Little Jeanne sobbed as if her heart was broken and would never be mended.

Having them on the ship made it feel more crowded but also more alive. Less serious. It was hard to be too serious while watching Oli practice sword moves against a loose sail corner—and being bested when it flapped unexpectedly, knocking him onto his back. Or when Little Jeanne startled Monster and sent her flying onto Guillaume's head. Or when Alexi made an apple appear to scuttle across the deck of its own accord, leaving Little Jeanne and Guillaume speechless—until Oli picked it up and pulled out the beetle that had been moving it all along. And all three screamed and fell over in fits of laughter. Jeanne smiled at the memories, smiled at having them here with her, finally safe.

It was like being home, watching her children grow into the people they were becoming. The life she'd imagined for herself before all of this happened. The only thing that would have made it better was if Louise and Geoff were with them too.

Pieter's voice broke through her thoughts. "M'lady. Ship on the horizon."

In seconds, she and her men were on their feet, practiced efficiency guiding everyone to their positions. The children had been watching Amée teach Alexi how to make an egg dance across the deck just like the apple, and Jeanne called to her first mate.

"Jacques, you're on guard duty."

Jacques was quickly across the deck and herding Amée

and the children down the ladder. As they sliced through the water toward the merchant ship, Jeanne joined her fighters at the rail and watched a handful of men throw themselves into the English Channel—presumably preferring to take their chances with the sea. She almost laughed aloud. Her reputation was now so fierce that men would rather drown themselves than face her.

The merchant crew who stayed behind put up an impressive fight for peaceful sailors who'd never before seen battle. Jeanne liked them in spite of herself. These weren't Philip's men. They were French, yes, and carrying French cargo for French purposes, but something about them was different. Perhaps because there weren't nobles onboard calling the shots.

But brave as they seemed, it took very little time to disarm them and take their ship. As Jeanne took in the faces of the survivors, one of her men emerged from the ship's cabin, waving an official-looking letter like a flag of surrender.

"What's this?" Jeanne asked, grabbing it.

Her man grinned. "I don't read, myself, m'lady, but it's the Pope's seal."

Interesting. Jeanne turned her attention back to the captive crew. "Where were you sailing?"

"Londres," a pale sharp-chinned man said. "The letter is for King Edward."

*Interesting.* What could the Pope be sending to Edward? The truce between Edward and Philip—the one they'd signed just before Philip took Olivier's life—was good for another few months yet. Was this a request to prolong it? *Merde,* she hoped not. She wanted Philip harried and hurt and distracted at every turn, so she'd been looking forward

THE LIONESS

to the day when Edward sent his armies back into France to take Philip's throne.

Jeanne broke the seal to read the letter. And burst out laughing. *God's nails.* Its tone was scolding—a father chastising an unruly child. France and Britain were in a truce, the Pope said, so Edward needed to stop harassing French ships, burning up merchant fleets, and destroying war galleys. The English Channel was not fair game, and how dare Edward break the truce.

Jeanne wanted to scream with delight. So they thought she was allied with Edward. They didn't believe—or didn't *want* to believe—that she was wreaking all this havoc on her own. Philip was annoyed. The Church was annoyed. Jeanne couldn't think of any more encouraging news she could have gotten. The Church that had betrayed her children to Philip was demanding she stop burning merchant ships? Well, she'd have to burn a few extra now to make a point.

Her heart light, she turned to the disarmed merchant crew. "Any man who doesn't support King Philip can join my cause here and now. Make yourselves known."

She was met with a wall of silence and raised eyebrows from both her crew and theirs, and then, all at once, shouts of men clamoring to be heard.

"Me!"

"I don't support him!"

"As far as I'm concerned, the king can go to hell!"

"Always thought he was a hedge-born bastard."

Since the merchant who owned the ship had jumped into the sea on Jeanne's arrival, there was no one left who cared enough to defy her.

The youngest sailor onboard—a skinny brown-skinned

boy barely older than Oli—screamed, "He's a big ol' dull-head, the king! Everyone knows he's a fopdoodle."

Alexi jostled the boy's shoulder in a friendly way. Jeanne had never heard anyone use slang for a common fool in relation to the king, and she was delighted. Fopdoodle, indeed.

She grinned at the boy. "And what do you know about me?"

The boy's eyes went wider. "They call you a lioness, m'lady. They say you cut the hearts of your enemies clean out and eat them. My maman calls you her own heart's root, says she'd like to cut out some hearts herself. Says she hopes you eat the king and the duke."

Jeanne was touched—calling someone your heart's root was the dearest kind of love. It meant you'd taken root there. It meant you'd be impossible to root out. It meant a heart somewhere in France, perhaps more than one, didn't fear her. It *admired* her.

"Why did your smart mother send you on a merchant ship knowing this lioness' den is on the Channel then?" Alexi asked, nudging the boy's shoulder again.

It was a good question. Why, indeed? Why risk this lively, precocious boy? The boy, held at sword point by pirates, who wasn't afraid but instead seemed *elated* to bad-mouth the king and praise Jeanne.

"Need the money, sir. My pa's dead in Duke Charles' wars, and my uncles too. They say the duke dragged Pa into a church to say one last Mass instead of taking him to the healer when he was injured in battle. Now I'm the oldest boy—the man of the family. Maman makes what she can as a seamstress, but we needed the money, so I took this job."

The duke's wars. Of course. This boy was yet another casualty of Charles' damn pride.

THE LIONESS

"What's your name, boy?" Jeanne asked.

"Louis."

"Louis, how would you like to join a pirate crew?" She grinned at the boy's large-eyed silence. "We could use a cabin boy, and my son could use a sparring buddy. I'll send coin home to your maman."

Louis nodded, speechless at his good luck. Alexi released his shoulder and patted him on the back.

Jeanne turned her attention to the scrappy merchant crew. "The rest of you get to keep your lives, though not your ship. In exchange, I need you to do something for me."

"Anything, m'lady!"

"Thank ye, m'lady!"

"M'lady is great and merciful!"

She held up a hand, quieting them. "The French Church betrayed me recently, as did Duke Charles of Brittany, and I'd like them to know what that betrayal buys."

She'd left more men alive on this ship than ever before, but it was hushed as the grave as she went on. "You're going to go to Charles' city and burn down a church."

## CHAPTER 27
# THE ENGLISH CHANNEL

Jeanne pinned the Pope's letter to her mast with a dagger and watched it flutter in the wind.

Her ship was slicing through the water again, this time bound for the French shoreline. Sprawled around the deck, her own men mixed with the merchant crew, eating the rough ship crackers and drinking wine they'd found in the belly of the merchant vessel that now burned behind them like a torch in the twilight.

Alexi held court in the center of a circle of men, his back to Jeanne. "You all know about Guy de Penthièvre, right?"

Jeanne's eyebrows flew upward in shock, and she stopped to listen.

"Married Jeanne after her first husband snuffed it, then told everyone she was lying about their marriage! He thought, *'Damn, that woman is intriguing'*—and then he saw her fight and thought, *'Damn, that woman's going to kill me.'* Took her to court and sued her for slandering him by saying they were married."

His tone was joking, but heat rose to Jeanne's cheeks. *Merde.* She'd married Guy in a rush, barely knew him,

168

barely had time to grieve for her first husband. He was a smart match on paper—a man with a claim to the title of Breton duke, strong connections, a powerful family name. But as soon as they were married, off he went telling the whole world she was a liar and that they'd never wed in the first place. The fool. Or, as Louis would say, the fopdoodle.

Jeanne didn't know what had given him those cold feet. All she knew was that from that moment—as she always did with her enemies—she'd done the exact opposite of everything he wanted. He wanted to talk publicly about what happened. She clammed up. He wanted to quiet things down and move on so he could marry again. She started talking.

Eventually, the church annulled the marriage, which was just fine with Jeanne. But damn if that year hadn't been irritating. And damn if she hadn't thought everyone had forgotten about it by now.

The men around Alexi were falling over with laughter and he was animated, energized, by their mirth.

"What an impotent muttonhead!" one of the sailors said between laughs.

"Wonder if that'd work for me," another pretended to muse. "Mister Pope sir, please, I didn't actually marry this woman. We've just been living together ten years and have four children."

Guy's foolishness *was* rather funny if you thought about it, but Jeanne didn't want her men joking about her personal life. Time to cut that off at the ankles. She stepped around the seated men, pulled back, and punched Alexi in the neck, knocking him into one of the sailors who laughed and also punched him for good measure.

"My love life is off limits," she said, turning on her toes and sweeping back across the deck.

When they took the sailors ashore later that night, each knelt in the sand before Jeanne and promised his loyalty. She knew it was unlikely that they'd all march to Charles' city and set churches alight, especially with how religious and superstitious sailors tended to be. Nobody wanted to get on god's bad side. But if even one took her seriously—and she did believe at least one would—the message would be powerful. It would demonstrate how her influence had grown, how far-reaching it had become. How much Charles had to fear. And now, after betraying her children, how much the Church had to fear, too.

As the men took off into the night, pockets heavy with coins from Jeanne's coffer, Jeanne turned to Amée. They'd planned for her to head ashore to check in with Amélie, Louise, and Jeanne's other allies in a few weeks' time, but since they were already on French soil, it made sense to go now. She'd head up the coast on foot toward the next town, its torches and candles flickering to life in the twilight. From there, she'd buy a fast horse and ride for Louise and Geoff to hear the latest gossip from the courts.

Jeanne grinned. "Ride safe, Merlin."

"Are you sure you don't want an escort this time?" Pieter asked, his voice tender.

"It's easier to go unnoticed without one." Amée squeezed both their arms and faded into the shadows.

Before Pieter even said anything, Jeanne knew what was coming. Ever since the nunnery, he'd wanted them to stop. Didn't understand that Jeanne *couldn't* stop. That she could sooner stop existing than stop going after the men who'd killed Olivier.

Amée had once told her that she'd started forgetting

THE LIONESS

things about Giselle—the sound of rain on her house, the color of her eyes—and Jeanne realized that the same thing was happening to her with Olivier. Not even two years since his murder, and she couldn't remember what it felt like to have his hand stroke the back of her neck, couldn't remember his laugh. She knew Pieter missed him too, but he didn't understand that her loss kept building on itself. First, the loss of Olivier. Now, the fading of his memory. If she stopped fighting for that, she'd lose herself too.

Pieter's voice was soft, pleading. "Have you thought more about what I said?"

"No, Pieter."

"Please—you have to see reason here!"

"I *do* see reason. I also see injustice everywhere I look."

"You can't fix it, Jeanne. We've been fighting for years, and we haven't fixed it."

"Then we keep fighting."

"And the children?"

"They still don't deserve a world where their father's murder goes unpunished." Jeanne's voice was calmer than usual. She was used to these arguments now, comfortable with them like a favorite dagger. "They're safe, Pieter. I promise you, they're safe."

# Meanwhile...

## PARIS, FRANCE

THE DUKE KNELT, BARE-KNEED ON GRAINS OF RICE, as he prayed at the front of the little chapel—and Catherine was afraid.

She'd been instructed to serve Duke Charles in whatever way he needed while the priest was away. She wondered what that meant.

Would he hurt her, like the king had hurt his mistress?

Catherine had been the one to tend to Nicole, her neck tender and bruised, angry red and violent purple. It was healed now, like it had never happened, but Catherine could see the ghost of the thing behind Nicole's eyes. Could see the way she flinched away from men at court, the way the spark died in her smile when the king entered a room.

Catherine's heart fluttered in her chest like a trapped bird. Her mother had told her to be careful when she got this position at the palace last year, when she was twelve, but this was the first time she'd understood that *careful* meant she could harmed physically. Not just lose her position, but lose her safety.

She'd been forced to kneel on rice as penance before,

172

and she knew the way it wedged into skin, pricking, burning, beating like a dozen little hearts. Was the duke invincible? A saint in his own right? Did he not feel the grains slicing through layers of skin? She shivered, willing her flighty heart to still. Unlike the king, the duke had never done anything to anyone except himself. She tried to believe that made her safe.

As if Catherine's very thoughts were magic—a dark sort of summoning charm—the doors to the little chapel flew open and King Philip entered. Her bird-like heart fluttered faster. *Two* dangerous men and nowhere to go. She bowed low as the king marched forward, trying not to let the fear show on her face.

Charles, ever devout, ever prioritizing god above all else, ignored the king, even as the more powerful man tapped a foot impatiently beside him. The duke finished his prayer, made the sign of the cross, and then slowly stood to face Philip. Painfully slow. A show of power. A clear message that he didn't have to rush to respond to his king like the rest of them.

Catherine kept her head down, hands clasped demurely in front of her skirts, trying to stop remembering the red bloom across Nicole's throat.

Finally, Charles spoke, inviting conversation. "Your Majesty."

"They're saying the children are alive." The king's voice was twice the volume necessary in the small space, and Catherine flinched.

"You're upset."

"Of course I'm goddamn upset. She lost nothing! She's back out there on the Channel!"

"Don't blaspheme," Charles scolded. Then, "She'll be

shaken, though. You found the children once, so she knows you can do it again."

"They say she's a witch." The king's voice rose again, echoing shrilly off the stone, the altar, the stained glass. "That she's out there eating hearts and calling the devil down to make darkness descend over the waters at will."

"Superstitious nonsense, Your Majesty. You know the how the peasants are. Storytellers, each one embellishing more than the other." Charles placed a comforting hand on the king's arm. "And even if she is a witch, witches are never more powerful than god. And god is on *our* side."

Catherine pressed her own hands together, a silent prayer slipping from her mind to the heavens. *Is it true, god? Are you on the side of a man who left red and purple welts across his mistress' delicate neck? Who sent men to burn children alive in one of your own holy places?*

No answer came, but Catherine hoped it wasn't true. Hoped that an all-powerful god hadn't sanctioned the murder of small children and his own nuns. Hoped that god saw this conversation—ironic under the stained-glass relief of Mary, woman, mother—as a sort of heresy. They'd all be safer if god struck these men down himself.

She prayed for it and wondered if that was blasphemy.

The duke was speaking again, his voice a conspiratorial whisper, his mouth a smirk. "We knew she'd return to the Channel, so we've already laid our traps, remember. She doesn't know what's coming. And if her children are with her, god rest their souls."

Catherine glanced at the king's face as it transformed from rage to something just as wicked.

Delight.

Nicole's words came back to her then, from when

Catherine had brewed her herbal teas and cleaned the scratches on her neck. *"The worst part wasn't even the pain. The worst part was the look on his face. Triumph. Power. Joy."*

This was the look she'd meant. The look of man with the power to kill.

## CHAPTER 28
# THE ENGLISH CHANNEL

A storm was brewing when the warship appeared on the horizon.

"Okay, little love." Jeanne detached Little Jeanne from her skirt. "Time to go below."

Little Jeanne scowled with exaggerated offense, then stomped expressively toward the cabin. Her brothers and their new friend and sparring partner, Louis, looked up from where they'd been watching Monster stalk a mouse and, knowing the rules, sighed and followed after her.

Jeanne turned to Pieter, who was walking the deck beside her. "Tell Alexi he's on guard duty for them."

He nodded and left, while all around, her men fell into formation. They were veteran pirates by now, and everyone knew their role. The archers stood at the ready. Fighting men fell into ranks and balanced boarding planks along the deck.

Fat raindrops started to fall, and thunder boomed loudly. It was a stroke of luck—Jeanne's men were now used to the whims of the English Channel's weather, but their opponents might not be. Jeanne shivered in anticipation. Taking merchant ships frustrated France's trade efforts, yes, but taking King Philip's warships felt so much more personal, so much closer to taking the king himself.

A whistle from behind broke her concentration, and she half-turned. Across the ship, one of her watchmen was waving frantically at her.

"M'lady," he said in a low voice as she approached, "there's another ship coming in from the other side."

She followed his finger and saw what he meant. A second ship was approaching, too far away to make out what it was yet but headed straight for them.

Pieter spotted her talking to the watchman and strode over, staring into the horizon with his eyebrows drawn together. "This isn't good."

"Do you think it's an ambush?" Jeanne asked. "Another warship?"

"Yes."

Her frown deepened. "Well, we've taken two ships together a few times before..."

"Not warships, m'lady."

"No, but it looks like we'll have to here." Jeanne shrugged, trying to look unconcerned, but her heart beat faster. She didn't love surprises. She preferred to be the one doing the surprising. There was no cause for alarm, though. It was two ships. Just two. And her men were exceptional fighters. So it was a bigger challenge than they'd faced before...so what? They'd handle this one as they handled them all—brave and right and fighting with every fiber of their beings.

Still, Jeanne wished Amée was there to give her a speech about how she was the storm or to show them how to light men on fire en masse.

Jeanne sent a third of her men to brace for attack on the

second front, putting Pieter in command. And then the first ship was upon them and so was the storm—slow drops of rain turning into a torrent, lightning arcing across the sky above—and Jeanne could no longer worry about large-scale strategies because her sword was out and she was bouncing on her toes, blocking blows and dealing them out in succession.

At first, it was like any other fight, except this time Jeanne stayed aboard her own ship, thinking it a better field from which to face two enemies at once. She danced and dove, weaved through flailing arms and singing metal. Her skirts and hair grew heavy with rainwater, sticking to her skin as she moved. She speared one opponent and then another. She saw men falling—some the king's, some her own—and she fought on, hair whipping, armor bumping against her skin.

But then, in a way it never had before, the battle turned.

The second ship was upon them and arrows and shouts came from behind. A stinging pain shot through Jeanne's left arm, followed by a wet heat. She sucked in her breath and whipped her head around to look.

An arrow had caught her, leaving a two-inch gash. It was just a flesh wound. In so many years of fighting, Jeanne had had more than one, so she turned and kept fighting through the burn. But something was different. Too many of her own men lay on the deck in pooling blood. Too many enemy sailors and soldiers kept piling in behind their fallen fellows. And Jeanne's gut wrenched in worry.

They weren't winning.

They weren't going to win.

As she dispatched another foe, stabbing him with her dagger and pushing him overboard, a heavy hand landed on her arm. She turned to strike—

It was Pieter, his face drawn with worry, rain cascading over his eyebrows and off his nose. "You have to go," he whispered urgently. "You have to take the children and go."

In any other circumstance, Jeanne would argue, but her instincts had already told her the battle was lost and the thought of leaving her children to the mercy of the man who'd already tried to burn them alive...

It was unthinkable.

Never before had she run from a fight—she'd always imagined herself dying in battle. But she couldn't today. Not with her children shut away in the cabin. Not with the king still alive and on his throne.

She nodded at Pieter and turned to follow, surprised to find that he'd already stowed the children in the rowboat and pushed them out to sea. Monster stood over them like a guardian, legs splayed and tail in the air, soaked to the bone, a black skeleton lit by white shocks of lightning.

Pieter took Jeanne's sword. "Jump."

With no time to think about it further, no time to ask if he would follow, thinking only—with an urgent kind of terror—that her children were floating farther away by the moment, Jeanne flung herself into the water and swam.

## CHAPTER 29
# THE ENGLISH CHANNEL

When night fell, Jeanne was still rowing. Soaking wet, shivering, and still rowing.

They'd slipped away through the water, everyone's attention focused on the battle, the storm hiding her retreat.

"Oli, what happened to Louis?" she'd asked as she started to row.

"He let go, Maman." Oli's voice was heavy with guilt, sharp-edged with defiance. "Pieter told him not to let go of my hand, but he did. It wasn't my fault, Maman. *Louis let go*." Then he'd kicked the side of the rowboat and buried his face in his hands.

Why was it so much more painful to watch her children hurt than it was to be hurt herself? Jeanne was sorry for Louis. She'd liked the boy. But seeing Oli bowed over by his loss threatened to break her.

"Pieter tried to save him, Maman," Guillaume whispered.

Oh god. *Pieter*. Pieter, who'd saved her children, sent her after them, and thrown himself back into the fray.

# THE LIONESS

Pieter, who'd been right all along that the children weren't safe with her.

He'd saved her and she'd left him.

And now her ship was burning—a vague orange glow through the pouring rain—and she knew he was gone. Lost to her forever. Pieter and Alexi and Louis and the rest of her men, all lost. Like Olivier. Like her children had almost been.

Her shoulders ached from rowing for so many hours, the wound in her arm throbbing in time with her heart, but she wouldn't let herself take a break. As the rain slowed, she thought she could still see the fire rising into the sky in the distance. The king hadn't hesitated to burn down a nunnery believing her children were inside. She didn't want to know what his men would do if they found them now—her armed with just a dagger and a heavy oar. They had to get as far away from the warships as possible.

Closing her eyes and breathing deep, she pushed into the pain. Pull, breathe. Pull, breathe.

She wondered if this was always how it ended for women like her. All loss and pain. A woman's fire drowned in a downpour of a man's power.

"Maman," Little Jeanne whispered.

"Yes, darling," Jeanne answered, breathless with effort.

"Did the bad men kill Pieter like they killed Papa?"

The words were like a knife driving the truth in deeper. She'd lost the battle. She'd lost her closest friend. She'd lost her husband. She'd left his best friend behind. The guilt was a weight on her neck, pushing the ache of her muscles all the way into her bones.

She'd never lied to her children about the harsh realities of their world. Perhaps protected them by keeping her silence sometimes, but never outright lied. And she wasn't going to now.

"Yes, my love. But we're here. We're safe. You're safe. Maman is taking you to shore—to Britain."

At least, she hoped they were pointed toward Britain. She was good at navigating by the stars after two years on the water, but the sky was hard to see through the storm, and it was possible she was wrong.

She'd been wrong about everything else.

JEANNE HAD BEEN ROWING for almost two whole days. Her arms were numb and cold and foreign, like something no longer connected to herself. She longed to stop, to rest, to close her eyes and never open them again. To be done with her quest. To be done with life. The unfairness of it. The cruelty of it. The loss piled atop loss piled atop loss.

Pieter was gone now. Olivier gone for years. Alexi. Louis. And the men who'd killed them were roaming free, sleeping on featherbeds and killing whomever they wanted without consequence.

Jeanne had never felt such a deep despair. Such bleakness.

But still, she rowed. For Oli. For Guillaume. For Little Jeanne. And for the men who'd died unfairly and still needed justice, who still deserved to have their stories told.

It was storming again, and all four of them were soaked through and miserable. The boat rocked wildly over black waves and Oli whimpered—her strong, brave child wide-eyed with fear. Guillaume held Little Jeanne in his lap and stroked her hair, whispering that it would be alright.

They didn't deserve this.

It was Jeanne's fault they were here, shivering in a rowboat, sleeping huddled together under a single blanket, sucking rainwater out of their hair and licking it off their fingers, afraid their tiny vessel would capsize at any moment and they'd all be lost in the depths of the Channel.

She pulled harder on the oars, the throbbing in her arms a form of penance. She'd gotten them into this, and she was going to save them if it was her last living act.

THE THIRD DAY DAWNED A RELIEF. The storms had passed, the Channel was calm, and the sun was out, bringing a welcome warmth to their faces.

At first.

It grew hot and hotter and after a few hours, their skin burned red, and Jeanne's tongue felt like wood in her mouth—dry and huge and unwelcome. Guillaume was curled under the blanket, his eyes closed. He'd been like that for hours, and Jeanne wondered if it was the heat he was hiding from or if it was just because he hadn't slept. She wished she could wrap her arms around him, but any moment not rowing was a moment not bringing them nearer to shore.

In the late afternoon, his skin blistering and lips cracking and bleeding, Oli started scooping water out of the sea and over his head.

"Stop, darling," Jeanne said, her voice a dry, grating, unfamiliar thing.

He ignored her.

"Stop," she said again.

His eyes narrowed.

"You're putting water in the boat." She looked pointedly at the water sloshing around at their feet.

In frustration, Oli punched the side of the rowboat, causing it to lurch back and forth.

"*Stop!*" Jeanne yelled. "You'll kill us all!"

Little Jeanne started wailing.

*Damn it all to hell.* Jeanne wanted to comfort her but forced herself to keep rowing. Rowing was the thing that would save them, not the temporary comfort of a mother's hug. And if she stopped rowing now, she wasn't sure she'd be able to start again. If she stopped, her arms might give out for good.

"Jeanne, darling," she whispered. "It's okay. We're going to be okay. We're going to get to Britain. I think we have to be almost there." The words stuck in her dry throat like barbs, and she coughed. And then she realized, with a shot of fear, that her shouting and Oli's boat rocking and Little Jeanne's sobs hadn't woken Guillaume.

"Guillaume," she said.

There was no movement under the blanket.

"Guillaume?" This time she was louder, but still nothing.

For the first time in days, Jeanne stopped rowing. With arms and legs shaking from exhaustion and an unnamed fear, she dropped onto all fours and crawled the couple steps between them, lifted the blanket, and put her hand on his face.

It was stiff and clammy, and Jeanne simultaneously knew and wished she didn't know that her son—her sweetheart son—was no longer breathing.

Like her husband and Pieter, Guillaume was gone.

CHAPTER 30

# THE ENGLISH CHANNEL

Jeanne held her breath and tried to still her horror. Was the boat rocking violently or was her world shaking around her? Guillaume was gone. Gone. Gone forever.

And she was trapped in the middle of the sea with two young children who couldn't know. They would panic. They would capsize. They would all follow Guillaume into death. She couldn't react. Couldn't show them her fear.

Jeanne leaned down and kissed Guillaume's face then looked at the other two, both quiet, both watching her. She forced a smile, pushed back the hair on Little Jeanne's soft, downy head, and kissed her hard on her warm brow. Then she squeezed Oli's hand.

"It's going to be alright," she said.

And then, trembling and terrified of getting off course, she dropped back onto her seat and forced her protesting arms to keep rowing. If she didn't get them to England soon, they'd all follow Guillaume into heaven. Except, she realized with a pang, the pope himself was writing to condemn her actions. Guillaume and Pieter and Louis and Alexi were all dead because of her.

She wasn't going to heaven.

BY THE TIME Jeanne saw land, she wasn't sure it was real.

Her head pounded and her skin burned, and the air seemed to shimmer in front of her with ghosts and angels, devils and sparkling cats. Little Jeanne had curled herself into Guillaume's stiff frame, and Monster had curled herself into Little Jeanne.

"Why won't Guillaume wake up, Maman?"

Jeanne couldn't answer. She kept seeing ships on the horizon too, but they never came closer, and she wasn't sure if they were actually there. Should she try rowing faster? No, she couldn't—her arms were trapped in a rhythm she doubted she could stop.

But the land...that was real, wasn't it? That strip of shoreline growing nearer. It didn't move or shimmer or disappear and reappear. And that made it real, didn't it? She tried to hold the thought in her head, but it was crowded out by the command she'd been repeating to herself for four days. Pull, breathe. Pull, breathe.

And then they were in shallow water. Almost there. If the land was real, all Jeanne would have to do was get out of the rowboat and pull it ashore. It was Britain—she knew it was Britain, not the rocky Brittany coast. She stood unsteadily and stepped, then fell, into the sea. If the land wasn't real, she'd just plunged into the deep.

But her feet found the bottom and she stood, waist-deep in shockingly cold water.

# THE LIONESS

Oli watched through half-closed eyes. Little Jeanne slept on. With the last of her strength, Jeanne towed them to shore and dragged the boat onto the sand. She had to get to the nearest town, to water and food and a doctor. Instead, the sparkles at the edge of her vision turned to black and crept across her eyes, pulling her into darkness.

∾

SHE WOKE with a bowl of water on her chest and concerned faces hovering over her—two men and a woman. They were checking to see if she was still breathing, the ripples in the water reassuring them that she was.

Someone asked a question in a language she didn't understand. English, she supposed, remembering where she was. And then the woman spoke in rough French. "Can you understand me?"

Jeanne tried to answer and found she couldn't. She hadn't realized how much strength it took to say a single word. Hadn't realized what exhaustion truly felt like. Everything hurt. She couldn't raise her arms, couldn't keep her eyes open, couldn't form the words.

*Have you seen my baby? Guillaume. Is he gone, or did I imagine it?*

He was, though. She knew he was. The question was a trick, her heart rebelling at what her mind knew.

The woman said something to her companions in their harsh, rocky language, before the three of them carried her to a cart at the edge of the beach, where a mud-packed trail led up into some trees. Jeanne felt them lifting Little Jeanne in beside her, then Oli. Warm, breathing. She'd saved them, at least. It was something, but it wasn't enough.

The cart moved beneath her, and the blackness at the edge of her vision came for her again.

When Jeanne woke, sick and dizzy and drowsy, stretched out on her back with Oli and Little Jeanne warm and still asleep beside her, she had one thought: if she'd rowed a little harder, Guillaume would be alive. If she'd been a better mother, Guillaume would still be here. If she hadn't tried to hide her children at the nunnery, hadn't taken them onboard the ship...if she'd listened to Pieter—poor, dead Pieter—and taken them and fled...

She should have let the king kill her before letting her son die.

She should have done something else. *Anything* else.

Jeanne went to sit up in the sand and realized there was no sand. No water. No boat. The three good Samaritans had been real, and they'd brought her somewhere. She was lying in a featherbed in a lavish room, the light around her golden as the sun set outside the window. She *should* want to know where she was now, but she couldn't muster the strength to care. How could the world still have things like featherbeds when Guillaume was gone?

She was a terrible mother. She was a monster and a failure. A failure at keeping them safe. A failure at avenging her husband. A failure at everything she'd believed herself to be. She'd thought herself a warrior, a fighter, the kind of woman who would take on the world and win. Like Isabella. Like her mother.

But she was nothing. She wasn't strong enough or brave enough. Wasn't smart enough to save the things she loved

THE LIONESS

most in the world. She didn't stand for mercy, but she couldn't stand for justice either. She wasn't enough.

She tightened her fists around the soft blankets and gave in to the unbearable heaviness in her chest—sobs turning to coughing fits in her dry throat. Everything was gone. Everything was wrong.

She'd burned ships and fortresses to the ground, beheaded the king's allies, given up her life to make right what was done to Olivier. And none of it mattered.

Guillaume had been the kindest soul in the whole world. He didn't deserve this. Didn't deserve a mother like her. And the king...if Jeanne hated herself, she hated the king more. This was no longer about a single injustice. It was injustice piled upon injustice. It wasn't men killing men or grown women. It was men killing *children*.

It was evil.

She put her hands over her eyes and tried to stop the flow of tears—she had to think of Oli and Little Jeanne now. Given the featherbed, it seemed she was among friends of some sort, so she wasn't worried for their safety, but she needed to check on them. To comfort them. To feel the telltale flutter of breath and heartbeats and wild aliveness.

She turned. Her back and shoulders protested at the movement, her skin hot and tight, her arms tender and sore. She reached out to Oli first, holding her palm to his chest, reassured by its rise and fall. He was shiny red with sunburn, cheeks hollow from days without food, but his breath was strong. His heart too. It was the same for Little Jeanne, whose face was already peeling thick white strips of dead skin, but whose heart beat strong.

Jeanne looked around for Monster, who wasn't on the

bed with them. The cat wasn't rubbing herself along the tapestries, wasn't stretched out in the patch of sunlight on the floor. Another soul lost then. She pressed her palms to her eyes and took a shaky breath. It was ridiculous to be worried about a cat, but there it was. Jeanne de Clisson was worried about the cat.

She forced herself to stop the tears, control her breathing. Deep breaths. In through the nose and out through the mouth, just like in training. Just like a fight. Isabella de Aquitaine wouldn't cry, she was sure of it. Jeanne's mother —falconer and diplomat and unyielding soul—wouldn't cry. And neither would Jeanne.

No. Jeanne was a fighter who was going to fight for what she had left. She'd finally listen to Pieter and send the children somewhere the king couldn't get to them. She hadn't been able to protect them before because Philip had too much damn power, but now...now she was in Britain. What was it Amée had said—dear, dear Amée who might be the only one of Jeanne's friends left alive? *My enemy's enemy is my friend.* Jeanne was in the land of her enemy's enemy. Now, perhaps, she had a chance to ally with a king of her own. If kings were the ones with power, she would use King Edward's to make sure Oli and Little Jeanne were safe for the rest of their days, no matter what it took.

The clearer her thoughts became, the more certain she grew—she'd go to the British king and offer him an alliance that would keep her children safe. An alliance she hoped he also craved. An alliance that would get her within striking distance of Philip so she could end this damn thing once and for all.

A small movement at the corner of Jeanne's vision caught her attention. There, perched in the narrow stone window as if by magic, Monster sat twitching her tail.

Jeanne probably shouldn't have felt so relieved, but the cat was back and that meant one of the thousand things that was wrong wasn't wrong anymore. One of a thousand losses wasn't a loss. It meant, perhaps, she could still make things right.

And Jeanne's battered heart took comfort in it.

## CHAPTER 31
# WINDSOR CASTLE, ENGLAND

J eanne stood before the king in the sweeping hall, her hair done up for the first time in years. Oli and Little Jeanne peeked out from behind her skirts, while Guillaume's body lay in front of them, embalmed and wrapped in waxed cloth.

The fishermen had taken her to a noble household where they'd immediately known who she was. They'd readily agreed when she asked for their help getting to the castle, which was so much like the ones Jeanne had known in France—from the tapestries and fashions to the throne itself, it was as if Britain had borrowed French designs and shifted them ever so slightly. Slightly lower necklines, slightly different shapes, but familiar enough to feel like home.

Jeanne supposed that made perfect sense—the French and British nobility were inescapably tangled. It was the whole reason for the war they were in. King Philip and King Edward were both related to the former king of France, both with potentially legitimate claims to the throne, one through the female line and one through the male. Of course empires run by family, constantly aligning via cross-channel marriages, would have much in common.

King Edward leaned eagerly forward on his throne. The courtiers lined the walls, wide-eyed and trading whispers, which floated to Jeanne from every angle. Jeanne was glad French was the official language of the aristocracy and she could understand every word.

"They say her ships are made of fog!"

"They say she beheads French noblemen herself with a single stroke!"

"They say she can transform into a lion thanks to the power of the devil!"

Well, one of those things was true. She'd beheaded a few noblemen.

Jeanne took a deep breath and spoke, clear and steady. "Sire, I come to offer my services to Britain." She swept a hand around the whispering edges of the room. "You've clearly heard of me, so you know what I'm capable of."

The king laughed and clapped. "Yes, m'lady! We've all heard how you dye your sails in the blood of the slain and eat the hearts of your enemies. I bet Philip pisses the bed every night."

The court roared with laughter until Edward held up a hand. "So what can I do for the fiercest pirate on the Channel?"

"I need three ships and the men to crew them. I want my children"—she motioned to Little Jeanne, still clinging to her skirts, and Oli, who was standing tall but staring at his brother's body—"to be raised here in the castle or with your most trusted nobles, kept safe at any cost while I cut your enemies off at the knees. I also require a nobleman's burial and a place to honor the death of my son, Guillaume."

Her heart twisted as she said it, and she blinked back emotion, pressing her lips together. This was not the time for tears and grief. It was a time for strength. For harnessing her rage and turning it into something that could destroy the king who'd stolen her life.

She breathed deep through her nose and continued. "For this, I pledge to continue wearing down France's forces and destroying our shared enemies, King Philip VI and Charles de Blois, the Duke of Brittany."

When she finished, the hall was silent. The whispering nobles stared at her and then at the king, while Edward's advisors furrowed their brows and tilted their heads, thinking. A beautifully arrayed woman with brown-gold skin that reminded Jeanne of a tiger's eye gem watched with interest from beside the throne. She assumed it must be Queen Philippa, the woman behind so many of England's strategic decisions. The love of King Edward's life, they said. The merciful half of the throne.

And then there was the king himself, stroking his beard and—Jeanne realized with relief—smiling again.

"Jeanne de Clisson," he said, letting his hand drop to the arm of the throne. "I never thought I'd meet you in person."

She inclined her head at his words, fighting to keep her face steady and her feet beneath her. Relieved at his response, hope warmed in her chest. He would give her the ships and her children their safety. And that was what she needed most now—to know her two smallest living children were safe.

But her feelings were so tangled up and wrong. Was this the only way? It had been so clear to her when she woke on that featherbed, when they'd ridden in from the coast. She'd

THE LIONESS

been so certain when she marched in here. But now, with the king so delighted to meet her, she wondered. Could she —*should* she—have asked to retire here with them instead? Would King Edward have let her stay? Would he have given her something—everything, in truth—for nothing?

No, that was ridiculous. He was only delighted because she'd promised to return to being a continual thorn in France's side. And she was Jeanne de Clisson—justice was her life. Her blood. The air she breathed. She couldn't have brought herself to stay anyway, could she? Not until Olivier and Guillaume and Pieter could rest in peace and the men who'd betrayed them were buried deep in the earth's endless darkness.

The king was still speaking, and Jeanne struggled to focus. "M'lady, you have become legend! Sometimes I thought you weren't real at all. The tales they told...skirts dyed in blood! Demon fighters! Black cats following at your heels!" He clapped again, charmed. "Of course, of course, everything you have requested will be done."

And so it was.

That very day, Edward appointed guardians over Little Jeanne and Oli at court. They were given splendid rooms with featherbeds and silk hangings. A private doctor visited each child, slathering their peeling sunburns with herb poultices and prescribing food and rest. He'd return to treat them twice daily. Arrangements were made for Oli to start training with other boys his age as soon as he was well enough to do so.

The castle doctors took Guillaume's body to be prepared for burial, and a ceremony was set for that afternoon. Jeanne was whisked away for a bath, rubbed with spices, and given a lavish new dress in bright splendid white. "For important funerals," a servant girl had explained, "we mourn in white here."

Two deft-handed servants tended to Jeanne's hair, braiding it into the most elaborate style she'd ever seen. "To honor your son, m'lady," the same girl murmured, placing a hand on Jeanne's shoulder.

During the braiding, Jeanne held Little Jeanne in her lap, her daughter's body warm against her chest, the thrum of her heartbeat steady and comforting as the little girl tucked her thumb in her mouth and fell fast asleep. Jeanne wished she could do the same—curl into a ball in someone's lap, warm, safe, and forgetting, at least for a moment, how much she'd lost.

Instead she watched her hair transform, and she thought of Amée. Though she was glad she hadn't been on the ship during the attack, Jeanne's confidence in the safety of anyone she loved had vanished. She wondered where Amée was now, if she was alright. Her stomach sank at the thought that perhaps Philip—or worse, Charles—had found her too.

Then there was Louise, and Geoff. Were they still safe? Had the king discovered that they'd been aiding her? Guilt tugged at her heart—had she been wrong to ask them to spy? Had she also put them at risk?

Then her worry for her oldest children slipped into thoughts of Guillaume, and the fragile, perfect moments they'd had before this mess. He brought her a tiny baby rabbit once. He'd found the poor thing in the fields, where the kids were playing under the watchful eyes of mother and nurses. It was like a toy, strangely calm wrapped in his pudgy arms.

His eyes had shone with wonder and he whispered,

# THE LIONESS

trying not to disturb the tiny ball of fluff, "Maman, I saved her!"

That was all Guillaume had ever wanted to do. Save and love. Hug his busy brother and snuggle up in his Maman's lap, gurgle to the fish and carry baby rabbits to safety. With a sharp pain, Jeanne remembered how he'd comforted Little Jeanne on the rowboat. Even as he was dying, he was looking to help someone else.

Her body felt heavy and disconnected from her mind as the servants finished her braids and bid her farewell, assuring her that someone would come to escort her to the ceremony. And then the door clicked shut and she and Little Jeanne—still asleep with her mouth open and her cheek pressed to Jeanne's shoulder—were alone.

Jeanne thought of her own maman and wondered what she would do if she were here. She'd lost three babies of her own and her husband when Jeanne was too small to understand, but she'd soldiered on, raising the unruly Jeanne, hawking, hunting, dancing, and defending her castle twice from raiders and British sieges. Somehow she'd gone on, still vibrant and wild and decidedly herself. How had she done it with so many babies in the ground?

Jeanne stroked her daughter's soft dark hair.

She had to go on too. For her children. For her husband. For herself, perhaps.

They could take everything from her, but the one thing they could never take without her permission was her self. That challenging, beautiful, unmistakably *Jeanne* part of her soul. That, they could only take if she chose to give it up.

Jeanne closed her eyes and breathed deep, smelling the sweet lavender of Little Jeanne's just-washed scalp and the cardamom she'd bathed in. She'd lost so much, but she still had this. Still had Oli and Little Jeanne, Louise and Geoff hopefully safe in their castle, Amée somewhere in France gathering information. She had risked them for revenge, and now she would protect them with it.

A soft knock sounded at the door and Jeanne rose, lifting Little Jeanne into her arms.

It was time for Guillaume's funeral.

HER PERFECT WHITE dress was ruined, splattered with ground-in dirt, wet with mud that had seeped in at the knees. Jeanne had stood tall and strong at the funeral. She'd held Oli and Jeanne's little hands, and she hadn't let them see her cry.

But now she was alone in a quiet corner of the castle gardens, with no one to see her. Now she could tear out those elaborate hateful braids, press her knees to the earth, destroy the horrible dress that meant her son was dead. She pressed her back to a fruit tree and pressed her hands to the dirt at its base. She was so tired.

A crunch of pebbles told her that she was no longer alone, and she frowned as a man—tall, thin but strongly built, his eyes a striking green against the garden backdrop—stepped into the little alcove.

She'd thought she wanted to be alone, but she now realized with a jolt that she wanted to fling herself into this stranger's arms and cry into his shoulder. She wanted someone else to hold her up. Someone else to be strong for her. Just for a few minutes. A few hours.

He saw her, and those bright eyes crinkled with kindness. Where the other nobles Jeanne knew would tell her to get up and get cleaned, this man crossed the distance between them and lowered himself, legs crossed, into the mud with her. He reached out and squeezed her knee, and it released something in Jeanne.

Tears flowed down her cheeks, slow at first, then faster. Her breath came thick and heavy and loud. The man took her hand into his own warm one, the dirt she'd been clutching now smashed between their palms.

They sat like that for a long time. The pink of sunset faded, and darkness fell over the gardens. The smell of cooking fires wafted past. Monster, who'd followed Jeanne into the garden, curled up in the man's lap as if she'd known him forever.

And then Jeanne spoke, her voice quiet and broken. "I've been fighting my whole life," she whispered. "My whole life. To train with the boys. To marry a man I love. To get justice for him. To have a say in my own damn life. But for what? So they can fight back even harder? So they can take even more from me?" It didn't matter that this stranger wouldn't know what she meant; the words rushed forth because they *had to*. She had to tell *someone*.

She shook so hard that even her breaths came out trembling.

"If I hadn't fought, Guillaume would be alive. He'd be chasing his brother through the training fields. Falling asleep in my arms at night. Dragging this damn devil-cat around the castle." She laughed through her tears. "He loved that cat."

The man squeezed her fingers, held her gaze, but didn't speak.

"I'm so tired. I'm so tired of fighting, but I can't stop. Because they killed my husband. They killed my son. They killed my best friend. And I can't live in a world where they get away with that." She covered her face, and a moment later felt his warm grip on her shoulder. Still there. Still listening. She dropped her hands and looked into those kind eyes. "They take and take and take and I don't know how to stop them. I take and take and take but it doesn't seem to matter. They always have more soldiers, more ships, more noblemen ready to take up their cause."

When the man spoke for the first time, his voice was as kind as his eyes. "What if you did stop?" he asked. "What if you stayed here?"

Suppressing her surprise that he'd followed any of that, Jeanne shook her head sharply. "No. Stopping means giving up on Guillaume, Olivier, Pieter, Louis, Alexi. Stopping means they win, and they *can't* win." She choked on the last words and coughed.

The man squeezed her shoulder.

"They can't win," she said again.

He nodded. "I imagine I'd feel the same way, in your shoes. I'd want justice. I wouldn't stop either."

And then, because right now that was what she needed to hear, Jeanne leaned forward and wrapped her arms around the kind-voiced stranger, let herself relax into the strength of him, the warmth. He held her until the moon rose high in the sky and the stars spread across the void to bear witness to her loss.

## CHAPTER 32
# WINDSOR CASTLE, ENGLAND

Amée arrived in England like a storm—swift and fierce and without warning.

Jeanne was in the garden watching Oli instruct Little Jeanne in his own version of chess, where the knights were the most powerful pieces and the entire board was trying to assassinate the king. One moment, she was alone. The next, Amée was flying toward her.

She wrapped her tiny arms around Jeanne and buried her face in Jeanne's shoulder, and something about the gesture made Jeanne want to laugh and cry at the same time. She wrapped her own arms around the girl's shoulders, then laid her cheek atop her head.

With so many things competing for Jeanne's attention, she hadn't even realized how much she'd missed Amée. Missed her quiet presence. Missed her musings about magic. Missed the way she saw the world so differently—a world where she embraced storms as cover and used ravens as a distraction. Most of all, Jeanne had missed the company of another woman who understood her, who knew what it was to need justice, who knew what she'd lost.

Amée pulled back, her face sticky with tears and pinched with the effort of staving them off. "I was so scared I'd find you on your deathbed or that the rumors you'd ended up here wouldn't be true."

Jeanne wiped a tear from Amée's cheek, and the younger woman took Jeanne's calloused hands in her scarred ones. Jeanne often wondered about those scars. She'd never asked where they came from.

"Is it true what they're saying in the city? Is Guillaume..." Amée glanced toward where the children's game had devolved into Oli crashing two knights against each other and muttering about tournaments, while Little Jeanne wandered off after a butterfly.

Jeanne closed her eyes. She wanted to laugh at Oli and Little Jeanne and scream into the sky about Guillaume all at once. What would he be doing if he were with her now? Watching his brother smashing knights? Helping his sister chase bugs? Her throat tightened and she pressed her lips together to keep from falling apart in front of the children.

"Yes," she whispered.

And then Amée was back in her arms like she could keep Jeanne together with the force of her will, and Jeanne's heart cracked open all over again. Amée had rushed across a country, across the Channel, to hold her up. How long had it been since someone had loved her like this?

When Jeanne finally let go, Amée spoke quietly. "Louise and Geoff are fine—the king doesn't think they're involved with you. Louise managed to stop him from confiscating their lands, but she said to tell you he's been throwing temper tantrums again. They're having problems with

THE LIONESS

trade because you keep burning their merchant ships, and now there's unrest in the capital because no one can get what they need."

*Good.* It was small comfort given how much Philip had taken from her, but Jeanne was still glad to know he felt what she was doing. That his supporters felt it. That the country felt it.

"Amélie sent funds," Amée went on, "but I suppose you don't need those now that you're allied with Britain? I didn't make it to any of the other allies. When I heard the rumors that your ship had been destroyed by the French navy, I rode straight for the coast. The people there said they'd heard you'd washed up in Britain, but no one seemed to know whether you'd washed up alive or not." She tried to laugh, but it came out like a sob.

"And the duke?" Jeanne asked, blinking away tears of her own.

Amée's face pinched again. "No new news of him, except that the countryside is currently obsessed with how he cut off the heads of Montfort's knights and catapulted them at their families over the walls of Nantes. It's an old story. Happened years ago. But the peasantry seems to just now have gotten going with it."

She waved her hand dismissively, but something in the gesture felt off. Before Amée could go on, Jeanne asked, "What's wrong?"

Amée looked startled. "What do you mean?"

"I mean something else is wrong. Something's bothering you. Is it just that Charles is still alive?" She searched Amée's face. "Did you see him on the mainland?"

Amée's expression was that of a rabbit flushed from the brush during a hunt. "It's nothing, not compared to what

203

you've endured. I feel foolish even being upset when Guillaume and Pieter..."

Anger—the kind that made Jeanne want to fight anyone who dared even think about hurting someone she loved—welled in her chest. What had the damned duke done now? The peasants liked to say Jeanne was allied with the devil, and now she wished it was true so she could curse the duke straight to hell. Instead she ran her thumbs over Amée's scarred palms and waited.

"When I was twelve, I ran away from home," Amée said. "My parents wanted to marry me off, and I knew that wasn't the right thing for me, so I left. As I was traveling, two men tried to...they tried to take me. When they thought I couldn't hear, they had a whole conversation about how they were going to sell me like they'd done to other girls before—sold them to nobles and merchants." She shuddered. "I'd run away to keep from being touched by a man, and now they were planning to sell me to another one."

*God's nails.* Jeanne's heart was a fist, hard and tight and clutching in on itself. When would this world stop serving up hell to little girls?

"They pretended we were friends, and I pretended I hadn't heard them, but when they fell asleep, I ran. But one of them woke up and came after me. I tried to hold him off with my knife...but what did I know about knives? He took it from me and gave me these." Amée showed Jeanne the scars stretched tight across her palms.

"But you got away," Jeanne whispered, wondering what had brought back all these terrible memories.

Amée nodded, her face folding in on itself with grief. "That's when Giselle saved me. She took me in and healed my wounds and gave me purpose."

Little Jeanne lost interest in the butterflies and sidled

over, looked up at Amée with curiosity, then fiercely wrapped her little body around her leg. Amée laughed through her tears and stooped for a proper hug. Jeanne crouched beside them, running her fingers through Little Jeanne's hair.

"The men who tried to take me," Amée said, "who gave me these scars...it turns out they're part of Charles' court, and he's just given them lands and titles in recognition of the services they've done him. I couldn't find out what that meant, though, before I heard about the attack on your ship and rushed back here. For all I know, he's buying children along with the rest of the nobility."

Every word was a dagger, and Jeanne's skin flushed hot with familiar rage. Amée's must have too, because when she went on, her eyes were sharp, her tone deadly.

"I should have killed them all, even if it led to my death. Because of me, they're all still alive, still kidnapping children, still killing people's only family, still—" A sob abruptly broke her words, and Jeanne wrapped both Amée and Little Jeanne in her arms.

"I know how you feel," she whispered. "Guillaume was my fault. And Pieter..."

Little Jeanne extricated herself from Jeanne's embrace and wandered toward Oli, whose chess game had now further devolved into throwing pieces against the garden wall.

"But you're strong!" Amée said. "You're fierce. You've killed dozens of men—maybe hundreds. You've made the king feel your wrath! And what have I done? Gotten caught trying to poison the duke, run away from some kidnappers, and had my hands cut so deep they took months to heal."

Amée was breathless now, her words coming fast, tumbling over each other. "That's when I started dressing as a man. I didn't want men to look at me like that anymore, so I cut off my braids and started binding my chest and Giselle helped me sew new clothes. It made me feel safe—powerful—then. But now? It's nothing. *I'm* nothing."

"No." Jeanne's voice was firm. "It's Charles who's nothing, not you. You—you're *everything*. You fought off an adult man when you were just twelve and survived a severe wound. You learned to do *magic*. You magicked your way onto my crew and befriended my fiercest knight. You've survived a half-dozen spy missions. Does any of that sound like something a person who's nothing could do?"

Amée closed her eyes, the storm on her face passing. "No."

"Damn right."

And then Amée laughed through her tears, and an invisible tension melted away from her. She swept an arm across her face and took a deep breath, steadying herself. "Jeanne, we need to talk about Pieter."

*Oh god.* Pieter. How could she tell Amée that he was gone? That Jeanne had washed up in Britain alive, but without him. That she'd gotten him killed. Amée would hate her. The one person who still loved her was going to hate her.

"Amée, he didn't make it off the ship."

"I know."

What did she mean? Had Pieter's corpse washed up in France? Had the duke been bragging about his death? Worse, had King Philip mounted his head in Nantes just like Olivier's? Jeanne felt ill at the thought.

"When I heard what happened, it was because they were marching Pieter into Paris."

*Merde*, so Jeanne was right. They'd probably mounted

THE LIONESS

his head on the wall. She lifted a shaking hand to her mouth.

"I'm sorry," Amée said, looking worried. "I thought you knew."

"I assumed they'd thrown the men into the sea. I never imagined they'd take Pieter's body to the king...I..."

Amée's eyes widened. "No! Jeanne, no! You misunderstand me. It's not Pieter's body they took to Paris. It's *Pieter*. They took him alive."

## CHAPTER 33
# WINDSOR CASTLE, ENGLAND

*live.* Jeanne hadn't even considered the possibility that King Philip would leave a man alive, though she supposed he saw it as a poetic sort of justice. She scoffed at her own hope. Pieter held in a dungeon, certainly interrogated, possibly tortured— it was a terrible thing. But he was *alive*.

Jeanne wanted to sweep Amée up in her arms and twirl her like a child. Her body filled with a sureness she hadn't felt since the battle. Pieter needed her. It was time to tuck away her grief and take action. She couldn't keep crying in garden corners and sleeping long hours and forgetting to eat. Love was action, and action was love. Jeanne was the only one who could save him—and save him she would.

She'd take the ships King Edward had offered her, and she'd burn France to the ground if needed. She hadn't been able to save Olivier. Or Guillaume. Or Alexi and Louis. But she could save what family she had left.

∽

THE LIONESS

THE NEXT DAY, Jeanne went to the port. The king had invited her to see her new ships, so two hours after waking—wearing a rich red gown he'd given her, and with her hair once again elaborately braided—Jeanne made her way across Londres to inspect the fleet.

When she swung down from her horse and onto the stone platform, Amée was already there waiting. Jeanne's heart lightened. She'd liked Amée since the day she'd confessed her disguise, but now Jeanne's gratitude for her Merlin had doubled and tripled upon itself. Amée was a lifeline and an anchor, the one person in Londres who'd known Guillaume and Pieter, the one person Jeanne could just be with. No mask. No act. No stone-faced fierceness.

Jeanne squeezed Amée's shoulder in greeting, and she smiled a little in response, one dimple appearing on her right cheek. Monster was there too, perched on a low stone wall, ignoring them as she watched a spider scramble for safety. On the river, three large cogs—each with a single large sail—were being repaired and prepared for Jeanne's return to piracy. She pursed her lips. Cogs were what Britain had, but *merde* were they slow. Before she'd even boarded, she already missed her Genoese warship. With a sharp pang, she thought of Alexi and Louis—inextricably linked to that ship and its demise. Everything about these vessels would be different, including the men.

"What do you think?" she asked Amée.

"I think..." Amée paused and studied the ships. "I think they're not fierce enough."

Jeanne furrowed her brow. "Well, it's not the ships that are fierce. It's the people on them."

"You're Jeanne de Clisson, a mythical monster as far as the French peasantry is concerned. Louise said the latest rumor is that you can breathe fire. Appearances matter,

209

Jeanne. It's like with magic—if you want people to be impressed, you dress in magician's finery or king's robes. If you prefer people to ignore you, you dress as a servant boy." Amée smiled wryly. "And if you want people to be afraid... you terrify them with your ships before they see your face."

Jeanne stared at Amée. It was just like that first storm— when Jeanne had turned toward caution, Amée had advised her to instead embrace the opportunity. To use the tempest to scare her enemies even more. Jeanne would never have thought to do that, but it was genius. Fearful men were more likely to flee and more likely to make mistakes when they fought. More likely to be defeated.

"That's brilliant," she said. "But how do we make them fierce?"

"Black paint, I think." Amée held a hand in front of her and squinted as if imagining it. "Yes, make the ships black and their sails red." Her eyes sparkled with mischief. "They say you dye your sails in the blood of your enemies, so make them believe they're right."

Jeanne laughed out loud. *Yes.* It was perfect. Before they even shot a single arrow, her ships would slide out of the fog and strike her enemies with terror. Amée was a genius. But as she turned to tell her so, her breath caught in her chest—walking toward them was the man from the garden. Jeanne's heart tripped over itself and reached out longingly at the sight of him. Surprised quickly followed. This man had seen her at her lowest, but seeing him again didn't remind her of that, only of the comfort she'd found in his arms. The uncomplicated relief of being seen.

Amée shifted, protective, to Jeanne's side as he approached.

"Jeanne." His tone was warm as he squeezed her hand

between his. Then he turned to Amée. "I don't believe we've had the pleasure yet."

"Arley," Amée said in a voice as low as she could send it.

"Pleasure, Arley. I'm Walter Bentley."

Walter Bentley. Jeanne had heard the name before. He was a knight, a military leader, a long-time ally of the king who was deeply respected in this court.

It was strange—Jeanne had been so careful not to fall apart in front of anyone, but she had with this man. By all rights, she should feel exposed and vulnerable, especially now that she knew who he was. She should wonder who he'd tell, how he'd judge her, how he'd present her to King Edward. But she didn't. She only felt a bone-deep sense of being known, being *safe*. She knew without asking the question that this man would keep her secrets, that when he'd taken her hand in the garden, he'd become hers. Like Pieter and Amée, this was a person she could and would trust.

He turned back to Jeanne. "The king asked me to help manage the process with your ships. Anything in particular you want done?"

Jeanne wished he'd be less formal, but it wasn't like they knew each other—at least not like she *felt* they did. They'd spent a few hours curled up in the mud together, that's all. A flush crept across her face, and she took a shaky breath before answering.

"Yes. Paint them black, and dye the sails red."

His face lit up, eyebrows flying toward the sky. "Truly, m'lady?"

Jeanne's blush deepened. "Are you mocking me?"

"No, no! Not at all! I'm...admiring you." He threw up his hands, a tiny act of surrender. "Truly! No one else would think to turn the ships into something from hell."

"Actually it was Arley's idea. He's the most brilliant illusionist the world's ever seen."

"Remind me not to get on your bad side either." Walter inclined his head toward Amée. "So black ships and red sails then. Is there anything else I can do for you? The king said to spare no expense—I'm to give you whatever you want."

*You could hold me again.* Jeanne's unruly heart stretched out in her chest and she wanted to roll her eyes at herself. *Really, Jeanne?* Pieter was in a dungeon being tortured, Guillaume was in the ground, and she wanted to be *held*? And by a stranger, no less. *Get yourself together.*

She cleared her throat and looked at Amée. "What else do we need?"

Something fierce flashed in the younger woman's eyes. "Can you get me ravens? Four or five dozen?"

Walter looked surprised, but he nodded.

"Also four additional barrels of spirits—but mark them as something else so the men don't drink them. I'll give you a list of medicinal herbs, and I need a small barrel of incense, and—" Amée gasped and pressed a hand to her mouth. "Jeanne, I know how to get us into the French castle."

Jeanne raised an eyebrow, held her breath.

Amée's eyes shone. "We're going in disguised as a troupe of magicians."

## CHAPTER 34
# WINDSOR CASTLE, ENGLAND

Jeanne leaned on the training yard rail as Oli sparred with another nine-year-old boy while their instructor circled them and called out commands. Little Jeanne held her hand, also watching on, her eyes bright and delighted. Monster had tucked herself into some hay in a nearby cart and stared unblinkingly at them through a slit in the wood like a shadowy demon.

Walter—*Sir* Walter, someone in court had corrected her earlier that day—sidled up to the rail beside Jeanne and squeezed her shoulder. "The king told me you're setting sail soon."

There was something about his voice that she liked, a calm that seemed like it would never break, no matter the storm. He was a little like Pieter that way. Jeanne's heart hurt to think it.

"Yes, we leave tomorrow."

"I'd like to come with you. I'm a scrappy fighter and I'm told that I'm quite the strategist, but my strongest skill is subterfuge. If you need to get friendly with some prison guards or bribe a soldier, I'm your man."

213

Jeanne fought back a laugh at the hopeful, childlike look in his green-blue eyes and the cute crooked snaggletooth that made his smile so boyish. She hadn't known Walter long and didn't know him well, but the relief of hearing him say he wanted to fight by her side was like being wrapped in a warm blanket. It was the feeling of winning a battle. The feeling of an ally's shoulder against your back, knowing someone was looking for you.

Before she could accept, Little Jeanne squeezed her hand excitedly, bringing her attention back to the sparring match. Oli had backed the other boy into a corner.

"Surrender, you dog!" he shouted.

Jeanne longed to ruffle his hair and tweak his nose, her heart so soft in that moment it could be broken with a feather. Oli may have been training for battle, but he was still such a child. Still imagining that he'd have the time, breath, or inclination during a real fight to puff out his chest and name-call.

"Maman," Little Jeanne squeaked, "he's winning!"

"Yes, little love." Jeanne squatted down, pushed the curls behind her daughter's ears, and studied her little heart-shaped face. It was the same shape as Guillaume's, the same as Olivier's.

She leaned in to kiss Little Jeanne's cheek, then stood just in time to see Oli disarm his opponent and launch into a speech. A small smile snuck onto her face. The instructor rolled his eyes and told Oli off for being so pompous, which made Little Jeanne giggle. The sun was warm on Jeanne's skin, and her muscles—so tense since their escape from the ship—finally started to unknot.

She turned to Walter, feeling soft and light and so very unlike herself. "Get your things together. Come morning, we leave as soon as the supplies and men are ready."

THE NEXT MORNING, they set sail on Jeanne's flagship—named *My Vengeance* on Amée's suggestion—with a hull full of ravens, barrels of alcohol "not for drinking," and two other ships newly painted, dyed, and dangerous. And as they sailed, they planned.

Jeanne and Amée sat at the table in the cabin where they'd taken up residence together, much to the scandalized whispers of the crew who all still believed Amée to be a young man. Sir Walter had joined them, the one man invited into the women's war council. He sat quietly in his own wooden chair, elbows on his knees, fingertips pressed together, listening. This was his defining feature, Jeanne and Amée had agreed—the man was always listening. It made him likeable, and it made him a good soldier. He always seemed to know what was going on.

As Amée outlined her plan, he broke his silence. "Why disguises and why magic?"

"We once snuck into a fortress dressed as kitchen servants, and I..." Amée glanced at him and let her sentence trail off, but Jeanne knew she was thinking of how she'd successfully passed herself off as a man for ten years.

Jeanne jumped in to cover the awkwardness. "It worked like a charm. Two people burned down an entire fortress and not a single guard stood in our way."

Amée shot Jeanne a grateful look and continued. "At first I thought the most logical disguise was guards, because if Pieter's in prison, we'd need to pass for people who could gain access."

Walter nodded. "It's a good plan."

"No," Amée's voice was firm. "Jeanne can't pass for a

guard, and neither can I, so we'd have to trust Pieter to men we don't even know."

The thought sent alarm spiraling through Jeanne. Amée was right—there was no way she could pass as a guard and no way she'd send in men she didn't know and trust with her life. She wished Alexi was there, wished Roland had been as trustworthy as she'd once believed. Both had been great fighters. Both were loyal to Pieter. Both would have done anything to rescue him. Her stomach clenched at the thought. Both dead, one as a traitor. How things changed.

"So...magicians?" Jeanne prompted, forcing her mind away from the man who'd betrayed her and the man whose jokes had burned up with her ship.

"Magicians." Amée's eyes shone in the dim cabin. "It's a way into the castle without a fight. They're unlikely to be treated with suspicion, and I already have the skills to put on a show. By the time magicians are brought in to perform, the court's half-drunk and raving. No one will know it's you, and no one will notice when we slip out of the hall."

Jeanne nodded, as did Walter beside her. It made sense. And not only did it get her closer to Pieter—it would also get her to the king himself. Because if she was honest with herself, that was the thought that'd been buzzing in the back of her mind ever since she'd decided to go after Pieter.

If she was sneaking into the castle, Jeanne wanted to kill the king. She couldn't come so close and let him walk away. She'd started her quest wanting him to suffer before he died; now she just wanted him to die.

For the first time, she voiced these thoughts to Amée. "However we get into the castle, we need a plan that gets Pieter out *and* gets me to the king. As long as he lives, nothing is safe. Nothing is sacred. I am not going to leave with him within the reach of my blade and still breathing."

THE LIONESS

As she spoke, Jeanne's resolve hardened. Something about declaring her decisions aloud made them real and solid and no longer tentative. She was going to kill the king and rescue Pieter, and then the one evil left in the world would be the Duke of Brittany. And how hard would he be to kill once the king's protection had crumbled around him like ash?

Amée looked like she might protest, but Walter's hand found Jeanne's in the dimness. "I suppose our rescue mission has gotten a bit more complicated then," he said. "But if there's one thing I've learned in two decades of fighting, it's that men are easier to kill than you'd think."

# MEANWHILE...
## PARIS, FRANCE

QUEEN JOAN WAS STILL TOO OLD FOR THIS SHIT.

Too old for her husband's temper tantrums. Too old for his peacocking. Too old for the scheming that only ever seemed to make them more enemies.

"She's dead, dead, dead," the king crowed at the duke across a table laden with every luxury. "I'm sure of it!"

They sipped wine from gold-dipped glass goblets and pulled tender meat from fragile quail legs arranged on little gold-swirled plates. The duke ate sparingly, daintily. The king ate with gusto, as always. Joan was too disgusted to eat at all. Hadn't her husband grown tired of crowing about things uncertain? He thought he'd stopped Jeanne three times now, four maybe. And every time he was wrong.

*She'll fall into line*, he'd said. *We've found her children*, he said. *We've got her*, he said. And every time, premature. Not the only thing premature about the man, if Joan was honest.

The duke was more cautious. "Let's not get ahead of ourselves. We need confirmation from our own men."

Philip frowned, pointing a fork back and forth between

THE LIONESS

them with vigor. "There's no way she survived the Channel! Anything else is rumor."

"Your Highness—"

Philip cut Charles off. "I know you're keen to keep her knight alive for questioning, but it's time to be done with him. He's not given up anything useful, and there is simply no way she survived the Channel anyway!"

Joan ran a finger along the stem of her glass. "My love, I too would like to urge caution here. We're fighting battles on multiple fronts—Joanna's causing trouble in the north, there are routier problems in the countryside because of the truce, and we cannot afford to underestimate Jeanne yet again. Until we have confirmation of her death, I beg you to listen to Charles."

Charles held up a hand to silence her, and irritation skittered across her skin.

"Thank you, Your Majesty. Philip, all I'm asking for is a few more weeks. If Jeanne is truly dead, then we'll never see her again. If she's alive, she'll come for her man, and if she does, it's a suicide mission. We smoke her and her army out. They march on us, and we crush them. With her knight alive, we force her into the open, but without that, she could lay low and strike at us at the worst moment. I understand that you don't agree with me, sire, and I respect it. I'm asking for some more time as a personal favor." Charles inclined his head, awaiting the answer.

Shrewd, the way he'd presented it. Joan had always thought the duke was the kind of man to keep on their side —she liked to believe it was her gentle urging that had helped Philip ally with Charles instead of his rival in the contested dukeship of Brittany. Kingdoms rose and fell on smaller decisions, and Joan liked to think this one had helped keep them in power. And more importantly, helped keep her and her children alive.

The look on Philip's face was a gratified one. The inclined head and the framing of the request made him feel powerful, even as he was about to give up some of his power. That was the duke's gift.

"Well, Charles," he said through a less-than-dignified mouthful of quail, "when you put it that way, I suppose I can grant you another few weeks with the prisoner. And then, if—as I suspect—Jeanne is dead, we'll kill him. Publicly. Humiliatingly. Just like her husband."

## CHAPTER 35

# PARIS, FRANCE

The moment the covering touched Jeanne's head, she wanted to scream and fling it off. Instead, she balled her fists and took a deep breath as Amée attached it tightly to her scalp then slipped out of the room to find a few more pins.

After years of letting her hair down, the head covering was hot, itchy, and constrictive. Jeanne reminded herself that she would walk through fire to get to the king or get Pieter back. Now she had her chance to do both, so what were a few pins digging into her scalp and the hot itch of the magician-assistant's dress?

In another hour they'd be in the castle, just like Amée had promised. They'd sickened the king's royal magician, and Amée had been hired in his place—along with her two assistants. Walter had taken the lead on getting soldiers drunk and talkative, and they now knew that Pieter was indeed alive and being held in the palace dungeons under the torture tower—a fact that made Amée flinch.

They knew where Pieter was. They knew how to get in. They had a plan. Now Jeanne just had to keep her excitement and the irritation of the pins at bay long enough to rescue him.

And kill the king.

The other two had tried to talk her out of it, but Jeanne was determined. They were here and they would accomplish both. A live Pieter, a dead Charles.

She shook her shoulders to dislodge the thrill of it, and Walter—perhaps reading her movements as nerves—crossed the room in two strides and took her hands. She tried to ignore her body's response, a warm flush dancing across her skin, an urgency in places she hadn't felt urgency for years. She shouldn't feel this way, shouldn't let anything distract her from the most important mission of her life. After she killed the king, maybe. But now...now it felt wrong. *Focus, Jeanne.*

She thought Walter might say something, but he simply lifted her hands to kiss them, tucked a rogue curl into her wimple, and stepped back.

She forced herself to break eye contact, then she broke the silence. "You know, I haven't heard how you became one of the king's lieutenants."

Walter grinned. "Really? The court is so gossipy, I assumed you already knew. I'm a lowly Yorkshire man, come from nothing, born with no titles—the courtiers love to talk about it."

Jeanne raised an eyebrow. That was unexpected. The nobles were the warrior class, trained from a young age to fight and defend, so it was rare for a common man to be more than a foot soldier. Pieter was an exception to that rule, but he'd befriended Olivier and become a ward of his father as a child.

"Go on," she said, interested and grateful to be distracted from her earlier feelings.

THE LIONESS

Walter shrugged. "I was a scrappy kid. Always starting fights with my brothers, usually losing. With both of them older and bigger than me, I quickly learned that my only chance was to outsmart them. I'd ambush them when they weren't paying attention, try to trick them into separating to make the battle a bit more even. Over time, I started winning. I'd still come home scratched and muddy, but they'd both have black eyes from tree branches I whipped around on them or limps from the time I tripped them into a pit."

Jeanne nodded, amused, and Walter went on.

"By the time I was nine, I was sneaking off to watch the noble boys train, trying to learn from the sidelines. Got strapped a good few times for stealing into places I wasn't welcome. One day, one of the knights took a shining to me. I was already a good knife fighter, already good with my fists, but he trained me up with the sword.

"And then in my twenties I signed up to fight in Scotland. Worked my way up, had a few good victories, and people started to take notice. The king knighted me by thirty and made me his sergeant in France for a while, but at my core, I'm still that scrappy kid fighting dirty, so it made sense to form my own mercenary band and work with Edward that way." He shrugged, then gave Jeanne a shy grin.

"It's what I loved about you the first time I heard the stories—another scrappy fighter telling the world how it is, surprising people. I knew I'd love you even before I met you."

A warm flush spread across Jeanne's cheeks, and she leaned back in surprise.

"You don't have to say anything," he said, his own

cheeks going rosy. "Truly, I don't expect anything. I just...I wanted to tell you."

Rather than tell Walter off for dropping this on her right before their mission, Jeanne was comforted by the revelation. It meant she was safe. It meant they were in this together. It meant hope. It meant that once her love for Olivier had reached its perfect conclusion—with the death of the man who killed him—she'd have a place to land. To rest.

Perhaps, to love again.

Walter was yet another reason to kill the king. To free her own heart.

IT WAS LATE—THE SKY INKY BLACK AND STAR-STUDDED—when the troupe was finally ushered into the castle to perform. It was as grand as Jeanne remembered, with eight central columns stretching to the double-arched wooden ceiling and polychrome statues of past kings lining the wall. King Philip and his retinue sat at a heavy black marble table with a half-eaten banquet laid out before them. Walter was at Jeanne's side, his fingers interlaced with hers, while Amée stood slightly in front of them, her eyes on the doors, ready for the show to begin.

And with a flash of sparks, it did.

Acrobats flew through the doors, flipping and dancing past lords and ladies and landing in deep bows before the king. Amée stepped slow and purposeful to the center of the hall, taking the place of the king's usual magician and sweeping her arms around her in a circular shape trailed by a line of fire. The whole hall gasped in unison.

Jeanne barely registered any of it—she didn't care

about acrobats or shows. *Couldn't* care about them. Not with King Philip mere yards away. She let go of Walter's hand, clenched and unclenched her fists, and ran her fingers over the dagger tucked beneath her skirts.

*Merde.* She wanted to bound across the hall and shove her dagger under his chin. To see the surprise and recognition in his eyes, see the life go out of them. Her skin flushed and heart raced at the possibility, her breathing shallow.

But if she killed him now, they'd never get Pieter out. The king's guards were also yards away, which meant she'd never get the duke. They wouldn't escape. Patience wasn't her strong suit, but she would wait for the right moment this time. She pressed her fingernails into her palms and stared at the king from under her wimple, half-wishing that he'd recognize her, that he'd know his doom was at his doorstep.

But just as Amée had predicted, he didn't.

"People see what they want to see," she'd said. "They don't see what they aren't looking for. If they expect a boy servant, they see a boy servant—even when you're a girl in disguise. If they expect a witch, they take you to trial as a witch, even if you're not one." Her tone had been bitter, but her voice strong. "He thinks you're in Britain or at sea. He'd never imagine you here, dressed as a magician's assistant, standing in his own hall. He won't see what he isn't looking for."

And she was right. Jeanne stood bare-faced in the king's hall, and not a soul sounded the alarm.

The acrobats kept the crowd awed with twists and flips and feats of balance that defied nature. A small boy, no more than nine, stepped to the center of the hall to interpret the stars for the king, promising him glory and triumph. Then Amée took over again—moving apples and eggs across the floor without touching them, using incense to blow a line of fire around her in a circle, making a nobleman's coin pouch disappear and reappear. As her assistants, Walter and Jeanne retrieved apples and handed her powders, heads down, invisible as Amée commanded the room's attention. She was brilliant, Jeanne thought, with the kind of pride her heart usually reserved for her own children.

Then, as Amée took her bow to make way for the next act—a sword-swallower—she gasped a little and clutched at her stomach. A stab of fear pierced Jeanne before she realized this was the act—an illness that would get them into the doctor's chambers. She was first irritated at falling for her own trick, then amused that it was so good, so worth falling for, that it caught her as well.

With her arms wrapped around her waist and her forehead creased in pain, Amée whispered with one of the servants. Walter held her elbow and knitted his eyebrows in concern. The servant glanced at Walter, then at Amée again, and then nodded somberly and led her by her other arm out a side door and into the castle's empty corridors. Jeanne followed.

When they reached the doctor's offices—a cluster of rooms filled with herbs and remedies—the servant girl said, "Wait here. I'll bring the doctor."

God's nails this was easy, Jeanne thought with a little thrill. She was finally going to get Pieter back, have her revenge, and see justice done. And then *she* could rest— she'd return to Britain to watch Oli train and see Little Jeanne grow up.

She was so close.

An old man with a round pale face, a wispy gray beard,

THE LIONESS

and a bored expression bustled in. "Alright then, show me where it hu—"

Though they were supposed to wait for Amée to spike the doctor's wine with a sleeping draught, hope made Jeanne reckless. Without thinking, she grabbed a metal pot off the nearest worktable and swung it hard into the doctor's head. He crumpled to the ground.

Amée and Walter looked on, shocked, until Amée uneasily whispered, "This wasn't the plan."

"Just as good." Jeanne's body hummed with impatience. "Spiking his wine would have taken longer anyway."

"We'll still need those sleeping herbs," Sir Walter said, catching Amée's eye. "When you hit a man like that, he doesn't stay down long."

"Doesn't stay down long?" Amée sounded dazed. "It looks like he'll never get up again."

But after another few seconds, she shook herself out of whatever was holding her back, reached a trembling hand into the pouch at her side, dropped some herbs into a glass, then poured in some wine from the carafe doctors kept in their rooms to help settle patients' nerves.

Jeanne and Walter watched—the former impatient, the latter intrigued—as Amée used a pestle from a nearby table to mash the herbs into the wine. Then the doctor groaned, and she jumped.

"See?" Jeanne said. "He's alive."

Walter stooped to the doctor and supported his head. "Doctor," he said, his voice tinged with believable concern. "Are you okay? You collapsed!"

The man's eyes rolled open, and he looked blankly up at Walter, confused.

Amée stood rooted to her spot by the worktable, and it worried Jeanne to see her so unsteady. She'd been with

Jeanne for years now, helped to plan battle strategies, had even tried to kill the duke with poison, but now Jeanne realized that she'd never been this close to someone they'd harmed. She'd always stayed out of the way—in the cabin, in a kitchen spiking drinks with poison, in a war council talking about death as if it were something far away.

"Arley," Walter said firmly, "give the poor doctor something for his nerves."

Amée stumbled over and tipped the contents of the wine glass into the man's mouth. The doctor swallowed it all down, closed his eyes, and took a deep breath.

*Good.* Now they could get on with their mission. But as Jeanne turned for the door, the doctor seized. His body twitched in a jerky movement, then a second, and then he began flailing. Foam formed at the corners of his mouth. His eyelids lifted slightly, revealing only white. The herbs meant to push him into unconsciousness had done something else.

"Let's go." Jeanne's whisper was urgent, but Amée just looked at her, wide-eyed with panic.

"Oh no, oh no! What did I do? Did I give him too much? Oh my god, did I use the wrong herbs? Perhaps they were just supposed to steep in the wine, not be pestled. Oh god."

"Arley," Walter whispered, taking her shoulders. "Come on, we have to go."

"I can't feel my arms." Amée was breathing too fast now, and Jeanne knew what that meant. She'd seen enough men pass out in training to understand the signs.

"Arley," she said.

The doctor fell still, his lips turning blue.

"Arley."

Amée stared down at him, her eyes unfocused, her voice

higher than usual. "It must be terrible to die by poison. He's choking..."

"*Amée.*" Jeanne's tone was sterner now, risking the use of Amée's real name to snap her out of her trance. And it worked—Amée's eyes locked onto hers. "We have to go. You can't help him, and you don't want to. Any man who works with your enemy is your enemy—do you hear me? This doctor works for Philip, and Philip protects the duke. We were fools to try and spare him in the first place; this would have been quicker with a dagger. But there's no second guessing on a rescue mission. We're here now, and *we have to go.* If you don't pull yourself together, Pieter is going to die."

Amée stepped back as if Jeanne had hit her, but the flush left her cheeks and her eyes focused again. At that moment, brisk self-assured footsteps sounded in the hall, moving their way. Walter grabbed both women and pushed them behind a heavy tapestry in an adjacent room.

"Don't move," he said. "Don't say a word."

He didn't need to say it—Amée was already silent as stone, and Jeanne knew better. Then he was gone, no doubt hiding elsewhere in the room since there wasn't enough space behind the tapestry. The footsteps stopped. The heavy door creaked open. A scream pierced the silence and then the footsteps pounded out of the chamber, down the corridor, and away.

The doctor, still lying blue and stiff and empty on the floor, had been discovered.

Which meant *they* had been discovered.

## CHAPTER 36
# PARIS, FRANCE

J eanne flew out from behind the tapestry and after the screamer—a young man who proved easy to catch, easier to kill. She tucked his body into an alcove, blew out its candle, and hoped no one would see him.

There was a chance someone had heard the screams, but it was also possible that the revels in the hall were too loud and they'd gone unnoticed. Unless she heard an official alarm, Jeanne decided to count on the latter and stick with the plan: Walter and Amée were going after Pieter.

Jeanne would take the king.

Which was how, minutes later, she ended up crouched behind a heavy wooden dresser inside Philip's own chambers. The damn self-assured bastards in the castle guard hadn't even posted anyone at the doors. Was it going to be this easy to kill the most well-protected man in France and end this thing once and for all?

She felt elated. Invincible. Was this how Isabella felt when her men captured her husband, the English king? How Sybil of Anjou felt when her forces swept away those of her enemies? Did Olivier know, somehow, that she was

230

about to avenge his death? She wondered if it brought his soul peace. She hoped it did.

Assuming they were right about timing, King Philip would be at least another hour, but Jeanne positioned herself right away—if he turned in early, she wouldn't be caught unawares.

She hoped, fleetingly, that he'd come without the queen. From what Jeanne knew of her, she was strong and scholarly, often ruling France while her fool of a husband was off fighting wars and ordering nunneries burned to the ground. The peasants called Joan evil, marked by the devil by her limp. But they called Jeanne evil, too, in most circles. Not to mention Isabella. So maybe Joan was evil, or maybe she was just sharp and strong-minded. Maybe she was just her own brand of wildcat.

Either way, Jeanne wanted her husband, not her, but she would do what she had to. Joan had chosen to throw her lot in with a killer, just like the dozens of nobles Jeanne had beheaded at sea. If the two retired to this chamber together, Jeanne wouldn't spare her.

The door creaked.

Jeanne tensed. Ready as she was, she was surprised the king was back so early—the other performers would still be in the middle of their final act. Unless she'd lost track of time?

A broad-shouldered man stepped inside and quickly, quietly shut the door behind him.

*Too* quickly, she thought. *Too* quietly.

This man was not Philip; he was an intruder like her.

Jeanne had a split second to decide whether to hide or take him down. Hiding was less likely to raise an alarm, but it also wasn't in her nature. In a matter of seconds, she'd stepped up to the surprised man's back, flipped him around, and pressed her knife to his throat.

"What are you do—" The question died on her lips as shock washed over her like waves in a storm. The unarmed intruder with a face like a boulder was none other than Roland—the man she'd thought was loyal, was hers, the man who'd attacked her in her cabin, the man she'd *drowned*.

Her thoughts swirled, none of them making real sense. How was he here? How had he survived?

Another wave hit her, this time of realization. It was *Roland* who'd told the king where her children were. Not the nuns, not the Church—it was a dead man who wasn't dead.

"Why?" she hissed, pressing her knife in harder. "How?"

He flinched, then spoke too loud for her liking. "A fishing vessel found me almost as soon as you were out of sight."

Jeanne knew enough about suppressed rage to recognize it under his forced calm.

"And what are you doing here now?" It was odd that he was in the king's chambers. Fear tugged at her—did they know she was here? Had they sent in a scout?

Roland's eye twitched. "I need money, so I was going to take one of the queen's brooches. I've...been gambling."

Jeanne almost laughed at the absurdity of it. Gambling debts and thievery, the attempted murder of children. Who was this man she'd once thought she knew?

"You told the king about my children?" Jeanne already knew the answer, but she needed to hear it from him.

"Yes."

"It was your idea to burn the nunnery?"

THE LIONESS

"No." He tried, unsuccessfully, to keep a sneer off his face. "That was the duke's."

God's nails. Just when she thought betrayal couldn't cut any deeper, in twisted the knife, all the way to her soul. Her old friend the duke, the *pious* duke—not just a murderer, but an attempted murderer *of children*.

"Why?" Jeanne hated how desperate the word came out. Here she was with a dagger at Roland's throat, his life in her hands, and it sounded more like she was begging for her own. "They were babies—no threat to you or to him."

"It was the only way to destroy you."

Rage and despair warred within her. She felt the same deep exhaustion she'd had after Roland attacked her on the ship, the sense that no matter what she did, she'd never win.

*Give up.*

The thought danced through her head, and she almost screamed aloud at it. How could she when she was steps away from killing the king? From winning?

But here was Roland, reminding her that winning wasn't always winning. She could try to take control of her men and watch them rebel. She could throw a traitor into the water and see him resurrected, intent on murdering her children.

How could she have been so foolish? She should have killed him herself that day on the ship. But she'd been so tired, so discouraged. And that weakness—that small mercy—had almost killed all three of her youngest children. *You stand for mercy, Jeanne*, her mother had said. Well this is what mercy had bought her.

Jeanne felt herself press the dagger harder and saw blood welling around the blade. As Roland opened his mouth to speak or to scream—Jeanne would never know which—she silenced him forever. Her whole body was heavy as she stepped back and watched him slump to the floor, grasping ineffectively at his throat.

The thoughts of the children cut at her. It was her fault. Her fault. All of it was her fault. She pushed out a long breath and tightened her hands on the dagger—she had to pull herself together. She was in the king's chambers, here to make right what had happened. She couldn't fall apart now.

And then came the bells, the alarm horns, the shouting.

They'd been found out.

What now? Were Walter and Amée on their way to the dungeons to meet her? Were they running for their lives? Were they—Jeanne's gut curled into a tight fist at the thought—captured? Killed? Were there more casualties because of her?

Should she stay and kill Philip even if it cost her life, or should she go and find Pieter, assume they hadn't made it to him in time?

*Pieter.*

She looked at Roland's body and knew she couldn't stay. The king would be better guarded with the alarms ringing through the castle—he might not even come back to his chambers. And no matter how much she wanted to kill him, she would never choose him over the people she loved.

Pieter, Amée, and Walter were somewhere in this castle.

Jeanne had to go.

Roland's body was blocking the door, so she lifted him under his arms and hauled. He was even heavier than he looked, and it took her too long to pull him halfway behind a dresser. It would have to do. But her dress was now streaked with blood and likely to get her stopped or ques-

THE LIONESS

tioned, so she chanced another minute to throw open the queen's bureau, choose the simplest dress, and leave her own bloody clothes crumpled inside. She tore off the head covering that marked her as lowborn and prayed her braids were elaborate enough to pass for a noble.

Then she arranged her face into what hopefully looked like confusion and concern and moved, as fast as she could without running, toward Pieter—the man who should have been her priority from the start.

## CHAPTER 37
# PARIS, FRANCE

Jeanne met three guards on her way to the tower dungeons, and not a single one recognized the queen's dress or Jeanne's face. They all ran right past her, single-mindedly focused on whatever alarm had drawn them.

Could they really be so oblivious? Or perhaps the alarm hadn't been about her at all? What else had happened? But before she could unravel the answers, she turned a corner and saw a scene that made her blood run cold. Amée was stooped at a door, presumably Pieter's cell, picking the locks. She was so engrossed in her work, she hadn't noticed a guard closing in from her left with his sword drawn. Walter was looking in the opposite direction and hadn't seen him either.

Jeanne reached for the dagger at her hip, only to realize she'd neglected to cut a hole in the queen's skirts. In her usual dress, reaching the weapon was easy through a carefully cut slit—in this one, she had to pull up the skirts to get to it. *God's nails*, how could she have not thought about this? She bunched the skirts toward her waist, but it was too slow. She knew she was being too slow. She wouldn't be able to save Amée.

There was a clang of swords as Walter fought with a previously unsighted guard who'd been approaching from the right. What villain put Pieter's cell at the intersection of so many damn corridors? At the sound, Amée instinctively flattened herself on the stone floor and, by pure chance, the second guard's sword missed her and embedded itself in the wooden door.

Walter made a startled noise, kicked his own attacker away with surprising strength, and skewered the man now reaching down to grab Amée. The dying guard fell backward, taking Walter's sword with him.

Jeanne's heart leapt into her throat as she finally unsheathed her dagger. The other guard was now back, but from this angle, Jeanne wouldn't be able to throw it without hitting Walter.

"Behind you!" she shouted, hoping her shouts wouldn't bring yet more of the king's men streaming down the corridors.

Walter turned. The attacker raised his sword above Amée as if in slow motion and Jeanne's heart seized. There wasn't enough time for Walter to pull the sword from the door, and the dagger he kept under his tunic wasn't enough to stop the blow.

Jeanne was going to lose Amée.

She was going to be the reason for another innocent death.

Her stomach clenched with the certainty of it.

And then Walter stepped in front of the cowering girl and viciously kicked the attacker backward. The kick pushed him just enough off course that the blow fell along

Walter's arm instead of his chest, wrenching a scream from him as it sliced from shoulder to palm.

There was so much blood, but he wasn't down, wasn't dead. Yet.

And then Jeanne was there, and before the guard even realized she was beside him, he was dead.

"We have to go," she breathed. "Amée, are you alright? Can you open the door?"

Jeanne's chest tightened, tears of rage and fear caught in her throat. The weight of all these people she had to get out alive threatened to crush her. Amée trembling as she worked the lock. Pieter somewhere behind that door. Walter turning whiter with blood loss by the second.

Despite Jeanne's shout and the noise of the battle, no more guards had arrived. Without any real thought, Jeanne found herself ripping long strips off the bottom of her skirts and wrapping them tight around Walter's injured arm as Amée worked the locks.

She had to stop the blood loss.

She had to get them out alive.

She *would* get them out alive.

## CHAPTER 38
# PARIS, FRANCE

The lock clicked, heavy and final, and Amée flung the door wide, whispering Pieter's name like a prayer.

And then suddenly, he was there. Tall and strong and so very himself, though limping and wincing from whatever he'd had to endure.

Jeanne rushed forward and kissed his cheek, her eyes glistening.

As she pulled back, he put a hand gently, wonderingly on the side of her head. "You're here."

"Of course we are," she whispered. "Let's go."

He nodded, a familiar determination finding its way back into his eyes, as he reached down and pulled Walter's sword from the dead guard and nodded for Jeanne to lead the way.

They all trailed after her into the dark corridor to the left. She'd studied the plans longer than anyone, so she knew the way least likely to be guarded. The alarms still resounded in the distance, and Jeanne's heart beat in time with their frantic calls. As they went, she blew out candles

239

and snuffed torches, leaving behind a darkness that would make it harder to be followed.

Right turn. Left turn. Right again. And then they were outside in a back garden, and Jeanne was hoisting Amée over a wall. Pieter followed, then Walter, then Jeanne herself.

There was supposed to be a boat waiting for them, but the alarm must have scared their boatman away.

Jeanne didn't hesitate. "Can everyone swim?"

They all nodded, though Walter looked faint, Pieter pained, and Amée afraid. Jeanne hoped they each had enough strength to make it just a little farther.

"Follow me," she whispered, diving into the water.

*Merde*, it was cold. Jeanne's lungs seized up, and she had to force herself to ignore her body's instinct to turn back. Instead of heading to the south bank as planned, she carved through the water to the north, toward the city. Going deeper into Paris was dangerous—they'd be sitting ducks, at the mercy of the king's loyal subjects. But those alarms, and the absence of their boat, had changed everything.

Jeanne had expected to take out the guards and escape with hours to spare before the next shift discovered something was wrong. But now the city would already be flooding with soldiers searching for them.

The boat—the first of three escape plans, and Jeanne's favored option—had either fled into the night or taken their money and never come at all. It was supposed to take them to a merchant ship bound for the Channel, but showing up there covered in blood and soaked through from their swim would cause too much stir to go unnoticed. The merchant ship plan would have to be abandoned.

Their second and third plans had both been horseback.

Jeanne had purchased horses that were now stationed at either end of the city, but with soldiers undoubtedly making their way through the streets and everyone much weaker and more injured than she'd hoped, they'd never make it through. Not looking like half-dead vagabonds. The horses were also out of reach.

And so Jeanne improvised, pulling her companions out of the icy black water and taking them to the one place she could think of that might be safe—the brothel where she'd hidden after Olivier's execution. They'd taken her and Pieter in then, so perhaps they would again now.

When she reached the brothel's door, she caught Pieter's eye, her heart flying into her throat at the sight of him. He was here. He was alive. He seemed mostly alright. She had the unreasonable desire to throw herself into his arms and weep with relief, and then immediately felt furious with herself for indulging in sentimentality when they were still so exposed. Pieter, oblivious to her struggle, nodded, which she took to mean the brothel was a good plan, so she pushed her way inside with the others crowding in behind.

She scanned the dim room, looking for the madam. Pieter stepped up beside her. He knew the madam better, caught her eye first, and stepped slowly toward where she stood at the side of the room chatting with a shabbily dressed man with his back to them.

The woman's eyebrows flew toward her hairline. She whispered a few words to the man, smiled kindly and patted him on the arm, then swept across the room to herd the disheveled group through a narrow doorway and into her office.

"Pieter, what is this?" she asked as soon as she'd shut the door behind them.

GIGI GRIFFIS

"Gabrielle, I'm very sorry to trouble you, but we've been —" He paused, coughed, and reached out to touch Jeanne's shoulder.

She wasn't sure what it meant. Was he was thinking of something to say, trying to keep her from jumping in, or calming himself? Perhaps assuring himself that she was real, he was out, and they were here. Safe, in a way.

"We were attacked," he finished, his voice low. "And we need a place to recover. Like before."

Gabrielle pursed her lips, eyeing them shrewdly. "And like before, I assume you can pay for that? I don't house fugitives for less than double-board."

*Fugitives.* Jeanne frowned. Of course Gabrielle knew what they were, who they were. Jeanne was famous, wanted in the city, and this woman had housed her before that became common knowledge—not after. She'd recognize Jeanne and know her name, and there was no assurance that she wouldn't turn them in. Knowing she was housing a wanted woman changed everything. Were they safe here? Even at double-board, Gabrielle could just keep them occupied until she called the king's guard.

Jeanne cleared her throat. "Make it quadruple board, and for a week. We'll pay half now and half when we leave. We'll need meals brought up." She glanced at Walter, his face pale and his breathing labored. "And we'll need someone to fetch some herbs. My colleague"—she motioned to Amée—" can give you a list."

Gabrielle inclined her head. "Sounds like we've got a deal, m'lady Clisson."

Jeanne raised her eyebrows. Bold of Gabrielle to make it clear she knew who she was talking to. It had been right to dangle more money in front of her, and wise to let her know that half was contingent upon their departure.

But was that enough? Would Gabrielle take their money and let them go or would she call the guards as soon as they'd stepped out her door? Another incentive for her silence seemed prudent.

"I'll also send a bonus with a messenger once we're safely away from the city."

Gabrielle looked delighted. "Well then, that sounds fair. I'd heard of your generosity, m'lady. Glad it wasn't a rumor. I'll go prepare a room. Stay here. Wouldn't want any of our friends in the main hall to recognize you. We'll wait until they're...occupied, then we'll take you up."

## CHAPTER 39
# PARIS, FRANCE

The four fugitives clustered in a dingy room with two cots. Pieter sat heavily on one, sipping water and nibbling on bread before falling asleep. Jeanne had demanded to know when they'd last given him something to eat or drink, and the answer was horrifying— days, maybe even a week. Pieter couldn't be sure because in a dark cell with no natural light, time's passing became a strange, unknowable thing.

Sir Walter lay pale-faced and shaky on the other cot, his arm still wrapped in the cloth soaked with blood and water. Amée was on her knees at his side, a pile of herbs, clean dressings, and a bowl of water she'd requested from Gabrielle on the floor beside her.

Jeanne stood over them, her stomach a mess of knots. Walter was too pale. He'd lost so much blood, and there was nothing Jeanne could do except watch and hope as Amée cleaned the wound, packed it with mashed-up herbs, and rewrapped it in a clean cloth.

"That's all I can do," she whispered to keep from waking Pieter. "The good news is the bleeding's stopped, so

I'm just hoping the herbs will keep out infection." Her face was drawn, exhausted, and it didn't surprise Jeanne when she added, "I think I need to sleep."

Jeanne motioned Pieter, who was now snoring softly. "I'm sure he wouldn't mind sharing."

Amée looked so scandalized that Jeanne almost laughed. Instead of answering, the younger woman curled up on a blanket on the floor and immediately fell into the same kind of exhausted asleep that had already claimed Pieter.

Jeanne marveled at her. So capable at such a young age. So much quieter and more patient than Jeanne had ever been. So smart. No, not just smart—brilliant. Jeanne never would have thought of half the things Amée had. Black ships and red sails. Sneaking into the castle as magicians. Chewing up herbs and packing them into Walter's wounds to stop the bleeding.

She looked down at the younger woman, her face so peaceful in sleep, and felt something fierce and motherly rise in her chest. She owed Amée her life and the lives of her men. And something else too—she owed Amée her *hope*.

Amée had appeared in that garden when all hope was gone. Yes, she'd reminded Jeanne of what they'd lost, but she'd also told her that Pieter was alive. Told her, through her tears, through the fear that had driven her across the Channel, that Jeanne was still loved and that someone still believed in her. It was like finding a long-lost daughter she hadn't known was lost.

Lost. Like Pieter had been.

Jeanne hadn't gotten a chance to talk to him yet. They'd all been so tired, he'd been so hungry and thirsty, and attending to their sore, aching, broken bodies had seemed more urgent than their souls. But as Jeanne stood there, she wished Pieter were awake so she could ask him how he was, ask if he hated her for taking so long. For letting him be taken.

Walter too. She wanted to comfort him and hold him. She wanted—she was ready to admit it now—to kiss him.

She wanted to wrap her arms around all three of them, to feel the solid warm aliveness of them, to be physically, viscerally sure they were okay. There was no way she could sleep—not with all these wants beating through her like a second heart and the adrenaline from their escape still racing through her body. So even though she didn't want to wake him, Jeanne eased herself onto the cot beside Walter and rested her head on his good shoulder.

"Thank you." Even as she whispered it, she wondered what she was thanking him for. For saving Amée? For helping them rescue Pieter? For coming with her? For loving her?

"You're welcome," he murmured, his voice faint but happy.

She was surprised he was awake, but glad to hear his voice. He tangled his fingers in the ends of her unkempt hair.

They stayed like that for a long time, neither speaking, and Jeanne felt a thousand tensions release. Olivier was gone and Guillaume was gone. And she would avenge them. She would honor their memory. But that didn't mean she couldn't let Walter caress her scalp. It didn't mean she couldn't feel the relief of having Pieter, Amée, and Walter here with her, unknotting her muscles one by one.

Jeanne lifted her face and pressed her lips to Walter's cool pale cheek. Then, as the last of the adrenaline faded, they both were claimed by sleep.

Hours later, drifting in and out of sleep, half-dreaming, half-planning their escape, Jeanne barely heard the soft knock at the door. By the time she stirred from the mattress to answer the second knock, Amée had opened her eyes and jumped to her feet.

"It's okay," Jeanne murmured.

But it wasn't.

Gabrielle stood in the doorway, her lips pursed and her face tight.

"You have to leave," she said flatly.

"What?"

"You have to go. Now. The king's men are conducting a door-to-door search. Whatever you did last night, they seem to know you're still in the city. They can't find you here. You have to go."

Jeanne's chest tightened, and Amée sucked in a breath. Would they never have a safe moment to rest? How in the name of the virgin was she supposed to get two battered, half-conscious men, twice her and Amée's sizes, out of the city?

She opened her mouth to protest but closed it again. Gabrielle wouldn't care, and it didn't matter—if the soldiers came here, they were all dead. Gabrielle had no choice. Which meant Jeanne had no choice. They had to run.

"How long?" Jeanne asked, her voice steady as her mind and body steeled themselves.

This was the reason she trained—so that when it came time to fight or fly, to move in the danger of the moment, her body and mind would obey. No fear. No confusion. Just the ability to make a decision and plow on through whatever stood in her way.

"Two hours. Maybe less. The soldiers are in this quarter already, so it won't be long. If they show up and you're here, I'll serve you to them on a platter."

Gabrielle didn't even blink when she said it, but Amée gasped again. Sweet Amée, thinking this woman was their friend and not just a paid secret-keeper.

Jeanne nodded. "We'll be gone well before that."

Gabrielle nodded curtly back and left, closing the door behind her.

Jeanne turned to face a wide-eyed trembling Amée. "I know you're scared, but I need you to focus. I need my Merlin. What do you think is the best way to disguise ourselves?"

Amée shook her head. "I don't know. I don't..." She paused, nervously licked her lips. "Wait. Alright. If they know who we are and what we look like from last night, then they're searching for three men and a woman—two brown-skinned people and two white. We can't be what they think they're looking for." Her breathing slowed as she reasoned. "What's the quickest way out of the city?"

The horses waiting at the city's outskirts were too far—they'd have to pass through too many neighborhoods to reach them, so Jeanne said, "The river."

"Alright. So we have to get ourselves to the river, and we can't be what they're looking for. Do you think Gabrielle has dresses we could buy off her? Pieter's too tall and conspicuous to pass as a woman, but I can wear a dress and so could Sir Walter if he shaved. Three women and a man aren't at all what they're searching for, so they might not look too closely."

It was a good idea, but Jeanne wasn't sure it would

work. How many limping and muscled black knights were in the city? Even with the rest of them in disguise, Pieter would be hard to smuggle through the streets without being noticed. Unless...

"What if we had a cart? We could cover Pieter with cloth, then we'd be three women pushing a cart to the docks."

Amée nodded. "If we can get one."

"I'll ask Gabrielle about the dresses and a cart," Jeanne said. "You wake the men and help Walter shave."

## CHAPTER 40
# PARIS, FRANCE

Walter was clean-shaven with his eyebrows plucked thin—as was the custom for Parisian women—and his lean muscled body was bundled into a scratchy light green dress. His hair was too short, but they hoped a traveling cloak and hood would mask that fact. They put his arm in a sling, hoping it looked like an everyday injury. A fall from a horse. A tumble down a staircase.

Amée and Jeanne also wore cloaks over dresses, hiding Amée's own short hair and Jeanne's possibly recognizable face.

Gabrielle sold them a cart and ushered them into a back alley, where the sunrise was turning the cobblestones a warm yellow. They swept greens off the cart, got Pieter settled inside, then piled the greens back on top of him before securing a cloth over it all. He wasn't fully covered, and if anyone lifted the cloth, they'd potentially notice a hand or foot or stretch of scarred midnight skin, but a cursory glance wouldn't give them away. Jeanne prayed it was enough.

THE LIONESS

Jeanne squeezed Amée's shoulder, hoping the younger woman understood that was her way of saying thanks. Briefly. Without a sound. Keeping inconspicuous. While listening for trouble. But a thank you all the same.

They set out for the river with Jeanne pushing the cart because Amée wasn't strong enough and Sir Walter was struggling with dizziness and weakness from blood loss. Twice they passed soldiers, and both times they were ignored as the men shouted to be let into homes and pubs and shops—the pounding of their fists on wooden doors reverberating through the fugitives.

Even after watching Amée for years, seeing how easy it was to fool people, even knowing that people didn't look for what they weren't expecting, Jeanne marveled at how they could pass through without so much as a glance. Did it never occur to anyone other than Amée that a dress and a hairstyle were both things that could be changed? That they weren't immutable indicators of gender?

The cart rattled over the cobblestones. Another group of soldiers appeared in a doorway and looked at them. Looked away. *Fools.* Jean almost laughed—perhaps being witless was a requirement to join the king's guard. And then a shout broke through her smug thoughts.

"Ladies, ladies!" The smiling soldier was standing unsteadily in the doorway of a tavern, his cheeks the bright red of a man whose drunkenness had survived through the night and into morning. "Your beauty exceeds the rising of the sun!"

"Keep walking," Jeanne whispered. "Ignore him."

"Whoa, ladies! What's wrong? No smiles for me today? You're breaking my heart!"

He stumbled down the single step at the tavern's entry, threw a hand across his heart, and moved to block the cart,

251

forcing Jeanne to stop. To her left, Amée's hand had started shaking. To her right, Walter stood calmly, his head tilted down to hide his not entirely feminine features.

*Merde.* The soldiers they'd passed just moments ago had stopped to watch. Jeanne could barely see them out of the corner of her eye, but she could tell that there were at least four of them. She wasn't sure she could take on five men with the rest of her party injured, sick, or untrained.

The drunk man squinted at them and Jeanne wanted to punch him in his blotchy red face. Instead she offered the smile he'd requested. "Thank you for the kind words, sir, but we must be going."

She lifted the cart's handles, hoping he'd take the hint and move. But when he did, it wasn't out of their way—he approached Walter and tucked a finger under his chin to raise his face.

*Damn.* Walter's disguise only worked if you didn't look too closely. Jeanne discreetly slipped her hand into the slit she'd cut in her skirts.

But the man didn't raise an alarm; he just smiled broader. "Gimme a smile, sweetheart," he said. "Those eyes are the prettiest eyes a man could ever wish to gaze into, and they deserve a smile to match!"

Walter, clearly as surprised as Jeanne, let a whispery laugh escape.

"That's it, m'lady," the soldier said, delighted. "A woman's laughter is a balm to a man's war-torn soul."

What. A. Fool. Jeanne pursed her lips, hoping he was done with his poetics and they could go now.

But he only craned his neck to look past Walter and shout to the soldiers watching on. "Hey, there's enough beauty over here to go 'round! I've found the sun, the moon, and the stars walking through our very streets! Come meet these nice ladies, boys."

*Merde* again. Jeanne was going to have to kill them all, even if it killed her too.

"Shut up, Gaston, you young fool!" one called back. "We're on duty, and you're on duty yourself in an hour. Go stick your head in the horse trough!"

The rest roared with laughter.

"Your loss!"

Jeanne had no idea what to do. They needed to get out of there before the sober soldiers changed their minds and came over, but the damn fool Gaston was still in her cart's way. If she ran him over, his friends would surely rush over. If he looked down at the cart, he might notice Pieter through the cloth and greens. And as much as she wanted to kill him, she couldn't without giving herself away.

In the end, Jeanne didn't need to think of another option because Walter leaned into Gaston and whispered in his ear. "Walk us to the river?"

Jeanne fought to keep from rolling her eyes at the exaggerated way he batted his lashes. Gaston clearly didn't notice—or care—though. He hooked his arm through Walter's good one and started toward the river.

"I've been a soldier ten years now, m'lady," he boasted as they set off for the river. "Fought a lot of important battles, y'know."

Walter made a noncommittal noise.

"Not married either. A man's gotta find the right woman. A woman like you, with those eyes. So green!"

They turned the corner, out of sight of his soldier friends, and Walter—smiling in a way that he clearly thought was coy—reached up with his good hand and smacked Gaston's head into a wall.

He dropped like a stone.

"Poor lonely fellow," Walter said, his eyes sparkling with mirth.

"It's not funny when there are soldiers right behind us," Jeanne snapped. "Let's tuck him into a doorway and get out of here."

When they reached the river, Jeanne's arms were screaming from the effort of wheeling Pieter the whole way. There weren't any merchant vessels or boatmen in sight at the dock—just a collection of tethered fishing boats with flat bottoms and high sides.

She wasted no time picking one out. "Pieter, get into the boat while no one's around. Walter, grab the cloth and cover him, then get in yourself. Arley, you next."

As soon as they were in, Jeanne untied the boat and rowed them fast and hard out of the city. The action made her heart ache for the last time she tried to row those she loved toward safety. Poor Guillaume.

Pieter smiled through a gap in the cloth. "Walter, you sure you don't want to stay? That sounded like quite the proposal back there."

Walter wiggled his neatly plucked eyebrows.

"Well, now we know who's the most beautiful woman among us," Jeanne said. "Next time I need a spy in a dress, I'm sending you."

CHAPTER 41

# THE ENGLISH CHANNEL

J eanne's black fleet was waiting for them as expected, and the four boarded with a collective sigh of relief. For a moment, Jeanne forgot herself and looked around for the children but realized her mistake seconds later.

Her heart throbbed like a bruise. She could never quite get all the people she loved safe and in one place; there was always someone missing.

And two of those someones were missing forever.

Why was it so hard to remember that Guillaume was gone? Why did she have to relive the realization over and over?

She'd never had trouble accepting death before, and when she thought of Olivier, her traitorous heart didn't leap with hope, just rage. But Guillaume—it was different with Guillaume. Sometimes, even though she knew he was gone, it felt like maybe it had all been a dream. Every time, her heart rose with the hope of it. And every time, she hated herself for it. Because it *hadn't* been a dream. Guillaume

255

was gone, and the sooner her heart accepted that, the better.

She shook her head as if she could shake off the sense of unreality, and she felt Pieter's huge warm hand on her shoulder. It was comforting and familiar, and she blinked away the tears that pricked at her eyes.

Everything had moved so fast, she still hadn't gotten a chance to talk to him. She squeezed his hand hard, hoping he knew what it meant. Needing it to communicate her fear and rage and grief and guilt and the depth of her relief—all of it beyond words and mashed together inside her.

"Thank you for coming for me," he said.

Not knowing what to say, she gave his hand another squeeze and began taking inventory. Everyone was now onboard: Sir Walter leaning, still pale, against the rail; Amée standing a half-step behind two crewmen as they prepared the sails, trying as usual to stay invisible; and Pieter beside her, stoic and calm even after everything. Even in his weakened state with his limp, he was a rock—strong and steady and reliable. In all her urgency to rescue him, she'd forgotten how much she *missed* him.

She squeezed his hand a third time then turned to her men. "Ready the ship. Let's get out of here."

WHEN JEANNE ENTERED HER CABIN, Monster was waiting on the bed. A flush of surprise and delight overtook her at the sight. *Merde*, she was getting soft—she'd again missed the goddamned devil-cat. Without thought, she strode over to stroke Monster who, purring, rolled onto her back and writhed under Jeanne's palms before swatting fiercely at them like the devil she was.

Amée followed Jeanne in, trailed by Walter and Pieter, who shut the door behind him. It was the first time they'd had a chance to breathe, to think, and to talk without danger nipping at their heels.

There were so many things Jeanne wanted to say. That she was glad Pieter was back. That Amée remained a genius. That Walter...what *did* she want to say to Walter? That saving Amée was the noblest thing she'd ever witnessed? That if he wanted to kiss her, now was his chance—even with an audience and his damn plucked eyebrows?

She hadn't even spoken yet, but still she flushed. She didn't want to say those things to the whole group—what she needed was time alone with each of them. But first she supposed she should tell them the plan.

So she did.

They'd race across the Channel to Britain, where the king's best physicians were waiting to see Pieter—and now Walter too. The crew had been instructed to ignore merchant ships and only attack warships if they stood in her way. And then, not knowing how to end a military strategy conversation with the one thing she had left to say—that her heart was so full of love for them, she thought it might burst—she gave a curt nod and dismissed the two men.

Once they'd gone, she wrapped her arms around Amée, the brave, slight, brilliant girl whose tricks with dresses and carts and magic shows had saved them. At last, she let the tears she'd been holding back flow warm and salty down her face.

## CHAPTER 42
# THE ENGLISH CHANNEL

"You saved us," Jeanne whispered.

Amée's eyes brimmed with tears. "You saved *me*."

Jeanne pushed Amée out by her shoulders and searched her face.

"I thought I was helpless," Amée said. "I tried to avenge Giselle, but I failed. And then you—this—came along and made me feel like I wasn't powerless anymore. You're the most powerful person I know, Jeanne, and you listen to me. You follow my plans even when they don't completely work. Before this, only Giselle had ever trusted me or seen me. But you trust me too."

"That's not a kindness." Jeanne laughed, pulling Amée back to her. "Anyone who doesn't trust you is a fool."

A thunder of footsteps sounded overhead, followed by a loud knock. "M'lady Clisson!" a muffled voice shouted through the door. "A warship—they've found us!"

*Merde.* Couldn't she have one damn moment of peace? Jeanne released Amée and threw open the door. "Ready the men," she told the sailor. "We're coming." Then she turned back to Amée. "You can wait here where it's safe."

"No, I can help."

Amée wiped the tears from her face, and Jeanne listened with rapt fascination as she explained why she'd brought along a hull full of magic tricks and ravens.

ON DECK A FEW MINUTES LATER—OUT OF THEIR DISGUISES and back in normal clothes—Jeanne and Amée stood by the mast as Jeanne's best archers launched arrows loaded with pouches of seeds and rotten meat onto the enemy ship. Each pouch burst on impact, scattering its contents in every direction.

"Imagine how confusing this is for them," Amée said, her voice brimming with pride. "They must think our archers have terrible aim—they haven't hit a single soldier."

Jeanne grinned as Amée signaled to the men around her, who in turn released the ravens. Dozens and dozens of birds, rising like a cawing black cloud into the air. Jeanne watched on in awe. For a moment, the birds blotted out the world, just as they had the day she'd first met Amée, who'd since explained that ravens were the devil's spies.

And Jeanne was the devil's wife.

If they wanted the king's men to fear them, they'd send them what they feared most: a supernatural sign from the devil himself. Unlike Jeanne's men, the enemy hadn't been living with a hull full of ravens for months, hadn't grown accustomed to them. Jeanne imagined the terror rising in each enemy fighter as the cloud rose into the sky, circling,

circling, and then diving to where the seed and meat called to them.

At once, the warship's decks were covered in a cawing, flapping mess of birds. The frantic shouts of men carried across the water as they flailed arms and swords at the persistent ravens.

"Demons!" someone screamed.

"She's in league with the devil!" another yelled.

By the time Jeanne's men boarded the warship, everything was chaos. The advantage was theirs.

They took the warship in record time, in Jeanne's easiest victory yet. Once the enemy's men were dispatched, she joined Amée again at the mast where she was clicking her tongue and tempting the ravens back with seeds and meat. About half flew off toward the now distantly visible coast, but the rest fluttered down around the women like a protective cloak, a dark omen for the French.

Jeanne hoped the sailor she'd left alive was terror-stricken in his rowboat. Hoped he'd tell the king that now even the birds were after him.

# MEANWHILE...

## PARIS, FRANCE

"KILL THEM! KILL THEM ALL! EVERY GUARD. EVERY SENTRY!"

Philip was in the hall screaming, flailing, practically frothing at the mouth, as Joan tried to calm him. It had been a particularly stiff day on her leg, and following him as he paced—even with the assistance of her cane—was wearing down both her patience and her energy.

"My love," she said, wishing her words sounded softer and less pained, "wouldn't it be better to wait and find out who is truly responsible?"

"They're *all* responsible! How could they let that woman just walk in here and take him? A woman, for god's sake! Why are women always such a thorn in my side?"

Joan clenched her teeth and slid into a high-backed chair, trying to find a comfortable position. She gritted her teeth against both the ache and Philip's ignorance. Even after so many years of her advising him, he *still* managed to underestimate women. She'd told him Joanna de Montfort wouldn't go down without a fight. Told him Queen Philippa was no wallflower. She'd warned him to send more men after Jeanne.

But no.

Every time it was a confident, "She'll fall into line," and then every time it was shock and horror when she didn't.

Were men incapable of learning, or was Philip just special? With each year that passed, he grew smaller in Joan's estimation. Soon he'd be less than grain of sand.

"My love," she said, "I'm only urging caution so that you don't inadvertently execute loyal men who didn't have anything to do with the escape."

"Loyal?! BAH! What kind of loyalty allows my worst enemy into my own castle? Have you forgotten your missing dress and the dead man found in our rooms?"

It was exhausting, watching her husband pick off their allies. He always lived so completely in one moment, it made him neglect the bigger picture. If service to the crown led to death, soon there'd be no volunteers, no soldiers, no nobles sticking their necks out. They'd have no one left on their side. Joan's safety—and that of her children—*required* those men and women to stick their necks out.

And here was Philip, killing them off one by one.

Joan didn't really understand Jeanne and Joanna—their rage, their vengeance, their single-minded hate for the man who killed their husbands. Joan wouldn't fight a single damn flea to avenge hers. A dead husband would be such a *relief*. She wondered, not for the first time, if she should have Philip assassinated and be done with this chaos once and for all.

As always, once her anger had simmered, the answer was no. Without him, her situation became too precarious, her children too unsafe. Her only choice was to keep trying to rein him in, to get him back into the good graces of the allies that remained.

So she gathered her frustrations and stuffed them deep

THE LIONESS

inside. "Dear one, didn't you yourself say the other day that Joanna de Montfort is the real threat, not Jeanne? Why don't we focus our energies on her? Leave the captain of your guard to deal with his men as he sees fit. Leave Jeanne and her man to retreat across the Channel."

Even though she knew it was the best strategy, she hated presenting him with reason as if it was his idea. Philip hadn't been the one to say Joanna was the threat— Joan had. Philip had merely agreed. But if he didn't think he'd come up with the idea himself, he'd dismiss it outright.

*Men.*

Philip flapped a furious hand in her direction, barely listening. He was too angry, too emotional, even for that most reliable of placating strategies. "I'm serious," he barked, this time toward the door where his captain of guard had just appeared. "Kill them all. Any person who was on duty during the escape. They're all accomplices."

The captain cleared his throat, echoing Joan. "Highness, we need the men's loyalty—"

"Not you too," Philip said. "Both of you, stop. I won't be diverted from my course! Let the other men learn from this: failure is death."

## CHAPTER 43
# LONDRES, ENGLAND

*Dearest Maman,*

*It is quite a gruesome thing I have to report, but Geoff says you'll want to know. The new bows that Britain has been employing against the king have the army in quite a terror, so he's ordered his men to remove the middle and pointer finger of any captured man suspected of archery. As a result, a new gesture has been sweeping through the peasantry. I must say they are quite rude about it, holding up those fingers at anyone they don't like who happens to be passing. It's meant as a threat, but since they're not even archers, the joke doesn't seem particularly sophisticated or threatening.*

*War really does bring out the worst in people.*

*Your magician boy left us to return to you only a week ago now, so I have no additional news to offer. But we have heard rumors of your demise, so I am writing to ask you to please reply to confirm that you and our younger siblings are indeed safe and in Britain.*

*Your Louise.*

J eanne pressed the letter to her heart. It comforted her to know that her oldest children were safe, comforted her even more that they were writing simply to confirm Jeanne's own safety. She'd write back quickly and send the letter with someone King Edward trusted.

They'd docked the ships in Londres less than an hour before, and all around her was activity. Men shouted across to each other as they unloaded. Some sang crude songs. Others grunted and stayed silent. Still others talked— about the sea, about home, about families and sweethearts left behind. Jeanne's English had improved during her months there last time and then at sea with her new men, and she could now understand the gist of their songs and musings if not every word.

Amée and Pieter were still with her on the docks. Sir Walter had been rushed off in a wagon since he was in the worst condition, but there wasn't enough room for everyone. So the three who remained watched Jeanne's men carry coils of rope and cages of ravens off the ship while they waited for another wagon to be sent.

Amée reached up to squeeze Pieter's shoulder, and Jeanne's heart reached out to them both. Pieter was too thin, unsteady on his feet, holding most of his weight on one leg. Jeanne wished the damned wagon would hurry up so that he could begin to rest and recover and heal.

And then a long, clear, and high-pitched shriek rang out. A woman with rich red hair peeking out from under her wimple, widened brown eyes, and a mouth in a perfect O dropped her parcels and rushed toward them.

Jeanne wasn't sure whether to draw her dagger or stand by to see what the fuss was about. The woman was empty-handed, so she wasn't a threat, was she? Jeanne glanced at

Pieter. His hand was fixed on the hilt of his sword, but his face remained impassive.

The woman threw herself to the ground at his feet and burst into tears. "Saint Maurice! Saint Maurice! Oh, all that is holy, you're here! You're here to bless us!"

Jeanne furrowed her brow, and Amée's mouth dropped a little. Both looked at Pieter, whose usually even gaze had turned to one of discomfort. He shuffled backward with a wince, away from the crying woman who was now grabbing at his feet and sobbing incoherently.

Everyone knew the story of Saint Maurice—the black Roman soldier who was ordered to massacre Christians but refused. He was martyred when he spurned the order to kill god's people. Now, the Church called him a saint. A man people prayed to for blessings and courage. The patron saint of weavers, dyers, swordsmiths, and soldiers.

*Merde*. This fool thought Pieter was some sort of resurrected Christian saint? It was like all those dunderheads over the years who'd challenged him to duels thinking he was the literal Black Knight of legend. What did this woman expect of Pieter? To bless her foolish life? Turn her into a master swordsmith? To help her find lost cheese like Saint Thomas Becket was said to do? Jeanne had no use for saints of any kind, but throwing yourself at the feet of a stranger and declaring him one seemed even more useless than believing in them from afar.

Everyone was watching now—the men had stopped their packing and passers-by were pointing fingers at the prostrate woman, some looking curious, others grinning.

Pieter glanced at Amée for something, but Jeanne wasn't sure if it was understanding, reassurance, or something else. Whatever it was, he must have found it, because

THE LIONESS

he seemed to draw strength before pulling the sobbing woman to her feet and peering into her face.

"I'm not him," he said in a low kind voice.

The woman looked startled, shocked even, and then embarrassed. "You're not?"

"No. He's a martyred saint, miss. He's gone with god."

"Oh. Oh, I..." The woman stood, swiping at her eyes with the heels of her hands. "I'm sorry...I..." She squinted at him. "Are you sure?"

"Yes. Whatever you were hoping for, I can't help you."

And then the woman looked around and realized how many people had stopped to witness her make a scene. Her face turned pink, and she mumbled something that might have been an apology. She scurried away to collect the things she'd dropped.

Amée put a hand on Pieter's arm, and the pair stood uncomfortably until the surrounding eavesdroppers decided the show was over and got back to their tasks. Then Pieter sighed and looked down.

"I'm so tired of that."

"It happens a lot?" Amée asked the question as though she already knew the answer.

"Well, not Saint Maurice—that's a rare one. Usually they think I'm a Saracen or a Black Knight, like from the stories." He tried to smile. "I guess I should be grateful that this one didn't challenge me to a duel."

Jeanne had seen the Black Knight thing happen more than once over the years, and though it irritated her, she hadn't known how much it bothered him. She'd never heard Pieter say anything about it, and she'd mistaken his calm for a lack of feeling. She'd assumed those men didn't get to him. It hurt to realize she was wrong, hurt more to

267

realize she'd never thought to ask. She wasn't a very good friend.

"God's nails, Pieter," she said, "I should have punched that woman in her fool teeth."

Both Pieter and Amée smiled and shook their heads.

"They ask me too," Amée said. "About being a Saracen, I mean." Pieter's eyebrows rose in surprise. "Truly?"

"Yes. Often. Mostly it's annoying, but there was one time at a church...You know the tale of the King of Tars— the black king who turns white when he becomes a Christian? Someone screamed at me that I couldn't be a real Christian, because I wasn't white yet."

Jeanne balled a fist. "*Merde*, what is wrong with people? Accosting you on the docks and in church over children's stories."

Amée and Pieter exchanged another knowing look.

Then Amée's eyebrows snapped up in surprise and delight spread across her face. It was the look she got when inspiration hit. "Pieter," she said, her breath catching a little, "everyone's afraid of the Black Knight, right?"

"Yes."

"And we want our enemies to fear us, right? So instead of correcting people, what if you embraced it? What if you told them, 'Yes, I am the Black Knight.' What if you *became* the Black Knight of legend? You could dress in black armor and be the very thing they're afraid you are."

Jeanne laughed out loud. Understanding washed over Pieter's face, followed by a hint of a smile and a sparkle in his eyes. Jeanne reached out and squeezed his arm, her own eyes dancing with mirth.

Encouraged, Amée went on. "It's like Jeanne's sails and the ravens. Instead of saying no to people's wildest ideas, we say yes. *Yes*, we are something to fear. *Yes*, we are something to remember."

To Jeanne's surprise, Pieter laughed and swept Amée into a hug, twirling her around. He stumbled a little when he set her down, as if he'd forgotten that he wasn't in any state to be twirling people. If any other man had done it, Amée would have panicked, but with Pieter she laughed along. Jeanne laughed too and touched her friends' arms. She was delighted to know them both.

By the time their wagon arrived, Jeanne had sent a man ahead to the best armorer in Londres to order Pieter's new armor—black as midnight, ominous, threatening, and beautiful.

# 1346

## CHAPTER 44
# WINDSOR CASTLE, ENGLAND

It took six months for Pieter to heal and return to full strength. To the express annoyance of the British king —off fighting his own battles but sending frequent messengers back to inquire about her—Jeanne stayed in Britain the whole time, while her dark, dangerous, myth-shrouded ships floated harmlessly in the port. After everything that had happened to Pieter, she refused to leave. Especially when Oli and Little Jeanne were also at the court, not to mention Amée and Walter.

Jeanne spent those six months bouncing between the people she loved. She'd sit at Pieter's bedside and tease him about the pretty golden-skinned healer with the heart-shaped face who always seemed to linger in his room. Walk with him around the castle grounds to stretch his legs.

When he was ready to test his long-dormant muscles and instincts, they sparred. After catching him in the side for the third time in a row, she half-joked, "When you start beating me again, that's when we'll know it's time to leave."

She'd started sparring with Oli too. He was outraged

when she knocked him over, dismayed when she ended each victory with a kiss to the top of his head.

"Maman!" he cried. "Everyone's watching!"

But Jeanne just grinned and kept going doing it. "Warriors need kisses, love. It keeps them strong."

"Hear, hear," Walter said from the sidelines, grinning like a fool.

Little Jeanne had taken to swords as well. Being only six, she wasn't in training yet, but she'd inherited Oli's role as Chief Mischief Maker, roaming the castle halls challenging stableboys and stray cats to duels. Oli's swordplay had always been fierce and serious, but Little Jeanne's carried a hint of dance. Where he'd mainly wanted to smack swords together, she was more interested in twirling away from and around her opponents—a practice only Monster put up with. She'd sit still and yawn enormously as Little Jeanne whirled around her, a storm of giggles and flyaway hair.

Jeanne had just finished a training fight with Oli—who'd marched off in a huff after one too many kisses—when Walter appeared at her side. He led her to a low stone wall where they could sit together, then took her hands and rubbed circles into her palms with his thumbs. It wasn't the only place he'd been putting those calloused hands lately, and Jeanne's temperature now rose to a fever pitch whenever she saw him.

He cleared his throat. "I have something to tell you."

Ah, *merde*. She could tell from his tone that it wasn't news she'd like. So much for the anticipation rising across her skin.

"Edward wants me to take on two British-controlled castles in Brittany..." He trailed off, reaching up to run a thumb along Jeanne's jaw.

Ah, so he was going to France. Jeanne was surprised at how much that stung. Was it so easy for him to leave her? So easy to say goodbye? But of course he was leaving— what other option did he have? He was a powerful military leader in his own right, not one of her men. He had his own agendas, his own favors to beg from the king, his own future to think about. She'd been silly to think otherwise.

And then he spoke again, softer this time. "Come with me."

"What?"

"Come with me to France. Isn't Brittany your home? Don't you miss it? Marry me, Jeanne. Marry me and come to France."

Jeanne's heart thrilled at the thought. They'd join forces, defend castles together. Her life could be like it had been before, with watches from castle towers and walks in Brittany's deep green forests. She missed the smell of ferns. She missed waking up with someone every morning.

But no. Jeanne closed her eyes. She couldn't go defend castles in France, not while Philip and Charles were still out there. If she didn't make things right, no one would. She was Jeanne de Clisson. Her whole life was about justice— she couldn't, *wouldn't*, choose anything else above it.

She looked away and sighed, the disappointment sharp and bitter in her mouth. "I can't, Walter. You know I can't. I owe it to my husband and my son to finish this thing."

There was a long silence. Jeanne glanced at him, afraid of seeing disappointment, anger, pity.

Instead, he nodded sadly. "I thought you'd say that. And I don't blame you. Justice in this world only happens if you make it happen." He lifted her hand and kissed the palm. "I wouldn't let something like that go either."

Jeanne's breath caught in her chest. Walter knew her so

well, understood her so completely in such a short time. *Justice only happens if you make it happen.* It was what Jeanne believed, and there something about him saying it out loud that made her feel seen in a way she'd hadn't before. Everyone knew her name, knew her story, knew exaggerated versions of what she was. But so few people really saw her.

She curled her finger around a lock of Walter's hair to pull him in for a kiss—

And then Little Jeanne marched up and proudly presented her maman with a large spitting rat held tight by the scruff of its neck. Jeanne's nose wrinkled in disgust as she stared at her dirt-smudged grinning six-year-old. Where in god's nails had she gotten this thing? She looked like she'd been crawling around in a gutter.

Walter dissolved into incredulous laughter that reddened his face and caused a coughing fit. Jeanne was less amused.

"What are you doing? Fling that filthy thing away."

"Nay, Maman!"

"Oui, little monster."

Little Jeanne drew her eyebrows together, huffed, and stormed away with the rodent held high. Jeanne could only guess she'd refuse to release it until she'd shown Oli.

"Little rebels," she murmured, her lips quirking up in the half-smile she'd recently found herself wearing so often.

She should probably follow after Little Jeanne and get rid of the rat herself, but she never could bring herself to deny her children their wildness. She'd had to fight for hers, so she wouldn't make them fight for theirs. She wanted them to be strong and willful, the kind of people who didn't take no for an answer. The kind who'd grab this world and make it something. And they were—both of them, wilder and more willful as they grew older. Something fierce and proud rose in her every time she saw them these days.

But there was sadness at the edges, and for a moment the happy thoughts faded, replaced by memories of those who should have been here but weren't. Olivier fighting. Guillaume, so different from the rest of them, gone before the world could ever benefit from his tender soul. But what had once been an all-encompassing crushing grief had become a dull ache—still sometimes breathtaking, but quieter and demanding less of her attention. She could miss them now without losing herself. She could prod the aching bruise without feeling like it was going to kill her.

Jeanne occasionally wondered if that meant she was forgetting them. If they deserved better. If they deserved to burn through her like fire with every breath, forever. But if she was honest, it was a relief for the flames to burn down to embers. They were still there. Still burning. Still driving her forward. But now there was space for her to exist outside of them.

Walter, who'd finally composed himself again after meeting Little Jeanne's rat, kissed Jeanne's wrist and stood. "I understand why you can't come, but I do hope this isn't goodbye. When you're done killing the king and the duke, I'll be waiting."

"You'll have met someone else by then."

"There is no one else like you," he answered, tugging gently on a lock of her hair.

Jeanne shook her head, but inside she was a tender ball of warmth.

≈

A FEW HOURS LATER, Pieter found her in the gardens where she'd come to be alone with her thoughts. The warmth of Walter's proclamation had faded, replaced by a tangled mess of feelings about him and an even more tangled mess of feelings about leaving the children again.

She was missing so much of their lives. Every time she left and came back, Little Jeanne in particular had shifted into someone new. Gleeful giggling toddler. Oli's shadow. Dancer with a sword in hand. Rat hunter. What would she be when Jeanne returned the next time?

Pieter settled onto the low stone bench beside her and looked out over the grounds. The frost of winter had been replaced by the earliest spring buds, and there was even a single white flower already blooming on the maze-like branches of the tree straight ahead.

Jeanne smiled, and the warmth in her chest returned. At least Pieter was here, had always been here, would always be here. No matter how much she'd miss Walter, no matter how much she'd miss the children, she'd gotten Pieter back from the king's damn dungeon, and he'd be by her side. She was loved. She had someone.

"Jeanne." His voice was low as he put his enormous hand on hers. "We have to talk."

"Of course. What's on your mind?"

She wondered if this was a strategy meeting or something else. If he needed something, she realized, now was the perfect time to ask her for it. She felt expansive, grateful for him, ready to acquiesce to any request. New armor. More weapons. A feast to celebrate their departure, which she couldn't help but think would be soon. Whatever he wanted.

"You know Robine?" he asked instead.

She thought on it. "No."

THE LIONESS

He frowned. "Yes, you do."

There was something lecturing in his tone, and the warmth in her chest cooled. "If I say no, the answer's no, Pieter. I don't remember a Robine, so how about you just explain yourself instead of frowning at me like that?"

"Robine is the healer you've been teasing me about for months." His lips pursed. "You couldn't bother to remember her name?"

This conversation was not going the way Jeanne expected, and she wanted to hit Pieter for ruining her mood. "Alright, what about her?"

"I'm in love with her."

Jeanne stared at him. What kind of response did he want? Congratulations?

There was a long pause before Pieter said, "I think we should stay."

Heat swept across Jeanne's skin, flushing her face, her neck, her chest. So that's what this was. She'd thought his objections would be over by now—the children were safe under Edward's protection, and she wouldn't be taking them back out on the Channel. She'd even told Pieter he'd been right about that. But it wasn't enough. Now he had to come up with yet another reason that they couldn't avenge Olivier.

A woman dressed in crimson appeared at the edge of the garden path, her hair piled in elaborate braids under a sheer covering. Jeanne ignored her. She was no doubt some noble out for a stroll in the garden who'd hopefully have the good sense to turn around, because there was no stopping this fight now. If she didn't leave, if she wanted to listen, Jeanne supposed that was her damn problem.

"Were you even his friend?" Her words were daggers

277

aimed at Pieter's honor. "Did you even mean it when you made that promise to him?"

Pieter looked horrified. "That's not fair."

Jeanne got to her feet and balled her fists. "Yes it is. What are your promises worth?"

"You know they're worth everything to me." When Pieter stood, he towered over her. "I didn't come here to leave you, Jeanne, I came here to talk to you! It's been three years! We've been burning and marching and fighting and raiding for three years, and we haven't once gotten close to killing the king. It's time to let go. Olivier loved you, and he wouldn't want you living like this. We can't get to Philip, but you want us to waste our whole lives trying. Do you want us to die just like everyone on the last ship?"

The words hit Jeanne like a blow. Alexi. Louis. Jacques. Her men. Her beautiful, fast Genoese ship. All gone.

"All this time I thought you were trying to protect the children," Jeanne shouted. "Turns out you were trying to protect yourself!"

"How dare you accuse me of cowardice! I fought by your side for years, Jeanne. God's nails, I saved your life! I saved Oli's life. Little Jeanne's. I rotted in that dungeon for months. The only person who talked to me was a servant boy who brought the food and the man who interrogated me." Pieter's inflection turned from anger to pain. "I gave up everything for you, for Olivier. But it's not enough for you, is it?"

Jeanne's fingernails cut into her palms as she squeezed her fists harder, and she bit down on her tongue to keep from screaming. Walter was leaving her. Pieter was leaving her. At this rate, Amée would march into the garden at any moment to announce her engagement to a court astrologer or something equally ridiculous. Jeanne was going to be alone at sea with men she didn't know on a fleet of too-slow ships.

When Pieter continued, his voice was controlled. "I love her, Jeanne. It's the first time I've felt this way since I lost my wife more than ten years ago. Would you really deny me my happiness?"

"You think this is easy for me?" Jeanne's voice remained sharp as cut glass. "Walter proposed this morning, but I turned him down. Because I *owe* Olivier. Because my happiness isn't the most important thing here. But go ahead"—she jabbed at him with her sarcasm—"stay. Choose love over duty. I see what you are now. I see how little you think justice is worth."

This Robine woman had ruined everything. Jeanne wished she'd never teased Pieter about it, wished he'd never met her. She wondered if she'd somehow encouraged him with her jokes. *Merde*. This was why she didn't joke.

Jeanne was furious to see tears building in the corners of Pieter's eyes. What was she supposed to do now? Did he think crying would change the fact he'd sworn to help her avenge Olivier?

"I can see you won't support me in this," he whispered, and the brokenness of it made Jeanne want to scream all over again. "But I can't keep fighting. Olivier would want me to stop. He would want *you* to stop. I'm not keeping my promise by helping you kill yourself."

Jeanne searched for a response that didn't involve screaming or punching him, but before she found one, Pieter turned and marched away, passing the crimson-dressed woman who'd been watching them curiously on his way out of the garden.

As the crunch of his footsteps on the pebble path faded, Jeanne pressed her fists to her face. She was doing the right thing for Olivier and Guillaume by giving up a chance at love, so why couldn't Pieter? Why was she the only one who cared this much? Her face throbbed with the pressure of her fists, and she let her arms drop to her sides.

To her surprise, the woman in red came closer. She was a little older than Jeanne, her braids as black and sleek as Monster's fur, her eyes deep brown, and her skin the color of frost. A burn scar, pink and webbed, snaked up her chest and neck. She was dressed finer than Jeanne had thought, and she realized this was someone important. Something about the woman nagged at her. Did Jeanne know her? Had she forgotten her name?

"Your man's right, you know." The woman's voice was softer than Jeanne expected. "You should listen to him. Love is the important thing."

The *nerve* of her. Now Jeanne knew she really must be important—only important people invited themselves into conversations to tell others what to do.

Jeanne held up a hand. "You don't know what you're talking about." God she was so familiar. It was the scars... Jeanne knew those scars.

*Oh.* God's nails.

It was Isabella. The She-Wolf of France. The woman Jeanne had idolized since her twenties. The truth was like being submerged in cold water. Like jumping into the river when fleeing the dungeons in France. It stole Jeanne's breath. Made her limbs clumsy. Shocked her into silence.

Jeanne's hero was standing here in the garden with her. Jeanne's hero had seen Pieter humiliate her. Jeanne's hero was telling her to give up.

Isabella tilted her head. "I do know what I'm talking about. I know what it means to fight for what's yours, and I know what it means to lose. You said your lover proposed? That means a lot more than killing kings."

Easy for her to say, Jeanne thought. If the rumors were true, she'd succeeded in killing *her* king. They said Edward II had been assassinated while under house arrest, and it was currently Isabella's son, Edward III, on the throne. Granted, he'd put her under house arrest of her own to get there, but now she was free. Her greatest enemy was dead. Her son was ruling Britain. She'd won. Jeanne hadn't yet, so how could Isabella think she would give up?

"You were my hero, you know." The words tasted bitter. "I can't believe you'd tell me to walk away from what's right."

Isabella looked surprised, then her expression softened. "I'm honored—not everyone can claim to be the hero of the fiercest woman alive. I didn't mean to tell you to give up on what's right, Jeanne."

Jeanne's heart thrilled against her will at Isabella saying her name.

"What I'm trying to say is that what we think is right isn't always right. But love—real love, the sort your friend has apparently found—*that* is always right. It's the one thing worth living for."

"I know," Jeanne said. And she did.

What Isabella didn't understand, what Pieter no longer understood, was that Jeanne was doing this for love. Love was an action. It was what you did to take care of people, both while they were with you *and* after they were gone. Love was rage. Love was fire. Love was being willing to burn the whole world to the ground.

Giving up on her quest would be giving up on her love for Olivier and Guillaume. And nobody—not even the woman she'd admired for decades—would make her give up on that.

CHAPTER 45

# WINDSOR CASTLE, ENGLAND

Jeanne stormed into Amée's room, a chaotic mess of skirts and feelings. Amée froze in place with her knees bent, heels off the floor. She'd clearly been practicing the fighting stances Pieter and Jeanne had been teaching her since their return from Paris.

"I need to be able to defend myself," she'd told them, her voice hard. "I can't rely on Walter to take a sword for me next time, and I won't stay in the cabin anymore during battles."

So they'd trained her with a dagger, correcting her flat-footed stances, practicing her lunges over and over, showing her how to disarm a larger opponent.

Though Jeanne had arrived angry, she now flushed with pride that Amée was taking her training so seriously. She wasn't dangerous with a weapon yet, but she would be.

Amée released her stance and rushed over. "You look ready to set the country on fire. What's happened?"

The reason she'd come returned to Jeanne like saltwater on a wound.

"Pieter's leaving us!" Her voice was pitchy, and she

283

hated herself for it. *You have to be stronger, cooler, a stone, a mountain,* her mother had once told her, but there was no cold hard stone to be found here—her rage had turned to screeches and heat across her face. It was the kind of rage that came not with power, but with tears. The kind Jeanne hated.

"What do you mean?" Amée asked.

"I mean *he's leaving us.* He says he's in love." Jeanne spat the word like meat that had soured at sea. "He's staying in Britain and giving up on justice for love."

Amée dropped into a nearby chair.

"Walter's leaving for a new assignment in Brittany, the children are staying here under Edward's protection, and Pieter's staying because of some woman." Jeanne eyed her. "You're not planning to marry a noble while we're here, are you?"

Amée made a face so horrified it cut through Jeanne's anger and made her laugh out loud.

"No, that's...not for me," Amée murmured. "I'll never marry."

The part of Jeanne that wanted to keep raging surrendered to the curious part. "Why not?"

"I can't think of anything worse than being forced to let a man touch me, to have his children, to live with him forever." Amée shifted in her seat, her face frozen in a cringe. "Like I told you, it's why I left home."

Jeanne pulled up another chair to sit across from her, elbows on knees. "Is it the physical part that bothers you?"

"It's the whole thing. The touching. The...childbirth. I don't understand why anyone would want any of it."

Despite her lingering anger, Jeanne was surprised and warmly curious at how differently Amée's mind and heart worked than her own. It was both strange and endearing. It was nothing Jeanne had ever heard before, yet it seemed so correct for Amée. It was also a *relief*—Amée wouldn't leave her for some knight they met along the way. She laughed again, and god it felt good to laugh. To be surprised. To feel these rushes of affection whenever she and Amée talked. To let the anger cool. Amée was a cold compress on a feverish brow, a dip in the Channel on a blisteringly hot summer day.

Amée changed the subject. "So what happens next? If Pieter's not coming, does that change things for us? You're not thinking of quitting, are you?"

"Of course not. I want justice."

"And what is justice for you?"

Jeanne was taken aback by the question. "Killing the king and the duke. Or failing that, making them as miserable as possible."

"That's justice for Olivier and Guillaume," Amée said gently, "not you. Is it justice to spend your whole life fighting? If the world were just, wouldn't you—wouldn't we both—be able to live in peace?"

"So you also want to give up." Jeanne was surprised at how much more she could hurt. Walter. Pieter. Isabella. And now Amée. She didn't have anyone left.

"No, I…" Amée paused. "Charles being alive is so unfair, sometimes I feel like I'm going to come apart thinking about it. I hate him. I hate everything he stands for. I hate the Church he funds. I hate the men he promotes." Amée searched Jeanne's face. "But I've been wondering if it's fair to you—to me—to give up our whole lives for men like that. I'm not saying we should stop, I'm just asking when will it be enough?"

She was right, of course. Amée had a way of turning a thing Jeanne had already thought about at an angle she'd never considered. If the world were a just place, Jeanne wouldn't have had to fight so damn hard her whole life. Hadn't she done everything right? Hadn't she fought harder, played shrewder, pushed herself to the limit? And yet the king and the duke were still out there unbothered, and here she was still preparing to fight.

When *was* it enough?

"What if you—what if we—simply walked away?" Amée asked.

There was no expectation in the question, and Jeanne loved the girl for it. She wasn't trying to force Jeanne's hand, wasn't trying to change her mind. There was no push or agenda behind the words, just a soul in conflict. Just a mind that filtered through every option, wondering if Jeanne had weighed each one herself, or—as was her reputation—whether she'd plowed forward with whichever led her to a fight.

For the first time since she'd watched Olivier die, Jeanne actually allowed herself to consider it. What would happen if she stopped? The king would live, as would the duke. But so would Jeanne. Her life would no longer be wrapped up in theirs.

But before she could answer Amée's question, Pieter arrived. He leaned through the doorway looking uncomfortable, and Jeanne's traitorous heart momentarily forgot she was mad, leaping fondly at the sight of him.

"M'lady," he said, stiff and formal, "I'm sorry to interrupt, but I thought you'd want to know right away." He took a deep breath and squatted to be eye level with the seated women. "It's the duke. The Church has—well, they've sainted him. He's been declared a holy saint because of his devotion to religion. They're calling him one of god's holiest..."

# THE LIONESS

Pieter trailed off, and Jeanne knew the rage and nausea coursing through her must be written on her face. She pushed to her feet. It was too terrible to be true. The man who'd killed her husband—a saint? The shifty, devious man who betrayed his own friends was one of god's holiest people? The Church had deemed someone who'd suggested burning children alive to be revered?

A stabbing pain pierced Jeanne's hands, and she realized she was clenching them so tight, her fingernails had broken skin. Amée was holding her own fists up like she could fight off the news.

"God, Pieter," Jeanne said, "how could they?"

With those words, something broke inside her.

Moments ago she'd been wondering what it would be like to stop hunting the men who'd destroyed her life. But she couldn't *ever* stop hunting them. Not until they were gone. Otherwise the world would just keep rewarding them, keep giving them more and more power, more and more strength. The world would forget what they'd done. They'd forget Olivier. They'd forget her.

She hadn't realized she was screaming out loud until Amée took her clenched fist in her own hand and stroked it with her thumb.

"I can't—" Jeanne broke off with a strangled sound and forced herself not to dissolve into tears. "I can't live with that man a *saint*—a living, breathing, worshipped, honored, hedge-born *saint*. We have to find a way to destroy them both. We have to go."

"Then we go," Amée said, her voice low and fierce.

Pieter turned his head away, and Jeanne knew he hadn't changed his mind. But it didn't matter—Pieter or no Pieter, Jeanne was returning to the Channel.

## CHAPTER 46
# LONDRES, ENGLAND

*Dearest Maman,*

*I am writing to warn you that the king is in quite a state after whatever your men did to pull that fellow out of the dungeons. He hasn't said anything about it publicly, but court gossip is that he found a dead man in his very own chambers. Quite the ominous warning, Maman, though I'm surprised your men got to his chambers and didn't take Philip himself.*

*They say he was terrible to behold after all that—worse when they didn't capture your men after a thorough search of the city. The people there are calling you ghosts, spreading rumors that you've died at sea and it's your spirit that's torturing the king. Silly peasants.*

*Philip ordered all the guards in that portion of the dungeons hanged, along with the servant boy who worked down there. They lined them up and hanged them all together. Some people objected to the child's hanging because he was only six and you can't hang a child until seven, but I happen to know he was nine. Anyway the king didn't care how old he was —he just threatened to hang any objectors until they shut up.*

*Geoff says to tell you they've sent us an envoy of soldiers, so please don't send any of your own messengers for now. Supposedly they're to protect us since we've gone against you in public, but obviously they're here to make sure we aren't secretly in contact.*

*They are less than delightful company, Maman, and I do wish you'd reconsider retiring. It's a real inconvenience for us to have the king so firmly in our day-to-day business.*

*Your Louise.*

J eanne finished reading it aloud and looked up at Pieter and Amée. They'd been with her on the docks watching her men load the ships when the messenger arrived with Louise's letter.

Amée's face was pinched, which wasn't surprising—she'd been a street child, likely in danger of being hanged herself at times. Children could be executed for thieving, and Jeanne doubted living on the streets came without thieving.

But Pieter's reaction was unexpected. Jeanne would have guessed his captors' fate would feel like justice for him, but his face had crumpled in on itself with grief. Tears streaked shiny down his cheeks, and his hand was over his mouth. It had been days since Jeanne had spoken tenderly to her oldest friend, but now her voice was soft.

"Pieter, are you alright?"

He opened his eyes and looked wildly around the dock. "I have to go." There was no chance to ask where before he was gone, striding back to his waiting horse.

"Do you know what that's about?" Jeanne asked Amée.

Amée shook her head, mute.

"Do you think perhaps he made friends with one of the guards?"

"Perhaps. But would he react so badly to the death of a captor—even a nice one?"

Jeanne had no idea.

Pieter didn't come to see them off. That was the worst betrayal, the part that made Jeanne want to scream and throw things into the river. She'd stared at the dock, willing him to appear, as her new men released the ship from its moorings and they drifted away. But he never came. She was leaving Londres without even getting a chance to say goodbye to her oldest friend.

She'd farewelled the children, waking them this time and explaining that she was going to avenge their Papa. Oli had saluted her, and Little Jeanne had danced a little jig, then their long-suffering nurse had attempted, unsuccessfully, to get them back to sleep for a few more hours.

Jeanne had also farewelled Walter, kissing him on the temple as he tried to coax her back into bed for just a few more moments. The attempt had made her unreasonably angry. It was another reminder of the way everyone wanted her to stop, to stay, to leave the goddamn king to live his life in peace.

But there was no goodbye with Pieter. No ending. Just an empty space where he should have been by her side.

He was the only one left who'd known Olivier. The only one who could picture him when she said his name. The only one who'd set sail for the same reason as her. Her men were here on their king's orders, and Amée was here seeking her own revenge on the duke. Without Pieter,

# THE LIONESS

Jeanne was the only one left to stand for Olivier. To remember him.

The weight of that reality made her feel fragile in a way she rarely did. Like the king had not just stripped Olivier from the world, but also every person who'd stood for him, until only Jeanne remained. She'd never felt so insubstantial.

As her men steered them toward the Channel, she finally turned away from the docks, watched the riverbanks slide past. She hated Pieter for leaving. Hated him for the heaviness she now carried alone. Hated him for how much she didn't hate him but instead missed him like someone had cut off a part of her.

Monster, warm and humming, weaved around her ankles. Without Pieter, the damn devil-cat was Jeanne's oldest friend. She wasn't sure if she should laugh or cry. But she had to stop thinking about it. Had to focus. She'd tucked away her sadness before, so she could do it again. She had to—

A whisper cut through her thoughts. "Jeanne, look." Amé touched her shoulder and pointed back to the docks. To *Pieter*. There he was, at the edge of the water in his new black-as-midnight armor, one hand on his sword hilt and the other raised in the air, calling them back.

Calling her back.

Relief and fury tangled in Jeanne's chest—a thick knot that made it hard to breathe. He'd come after all, and from the way he was dressed, it wasn't to see them off. He'd come to join them.

Yet part of her wanted to leave him behind. He'd betrayed her, so she'd betray him right back. *You wanted to stay with your pretty healer?* she'd say. *So stay. Stay and choke on your betrayal.*

"Jeanne." Amée looked at her with concern. "We have to go back for Pieter."

"Why?" She was glad her voice came out low and cold, betraying no feeling. "He wants to stay, so perhaps we should let him."

Amée's eyebrows drew together. "You don't mean that."

She was right. Jeanne didn't even have the heart to keep up the ruse. Pieter was fast disappearing from sight—now a black speck in the distance—and Jeanne's fear of losing him again snuffed out her anger like a candle.

"Gilbert!" she called to her new first mate, her voice a commanding echo across the deck. "Turn the ship around! I've left something important behind."

"What changed your mind, Pieter?" Amée asked as the ship sped back toward the Channel.

The three were clustered on the deck—Pieter a powerful presence in his ominous new armor, Jeanne and Amée slight and easy to underestimate in comparison.

"Jehan." Pieter's voice cracked on the word. "He was the boy they hanged. A servant in the king's dungeons who brought me food. He wasn't supposed to talk to the prisoners, but when no one was there to listen, he'd tell me about his life. He was like me—came from one thing and wanted so much to be another. Wanted to be a knight someday.

"We were friends. I should have gone back for him. Should've found him in the city and told him to flee. He wasn't responsible for keeping me there, so I didn't think they'd punish him too. I didn't know." The last sentence was a whisper, and both women reached out to squeeze one of his hands.

# THE LIONESS

"Oh, Pieter," Amée whispered.

"You couldn't have known what the king would do," Jeanne said firmly.

"Yes, but it reminded me why we're doing this. Why Philip *can't* stay on that throne. I went home to Robine, and I told her everything about those months in the dungeon, about how no one touched me except to cause me pain...but sometimes Jehan would squeeze my hand through the slat when he gave me my food. No one talked to me, except sometimes Jehan. The king killed him for just to make a point. Like Jehan was nothing. Like he was bones leftover from a meal, tossed to the dogs and forgotten."

Pieter shifted his weight, his armor catching the newly risen sun and taking on an orange hue. "I don't want Jehan to be forgotten. I don't want Olivier to be forgotten."

"They won't be." Jeanne's certainty had returned. "We'll make sure of it."

Pieter nodded.

Always more sensitive than Jeanne, Amée asked, "How did Robine take it?"

"She understood, just like she always does. I've never had anyone understand me so well in my life."

Jeanne had been so angry that Pieter was staying in Britain, she'd never considered that perhaps this woman who'd enchanted him might understand him, understand *them*, understand justice. Perhaps she should have gotten to know Robine instead of accusing Pieter of being flighty. Pieter had been wrong to leave Jeanne—she'd never change her mind on that—but perhaps she'd been wrong to not try and understand why.

She squeezed Pieter's hand again. "I'm glad you came." Hopefully he knew what she'd left unsaid—that Jeanne de

293

Clisson, who was rarely sorry about anything, was sorry about this.

He returned the squeeze, then headed below deck. In the still-orange light of sunrise, his new armor was dazzling, and Jeanne was awed. Amée had been right once more. Pieter had embraced a reputation he'd never asked for, that of the Black Knight of legend, and he was every inch a legend himself—dangerous, strong, and stunning.

The damned king didn't stand a chance.

## CHAPTER 47

# THE ENGLISH CHANNEL

A few days after they left the comforts of Londres behind, a ship appeared on the horizon—a dark smudge against the sunrise.

"Ready the men," Jeanne said, and it was done.

Archers stood at attention. Fighters lined the rails. At the bow, Pieter stood gleaming in his powerful black armor. Amée stayed back near the mast, a nervous hand on her dagger and a look of determination on her face. And Jeanne watched on, hair dancing in the breeze, her cheeks flushed by the cold and the anticipation.

Then the other ship drew closer, and Jeanne realized it wasn't a French merchant ship or enemy warship at all—it was a simple dark-wood cog flying an English flag.

A friend then.

But a strange one, because there on the deck was a tall slender white woman, feet planted, hand shading her eyes, dressed in armor, and grinning from ear to ear. Her hair was a rich shade of dark brown, braided and tucked neatly out of the way. Her nose was long and aquiline; her eyes were like flint.

"Stand down," Jeanne ordered her men as the ship approached. Because she knew who it must be—there was only one other lady pirate on this channel allied with the English.

*Joanna la Flamme.*

Isabella was the She-Wolf. Jeanne was the Lioness. And Joanna the Flame was a raging fire. A woman so very like Jeanne—her husband betrayed and then killed by King Philip just a year past, her lands taken by the duke a few years before that. She'd allied herself with the English to win her son the dukeship, and she wanted the king's head as much as the rest of them.

Seeing Joanna left Jeanne feeling breathless and young. What news was this kindred spirit here to deliver? What power might they have as allies—two women with shared enemies?

Amée whispered, "Is that who I think it is?"

"Indeed."

"What does she want?"

Jeanne couldn't help but smile. "I think we're about to find out."

With the ships now within shouting distance, Joanna cupped her hands around her mouth. "If I come aboard, you won't maul me will you, Lioness?"

Jeanne laughed, her mood light and almost playful. "My taste runs more to French kings and Breton dukes, Lady of the Flames."

Jeanne's men retreated in earnest as Pieter helped Joanna aboard. Her own ship pulled away to a safe distance, ready to return for her when the two women were finished.

Without preamble, Joanna threw her arms around Jeanne and pounded her on the back. "They said you were traveling with the Black Knight of legend!" She laughed and motioned to Pieter. "I always think they're exaggerating these stories, like they do with mine, but it seems in your case the myths have merit."

"They've exaggerated your stories?" Jeanne joked. "How disappointing! I was hoping you really could call down fire from heaven on command."

Joanna's grin widened and, dark eyes dancing, she grasped Jeanne's arms. "You are just as I imagined."

"Let's go somewhere private and talk," Jeanne suggested.

The two women settled at the table in Jeanne's cabin, while Pieter and Amée hovered in the doorway. Jeanne waved them in—they were her war council, so of course they were welcome. They were both being so strange, waiting for permission. Jeanne supposed it was for appearances' sake, but Joanna hardly seemed the sort to care about appearances. No woman in armor could afford to.

Joanna began. "Our mutual friend Amélie said if I ever saw you, I should stop and introduce myself."

Another thrill shudder ran through Jeanne. The web of angry nobles she'd woven across France was still working hard for her cause. She glanced at Pieter, hoping he knew how grateful she was for his push toward such diplomacy —Jeanne never would have attempted it on her own. Without him and Amée, Jeanne would be a raging bull, a fierce storm. With them, she was smart, strategic, connected.

Her mother would be proud.

Joanna leaned forward and went on. "France is going after Aquitaine—the She-Wolf's homeland, the English stronghold across the Channel. The Duke of Normandy is leading the siege, so I've suggested that Edward sail on Normandy since it'll be undefended. They'll expect Edward to move south to defend Aquitaine, but instead he'll go north to take the Norman shores."

She chuckled, delighted with her own cleverness. "That's the big news. I'm currently enroute to Normandy, with more of Edward's forces on their way, but when I saw your ships...well, they're pretty distinctive, so I thought I'd stop to give you an update. And, of course, I wanted to meet you." Joanna's expression grew more serious, though her eyes still danced. "They're calling you the most powerful woman in France."

Jeanne laughed again. God, it was good to laugh so much, and even better to talk with someone so similar to herself. "Funny, that's what they say about you too."

"In that case, I guess we're both the most powerful woman in France," Joanna said. "Just depends on who's had the biggest victory that day."

"So...you on the day you snuck your men out of under-siege Hennebont, burned Charles' undefended camp to the ground, then resupplied in the next town, snuck back into Hennebont, and somehow held off his forces until rein-forcements arrived to defeat him?" Jeanne's eyes sparkled as she waited for Joanna to confirm her role in that brilliant win. "The peasants said you could walk through walls."

Joanna chuckled and nodded her confirmation. "And you on the day you plucked your knight out of the king's dungeons right under his nose—like a phantom." She glanced at Pieter who smiled and inclined his head, then she clasped Jeanne's arm. "Wait, I have more news. The king knows your children are Edward's wards."

She paused for dramatic effect, then laughed like she couldn't help herself. "Philip apparently threw a fit like a small child—he's worse than my toddler—and then he had the messenger killed on the spot." With that, she sobered a little. "The poor page boy's family are furious. They've sent an official refusal to pay fealty to the king anymore. It won't last, but it's a nice sentiment. I swear that man makes more enemies every day." By the end of the sentence, a ghost of a smile was back on her lips.

Joanna's delight at Philip's fast-declining support was evident, and Jeanne was buoyed by it. She may have failed to kill the king last year, she may have been forced to flee, but he was still vulnerable, still foolish, still making enemies at every turn. Jeanne was not alone in wanting him dead, and the more people who shared that goal, the closer she was to killing him.

"So," Joanna continued, "now I've seen you and know you're everything they say, I'd like to propose that you join us. We could use another fighting force when we take the Normans by surprise, and yours seems more than adequate." She looked pointedly at Pieter, then paused. "All the better if you could bring along some raven spies, blood-dyed skirts, and demons too. And did I hear correctly that you own a flying lion?"

Jeanne snorted.

"Who knows," Joanna whispered, raising an eyebrow, "maybe the king will come and try to stop us himself."

It was all the incentive Jeanne needed. "I can't promise any flying lions," she said, "but this lioness is all yours."

## CHAPTER 48
# NORMANDY, FRANCE

Amée dangled a piece of meat into a cage where two ravens neatly pulled it apart and swallowed it down. "We're going ashore soon," she told them, running her fingers over the rough metal. "And there's no way to transport all of you overland, so you'll be free."

Leaning against the mast, Jeanne watched on. She'd seen Amée talk to her ravens before, but it was always sweet to watch. What a strange and wonderful person she was.

She was only half-right about their plans though—a small contingent of Jeanne's men were going ashore to fight alongside King Edward and Joanna, but the rest would stay on the ships to resupply the English troops as needed. Still, she and Amée had agreed that leaving the crew in charge of the ravens was a recipe for raven neglect. They'd be better off free.

"I'll miss your company," Amée cooed to the birds. "You remind me of Giselle. You make me feel bigger than myself."

Jeanne wondered if she should move away—Amée didn't know she was there, and the conversation seemed private, even if it was with a unkindness of ravens. But at that point, the men began reboarding the ship, and with a deck full of people, privacy seemed unlikely regardless of Jeanne's presence.

Pieter joined Amée and tapped on a cage. "I'll miss these little scoundrels."

The movement unsettled the birds, and they restlessly cawed and flapped. Something about the noise was comforting to Jeanne, a reminder of the battles they'd helped her win, of the power of looking at things in unique ways.

"Goodbye, friends," Amée said.

She and Pieter set about opening the cages, and then—on Amée's instruction—Pieter flung a bucketful of meat and stale bread and seed into the air. All at once, the ravens mobbed the doors and took off, swirling, diving, swallowing, cawing, then spiraling upward in a swarm, moving inland as one.

Amée had told Jeanne she hoped they'd fly over the towns and cities their armies planned to take. She hoped residents would see them as an omen. She hoped they'd make surrenders quicker and more likely. She hoped—as she always did—that fear would be on their side.

As the birds disappeared into the distance, Pieter put a hand on Amée's shoulder. Comforting her, Jeanne thought, since she'd be sad to see the ravens go.

Jeanne liked that about him. He was a knight—strong, fierce, enormous—but there was something motherly about him too. Something that made him the one Jeanne always entrusted with her children. Something that made him the person everyone onboard went to for reassurance. Something protective of Jeanne and Amée, but not in the same way that Jeanne was protective. Pieter's was softer and less angry around the edges. Where Jeanne was a wild-cat, he was a wall. Someone you could lean on.

It made Jeanne feel safe and grounded, and she wondered Amée felt the same. And then Amée spoke, and Jeanne's eyebrows rose involuntarily at her next words.

"Pieter, can I tell you a secret?"

Pieter turned his full attention to her. "Yes, of course."

Jeanne listened, protective and maternal, as after all this time, Amée's story poured out. Pieter already knew about Giselle, but now he heard about the kidnappers and Amée's decision to cut off her braids and disguise herself as a man. When she was done, she told him she trusted him and asked him to keep her secrets.

Pieter, being Pieter, nodded slowly, seriously, then he smiled just a little. "Did I ever tell you I had a daughter?"

Amée's eyes widened. "No."

"She died the day she was born," he said, his voice low. "My wife too. And while I never got to know my girl...if I had, I'd be proud if she was like you."

Tears formed in Amée's eyes, and Jeanne wondered again whether she should discreetly leave. But she also couldn't look away—there was something powerful happening, and she wanted to be part of it, even if from afar.

"Is your name really Arley, then?" Pieter asked.

"No. It's Amée."

"Well, Amée, it's nice to finally meet you." He searched her face. "Would you mind if I thought of you as a daughter?"

At once, something about Amée changed. She seemed to grow taller, brighter. Whatever had been holding her tightly together released, and her body relaxed from fore-head to feet, smoothing the lines on her face, softening her stance. Was this the first time a man had said something like that to her? All her stories about men were harsh and difficult. Charles' indifference, her kidnappers' evil intent, the priest who'd accused her mentor of witchcraft. She'd mentioned her father once, and he hadn't sounded kind or approving either.

Pieter crouched down to be face to face with her, and Amée—who never liked to be too close to men, who always kept a half-step away, fading into the background—stepped in and wrapped her arms around his neck.

She didn't let go for a long time.

## CHAPTER 49
# NORMANDY, FRANCE

As Edward's armies came ashore around her, Jeanne was swept up in their combined power. Between the English, Welsh, and mercenary troops, they were fourteen-thousand strong, each individual a force to be reckoned with.

Joanna la Flamme was mounted at the front of a marching regiment. Her eyes sparkled with mischief and her glaive—a long, sharp, one-sided blade at the end of a pole—glinted wicked in the sun.

Jeanne had likewise been given a horse—a black charger with a bright white mane and a saucy attitude. He danced lightly on his feet, eager to move, while Monster rested on his haunches behind her, a witch's familiar for all the enemy knew. Jeanne's sword hung heavy and solid and perfect in its sheath.

To her right, Pieter's black armor flashed like a warning. Amée rode toward the rear, dagger at her side, carrying flint, candles, and incense for tricks the enemy didn't yet know. Edward's men carried ten thousand longbows and pushed heavy volley guns that resembled pipe organs but delivered fatal volleys of iron shot.

They were a force like none Jeanne had ever imagined.

They were, she was certain, going to finally kill the king.

When they made camp the first night, they could still smell the sea. Tents sprung up in clusters for noblemen and knights, Jeanne and Joanna. Scouts sped on ahead to pave their way, and soldiers dropped to the ground to sleep where they fell. Amée—exhausted from a long day in the beating sun—was already asleep on a thin straw mattress. Jeanne smiled to herself and pressed her lips to the girl's warm forehead. Amée looked so young as she slept, so much younger than twenty-four.

Jeanne's thoughts drifted to her youngest children, and she wondered what they were doing now. Were they asleep too, or was Little Jeanne dancing around with her practice sword while Oli made speeches to unsuspecting servants? She missed them. She loved them. Her heart fluttered at the thought that this might soon be over—their father, their brother, avenged; their mother kissing them goodnight.

She also thought about Geoff and Louise, but it was tinged with worry. Jeanne hadn't heard from them since Louise's note had reached her in Britain. Did Philip still have his men at their castle making it unsafe to send word, or was there some other reason they'd suddenly gone completely quiet?

There was a rustle at her tent's opening, and Jeanne turned, expecting to see Pieter or Joanna or perhaps a messenger from Edward come to call her to a war council. Instead, the flap closed behind a slender well-built man whose eyes flickered blue and then green in the candlelight.

*Walter.*

It was months since she'd last seen him, but he was the same—handsome, bearded, a smile playing across his lips. She hadn't considered that he might be here, that he and his mercenaries could be part of Edward's plans. Something light and breathless rose in her chest as her mouth opened in surprise.

He laughed, and she placed a finger to her lips, motioning toward Amée with her eyes. "Don't wake him."

"Her," he corrected.

Jeanne's heart tripped over itself, and she could only stare.

"You said her name in Paris when she was panicking," Walter whispered. "And it made so much sense."

"Why didn't you say anything?"

He shrugged. "She can tell me in her own time. I'm sure she has her reasons for being in disguise."

Jeanne smiled at how gentle, how thoughtful he was. God she'd missed him. Somehow she'd fallen for him more since she'd been away.

"Is that a new sword?" he murmured, touching the weapon strapped to her hip.

She stroked the scabbard with her thumb. "Edward gifted it to me when we landed."

"The scabbard is beautiful."

"So is the sword."

"So are you." He grinned, and they both paused, drinking each other in.

"I'm glad you're here," she said.

"I'm glad *you're* here," he answered.

"Walk with me?"

They slipped out into the torchlit camp, hand sliding into hand, feet falling into step—a nightly walk that would become their ritual, tucked between war councils and battle preparations and Jeanne's non-negotiable long dinners around the fire with Pieter and Amée.

FOR OVER A MONTH, the company took any town it wanted, but now France's armies had mustered and were headed their way. King Edward ordered them to fortify the camp at Crécy and prepare for a fight.

And prepare they were, training men, sharpening blades, strategizing positions. In a pause during a strategy session, poised on a rickety wooden chair in Jeanne's tent, Amée turned to Jeanne. "What does a real battle feel like?"

"You know what it feels like," Jeanne answered, perplexed.

Amée had been with her for years. True, she'd mostly stayed out of the way during clashes, and she'd spent a lot of time away on spy missions in France, but she'd still seen fighting, hadn't she? She'd been there to break Pieter out of the king's prison cells. She'd poisoned a doctor. She'd tried to kill Charles.

"Not like this." Amée said. "Not at scale. I've never been close to seeing so many men dying at once."

Jeanne supposed that was true. Over twenty thousand French soldiers were on their way to face the fourteen thousand English. The numbers were staggering. Jeanne's own battles had all been on a much smaller scale.

"You won't have to see the full fight this time either," Jeanne said in what she hoped was a comforting tone. "You'll be safe back here in my tent." If everything went according to plan, Amée wouldn't see any action—she'd stay at camp with the cooks and prisoners, guards and servants while the soldiers rode out into the fray.

"But what if I wanted to come with you?"

Jeanne blinked in surprise. "That's not a good idea. It won't be safe out there, and you're not a trained soldier."

"I've been training!" Offense crept into Amée's tone. "I've been training for months!"

"And we've all been training since we were six, seven, or eight years old. You're getting good with that dagger, Amée, but you wouldn't make it on a battlefield."

Amée pursed her lips and leaned back in her chair, rubbing a small piece of leather along the edge of her blade.

"What is that?" Jeanne asked.

"Poison. Just a nick would finish someone off."

*God's nails*, she was clever. "Always good to have a backup plan—if an enemy makes it into camp, I don't like his chances." Jeanne beamed at her. "Do you think we should get the archers to lace their arrows?"

Amée returned the dagger to its sheath and adjusted her gloves. "There's not enough."

At that moment, Pieter swept into the tent, an enormous imposing shadow. "They're coming." He turned to Amée. "You've got your dagger? Candles and incense in case you have to scare someone off?"

Amée nodded but looked disgruntled. "Jeanne, I really think I could help."

"And *I* think that this is it. I can feel it in my bones—this is the day we take the king." She adjusted her chain mail and tightened her belt, then added, "And I need you safe while we do."

Amée sighed.

And then Jeanne was out the tent flap and gone, leaving Amée alone, safe and sound while Jeanne took her shot at King Philip.

## CHAPTER 50
# CRÉCY, FRANCE

Dark clouds gathered overhead as Jeanne sat tall on her mount at the rear of King Edward's forces, Monster purring in her saddlebag. Joanna caught her eye and winked. Exhilarated by the charge in the air, by the coming battle, Jeanne winked back.

There were two contingents of longbowmen spread out ahead of them, with wicked-looking wooden spikes buried in the ground, angled toward the oncoming French. The field was full of holes the troops had been digging all morning—traps to catch unwary French soldiers and trip their horses. And behind the arrows and the spikes lay an army. Jeanne, Joanna, Walter, Edward and thousands upon thousands of their men.

Rain began pouring down, and across the battlefield, a contingent of Italian archers—paid members of the French army—advanced in formation, nocking their arrows in unison. And when the first volley came with the faint cry of "Loose!" echoing across the space between the armies, a staggering four thousand arrows flew through the air at the English line.

All around Jeanne, soldiers sucked in their breath. But every single enemy arrow fell short. Either the archers were too far away or the rain had thrown their arrows off course. The English army had no such problems—their longbows had more extensive range and quicker loading times. Ten thousand arrows flew into the Italian archers, killing more than half on the first volley alone.

Jeanne watched through the rain as the Italians turned and fled back toward their own forces, tripping over each other in their haste, twisting ankles and tripping in the field's many holes. And then the French screamed and charged, cutting down the bowmen they'd hired on their way across the field.

Jeanne shouldn't have been shocked—King Philip had always been a monster, had always been willing to kill his own men for slights both real and imagined. It was why she was here. It was why his kingdom was filled with nobility who sent her, Joanna, and Edward funds and men and secrets.

Still, in that moment, she *was* shocked. Taking out your own fighters at the start of a battle was the height of cruelty and foolishness. The Italian archers were no friends of hers, but she felt for them in their deaths. They hadn't deserved to be cut down like that. No one ever deserved the hand King Philip dealt them.

"Hold," Edward shouted. "Hold!"

Jeanne and the rest of the mounted forces held steady as the French came roaring forward through the rain and into the sure arrows of the longbows. Almost every charger died before they reached the front line—some by arrows, the rest dispatched by swords or the sharp spikes.

Jeanne marveled at their foolhardiness. Marveled at how her allies barely had to put up a fight. In two attacks, the French had already lost thousands, while the English were yet to lose a single man. The justice of it was a song beating through Jeanne's heart and dancing across her skin. Charge by charge, they were going take Philip down.

Then again, seeing his men cut down like this, Philip would never take to the field himself. The thought left a sour taste at the back of Jeanne's throat. If the battle continued going so well for the English, the cowardly French king would retreat, and he would survive. Jeanne wouldn't have her revenge.

She pushed the wet hair from her face and licked her lips—she would not walk away from this battle without watching him die. And if she was right, the way to kill him was to come up from behind.

Motioning for Pieter to follow, she steered her horse toward a stretch of woodland bordering the field.

"Where are we going?" he asked as she led them deeper into the woods.

"To finish it once and for all."

JEANNE AND PIETER stopped in the shadows of the trees on the French side of the battlefield, their horses quiet, waiting for the right moment. For the king to get close enough for an arrow. For a dagger. For a rush of swords. They watched as time and time again, he sent his forces barreling to their deaths. Thousands were now sprawled on the ground, their lives finished. Thousands more looked on, angry or restless in the day's dying light.

And then the fool—unable to see that he'd already lost—plucked up his courage and led the next attack himself.

Jeanne's body sparked with impatience as Philip

charged onto the field. Part of her hoped this was his end, but most of her hoped he'd retreat. That he'd turn his horse around and bring himself within striking distance of her sword. She wanted to do it herself. She wanted to be the last thing he saw. She wanted him to die knowing that killing Olivier had been his doom.

Instead, she watched as first one horse and then a second died beneath him, each quickly replaced by a nearby knight. She hadn't thought much about her own horse, but she hated Philip for leaving his behind so casually. Hated him for being so out of shape that both times a horse went down, his men had to help him mount the next one. That this bumbling thoughtless fool was the man who'd been beating her made outrage race across her skin.

*Come closer,* she willed, tracing her finger along her sword's cold hilt. *Turn and run.*

Suddenly, *finally*, an arrow sliced through the air and pierced Philip's jaw, knocking him from his third horse. Time slowed, and Jeanne's hope froze. Was he dead? Was the devil finally, irrevocably dead?

Men came to a stop all around him, creating a barrier with their bodies, armor, swords until Jeanne couldn't see him anymore. She glanced at Pieter and raised a questioning eyebrow. The whites of his eyes were ghost-like in the dimness of the storm and the shadows of the wood as he shook his head. No, despite being a head taller, he couldn't see either. No, he didn't know if the king was still alive.

Jeanne again faced the battlefield and watched the mass around the king shift and disperse. The men fanned out, and Philip was rising, remounting his third horse, riding away from the fighting. He wasn't dead.

He was coming her way.

# THE LIONESS

Was she enraged he'd survived or elated she'd have her wish? All she knew for certain was that the feelings warred inside her like a fire, making her stronger. Surer. She drew her sword and heard the scrape of Pieter's own sword beside her. They were ready. At last, the king would be hers.

And then a slight figure stepped out from the tree line, drawing Jeanne's gaze away from Philip's retreat. Time stopped completely. Her heart pounded in her ears, beating out a terrified rhythm that blocked out everything else.

*Amée.*

Amée was on the battlefield, just visible at the edge of the wood.

What was she doing here? She was supposed to stay at camp! Jeanne could tell by the confident way she moved along the tree line that Amée was coming to find her. But why? At the corner of her vision, the king was now being redirected to safety—away from the trees, once more out of reach.

Jeanne wasn't the only one who'd noticed Amée—the surviving Italian archers were turning, nocking their arrows, focused on proving their mettle. Time sped up again, and Jeanne sheathed her new sword and urged her horse onward. She didn't have time to untangle what Amée was doing here. She didn't have time to curse god for keeping Philip from her yet again. She barely had time to register the archers taking aim at the slight girl in her page costume.

All she could think was that there wasn't enough time to reach her.

## CHAPTER 51
# CRÉCY, FRANCE

*Run. Run. Run into the trees! Hide! Please, Amée!* Jeanne couldn't scream the words out loud without drawing attention to her and Pieter, but she screamed them in her head as she galloped along the edge of the forest, desperate to reach her friend.

Why had she come?

Amée had never done anything so foolish before. But Jeanne would never know the answer, because the archers were releasing their arrows and Amée wasn't running, wasn't hiding, wasn't darting into the cover of the trees. She was so fixated on getting to Jeanne, she hadn't paid attention to the field, hadn't realized she was visible.

Three arrows arced through the air, and one found its target, throwing Amée to the ground. A cry wrenched from her that made every part of Jeanne hurt. But as the archers nocked their bows again, a figure in skirts and armor materialized beside Amée, lifted her like a child, and disappeared back into the trees. Jeanne choked back a sob.

*Joanna.* Joanna la Flamme. Jeanne could see now why they called her that—when she emerged again, her eyes were fire. She nocked her own bow and fired at the archers. Nocked, fired. A man cried out. Then another.

Jeanne finally reached them, and they retreated together into the trees. Jeanne and Pieter rode at Joanna's side, while a half-conscious Amée lay draped across her horse, eyes fluttering. There was an arrow lodged between her shoulder and chest, but she wasn't dead. *Not gone,* Jeanne told herself. King Edward's doctor could save her. He had to save her. Jeanne would kill him if he didn't.

Threatening a man already on their side was absurd, but it made Jeanne feel less helpless. Made her believe that Amée, now soaked in blood, unconscious, slipping away, could still be saved by the only weapons she possessed— swords and fists and daggers.

THE STORM HAD PASSED. The battle was over. The enemy had followed their coward king into the night, with the English cutting them down as they fled. The estimate was ten thousand French dead. A hundred for the English.

Jeanne didn't care about any of it.

All Jeanne cared about was the small, blood-soaked, feverish girl mumbling nonsense in her restless sleep. She squeezed Amée's clammy hand and hoped she knew, even through her delirium, that Jeanne was there. That she wasn't alone.

Joanna pushed open the tent flap and ushered in the king's personal doctor. "Well?" she said before he'd even knelt beside the cot. "Do something,"

Jeanne shifted slightly to give him space, while Pieter paced in her peripheral vision, more worried than she'd ever seen him. Walter stood to the side, his face pale and drawn.

A young man bustled in carrying an armful of supplies, and the doctor looked shrewdly at Jeanne, then at Pieter. "Both of you, out. I need to remove the arrow, and you look like you'll throttle me for even trying. I've been at this long enough to know better." He shooed them away with his hands, then beckoned to Joanna and Walter. "You two look less murderous, so you can stay and hold him steady for me."

Jeanne tightened her grip on Amée's hand. "I'm not going anywhere."

"Oh yes you are, or you'll lose your page boy, because I'm not doing a thing until you leave."

Joanna placed a hand on Jeanne's shoulder. "Go and get some air. I'll make sure he's alright."

Then Walter's hand was on Jeanne's, warm and steady, and he was whispering in her ear. "I'll take care of her and make sure the doctor knows—and doesn't—whatever he needs to about her disguise."

Moments later, Jeanne found herself outside, staring at the tent flap. She wanted to go back in. She wanted to make sure Amée wasn't alone. And yes, she wanted to throttle the doctor should he harm so much as a hair on her head.

But Amée needed help, needed it desperately, and Jeanne couldn't risk him keeping his word and not helping if she was there. So she sank to the ground, crossing her legs under her skirts, feeling the mud seep through to her thighs, and watched the tent for any sign that she was needed. Pieter lowered himself down beside her and wrapped a huge arm around her shoulders. They both shook with cold and fear and silent tears.

Amée would live.

When the doctor told her, Jeanne burst into uncharacteristic sobs and threw her arms around him. The look on his face plainly said that he thought her hysterical, and he deeply disapproved. Jeanne didn't care. She could have kissed his sour, pinched little face. He'd saved Amée, and that was all that mattered.

"The pain," Amée murmured, "was like a dance. It was like a storm. Uncontrollable, undefinable, unstoppable. Like magic."

Kneeling beside the cot, Jeanne stopped running her thumb over Amée's scarred palms to instead feel her cheeks. Still hot. She supposed the poetic musings were a symptom of the fever. The doctor said it would pass, but Jeanne's heart chilled to feel the younger woman's face so blazing.

"Why did you leave the tent?" Jeanne asked, the question edged with desperation.

Amée closed her eyes and took a shaky breath. "I thought I could help. I've been training so hard, and I've been feeling like if I just helped more, we could get to Charles. I've been having nightmares—about him, about the men who kidnapped me—and I thought the only way to make them stop was to be braver. I wanted to be braver."

"But why leave the shelter of the trees?"

"I figured I'd find you quicker if I could see better. I thought I was still concealed by shadows." Tears formed at the corners of Amée's eyes, flicking off her lashes as she blinked. "I didn't think I'd ruin your chance at the king. I'm so sorry, Jeanne."

Of course Jeanne hated that he'd gotten away, but

losing Amée would have been worse. She didn't blame her; she was just glad she was alive. Glad Philip hadn't stolen one more thing from her. She didn't know how to say all that, though, so she just pressed on Amée's palm, wishing she was better at comfort and said, "You *are* brave. Don't you dare think you're not." As if that settled everything, Jeanne kissed Amée's too-hot forehead and started gathering their things.

Amée spoke softly. "Walter knows about me. Apparently he figured it out ages ago."

"I know," Jeanne said. "He told me he wanted to wait for you to share it with him in your own time."

"I guess we didn't have that luxury." Amée smiled weakly. "He fought with the doctor about removing my tunic. They wound up compromising by cutting off the sleeve and half the neck area."

A rare feeling of gratitude spread warm across Jeanne's skin. Somehow she'd gotten lucky twice—loved by two men who were both fatherly and fierce, tender and strong. When she looked back at Amée, her eyes were closed and her breathing was steady. The tension in her face had melted away in sleep, and Jeanne's heart settled into something resembling relief.

Outside, Edward's host were readying to march. Jeanne could hear tents coming down, wagons being loaded, prisoners being shuffled along. In the wake of his great success, the king would now try to take the important shipping port of Calais, while Jeanne and her men would sail for Britain where Amée could recover. This was where they would part ways, everyone packing up and soldiering on in different directions.

"So this is goodbye." Joanna appeared tall and steady at the entrance to the tent, with Walter a half-step behind her.

THE LIONESS

Joanna and her men were riding to Calais with King Edward. *Merde*, Jeanne would miss her. The fire in her eyes. The sharp edges of her jokes. The knowledge that another woman had Jeanne's back.

"For now," Jeanne said. "I hope we meet again."

Joanna returned her smile. "Me too, Lady Lioness." And then, unexpectedly, she crossed the space between them, wrapped an arm around Jeanne's waist, and kissed her full on the lips. It was warm and swift and hard enough to bruise.

Jeanne laughed in surprise while Walter's eyebrows flickered upward and his jaw dropped. Ignoring the man behind her, Joanna stepped back and gave a little bow. A sly grin played across her face. "You, m'lady, are even more than they say. King Philip should quake in his boots."

Then she was gone, sweeping out through the tent flap, swallowed into the camp. Walter watched her go, his face frozen somewhere between amusement and shock. Jeanne laughed again, louder, and kissed him on the cheek.

"Guess you've got some competition for my affections," she teased.

"I sure hope not." Regaining his composure, he wrapped a strong arm around her and motioned at Joanna's retreating form with his chin. "I could never compete with that."

# 1347–1350

## CHAPTER 52
# WINDSOR CASTLE, ENGLAND

Queen Philippa was on the throne, her golden-brown face a perfectly serene mask, though Jeanne knew it was unlikely she'd summoned her here for calming news.

Amée must have sensed Jeanne's unease, because she placed a reassuring hand on her shoulder. Jeanne put her own hand over Amée's, pressing back, glad she was there. A few months before, it had seemed as though she mightn't be—not only when she'd been injured and the doctor put her back together, but on the way across the Channel when the infection set in. Her fever had soared. Her cheeks hollowed. And Jeanne had again thought she'd lose her.

In the end, Amée had saved her own life. The doctors in the castle did what they could, but it was Amée who'd sent apprentices scurrying to the forest and the markets for herbs said to draw out the pain. It was Amée who'd burned rosemary in her room every night, even at her most delirious, to smoke out the infection. It was Amée who'd asked Pieter to hunt down magic books in the Windsor Castle library and bring them to her in the dead of night. It was Amée who'd carried out the spells.

She'd healed herself by sheer force of will, and Jeanne respected her even more for it. She couldn't believe she'd once thought the girl weak and refused her request to join the crew.

Now, in the great hall of Windsor Castle, Philippa surveyed the room, her eyes stopping on Jeanne and Amée. The corners of her mouth lifted. With Edward off leading the siege of Calais, she was the queen regent—ruling England, leading forces to stamp out Scottish rebels, judging disputes. The peasants called her fair and merciful. Most of the court agreed she was even better than Edward, who was himself known as one of the better regents in living memory.

Jeanne hadn't spoken to Philippa often, but she liked her. She was strong and fierce but also cool-headed in a way that reminded Jeanne of her mother—a natural diplomat in addition to a warrior.

"Dear Jeanne," Philippa began, her voice strong and warm. "I've just had good news from the battlefields. Duke Charles de Blois has been captured. He's on his way to Britain under the care of Thomas Dagworth."

Jeanne's breath caught in her chest and Amée's hand tightened on her shoulder. God's nails, *finally*. It had taken so long.

Five years.

Five years of fighting. Five years of struggle. Five years of loss. But finally, they'd gotten to him. Finally, she'd be able to kill the man who'd killed her family.

"When will he arrive?" she asked.

"Soon. I expect the messenger only beat them by a day or two."

THE LIONESS

"And when will we execute him?" Jeanne's voice was high, excited, impatient.

Philippa went silent, and the cheerful corners of her mouth turned down before she answered. "We won't be executing him, Jeanne. In the end, he surrendered, and we show mercy when we can here. We'll keep him away from the battlefield, perhaps ransom him back to France someday when we need funds or an advantage."

Her tone remained warm, but it was decisive in a way Jeanne hated. Was she really going to deny Jeanne this justice? After so many years and all her sacrifices? Heat rose along her skin, the familiar rage so easily sparked.

"This is the man who betrayed my husband and tried to kill my children," she said, the last three words coming through gritted teeth. "The man who had an innocent woman executed for heresy, leaving my friend alone in the world." She motioned toward Amée. "The man who killed thousands at his siege of Quimper. Don't you care about the people you lost?"

"Of course, but war is always tragedy, and those thousands weren't ours," Philippa corrected. "It's unfortunate that he killed his own people who stood against him, but he ransomed the English back to us. He's shown our people mercy, and we—the king and I—have chosen that same path for our reign." The queen calmy surveyed Jeanne. "You of all people should be grateful that this is how we do things. I happen to know your own husband was our prisoner five years ago, and we treated him well. Charles will be too."

Jeanne clenched her jaw, wondering if they'd throw her in the dungeons for smacking Philippa's infuriatingly calm face. Olivier had been captured in a siege, following orders, whereas Charles was the man leading the damn war. Mercy belonged where it was *deserved*. And Charles deserved none.

The silence sat thick across the throne room as Jeanne stared at the queen. Her ally...now the person standing between her and the man who'd sent Olivier to his death. At last, she opened her mouth to speak, to cut the tension and let it snap back where it would, but two hands gripped her elbows. Amée and Pieter. Both knowing her too well. Both warning her not to do anything rash.

For once, she listened to their unspoken plea.

"Is that all, my queen?" Jeanne tried to file the sharp edges off her words.

Philippa's smile held a hint of relief. "Yes, Jeanne. You may go."

BACK IN HER CHAMBERS, Jeanne was every inch the lioness they called her—pacing her room in fury, kicking at the lavish bed skirts, knocking things off the desk and the table at the end of the bed, and sending a hissing, irritated Monster scrambling past Amée and through the open door.

Jeanne stormed to the window and glared out over the grounds. Men were busy bringing in building materials and digging foundations for the expansion of the Chapel of Saint Edward the Confessor, where Edward was founding a new college—his and Philippa's pride and joy. Jeanne had a wild impulse to run out and tear down their neat piles of materials, to keep something important from Edward just as he was keeping something precious from her.

"The damn duke," she growled, holding up her fists. "Finally captured! And now they won't let me near him?

After all I've done for the kingdom, they won't let me near him!"

The only thing left on the table was a cup of tea and Jeanne screamed as she snatched it up and threw it at the wall. It broke cleanly into three pieces and sent tea sliding across the floor.

Pieter slipped into the room behind Amée, closed the door, and crossed the room to take Jeanne's hands. "If he's captured, he's lost his power," he said. "So even if you can't get to him, you've won. *We've won.* He can't hurt anyone else."

"I don't want him powerless," Jeanne spat. "I want him dead." She jerked her hands away. "He's a damned saint now. The Church will do everything they can to free him, and then we'll be right back where we started. Why, when I'm so close, won't the English give me this? I'm their ally. I've helped them win battles. I've been resupplying them, battling beside them..."

She trailed off, having finally run out of things to say, but the anger kept pulsing off her in waves. Amée looked equally furious. Her lips were pressed tight together, her body taut, coiled like a snake ready to strike. Charles had killed her mentor, and she wanted him dead just as much as Jeanne did. Jeanne loved her for it with the same intensity that she hated Charles. She grasped the younger woman's hand and hoped she knew that Jeanne's anger wasn't reserved for Olivier and Guillaume, but also for Amée's own loss.

A soft knock sounded at the door.

*Merde.* Couldn't people hear the shouting and know they should leave her well enough alone? She waved her hand at Pieter to open the door.

The young servant woman on the other side looked

understandably nervous. "Queen Philippa has requested you return to the throne room. She's just received a messenger and has more news that will interest the Lady Lioness." When Pieter nodded, the girl fled.

Jeanne sighed in frustration and stomped out of her chamber, back toward the hall, and the whisper of footsteps behind her told her that Pieter and Amée were following. When they arrived, Philippa stood and crossed the room, wrapping her hands around Jeanne's. She looked at Jeanne with eyes so sad, Jeanne's anger-hot skin turned cold with fear.

Someone was dead. It was the only thing that look could mean. Someone was dead.

But who?

Oli and Little Jeanne were safe, housed with nearby nobles, away from the fighting. Amée and Pieter were both with her. Pieter's love, Robine, the woman he'd been spending every moment with since disembarking, was also here in the hall. And Walter...

*Walter.*

Visions of him crushed under a boulder or shot through with arrows filled her mind. He was the most vulnerable of the people she loved.

In denial, Jeanne's heart screamed that perhaps it was Charles. Philippa had thought she'd be happy about his capture, so maybe she was also foolish enough to think she'd be saddened by his death. Maybe the ship transporting him had sunk. Maybe the men aboard had tired of his holiness demanding Mass every three hours and stabbed him through the heart. If so, she'd find the man who did it and shake his hand.

Yes, that had to be it. Walter was fine. It was Charles who was dead...

THE LIONESS

But when Philippa spoke, it wasn't about Charles. "Jeanne, I'm so sorry," she said, and Jeanne hated her closeness, the fragility in her voice, so much more than she'd hated the infuriating calm and strength. "We've received word that when we captured the duke in the battle of La Roche-Derrien, your son Geoff died."

Jeanne's vision narrowed until all she could see was the queen's concerned face and all she could think was how she wanted to shove it away. If she could stop that pitying look, she could stop everything. If she could stop Philippa from saying Geoff was dead, he wouldn't be dead.

Even as it flickered through her mind, she knew it was foolish. Philippa wouldn't tell her Geoff was dead unless she was certain, and punching the person who pitied her wouldn't bring her son back. It would probably get her locked in a cell.

Jeanne couldn't feel her body, but she could hear herself breathing—too hard and too fast. Pieter wrapped his arms around her from behind to hold her up, and she clutched onto his arms as if he could anchor her to this world.

"I haven't heard from them in so long." Jeanne's voice was small, missing its usual power. "They said not to write because they were under house arrest. When did they break free? Do you know when Geoff joined Edward's forces—or was it Joanna he aligned himself with?"

Philippa's eyes widened. "Oh, Jeanne, you didn't know? Geoff wasn't fighting *with* Edward and Joanna; he was fighting on the side of the duke."

## CHAPTER 53
# THE ENGLISH CHANNEL

It took two days for Jeanne to gather her men and take to the Channel, slicing through the water toward France as fast as the cogs could go. Two days of pestering Philippa for information she didn't have. Two days of screaming into her pillow at night. Two days of feeling like the world had turned on its head.

Her son was fighting on the duke's side. Her son had been *killed* fighting on the duke's side. It didn't make sense. It couldn't be right. Jeanne's heart screamed and twisted away from the very idea. It couldn't believe Geoff had betrayed her. Wouldn't believe it. Refused to believe it until she saw for herself.

Now Jeanne was racing toward France and her grown-up daughter. Toward answers. Had Louise been in on Geoff's plans? Had she really been under house arrest? Had they turned on their own mother? Or had King Philip found them out and forced their hand? Did Louise need saving? Jeanne couldn't believe she hadn't thought of her adult children right away, hadn't wondered about them at all. She'd been such a fool, thinking their silence meant safety.

THE LIONESS

She leaned on the rail, facing their destination, willing the cog to go faster. She'd never missed her Genoese warship quite so badly—if King Philip hadn't sent it to the bottom of the Channel, she could reach Louise twice as fast.

Pieter and Amée leaned along the rail on either side of her, watching her face.

"You've been quiet," Pieter said, soft and fatherly.

"What is there to say?"

"That you're furious, sad, about Geoff. That you're worried about Louise."

"You already know that," Jeanne snapped.

"Sometimes it helps to say things out loud."

"Saying I'm sad won't get us to Louise any faster. Telling you how I want to rip out Charles' fingernails one by one won't bring Geoff back."

Pieter went quiet.

"What will you do when we get there?" Amée whispered.

"Depends what we find."

Jeanne couldn't bring herself to give voice to the various scenarios that stabbed at her gut. The thought that maybe Louise had turned against her. Or that Louise was being held against her will, cold and half-starved and hurt in a cell. And the one she wished she could scrub from her mind —that Louise might also be dead.

*Louise. Louise. Louise.* Jeanne's horse's hoofbeats kept time with the refrain in her head. She could see Châteaubriant in the distance—the thick green trees of summer standing sentry around it, its stone walls mottled cream and brown, rooftops gray but seeming almost blue against the clear blue sky.

Jeanne's scouts had ridden ahead and came back reporting no sign of the king's army, just the usual soldiers at the gate and along the wall.

"Perhaps you should go in disguise," Amée suggested. "Or send a messenger in case it's a trap?"

But Jeanne's patience, which was limited to begin with, had been exhausted by the journey, by the news of Geoff's death, by the unending questions about what had happened. She had none left for subterfuge. This time, she would march right up to the gate, fully herself, completely recognizable. And if Louise had indeed betrayed her...well, she supposed this would be the end of it.

She took two men with her—both stout English fighters who didn't understand a word of French between them—but left Amée and Pieter behind. It was reckless, but if Louise was now her enemy, she couldn't put them at risk. She'd face her daughter with a guard of two men she cared nothing for. That was how it had to be.

And so, as her horse's hooves pounded out her daughter's name, Jeanne forced herself not to cry. She was appalled that she even wanted to. Her fists clenched so tight on the reins, the leather cut grooves into her palms, and when she reached the gate, she shouted, "Tell Louise that her mother is here."

The sour-faced gateman grunted and showed his yellowed teeth. "Lady of the castle said to turn ye away if you ever came calling. So turn 'round, lady pirate. Go back to the sea yer so fond of."

Jeanne held back her fury. How dare this guard deny her access to the last living child from her first marriage? She wished she'd brought a grappling hook from the ship to

# THE LIONESS

throw up to his perch and yank him down. And if he survived the fall, she'd claw out his eyes with her bare hands.

"Let me in, sir, or I'll have your head."

"I dunna answer to ye. I answer to the lady of the castle, and she says go back where ye came from."

Jeanne guided her horse closer and savagely kicked the wooden gate. "You won't tell her I'm here?" she asked, incredulous.

"She already gave 'er orders. No need to trouble 'er now."

"Well then, I suppose you'll just have to tell her that this gate is blocked from all entry and exit until she deigns to see her mother." Jeanne drew her sword and was satisfied to hear her two guards drawing theirs beside her, ready for whatever fight she dared pick.

The gateman's smirk faltered.

"I'm staying here until I see my daughter or I die," Jeanne said, her voice a warning. "And if anyone attacks me, you're the first person I'm going to kill. I might not make it in a battle, but neither will you. Go tell that to your mistress."

The man's eyes narrowed, and he turned to speak with someone out of sight.

Jeanne backed her horse away and settled in to wait. If they thought she'd leave so easily, they'd vastly misunderstood her. If Louise was alive and well and in control here, she'd have to tell Jeanne herself that she wanted her gone. And if she wasn't, Jeanne was not going to let them fool her into leaving.

FIVE HOURS LATER, when they must have realized Jeanne wasn't going away, the gateman called down to say Louise would see her now. The gate opened maddeningly slowly, but finally—*finally*—Jeanne and her men were through. They left their horses inside the walls and strode into the hall where Louise was standing as usual, her foot tapping with either impatience or nerves.

*God's nails*, it was her. She wasn't dead. She wasn't under house arrest being held at knifepoint. Relief quenched Jeanne's fear like cold water, but it was followed quickly by dread—if Louise wasn't in danger, it meant turning Jeanne away at the gate had been her idea.

If Louise wasn't in danger, then Jeanne was.

When Louise spoke, her voice was an octave too high. "What do you want, Maman?"

"What do I want?" Jeanne's incredulity returned. "I thought you were in danger! I came to make sure you were alright."

"And now you have, and I'm fine, so you can leave."

"Louise! What's wrong with you? Tell me what happened. Why was Geoff at the battle of La Roche-Derrien? Why are you turning me away? Explain yourself!"

"Maman, if you don't leave, the king is going to find out and it'll ruin everything!" Louise's face pinched. "You're so selfish; you only think of what *you* want. But what about us? Geoff wanted to be remembered, to have a place at the duke's side. Me? I want to be secure, to be part of this France—a France I believe in. We joined the duke's fight because we matter just as much as you!"

Jeanne couldn't believe what she was hearing. "Of course you matter! Everything I do, I do for you! For us! For my family! The king and the duke don't care about you, Louise. They let Geoff give his life for nothing, and they'll trade you into some marriage that benefits only them. You've been taken for a fool!"

Louise's volume rose to match her mother's, her shouts echoing in the cold stone hall. "I've arranged my own marriage, thank you very much. It's a fortuitous match that wouldn't have been possible without Geoff's sacrifice. He stood by me when you didn't. You make the king and the duke out to be such villains, but have you looked in the mirror lately? They say you've killed a thousand men by your own hand. A thousand *French* men. A thousand of your countrymen for some fool English king who thinks he can rule over us better than Philip? You've lost your way, Maman, but that's not my problem, and I will not give up my life for it!"

Louise had always been Jeanne's most difficult child—the one who knew which thread would unravel her calm, the one she couldn't reason with or control. But this was beyond what she'd ever imagined.

Louise thought her mother was a monster and a fool. She and Geoff had betrayed her. They had sided with Philip and Charles.

Was this it, then? Was this Jeanne's reward for loving her family so fiercely? For fighting for their honor, their memories, their lives? For throwing every weapon she had at the men who'd killed her husband and her son? She'd fought with every fiber of her being, and now her oldest children had embraced the very thing she'd been fighting against.

"Louise, please, you have to see reason. Philip killed Olivier without cause and without a trial. Do you think he'll give you more consideration on the day he casually decides you've betrayed him?"

"From what I've heard," Louise snarled, "Olivier was

guilty as sin. It's the king's prerogative to skip the trial. He's not the fiend you think, just a man who outsmarted your villain of a husband."

The words were like a physical blow. So there it was—Louise didn't believe her. Didn't understand her. Didn't see that nobles deserved trials because Philip wasn't infallible and shouldn't have the power to simply dispatch whomever he pleased.

Louise trusted a system so broken that it had destroyed her mother's life, and there was nothing Jeanne could do about it. Louise never backed down once she'd set her mind on something. They could scream at each other for another hour, but Jeanne knew with perfect clarity that she'd already lost her.

"You should go, Maman." Louise turned away to stare at the stone wall. "My fiancé, Guy de Laval, won't like to hear that I've seen you and not had you arrested. Go now, before I do."

*Guy de Laval.* One of the duke's most important allies. Louise really knew how to turn the knife. Jeanne's throat burned and tears threatened to spill out as she pushed her chin into the air and marched out, the hall's heavy door slamming behind her with a finality that threatened to snap her in half.

## CHAPTER 54
# BRITTANY, FRANCE

A man had threatened Louise as a child, and Jeanne had killed him. Now another threatened, and Louise was marrying him. The irony was a barb under Jeanne's skin, stabbing, irritating, leaving her rough and raw.

She and her troops had stopped in the forest a half-day's ride away, making a rough camp in a copse of trees. With the archers off in search of game and the swordsmen stoking a small fire, Jeanne pulled Pieter and Amée deeper into the trees for a private word. She explained what had happened at Châteaubriant and was met with identical looks of pity. It made Jeanne want to knock them both over —pity was such a useless emotion; just like sadness, just like grief. Painful yet static. They tore you up inside without changing a damn thing.

Not like anger. Anger was useful, a driving force, an energy that spread through the body and set it ablaze. Anger made men pay. Anger made them remember what they'd done. Anger *changed things*.

"Wipe those looks off your faces. This is not the time for

sadness." Jeanne balled her fists at her waist. "Louise—fool that she is—has made her choice."

"What do we do now?" Amée asked quietly.

"Charles. He's the culprit. He's the target."

Jeanne's rage wrapped around her like a cloak, comforting and hot. Like armor. Like a fire finding its way through the brush. She welcomed it. Without it, she felt naked. Exposed. If all she had was sadness over Louise, over Geoff, over Olivier and Guillaume, she'd be vulnerable to attack. But she had anger, and anger made her strong.

Pieter spoke up. "Except Charles is being held captive in the Tower of Londres. We can't get to him."

"I know that," Jeanne said, irritated. "I know we can't go after Charles without risking our alliance with England, without risking Oli and Little Jeanne. I'm not a fool. And I'm not talking about going after Charles himself. I'm saying he's taken something else from me, so I'm going to take something from him." The pause stretched long between them before she turned to Amée. "What does Charles love above all else?"

She answered immediately, her eyes sparking with an anger and understanding that warmed Jeanne's heart. "The Church."

Pieter seemed to catch her meaning too, but he looked uneasy. "What are you planning?"

"Charles is the patron of a good dozen churches in central Brittany, and last I heard, one was installing a stained-glass window in his honor. I say we burn it to the damn ground. He attacks my children; I'll attack his god."

Amée's eyes narrowed dangerously, and Jeanne smiled at her. When it came to Charles, they were aligned. Always, ever aligned. Pieter was another story, though.

"Do you really want to make an enemy of the Church?"

THE LIONESS

Jeanne made an annoyed noise—the man should have been a damn diplomat. "Pieter, the Pope doesn't send cease and desist letters to people he supports. The Church already hates me. Charles has their favor with his rock-filled shoes and his twice-daily masses and his habit of dragging dying soldiers into chapels for last rites instead of treating their damn wounds."

She spat on the ground. "Let's show them what it means to align themselves with a man like that. I can't get to Charles, but I *can* send a message. And the only way to get it to him—to make him feel as helpless as he should—is if I send it with fire. I'll melt that stained-glass window in an inferno."

What she didn't say was that she wanted him to feel helpless because *she* felt helpless. Helpless as Louise chose to align herself with unpredictable and untrustworthy men. Helpless knowing Geoff was gone, and she wouldn't even be invited to the funeral. Helpless knowing Charles was in captivity but had somehow become even more infuriatingly untouchable.

She didn't have to say it, though—Amée's expression told her that she, at least, understood. Understood what it was to need revenge and find it always, ever out of reach. Understood that if nothing else, the Church had one thing right: justice meant an eye for an eye, a tooth for a tooth, a life for a life. Mercy only belonged where it was deserved.

Pieter—mountain that he was—had always been softer. But he'd come around. He'd stand by them, even if his vision of justice was simpler and less destructive. He'd fight beside them.

He always did.

THE KING HAD BURNED down a nunnery to get to Jeanne, and there was something satisfying about lighting fire to the curtains, the furniture, the scrolls in the duke's favorite Church. Yes, Jeanne was sending the message to Charles, but she hoped Philip felt it too. They were not the only ones capable of burning the sacred. Not the only ones willing to cross the lines that decent society feared to cross.

If the night's darkness was a cloak, Jeanne and Amée were the daggers, cutting the town at its core. The whole place was asleep, dark, still. Clouds obscured the stars, and Amée said that was a good sign—even the sky was on their side.

Amée lit the first fires, and there was a strange reverence in her movements. The lighting was a prayer, a dance, a sleight of hand—Amée the magician, here to disappear the sacred. The church there one moment and gone the next. Now you see your god, now you don't.

Jeanne's movements had less in common with magic and more with her namesake lioness. She ripped tapestries from the wall, toppled candles, and smashed chairs. If only a priest had been there so she could make him watch. Instead, she grabbed a burning chair leg on her way out and used it to mark a J on the fountain opposite the church.

Pieter was waiting for them outside, standing guard but unwilling to participate. "The Church didn't kill Olivier," he'd said. "The Church didn't kill Jehan, Guillaume, or Louis. The *king* is my enemy, and I'd prefer if god wasn't on his side."

Still, he made no move to stop them. Didn't beg them to leave the church alone. And when it was bright and burning, he stood with them and watched until the village began to stir and scream, and people rushed toward the blaze.

THE LIONESS

Jeanne grabbed the first man who came running into the courtyard by the front of his tunic, and she lifted her dagger to his neck. "Tell everyone that this is the work of Charles de Blois. Your blessed saint is no saint at all." His eyes were wide and white in the light of the dancing flames as she shoved him away.

Jeanne followed Pieter and Amée through the maze of the village to the old dirt road where their men waited. She'd expected the fire to fuel her rage. She expected to feel powerful as she mounted her horse and raced for the coast. But instead, her fury—so hot as she'd torn down tapestries and hurled chair legs through that damned stained-glass window—flickered and cooled.

This wasn't what she wanted to be doing, and her heart knew it. What was it Amée had said? How was it justice for Jeanne to throw her life away stabbing at out-of-reach enemies? The question tugged at her as she rode. None of the answers made sense. She *had* to get justice for her family because that's who she was, but Amée was right, as she usually was—justice for Olivier and Guillaume, and for Geoff and Louise, was not justice for Jeanne. If the world cared about justice for Jeanne, she'd be retired in the countryside. She'd be tucked up warm with her family, slipping away for long rides and walks along the fern-draped shores of the river alongside Clisson Castle.

But the world didn't care. If Jeanne wanted justice for those she loved, it required her to make sacrifice after sacrifice. It required choosing their justice over her own.

In the end, it was no kind of choice at all, and the flame Jeanne had nurtured for so long died in her chest, fury replaced with a cold, hard exhaustion and the feeling that even if she succeeded, it wouldn't feel like winning.

## CHAPTER 55

# LONDRES, ENGLAND

When they reached Jeanne's ships, the crew had news—King Edward's siege in Calais had been a success. He was returning to Britain, leaving behind a contingent of men to keep their newly acquired port town. It was another stunning victory for Edward, and another stunning victory for his allies.

Hoping that perhaps the king would be in a generous mood and Jeanne could convince him the time was right to execute Charles, she set sail for Londres. Better a thin hope than the cold doubt she'd been riding with for days.

Upon their arrival, they picked their way past the freshly dug foundations of Edward's college and slipped into the hall where Edward and Philippa stood before three kneeling noblemen. Captives from the siege, Jeanne realized as she slipped to one side for a better view.

The men were white, dark-haired, dark-eyed, and broken, their heads tilted downward, hands tied behind their backs, faces mottled dark with bruises and red from the hall's heat. So this was the nobility that had held off

THE LIONESS

Edward's forces for nearly a year. It was almost humorous how small men looked once they'd been defeated.

Edward's usually cheerful voice was deadly serious, his mouth firm. "I sentence you to execution, to be carried out tomorrow at dawn—"

Philippa cleared her throat. "My love."

She took Edward's hand, and lines of his face softened as he faced her. Jeanne's heart cracked at the sight. The way they looked at each other reminded her of ruling Clisson with Olivier. They were equals, lovers, rulers, a pair knit together by something more than political expediency. Jeanne only knew a few couples like that—their power woven through with tenderness—and she wondered if it would have been like that with Walter. A marriage that started with love but became two people aligned in purposes, ruling their slice of the kingdom together.

Philippa was speaking again, and Jeanne forced herself to pay attention.

"—did what was right by their king. They didn't fight you out of hate but to try to save their home. We'd do the same. So why not ransom them back to France? Why not show the mercy we're known for? It can only strengthen our position both here and in France."

The longing in Jeanne's chest turned cold. These were King Philip's men. Enemies. They deserved death. She gritted her teeth and closed her eyes. Philippa was strong— a woman who'd led armies to crush Scottish rebellion while Edward was away—and Jeanne couldn't understand why she was granting mercy all over the place instead of grinding her enemies into dust. In her place, Jeanne would behead them herself.

But Edward clearly saw things differently. He lifted a

341

hand to his wife's cheek and said, "Of course, you're right. Showing mercy now might buy us our own men later...and some goodwill from the French nobility when at last we take the throne from Philip for ourselves." He motioned to the silent noblemen. "You will be kept in the dungeons until we can ransom you back to your countrymen. Take them away."

Jeanne held back a frustrated sigh. This probably wasn't the best time to ask about executing Charles. She'd have to wait. Perhaps if she could get Edward alone and leave Philippa out of it she'd be able to—

Her thoughts were interrupted by a pair of lean muscled arms that wrapped around her from behind. She turned, hand going for her dagger. Until she saw the face attached to those arms and her body relaxed. *Walter*. Bright-eyed, fool-grinning Walter. He took her by the shoulders and kissed her, his beard scratching pleasantly on her cheeks and chin.

A warm relief spread through Jeanne. She hadn't realized how much she missed him, had forgotten how good it felt to have him pressed against her. His nearness chipped away some small fearful part of her that was always expecting the next bout of terrible news.

But Walter was here, alive, warm, and well. Strong as he pulled her close and buried his face in her hair. The tenderness of it drew Jeanne's doubts back to the surface. What was justice for her if not staying here in Walter's arms?

She'd lost track of what was happening in the hall, but a collective intake of awed breath pulled her attention back. Two men in fine clothes knelt before the king and queen, presenting themselves while a spokesman's voice echoed through the room.

"Sires, these men are the ambassadors from Flanders

come to negotiate new trade treaties with your highnesses."

Jeanne listened with interest. Flanders was one of the few regions of France that refused to let King Philip trample them down. The men were both nobles, both with knighthoods, and both from families whose names Jeanne had previously heard cursed by Charles. They'd been barbs in the side of Philip and the duke for years. Jeanne felt an immediate kinship with them.

Albyn, the younger of the two, was short and broad-shouldered with a small red birthmark at the corner of his right eye, stark against his white skin. Gillis was older, his skin tawny, his black hair peppered with gray that matched his eyes.

When he turned and caught Jeanne's eye, he looked delighted to see her. She wondered if it was a poor attempt at flirtation or if he knew who she was. God, she hoped for the latter. If so, maybe the delight on his face meant another ally, more information, a way to get to Philip and end all of their suffering. Some way to finish this and crawl into Walter's arms and never leave again.

~

IT WAS LATE when a soft knock sounded at her door, and Jeanne's slyest smile quirked upward at the corner of her mouth. She knew who it would be, and her body hummed with the excitement of it.

Walter had spent all evening in strategy meetings with Edward—so much nearer than usual yet still out of Jeanne's reach. Now, he must finally have finished. She ran a hand through her hair, reveled another moment in the heat flushing across her skin, and opened the door.

"It's about time—"

The words ended abruptly as a man in a black mask shoved her backward onto the floor, stepped into the room, and closed the door behind him. Jeanne struggled to catch her breath. *God's nails*, what was this? Her hand instinctively went to the dagger at her thigh, but it wasn't there—she'd expected a visitor who'd prefer her thighs danger-free. *Merde*. Had she killed herself with her desire?

The intruder drew a dagger that shone in the room's candlelight. With no weapon of her own, Jeanne made the split-second decision to play up her weakness. If he thought this was going to be easy, perhaps he'd make a mistake, give an arrogant speech like a child, buy her enough time to gain the upper hand.

He stepped toward her, and she curled her feet away from him. Interpreting the movement as fearful, his eyes—the one thing visible through his mask—crinkled with a smile. There was a small red birthmark at the corner of the right eye, and Jeanne's memory sparked with recognition—it was the young broad-shouldered ambassador from Flanders.

Damn.

Albyn took another step forward, and Jeanne kicked out with all the force she could muster from her prone position, smashing her heels into his kneecaps and marveling at the loud pops and the quiet scream. The force of it pushed her backward, and she used the momentum to flip her feet over her head and roll up onto her knees.

The man had fallen to his own knees and was gripping his dagger hard, breathing harder. Jeanne's dagger was hanging from a bedpost behind her, but reaching for it would only give Albyn time to throw his, so she did the exact opposite of what she thought he'd expect—she launched herself at him. She aimed her kick for his knife hand's wrist, and he lost his grip on the blade. It skittered across the floor.

And then—just like the last time Jeanne had faced down an attacker alone in her chambers—Monster flew out of hiding and attacked him, all claws and teeth and spitting noises. Albyn threw up his hands to protect his face, and Jeanne took the opportunity to land a kick to his stomach. As he launched backwards, he twisted himself to land on his front instead of his back. He scrambled to his feet between Jeanne and the door, but instead of continuing to fight, to keep her from running and sounding an alarm, he turned and made for the exit himself.

Jeanne whipped around to grab her dagger and rushed after him, planning to throw it at his retreating figure. But then the man was back, filling the doorway. In a flash, Jeanne changed her grip, turning the dagger in her hand ready to strike—

"Whoa, stop!"

She stopped just in time, realizing the man in her doorway wasn't the masked assailant. As Walter placed his warm hands on her shoulders, the adrenaline fled Jeanne's body. All she could feel was a pounding headache, soreness in her tailbone where she'd fallen, and the throbbing in her feet where she'd kicked the man again and again.

Walter searched her face. "What happened?"

"Assassin," Jeanne croaked, her throat dry.

His face went ghostly white. "Guards!" he shouted into the hallway. "Guards!"

They arrived moments later, and Walter sent them to search the castle. Then, he led Jeanne back into the room and closed the door. "Tell me what happened."

"It was the ambassador. Albyn. He's the shorter one, the

broad-shouldered one with that red mark by his eye. He tried to kill me."

*Merde.* Only hours before, Jeanne had felt such kinship with that man. She'd even hoped to ally with him. Could she possibly feel more foolish? She'd let her guard down, and yet again a man had immediately tried to take something from her. Who was Albyn really—was he a Flemish ambassador who'd been bought, or was he an imposter? And what of his colleague?

A strong knock sounded at the door and Walter answered, his sword drawn. But it was only the guards, back to report that they'd found no trace of Jeanne's attacker.

"It was Albyn of Flanders—the ambassador." Walter's voice was steady. "Arrest him at once."

Looking concerned, the guard shifted on his feet. "Sir?"

"You heard me."

"Sir, we can't arrest an ambassador without King Edward's orders."

"Then wake him and get them."

"I'm sorry, sir," the guard said, "but he isn't to be woken unless there's a threat to his own life. We haven't found anyone in the halls, and the lady Clisson seems unharmed. The king will want to wait until morning to address this."

Walter growled in frustration and opened his mouth to argue, but Jeanne interrupted him.

"We understand." The pounding in her head had dulled any rage or sense of unfairness she had left. "We'll see the king when he rises."

In a low voice, Walter said, "At least post an additional guard in the hall to keep Lady Clisson safe for the rest of the night."

"Post extra guards for Arley and Pieter too," Jeanne

added. "And can you please send a servant to bring me some water?"

The guard looked from her to Walter and back again and nodded his assent, and a minute later, a servant girl arrived with the water. The relief of it was stunning—Jeanne's throat cooled and the pounding in her head softened.

Once they were finally alone, Walter wrapped Jeanne in his arms. "Are you hurt?"

"Only sore."

"I can't believe they won't wake the king. By the time the sun rises, those traitors could be long gone!" Walter began to pace. "I should take care of the ambassador myself. Drag him out of his rooms and kill him."

His voice was fire, and it warmed Jeanne to hear it. She knew what it was to carry such passion and fierce protectiveness for someone, but she wasn't sure she'd ever felt it so acutely directed at her before.

Under normal circumstances, she would have joined him in his rage, but something about the fight had left her barely able to keep her eyes open. Adrenaline gone, all that was left was exhaustion. So she put a calming hand on his arm, blew out the nearest candle, and curled up on the bed. Walter climbed in beside her and wrapped himself around her, warm and strong and safe.

"You don't have to stay," she said, even though she desperately wanted him to.

"Are you serious? You've just been attacked. I'm going to protect you."

Despite her exhaustion, Jeanne's irritation welled. "I don't need your protection."

Walter paused, and when he spoke again, she could hear his smile. "Alright, so you protect me then. I don't want to be alone in my chambers with killers lurking in the castle."

That was more like it. Jeanne murmured her assent, and with the fight draining her of everything except the will to sleep, she slept.

## CHAPTER 56
# WINDSOR CASTLE, ENGLAND

"There's a traitor among us, Your Majesty" Jeanne's voice was steel, cutting through the packed hall where she'd called for an emergency audience with the king.

Philippa and Edward were perched on their thrones, both richly arrayed and looking well rested. Pieter and Amée stood off to the side, both just woken and seeming uncertain, while Walter was at Jeanne's elbow in the center of the hall. A crowd of nobles, guards, and servants formed a ring around the room, and among them, the two so-called ambassadors.

"This man"—Jeanne pointed at Albyn, who was favoring one knee—"attacked me in my chambers last night. Sir, account for your crime."

The hall went quiet. Edward and Philippa both raised their eyebrows and looked at the ambassadors. Albyn attempted to appear surprised, but Jeanne thought his mouth hung open for too long to be convincing.

The older man, Gillis, stepped forward looking furious. "How dare you accuse my cousin like this!" he shouted.

349

"Now calm down, everyone." Edward lifted a hand. "Jeanne, this is a serious accusation. What proof do you have?"

Proof? Jeanne was taken aback. "Sire, I'm telling you that this man attacked me. He came into my chambers with a dagger, threw me to the ground, and would have murdered me in cold blood had I not kicked out his kneecap and ruined his plan."

"And you're sure it was him? The room was lit? You were fully awake? You saw his face?" Gillis' questions dripped with disdain.

"The candles were lit. I was awake. He was wearing a mask, but he had the same build, same movements, same mark beside his eye. It was him."

"Oh? So why didn't you detain him? Why not call the guards? If there was an attack, I imagine the whole castle would have known about it right away when it happened, not calmly in the light of morning." Gillis gave the king a look as though they were long-suffering brothers, burdened by false accusations.

"How dare you?" Jeanne's temper was hot and her volume higher than it should be. "We did call the guards. They posted extra sentries. We asked them to wake the king and were told to wait until morning. And if I say I was attacked, I was attacked! Ask your colleague to account for his whereabouts!"

"Albyn?" Gillis asked, his tone longsuffering, the answer —in his mind—clearly a foregone conclusion.

The younger man addressed the king directly, his voice a mockery of pity. "Sire, you cannot believe I would harm any of Your Majesty's allies. Flanders has been on your side since the beginning of this mess, and we are here to nego-tiate a new treaty. Why would we turn on you now? This

## THE LIONESS

woman"—he motioned toward Jeanne—"is gravely mistaken, and I'm very sorry for her, but I did not do such a terrible thing."

"Then why are you limping, sir?" Jeanne shouted. "Yesterday you walked with confidence, yet today your knee can't hold your own weight, because I kicked it out last night when you attacked me!"

Gillis laughed. "Oh, m'lady, I assure you Albyn has had knee troubles on and off for many years, I believe following a fall from his horse. It's not from an attack by a *woman*."

The emphasis on the last word made Jeanne want to end him right then and there. Instead she turned to King Edward, war in her eyes. He looked concerned but said nothing.

Gillis went on, now addressing the whole crowd. "Are we supposed to believe she fought off an attacker without receiving a single scratch? Look at her—no bruises, no cuts, no limp." He smirked at Jeanne. "Does this mean the rumors are true? You've sold your soul to the devil in exchange for immortality? Do you also drink blood and send a black cat out to collect the spirits of your enemies?"

Laughter rippled through the court, and Jeanne's anger pounded in her ears. *They didn't believe her.* None of them, the hedge-born fools. She'd brought so many men to their knees, and this lot still thought she was a joke, a myth, something blown out of proportion. Nothing to fear. Nothing to listen to.

"How. Dare. You," she said through gritted teeth, going for her dagger.

But Walter pushed her hand away, his strength a warning—she wasn't thinking straight. She couldn't draw a weapon on them here.

"Your Highnesses, please. I saw Jeanne right after the

attack, and this isn't something you should take lightly." He glanced pointedly at Albyn. "We may all be in danger here if there's a traitor in our midst."

"This is true." Philippa spoke for the first time, her words measured. "The matter is serious, and the court would do well to keep its jokes to itself."

The leftover tittering laughter ceased, but it only left Jeanne even more enraged. The person in the room who'd silenced them was Philippa, not Jeanne. They still didn't believe *her*.

Gillis spread his hands expressively and bowed in Philippa's direction. "Sires, this woman probably just had a bad dream. We've all seen hysterics like it before, I'm sure. But *if* she was attacked—though she certainly *looks* well enough to me—she's already admitted that she didn't see the attacker's face, so I can't imagine how you could believe it was Albyn, a fine young man and your ally his whole life."

Philippa and Edward exchanged a significant glance, leaned in for a whispered consult, then faced the court again.

"Jeanne," Edward said, "I'm sorry for what happened to you. We'll keep an additional guard on you at night until we resolve this. Monsieurs Albyn and Gillis, I hear you, and I agree that we cannot convict you without proof, but these are serious accusations. Therefore, we will convene tomorrow for a trial. Jeanne, please gather any evidence you have."

With that, the audience was dismissed, and people scattered in every direction. Gillis helped a hobbling Albyn from the room, his words floating back to Jeanne. She wondered if he'd meant them to.

"See?" he said, triumphant. "They won't do a thing to you without proof—and she has none."

Jeanne's skin flushed and her dagger's hilt dug into her clenched palm. She might have misjudged the king—thought he'd take her side, imagined the assassin would be dispatched from the world by nightfall—but they'd all misjudged her too. The court might not do anything, but she had never been afraid of doing things her damn self.

"I KNOW WHAT YOU'RE THINKING." Pieter caught up to her as she flung open the doors to the garden and stomped out onto the grounds.

Amée was close behind him and Monster, who'd appeared seemingly from thin air, leaped onto her shoulder, curling herself around her neck like a furry black shawl. Despite her anger, the sight made Jeanne want to laugh. She loved that damn devil-cat and was glad she'd made it through another attack unscathed.

"Jeanne, are you listening to me?" Pieter took her arm and turned her toward him. "You can't kill him."

"Who said I was planning to?"

Pieter rolled his eyes. "I've known you for a long time. I know your..." He paused, searching for the right words. "Your war face."

Amée snorted.

"Pieter, I do not have a *war face*," Jeanne said with a sigh. "This is my normal face. No—this is my furious face, and you're familiar with it because the world is a damn mess. And because you're currently making me furious. So make your point and be done with it."

"I already made my point—you can't kill him. Flanders is an important ally for England, for us. Not to mention that King Edward is the protector of your children, so if nothing else, harming that man would put them in danger of being turned out. Please, don't do it."

"Stop treating me like a fool," Jeanne snapped. "I would never put Oli and Little Jeanne's safety at risk. Now leave me alone. I want to walk in the garden."

She waved her hand to dismiss him and continued her stomp across the grounds. Pieter was right—about her intentions and about the risks. But he was wrong to think she couldn't have both safety for her children and revenge on the man who'd tried to end her life. She *could* have both. She *would* have both. She might not be able to get to the king who'd sent him, but she wasn't going to let a man in his employ live through another night just a few chambers away from her own.

"Pieter's right, you know." Amée slipped into Jeanne's rooms with Monster at her heels, closing the door behind her. "You shouldn't kill that man."

Jeanne sighed. *Merde.* Another lecture.

"But if someone *were* going to kill him," Amée continued, "they'd need to hide the body. If the court demands evidence of crimes...well, no body means no death. For all they'd know, he was guilty as sin and fled rather than face trial." She shrugged, a slight smile playing at the corners of her mouth.

Jeanne laughed out loud. So Amée wasn't here to lecture her after all—she was here to give advice. And if the woman who'd terrified men with ravens and suggested she dye her sails red was giving advice without trying to deter her, then Jeanne would listen.

"Where might one hide a body?" She motioned for Amée to go on.

Without hesitation, Amée said, "The foundations of the new college. Where better for a corrupt man to rest than under a corrupt church?"

Jeanne nodded.

"And if someone perhaps wanted to find out the truth before taking him out, this little pouch of herbs"—Amée lifted a small bundle in the air—"would incapacitate him without keeping him from speaking.

"Of course guards could be a problem, but there *might* be a convenient distraction in the corridor to draw them away when the moon reaches her peak. There *might* be some former street children in the kitchen who owe me a favor for getting them their positions, and they *might* already have a collection of rats to set loose."

Amée's teasing tone turned serious. "All you have to do is say the word, Jeanne, and I'll make sure these herbs make it into his nightly glass of wine. I often wander around the kitchens when we're here at the castle, so no one will think it's odd."

"Do it," Jeanne whispered. Her body hummed with the power of what she was about to do. What *they* were about to do. Justice never came easy, but she was going to take it. "But why are you helping? I thought you were against this, like Pieter."

Amée's expression was somber. "He's not wrong; it's an enormous risk. But any man who attacks a woman deserves to die. If you are going to do it, though, it has to be perfect —otherwise Pieter's ominous warnings will become prophesies."

## CHAPTER 57
# WINDSOR CASTLE, ENGLAND

"How's your knee?" Jeanne's voice was the barest whisper in the dark room.

The man jerked awake and then froze, feeling the dagger at his throat.

Jeanne purred. "Mmm, I wouldn't make any sudden movements. Or make any noises. Or I might. Just." She pressed the dagger harder, drawing the barest amount of blood. "Slip."

His eyes darted frantically, and his breathing came faster. An empty wine glass lay tipped over on the floor, lit by the moonlight beaming in through a window to the left of the bed on which Jeanne straddled the man, pinning his arms.

"Now you're going to tell me who you are," she said, her voice menacing.

"Albyn de Flanders," he whispered. "I'm an ambassador—"

"Liar. If you're an ambassador, you're one who's been bought. Or has Flanders turned on us?"

THE LIONESS

He nervously licked his lips. "If I tell you the truth, you'll let me go?"

Why did men always think she'd be so easy to move toward mercy, even after proving over and over that she was not the merciful Clisson? They kept mistaking her for the Philippas of the world.

Jeanne smiled, tried to look compassionate. "Yes, you can go if you never return."

If Albyn could move, she was sure he would have nodded. As it was, the truth flooded out in a rushed whisper. "We're not Flemish. We attacked the ambassadors and took their ship, their clothes, their official papers. King Philip sent us here to dispatch you...and the English king if we could get to him. He wants an end to the war. You can understand that, can't you?"

Jeanne made a noncommittal noise. Why did they always think she'd understand? "What else?"

"The Black Knight—the one who travels with you—we're to kill him too. Since the first attempt was foiled, Gillis' new plan is to poison you both."

Fear stabbed at Jeanne. "Poison us how? When?"

"Tonight, with the wine in your rooms." Albyn sucked in a breath as Jeanne pressed too hard on the dagger.

*Pieter.* If the wine was poisoned, he might already be dead or dying. Jeanne hadn't poured herself a glass because she'd wanted to be clear-headed for this. But Pieter could be pouring a glass even now. Jeanne's stomach lurched at the possibility. She hadn't considered that he might be in danger—she'd been too consumed with keeping her plans from him in order to avoid another fight.

Albyn might have had more information, but Jeanne had no more time. She needed to finish this and get to

357

Pieter. Her intentions were to be careful—strangle him so that he didn't bleed, use the rope she'd brought along to lower him out the window and into a cart. From there, she'd wheel him to the chapel's construction site to bury him in a shallow grave. Instead, she plunged her dagger into his windpipe, cutting off his life and any scream he might have let out. Speed was more important now than stealth.

She would have to leave the body here and hope no one discovered it before she got back. Why couldn't her plans go smoothly for once?

Once Albyn stopped shuddering, Jeanne lifted herself off him and cracked open the door to see if any guards were about. No one was in sight, so she stepped into the hall. Out of nowhere, a small shape barreled into her, pushing her back inside the room. Jeanne reached for her dagger before realizing it was Amée.

She pressing the door closed with her back and stared at Jeanne in horror. "What are you doing?"

"It's Pieter—the ambassadors poisoned the wine in his room. We have to get to him before he has a drink!" She started for the door again, annoyed that Amée was wasting precious time making her explain, but Amée put up a hand to stop her.

"You can't go like that, Jeanne. *Look at yourself!* Your dress is covered in blood. I'll go. You stay here and clean up."

Jeanne startled and looked down at her stolen servant's clothes. *Merde*, how could she have almost marched into the halls like this? Hard to feign innocence when she was dripping blood. It was fear—another useless emotion. Fear made her foolish.

Amée left the room as quiet as a whisper, and Jeanne stepped back to the bed to deal with the mess. She pulled up the corners of the blankets to wrap around Albyn's body, grabbed the rope, and used it to bind the blankets around his ankles, waist, and neck. *Merde*, she thought as she tried to drag him toward the window. He was too heavy.

She almost laughed. She'd killed so many men in her life, but the only time she'd tried to move a corpse herself was Roland. This man was much smaller, but just as immovable. What a fool she was, thinking she'd be able to carry him herself. It was like death had stuffed him full of stones.

*Death.* She thought of Pieter then, with a jolt. Amée had been gone too long. Had she been too late? Had the king taken yet another loved one from Jeanne? Would she have anyone left by the end of this? Her stomach turned—she needed to go after Amée, see for herself whether Pieter was safe.

She stripped off the bloody dress and the almost-as-bloody linen underdress, using their dry backsides to wipe her face and neck before throwing them into Albyn's fireplace. Though she wrinkled her nose at the thought of sharing his water, she plunged her hands into his wash basin and scrubbed her skin with a wet cloth until what was left of the blood could pass for a rosy flush. The cloth followed the dresses into the fire.

Wearing Albyn's clothes was even worse than washing in his water. Strong-smelling, still damp with old sweat, and too large for her frame. But she had to get to Pieter, and Albyn's horrible clothes were preferable to flying through the halls of the castle naked, so she fought the instinct to rip them off and headed for the door.

It opened before she got there, and in walked Amée, followed by Pieter and Walter—the former irritated, the latter looking bewildered.

"Pieter," Jeanne breathed his name, and the tightness in her chest eased.

"What have you done?" Pieter's response was strained. "I thought we talked about this."

The unfairness of his words left a bitter taste in her throat. "He was going to kill us both! I just saved your life."

Walter craned his head to peer around Jeanne at the tightly wrapped bundle on the bed. "Is that what I think it is?"

Jeanne narrowed her eyes at him and balled her fists on her hips. "Don't you lecture me too. I interrogated him and found out they'd poisoned our wine. Pieter and I were to die tonight. They're imposters, not the ambassadors. We're only safe because Amée and I took matters into our own hands."

Walter glanced at Amée, then back at Jeanne, and he raised his hands in supplication. "No lecture; I'm just catching up. Amée didn't have time to explain when she came to my rooms."

"This is a bad time to fight," Amée broke in. "We need to hide the body, and you"—she handed Jeanne a small bundle—" need less conspicuous clothes."

As if released from a trance, everyone started moving. Pieter and Walter went to the bed, lifting the bound body and using the rope to lower it out the window. Jeanne ripped off Albyn's clothes and kicked them viciously across the floor, pulling on the dress instead. Amée grabbed the discarded clothes, balled them up, and threw them out the window after their owner.

"He would have taken his clothes," she explained at Jeanne's questioning look. "If we want them to believe he ran, we have to bury them with him." "Jeanne." Walter motioned to her. He'd secured the rope to the heavy wooden bed, and Pieter's head was now disappearing through the window. "You next."

Amée nodded. "Go. Once you're all down, I'll untie the rope and drop it to you. You three take care of the body; I'll clean up here."

Jeanne assessed the blood-soaked bed, the trail of blood she'd left from bed to door to basin and back again, and she furrowed her brow. "Won't you need help?"

"The blood's fresh, and the floor's stone. If I get it done quickly, it shouldn't be that hard. The mattress is the real trick, but every herbalist knows which herbs remove blood-stains. I can do this."

"Alright." Jeanne embraced Amée and kissed her hard on the head. "Be careful." And then she was through the window, shimmying down the rope with Walter close behind her. It wasn't unlike climbing the ropes up the mast of her ships for a better view, and she felt comforted by the feel of rough rope on her palms.

When they reached the ground, the rope followed, its end frayed. Clever Amée must have realized it'd be quicker to cut than untie it, and every second they stood around was another second they could be caught. Jeanne's body warmed with a familiar admiration for her friend.

Walter and Pieter hoisted the bundle between them and set it in the waiting gardener's cart—Jeanne had at least planned that far, even if she hadn't understood how heavy the body would be. The walk to the construction site was longer than she expected, but it was late and dark and no one else seemed to be on the grounds. Guards would be at their stations, on the wall, at the gate, guarding Jeanne's currently empty room. And apparently no one else craved a post-midnight stroll.

When they reached the churned-up dirt around the

chapel where the building's extensions were going in, Pieter wordlessly grabbed a shovel and began to dig. Walter and Jeanne followed suit and before long, all three were shining with sweat in the moonlight. There was power in numbers, though, and Jeanne marveled at how fast the hole grew. It wasn't as deep as a normal grave, but workers would soon be piling on more dirt and stone, taking the fake ambassador farther and farther out of reach.

They rolled Albyn in, piled the rope and clothes on top of him, then re-covered the hole with dirt. Pieter carried the leftover shovelfuls to a nearby mound, while Walter used his boots to smooth the top of the impromptu grave. Jeanne wheeled the garden cart over to a group of other carts piled with rocks, transferring some onto hers to make it fit in visually with the rest. There was blood on her cart, but it would be dry in a few hours, and most of the other carts were covered in mystery stains anyway. Jeanne rubbed some dirt on it as an extra precaution, hoping it would go unnoticed.

She set one final rock on the cart and turned to find Walter and Pieter striding her way. Walter took her hand and led them both back to the castle, pulling them into the shadows at the wall.

"We need to get back in without raising suspicion," he whispered. "The guards at the door know me, so I think our best chance is for me to distract them. When I say the word 'wine,' come in and take the hall to the right. It's the fastest way out of sight."

Jeanne and Pieter nodded, and Walter stepped out from the shadows to rap at the door.

It cracked open, and a cranky voice asked, "Who's there at this time of night?"

Walter smiled sheepishly in the other man's torchlight.

"Just out for a stroll, lads. M'lady kicked me out of her chambers, and I needed some fresh air. You know what it's like."

The other man's irritation turned into laughter. "God's nails, man. We've all been there." He pounded Walter on the back and ushered him inside.

"What a night." Walter's voice floated out through the still-open door. "I sure could use a drink. Don't suppose you have any spirits do you, fellas?"

"You know they don't let us keep anything here."

"Aye, pity. Perhaps we could get something and sit and have a drink together? It's not like there's much going on at this time of night."

"I could use a drink," a third voice chimed in.

"Aye," the first said.

"Right, you lads go get your stash, and I'll watch the doors," Walter suggested.

Jeanne marveled at how casual he sounded, how innocent. There was no tension in his voice, no indication that this was subterfuge. Warmth crept across her face and goosebumps rose on her arms and legs—she was going to do such wicked things to that man later tonight.

"Bring some wine if you can," Walter called out softly.

At the word, Jeanne darted out of the shadows, through the door, and into the hall to the right with Pieter hot on her heels. She briefly caught Walter's eye on her way past. He grinned and winked.

WHEN THEY NEARED HER ROOMS, Jeanne waited around the corner while Pieter approached the guards stationed at her door.

"I need a moment alone with her," she heard him say. "If you don't mind stepping away for a few moments? I'll keep her safe."

The guards must have agreed, because their footsteps echoed down the hall. Jeanne was disconcerted and a little angry at how easy it was for someone to get rid of her protection. Granted, this time it was Pieter and Pieter would never mean her harm, but she couldn't imagine Edward would be happy about his guards so readily walking away at anyone's request. Though perhaps, she thought ominously, they were expecting to be asked. Perhaps they'd been bribed to walk away at anyone's request.

As the footsteps faded, Jeanne slipped around the corner and followed Pieter into her room. Amée was already there, sitting in the center of Jeanne's bed with her legs crossed and Monster curled up in her lap purring loudly. Jeanne couldn't wait to tell Amée that her plan—her glorious plan—had worked. She felt powerful. Strong. Capable of anything.

Between Amée's plans, Pieter's strength, and Jeanne's determination, they were finally going to take the king. Jeanne knew it. They'd appear for the sham trial the next morning and set sail the day after. She decided they would break into the castle in Paris again—it had been years since the last time, and Philip must surely have let his guard down by now. This time, there would be no dual purpose. No one to rescue from the dungeons. This time, it would be just Jeanne and the king, and she'd turn him into a corpse. And no matter what went wrong, they'd already proven they could get out of it. If she had Amée and Pieter and Walter at her side, they could do anything. They could end this.

THE LIONESS

But before she could say any of it aloud, Pieter spoke, his voice imbued with an anger she hadn't expected.

"You risked everything tonight, Jeanne."

Her rush of adrenaline gave way to irritation. "As I said before, I *saved* you."

"You couldn't have possibly known that, so don't pretend you did it for me. You did this for you. You did this despite the fact it put your children at risk. Put me at risk. Put Amée at risk." He waved a hand toward the bed, where Amée was holding both hands nervously over her heart. "And for what? Your *pride*. What if you'd been caught? What if Edward imprisoned you? How do you think your children would be treated then?"

"I think Queen Philippa the Merciful would treat them very well indeed." Two could play at this game, and Jeanne's voice went dangerously low. She was tired of Pieter questioning her commitment to her children. Tired of him thinking he knew what was best for everyone.

"Why do you even keep me around if you're never going to listen to me?" he asked, his tone softer now. "Worse, if you're going to lie to me? You put Robine in danger too, you know. By aligning herself with me, she's aligned herself with you, and the more risks you take, the more you expose us all."

Jeanne glanced at Amée who was studiously staring at the cat, staying far away from the conversation.

"Pieter—"

He cut her off. "I can't talk about this now; I'm too angry. We'll talk tomorrow. Sleep well, Jeanne. Amée."

Then he was gone, and Jeanne's certainty—the rush, the elation of taking out the would-be assassin—was gone with him. Jeanne never could just win without a fight.

## CHAPTER 58
# WINDSOR CASTLE, ENGLAND

The hall was full to bursting with nobles, servants, guards, and knights—everyone in the castle wanting to know what would happen with the trial against Ambassador Albyn.

The only thing missing was Albyn himself.

A large knight knelt before the king and gave his report. "We've searched the castle, the grounds, and the town, sires, but there's no sign of him." Murmurs rolled through the gathered crowd, and various theories were shouted out.

"Must have fled during the night!"

"There's the proof—innocent men don't run!"

"But no one saw him go. He must still be hiding somewhere in the castle!"

Edward and Philippa exchanged a look, and Jeanne stifled a smile.

"Well, that tells us something," Philippa said, her normally measured tone tinged with anger.

"It most certainly does not!" The voice echoed through the hall, dripping indignation. Gillis pushed his way to the front of the crowd and came to a stop before the regents.

366

THE LIONESS

"Albyn is missing because she"—he pointed dramatically at Jeanne—"did something to him!"

Jeanne's eyes narrowed. "Your man tried to kill me, then fled like a coward into the night. Don't try to shift the blame."

"This woman falsely accused him, and when none of us believed her fanciful stories, she kidnapped him! There's no other explanation!" Gillis' voice pitched high at the end, and Jeanne shook her head. The fool didn't know he'd already lost.

"Just yesterday you said I couldn't possibly have fought him off," she said. "So which is it? Am I strong enough to kidnap him, or am I too weak to fight off an attack?"

The crowd tittered with a mixture of agreement, amusement, and intrigue. Gillis opened his mouth to speak again, but having heard enough, Philippa put up her hands. "Ambassador Gillis, we'll keep searching for your colleague, and we will find the truth. But the accusation you've made is very grave indeed. Yesterday we asked Jeanne for her proof, and I ask you now for yours."

Gillis' face reddened. "My proof? She accused him and then she disappeared him! It's the only logical explanation."

There was a stir behind Jeanne as Walter weaved his way through to her from the back of the hall. "No, sir, it is not," he said, stopping by her side. "It's perfectly logical to assume Albyn didn't want to face justice for attacking one of England's most trusted allies."

Jeanne was gratified to realize how deftly he'd reminded the royals of her value to them, and how much it mattered that they side with her on this.

"How dare you. How dare all of you!" Gillis shouted, any composure he'd arrived with gone as he shook his fist at the onlookers. "I'm telling you this woman is responsible for Albyn's disappearance!"

"And just yesterday you told us a man couldn't be taken down by a woman—let alone a woman who came out unscathed. As you'll see, Ambassador Gillis, I still don't have a scratch on me." Jeanne's demeanor was ice. Her soul was triumph.

At last, King Edward spoke. His voice boomed through the room, a threat implied by both his words and his tone. "Guards, please escort Ambassador Gillis to his rooms and keep close watch—we wouldn't want his safety compromised." He nodded to Jeanne. "Jeanne, we apologize for doubting your story yesterday."

Jeanne inclined her head and bowed slightly. "Your Highnesses, if you have no further need of me, I think King Philip is feeling too safe on the Channel. My men and I will return there tomorrow."

Edward nodded again, and without another word, Jeanne turned on her toes and marched from the hall, making sure to pass Gillis on her way out. She leaned in close, her parting words a whisper just for him.

"Perhaps you just had a bad dream. We've all seen hysterics like these before."

"Why didn't you simply tell them the men are traitors?" Walter ran his hand along Jeanne's jawline, wrapped a loose curl around a finger. "You could have told them about the poisoned wine, the pirated ship, the stolen identities…"

He'd followed Jeanne to the garden, and they now stood beside a row of perfectly aligned flowers and freshly turned dirt.

"If they didn't believe me yesterday, why would they today?" she asked. "And I can't give them any proof without giving myself away."

"I suppose that's true."

"Anyway, if the king means what he said about having Gillis watched, I doubt he'll be able to make another attempt." Jeanne shrugged. "When we're safely out on the Channel, I'll send word back to Edward that the ambassadors' ship was taken and that the man is an imposter. He can decide what he believes then."

Having won another battle against another small man, Jeanne had gone to the garden triumphant. Strong. But these days, her triumphs felt so fleeting. Where the fire of her anger should have been, instead she found a quiet, empty, exhausted space. She wanted to be defiant and wild. She wanted to hate the king and queen for doubting her. But those feelings slipped through her fingers, and all she could summon was a desire to curl up beside this kind-eyed man and sleep for a year.

"I love that you always wear your hair down," he murmured, twirling the curl around his finger.

She smiled. "Walter, you once asked me to marry you."

His gaze snapped to meet hers. "Yes."

"Do you still feel the same?"

"Without question."

"I'm going to kill the king. He sent assassins for me, and I need to return the favor. This time it's either me or him, and if it's him—if I finally kill him—I'm coming back for you. For us."

Jeanne's tired, hopeful heart reached for Walter, and he answered by pulling her in for a kiss.

"Two years ago, I told you that you can have me whenever you want me, and I'll never change my mind," he said, smiling. "Edward is sending me to the north tomorrow to assess a situation with the Scottish rebels, but I'll be easy to find when you're ready."

Jeanne's heart purred and stretched happily like a cat in the sunshine. She leaned in for another kiss, but the moment was broken by the unmistakable sound of Pieter clearing his throat behind her.

Walter kissed her nose instead, then shook Pieter's hand. "You're well, I hope?"

"As well as I can be under the circumstances."

*Merde.* So Pieter was still upset. Annoyance rippled through her. She'd saved his damn life, but he couldn't get over his bruised ego.

"Jeanne, I came to tell you this will be our last journey together." Pieter's back was straight and his voice formal. "You said you're going after Philip—and I'm coming with you. But after that, no matter what happens, I'm finished."

Despite also feeling like this was their last attempt, something about Pieter's lack of belief in their success stabbed at her like one of those fool hairpins she used to wear. She wasn't sure what to say. *Goodbye? Good luck? Good riddance?* She wished he hadn't said anything. They could have killed Philip and all retired without her ever knowing that he'd been intending to leave her again. Everyone would have had their peace.

Instead...this. Telling her he was going with her one last time felt like unwanted charity. Pity. And he knew how she despised pity.

Before she could find the right words, Pieter spoke again. "Robine is pregnant."

Jeanne's mouth dropped open, and Walter laughed with delight.

"Congratulations!" he cheered. "That's wonderful news!"

And with that, Pieter's formality melted away, and Jeanne realized that he'd been steeling himself for a fight he didn't want. She wondered at her ability to fail to see things that were right in front of her. Pieter's life had always revolved around children. The loss of his own child. Protecting Jeanne and Olivier's brood. Telling Amée he wished he had a daughter like her. Carrying a torch for the memory of that servant boy King Philip had hanged.

Now he was going to be a father again, and, *of course*, he wasn't going to be an absent one. He was here to tell her he was still her friend. He still cared about Olivier. Still cared about justice. But if they failed, he couldn't try again. His fatherly heart wouldn't stand for it.

Jeanne couldn't be angry with Pieter for that—it was who he'd always been. It was like staying mad at the winter for being cold or with the wind for whistling.

She took a deep breath, stood on her tiptoes, and kissed him on the cheek. "Congratulations, Pieter. That child is lucky to have you as its father."

## CHAPTER 59
# THE ENGLISH CHANNEL

I t was a sunny morning on the Channel, only a few days after Jeanne had left Londres, when an English warship sliced through the steel-blue water to come alongside her flagship. The action was a strange one—she and her allies usually just passed each other on the water, sails flapping in the wind like a distant greeting.

As soon as Jeanne sighted the deck, she knew why this time was different.

Sir Walter stood at the rail, his mouth twitching upward at the sight of her loose hair whipping in the wind, her cheeks pink from a rare three consecutive days of sunshine. It was a surprise to see him, but her heart thrilled at the sight. There was something so breathtaking and earnest about him sailing after her.

Unless...

It suddenly occurred to her that he could be coming with bad news. She looked closer—was he smiling, or had she only imagined it? Had the king discovered Albyn's body? She searched her mind for what else it could be. Aside from her children, everyone she loved and hadn't yet lost was here with her. Pieter was napping in the sunshine at the side of the deck, Amée was leaning on the rail watching the English ship's approach, and now Walter was here too, safe as far as she could tell.

No, if something was wrong, it was with either her allies or her children. *God's nails*, please don't let it be the children. When Walter boarded, it was the first thing out of her mouth.

"The children?"

"They're well," he reassured her, pushing a wild strand of hair out of her face.

She exhaled in relief. "What happened to Scotland?"

"I asked Edward to send someone else. This was more important."

So he was here for her. Because he missed her. Or perhaps he'd brought news of the war, some helpful information to get her closer to Philip. With Walter's own ship now slicing back toward the British shore without him, it was clear he was staying. He was coming with her to take out the king, she realized with a flutter in her chest. They were going to end this together.

"I've missed you," he said.

Jeanne flushed at the words, and she leaned in to kiss him softly on the mouth. She smiled through it, her body unknotting itself, tension releasing one muscle at a time.

He pulled back and examined her face, and then he sighed. "As much as I want to stay like this, I'm pretty sure you'll hate me if I don't give you the news right away."

So there *was* news. Jeanne's flush cooled, and she took a deep breath, preparing herself for the inevitable blow or challenge. News that had brought Walter halfway across the Channel probably wasn't good.

"Charles de Blois attempted an escape—"

Jeanne made a strangled noise, but Walter threw up his hands to stop her. "Don't worry, he didn't make it. He's still in captivity. But I thought you'd want to know."

That was it? A failed escape? As long as there wasn't a real one, she didn't see the problem. When she'd first heard about the duke's capture, she'd wanted to kill him herself. Wanted to wipe that smug half-smile off his face once and for all. But since burning down his church, she hadn't even really had the time to think about him, and now she found she didn't care as much. He was defeated, locked in a tower. A prisoner. Jeanne's allies had taken his power and his freedom. And wasn't that exactly what a man like Charles deserved? To suffer knowing he was nothing? Death was too kind for him, she'd decided. This was better.

Her focus had now entirely shifted to the king. She, Pieter, and Amée had talked strategy every night. They'd gotten into the castle as performers once, but they didn't know if the king had figured out that ruse, so they needed a new one. A plan was starting to take shape involving guard uniforms and servants' clothes. They would dock in Brittany the next day and ride for Paris, and now with Walter here, Jeanne had yet another weapon in her arsenal.

Walter was speaking again, but this time his voice was strange, carrying a note of something like triumph. "That was the bad news, and this is the good. Jeanne...are you listening?"

She shook her head to clear the thoughts. "Yes, of course. Good news?"

"King Philip is dead. He's gone."

With those words, Jeanne's world stopped. Walter was squeezing her hands in excitement, but Jeanne barely felt it.

*Gone.*

*King Philip.*

*Dead.*

Her stomach sank, and a familiar boiling rage rose, heating her skin inch by inch. She hadn't felt this kind of fury since learning of Charles' capture, and she didn't understand herself. Didn't she want the king dead? *No*, her body screamed, muscles tensing, blood pounding in her head. *This isn't good news*. It was supposed to be *her* who killed him. Philip was supposed to die knowing and regretting every miserable thing he'd done to her. He was supposed to die slowly and painfully.

"How?" she demanded. "How did he die?"

Walter seemed taken aback. "Natural causes. They say it was in his sleep."

Her breath hissed through gritted teeth. "So he didn't even suffer."

Walter opened then closed his mouth, looking at her with pity, and Jeanne wanted to scream. Didn't he understand? This wasn't how it was meant to go. The king had cut Olivier's body apart—desecrated him—and he'd tried to burn her children alive. But his own death had been quiet. Peaceful, even. Now he'd be honored, mourned, buried wreathed in gold.

Jeanne could picture the court preparing his body as was tradition. Preserving it in vinegar and salt with aromatic spices. Dressing him in gold with a crown on his head, a ring on his finger, and a scepter in one hand. In the other, they'd put the Staff of Justice—ha! Justice. The word stabbed at her like a knife.

Where Olivier had been picked at by birds, his killer would be mourned by wealthy nobles in black hoods. Where her youngest children had almost been reduced to ash, their attempted murderer was being preserved for the resurrection. Where Geoff now rotted in the ground, the king would be wrapped in jewels and finery. They'd probably saint him like they had Charles. For the rest of Jeanne's life, she'd have to listen to fools around her invoking his name as they prayed for good fortune.

She wasn't sure if she wanted to scream, cry, or vomit.

Jeanne's insignificance washed over her. She'd been terrorizing France for years, and for what? They said he trembled at her name, but they also said she commanded a fleet of demons and sent ravens out as spies. For all she knew, the king had lived a fortunate life—blessed by the Church, blessed by the nobles, blessed even in death, afraid of nothing.

The familiar urge to hit something pounded through her, and she smacked her hand against the rail. Walter startled, staring at her wild expression with concern.

"Don't look at me like that!"

"Like what?"

"Like you pity me. Like you think his death is justice. Like you don't understand that a peaceful death is not justice for that man."

"It *is* justice. He's dead, Jeanne. It's what you've wanted for years."

She smacked the rail again, closed her eyes tight. "He died peacefully, Walter. *Peacefully*."

At that exact moment, as if by magic, as if whatever god was out there had heard Jeanne's heart screaming, a voice rang out across the deck. "M'lady! Merchant fleet in the distance!"

Her base desire to hit something had found a target. "Take them," she hissed. "Take the ships and burn them all."

And so another battle began, with the Lioness—wilder than any alive had ever seen her—at its head. Fire in her bones. A storm under her skin. On Amée's command, arrows slung with gunpowder pouches flew onto the merchant decks, followed by flaming arrows and blinding blasts. Jeanne's men hurled jars filled with the alcohol marked not for drinking after them, and as they smashed, the fires spread.

There were no ravens aboard Jeanne's ship, but Monster prowled along its railing, and Pieter stood behind the black cat, a mountain in his black armor, the Black Knight of myth. Standing behind Pieter, Sir Walter was less intimidating but just as deadly. The enemy sailors watched in horror, scrambling to put out fires as they approached.

Jeanne screamed like a banshee as she flew across the gap and onto the nearest merchant vessel, not even waiting for the grapples to latch on first.

CHAPTER 60

# THE ENGLISH CHANNEL

I t was the fiercest Jeanne had fought in years. She was a storm, a fire, rage made flesh. The fury that had recently been slipping through her fingers instead enveloped her as she cut down man after man. Her focus was perfect, her methods reckless. Swords narrowly missed her. Men hit her with their fists, and she barely felt it. An arrow pierced her arm and went straight through. It was nothing. A pin-prick. Her anger rose and pushed back the pain.

The largest, heaviest fighter onboard had already taken down two of Jeanne's men when she turned to face him. Muscles bulged tight under his scarred mottled-red skin. A single eye glared at her from a face that had clearly been hit one too many times. Nose broken. Ears curled in on themselves. A man that was hard to kill. Many, his face told her, had tried and failed.

He brought his sword down. Jeanne sidestepped, but before she could swing her own sword up, the mountainous man had hooked his free hand around her skirts and thrown her heavily to the deck.

378

Cold fear stabbed through her hot rage. Was this it? King Philip was dead, and now Jeanne would follow him to hell and continue tormenting him there? There was something almost funny about the idea. Something almost fitting.

For a moment, Jeanne was ready to embrace it, but then she saw Walter trying to reach her, and her acceptance flickered back into fear. She didn't want to die. She wanted him. She wanted to see her children again.

The fighter triumphantly raised his blade for a finishing blow, and Jeanne tried to get her feet beneath her, to spring away. But she was trapped, his boot on her skirts. As his sword plunged toward her, all she could think was that if she was going down, he was going with her. She'd be the woman who killed the unkillable man. Her fist closed over an unexploded pouch of gunpowder, finger looping around the twine that held it closed, and then she whipped it up, the powder flying free and straight into the man's face.

He screamed, but the sword didn't slow. Whether Jeanne wanted to or not, she was following Philip into hell.

Then her vision was shining and black. Black armor standing over her, protecting her. Pieter taking the blow on his own sword, his equally mountain-like size absorbing it easily. And then he was pushing the brute backward and Jeanne was on her feet again, her instincts still swift, punching her dagger into the now-blinded man's side and dancing away as Pieter brought his own dagger up to his throat.

"Were you trying to kill yourself?"

Jeanne had never heard Amée's voice so high-pitched,

so poorly controlled. They were in her dimly lit cabin, Jeanne seated on a chair while Amée attempted to clean the arrow wound in her arm and pack it with herbs. Pieter leaned against the doorframe, while Walter stood in between them, looking lost.

Amée's skin was hot against Jeanne's, her movements jittery, agitated. "What is wrong with you?"

"The king," Walter said. "I told her the king is dead."

Amée froze, her face drawn with an understanding Jeanne hadn't expected. *Charles*, she realized. Amée understood because of Charles. She knew what it was like to watch an enemy slip through her fingers. Knew what it was like for him to be out of reach. Knew what it was like to be denied the satisfaction of watching him die.

"I wanted to kill them myself." Jeanne held Amée's gaze as she said it. "I wanted to kill both of them myself."

"What will those herbs do?" Walter interrupted, his voice shaky.

Amée kept her eyes on Jeanne. "Stop the bleeding and dull the pain." She paused. "Though I'm not sure I *should* dull the pain—it's nature's way of slowing a person down, and it sure seems like Jeanne needs to slow down before she gets herself killed."

The rebuke scratched at Jeanne, irritating her ready temper. If Amée was going to try and mother her, maybe she didn't understand as well as Jeanne had thought.

"You could go home now," Amée added softly. "Go be with your children."

"I can't," Jeanne said, her rage and ferocity still audible.

Pieter spoke up from the doorway. "This isn't what Olivier would want, Jeanne. Your life is more important. His killer is dead, and the threats to your safety—to the children's safety—are all gone. He'd want you to live. He'd want you to be with Oli and Little Jeanne."

Jeanne wanted to punch him. Why was he constantly trying to drag her away from the only thing she knew, the only thing she *was*? *You stand for mercy*, her mother had said, but it was a lie. Jeanne was justice—from head to toe, down to her marrow. She'd chosen it. She'd become it. Without it, she was nothing.

"Don't tell me what my husband would have wanted." Jeanne's voice was steel now, and a brief flicker of hurt passed across Pieter's face.

"Then what are you going to do?" Amée asked.

"I'm going to..." Jeanne's words trailed off, because what would she do? She couldn't cut down a dead man. But everything inside her screamed that it wasn't over. The room stayed silent as she seethed, then snarled her answer. "I'm going to keep fighting. I'm going to punish the French for supporting him, for grieving him. Someday, somehow, I'm going to find a way to kill Charles. I will not give up on Olivier—or Guillaume."

Pieter punched the doorframe, and Jeanne jumped at the crash of fist against wood.

"You're not giving up on them, Jeanne! They're avenged! There's no one left to stop."

It was so unlike him to lose control, even for a moment, but his frustration was pointed in the wrong direction. Jeanne wasn't the enemy; *France was*. Anyone who'd supported their king was. She'd been wrong before to think it was only Philip and Charles. She'd been wrong that this was it, that she could retire. Philip had side-stepped justice, and now Jeanne could never stop.

The only way to make France remember what they'd

done was to burn the whole goddamn lot of them to the ground.

## CHAPTER 61
# THE ENGLISH CHANNEL

They took three more ships before it happened.

Three more merchant ships—two burned to ash and scattered across the water, one still being pillaged by Jeanne's men. Three more crews at the bottom of the Channel. Three more fights with Jeanne clinging to her rage.

The third battle had just been won, and Jeanne and Amée were in her cabin, the younger woman's face drawn as she tended to yet another careless battle wound. A frantic knock sounded at the door. Jeanne jumped to her feet—her skin still tingling with the heat of battle—and Amée followed, scrambling to tie off her bandages.

"Come in!" Jeanne commanded, and her first mate, Gilbert, flung the door wide, his face dirty and blood-splattered from the fight.

"M'lady, they've found a nobleman! He was hiding below deck but came up crying when we lit the ship on fire."

Without waiting to hear more, Jeanne grabbed her axe and swept out of the cabin. The previous two ships had carried only merchants, no nobles. She may not have been able to kill the king, but the fury in her chest hummed at the idea of beheading another of his lackeys, striking at Philip even after death. She'd chop this one into pieces like they'd done to her husband. She'd send his head to Paris in a box. She'd—

Jeanne reached the deck, and her thoughts stopped short. All the heat, the rage, the despair wrapped in fury coursing through her body froze cold. Her crew had formed a ring around the nobleman, who must have been only thirteen or fourteen. His brown hair was mussed by the wind, his face was heart-shaped and friendly, his eyes were wide with fear, and his cheeks stained with tears. But it wasn't the tears that stole Jeanne's breath.

It was his face.

*Guillaume.*

The captured nobleman looked just like her son.

Over the years, she'd dreamed of that face thousands of times, hundreds of thousands of times. What would he look like now? What would he have grown into? Her son who would have been twelve now, had he lived. Her son who'd spent his days talking to fish and saving rabbits and carrying a cat around in a perpetual hug. Her son who would have made an incredible father, an incredible friend.

This was so close to the face she'd imagined, the one she'd held close to her heart.

The boy was kneeling before her now, trembling, his round cheeks shiny with tears, and something inside Jeanne broke. She couldn't do this. She couldn't take another Guillaume from the world.

This boy had a mother just like her. He had a life. Perhaps a cat he carried around in a perpetual hug. Perhaps a river full of fish he'd gurgled at. Perhaps a father who'd

THE LIONESS

carried him on his shoulders while he laughed until he could barely breathe.

Her men stared at her expectantly, and where once Jeanne would have taken that as a challenge, she found—as another crack opened up in her heart—that she didn't care what they thought. Instead she turned to Amée and Pieter, still with her because they hadn't stopped to re-stock the ship yet, and Walter, each standing quietly, bearing witness. Waiting. The only three people on this ship who mattered. The three who saw the king's death as Jeanne's triumph. The three who'd expected her to walk away.

If she walked away now, they would see it as strength, not weakness. They'd see it as justice. Could she see it that way too? She'd said mercy belonged where it was deserved. Wasn't this it?

She lowered her axe and spoke, her voice oddly soft to her own ears. "Stand, boy. Tell me your name."

The surprised crew shared a glance before releasing him. Jeanne's heart leaped as he stood before her and looked her full in the face. His eyes were so much like Guillaume's. The same shape. Same color. The same emotional depths.

"I'm Jacques, m'lady." His voice was so small.

Jeanne knew if she looked around, she'd see shock at every turn, but she only had eyes for the trembling boy. "Jacques," she said, "you look just like my son."

A strange tangle of feelings welled up inside her. She almost laughed, almost cried—she couldn't tell which emotion wanted to come out. She wanted to draw the boy into a hug, to kiss him on his sweet cheeks. And then suddenly, she longed for more than just Guillaume. She always missed Little Jeanne and Oli, but in that moment, it consumed her.

Blinking away the tears threatening to fall, she looked to her right where Pieter stood, calm and steady. Her mountain. Her friend. And she knew he was right.

She had won.

The king was dead. Charles was in custody. If she kept going—kept burning ships and beheading nobles—then it would no longer be about justice. She would be the one taking sons from their mothers, husbands from their wives. She would be putting the people she loved in danger for nothing more than her own warrior pride.

The other two cogs were floating a short distance away, so Jeanne motioned to her first mate. "Gilbert, choose a ship. Take whatever supplies you need, and whichever men. Return Jacques home to his mother in France, then return to Britain."

She glanced again at Jacques, and her heart swelled with love and grief. Guillaume was gone, but she wouldn't take another boy from his mother. The relief of the decision was astounding. It was a tension she hadn't even known she was carrying—but now it flew away, releasing her. The longing for Oli and Little Jeanne expanded in her chest. She wanted to see them. She wanted to be with them.

It was time for Jeanne to be Jeanne de Clisson. Not the bloody Lioness, but the mother, the lover, the friend.

## CHAPTER 62
# THE ENGLISH CHANNEL

J eanne left piracy the same way she started it—wholeheartedly and without looking back.

She stood on the deck that night, peering through the darkness toward the English shore, feeling the light breeze on her face. Amée was beside her, staring up instead of out, perhaps reading the stars.

"What do you see up there?"

"Nothing," Amée whispered, as sad as Jeanne had ever heard her. "I'm asking them what a person does if their life's purpose disappears, but they have no answers."

Jeanne's forehead wrinkled. "What do you mean?"

"I felt safe here." Amée smiled wryly. "Ironic, isn't it? The safest I've felt since Giselle died is on a pirate ship commanding ravens and treating wounds and playing cards with Pieter. I was part of something bigger than myself here. I was powerful. Essential. This ship gave me purpose, but now there's just emptiness ahead."

She glanced at Jeanne before continuing. "I was so scared you were going to die, I kept thinking I should talk some sense into you, convince you to stop. But if I'm honest, I didn't want to stop. I wanted us to go on like this forever, because now that it's over, who are we? Who am I?" She paused. "You know, I think I understand why you couldn't stop after Philip died. It's because it wasn't really about him anymore. Or the duke. It was about having a purpose."

*Merde*, Jeanne thought. Amée was right.

Jeanne's rage at the king's death hadn't entirely been rage—there was fear there, underneath. In truth, there was *always* something else underneath. Rage wasn't only rage, it was also fear and sadness and grief. Bottomless grief. Her anger had kept her floating above them all for years, but it didn't mean they weren't there.

"We'll find a new purpose," Jeanne's said, her voice suddenly strong. "If we keep going, then the duke has stolen not only Olivier and Guillaume's lives, but mine, yours, and Pieter's too. Not to mention the lives of all the nobles and merchants I've fought. You taught me that, Amée, when you asked me what justice looked like—not for them, but for myself."

"I know." Amée's voice was barely a whisper.

Jeanne took a deep breath, and some unnamed emotion —regret? release?—stole over her. "As a child, my mother taught me that my role was to rule my lands and balance out my husband's justice with mercy. The whole idea chafed at me; it was so wrong. But now I think maybe I understand that she didn't mean I had to *always* stand for mercy, but that I *could* stand for it where it was warranted. The king didn't deserve my mercy, but that boy did. His mother did. I couldn't kill him. I never felt like that before. I was just...done."

"I know," Amée said, "and it's selfish of me to be sad when you're getting your freedom and your life back. It's

THE LIONESS

just...there's nothing for me in England or in France. Giselle is dead. I ran away from my family because they're not safe. My place is here. I felt listened to here, valued, the right-hand man of the most powerful pirate on the Channel. The illusionist who'd created the greatest mythology of our time." She frowned. "Does that sound too proud? That I loved the power of being the one to give you blood-dyed sails and raven spies and the Black Knight of legend? But now I have to start over, and I'll be small again. Vulnerable again to men like Charles."

Jeanne's heart tripped over itself. How she loved Amée, not just for her tricks and cleverness, but for these moments, for letting Jeanne see her, for seeing Jeanne in return.

"You won't ever be small."

"But you're leaving me." Amée's face closed, the words a wall dropped between them.

Jeanne startled—she'd just assumed that wherever she went, Amée would come along. Pieter would go to Robine and once again be a father and a husband, but Walter and Amée would stay with her. She'd never imagined anything else. They were hers.

"Amée, no," she said with a laugh. "You're coming with me."

Amée blinked. "What?"

"I would never leave you behind."

Then Amée laughed aloud too, and tears tumbled down her cheeks. "So you weren't leaving me, you were just too presumptive to tell me?"

Jeanne shrugged. She supposed it had been presumptuous.

"Where are we going?" Amée asked.

"King Edward has offered us British-controlled lands in

Brittany, at a place called Hennebont." The familiar half-smile tugged at the corner of Jeanne's mouth. "And I think Hennebont could use a good astrologer."

And then Amée was crying in earnest, and Jeanne wrapped her arms around her—her heart fierce and motherly and protective—and the conversation shifted from what they'd lost to what they could now have. A castle. An herb garden. Ravens without cages. Lives without secrecy. Love without war.

# EPILOGUE
## HENNEBONT, BRITTANY

Alone in the woods, Jeanne breathed in the earthy green of a rainy spring. Somewhere along the way, she'd forgotten how much she loved that smell. Loved everything about the Breton countryside. The sight of ferns tumbling bright down the hillsides, the sucking sound of mud around her boots, the way the trees bent to dip their leaves into the rivers. And the quiet.

*God's nails*, she'd missed the quiet.

Every day, she walked the paths around Hennebont. For the rest of her life, she wanted to remember everything she loved. And not just remember them—revel in them.

The forest. The castle. Her people.

Pieter, to whom she'd given her lands on English soil and who'd promised to visit in the summer. He and Robine had married, and they now had two beautiful daughters. He'd been so effusive in his letters about their life that Jeanne half-suspected someone else had written them. Stoical Mont Pieter had become a poetic and enthusiastic father.

Little Jeanne, now seventeen, had married Jean

Harpedane, Lord of Montendre, and was a new mother herself. She'd grown into a graceful, joyful woman—not a fighter but a dancer, always sweeping through her gardens light on her toes with a baby on her hip.

Oli had grown up to be what everyone who knew him expected: a fierce warrior like his mother. He'd solemnly promised her that he wouldn't rest until he finished her work, and the duke had been dispatched to hell. The proclamation stirred something in Jeanne. Pride. Fear, maybe. She hadn't told him not to—he wouldn't have listened any more than she would have—but she hoped he didn't lose himself in the quest. That he still made space in his life for more than just revenge.

Or that life would conspire to make that space for him.

After all, her own life had been filled with people she loved, not because she'd put aside her revenge, but because they kept showing up and sneaking their way into her heart regardless.

Jeanne took one last inhale of the forest's greenery and started for home and two of the people who'd lodged themselves deepest in her soul.

Walter, her husband. A warrior and a quiet listener, the man who loved her for both her fierceness and her tenderness. The man who'd waited years for her to be ready for him.

And Amée. There weren't words for how Jeanne felt about Amée. Another daughter, given to her not by birth but by fate. The smartest person Jeanne knew. The one who'd given her the legends that swirled around her even now. Jeanne was grateful every day that Amée had come to Hennebont with them, and that gratitude took up all the space in her heart, pushing out the rage and grief and lingering guilt at justice not fully served, a quest never fully realized, that sometimes still tugged at her.

She turned along the path, and her castle came into view. Amée and Walter were both outside. Amée was in the dirt, close to the earth as usual, tending the herbs that grew along the property line. She wore skirts sometimes now at the house, though she still kept her hair short and ran her healing and astrology business in town as a man.

Walter walked toward Jeanne, his eyes alight with the same admiration they'd held the day they met. Jeanne marveled at how little changed—and how much—as the years piled atop each other.

Trailing him, a shadow within his shadow, was Monster—who'd borne witness to even more than the humans. She still slept in Jeanne's bed, despite Walter's complaints.

"You can leave," Jeanne had answered flatly the week before. "The cat stays." And the matter was resolved.

Thinking about it now, a smirk tugged at the corners of her mouth. But then Walter was in front of her, sweeping her into his arms and kissing her. Hand in hand, they walked back toward the castle, now with Monster in the lead.

As they passed Amée, she wiped her hands on her tunic, looped her arm through Jeanne's, and matched their pace —the lioness, the magician, the commander, and the damn devil-cat.

# Historical Endnote

The real Jeanne de Clisson died in 1359, a few years into her retirement with Sir Walter, who was her third or fourth husband depending on how you're counting. Despite being ten years her junior, he passed away that same year. I like to think they were meant to go on together.

The Duke of Brittany, Charles de Blois, was ransomed back to France in 1356. He was so grateful to god for his release that he decided to do a long pilgrimage barefoot in winter. When peasants tried to put down straw in the streets to soften his path, he apparently took another route. They say the man couldn't walk for fifteen weeks afterward.

Speaking of Charles—in reality, he was sainted *after* Jeanne's death. I chose to move the sainthood into the story because I couldn't stop thinking about how furious she would have been. You may be glad to know, as Jeanne would surely have been, that the sainthood didn't last—the Church was talked into rescinding it years later for political reasons. Today, Charles de Blois is beatified but not sainted.

Another fact Jeanne would have enjoyed is that her son

# HISTORICAL ENDNOTE

Olivier (known here as Oli) was instrumental in the battle that finally killed the duke in 1364 (the Battle of Auray), though he didn't strike the killing blow himself. He was as fierce as his mother and later became known as The Butcher.

Louise married one of Duke Charles' allies, inherited her brother's estate upon his death, and became a baroness. She died in 1383, likely having never reconciled with Jeanne.

Joanna la Flamme returned to England, and the rumors were that she lost her mind. It is perhaps more probable that this powerful woman had a disagreement with Edward and was held against her will to prevent her defying him as she had the French. She was confined in England until her death in 1374.

None of the people mentioned in this book would have known it then, but they lived against the backdrop of what we now call the Hundred Years War. It started with Philip and Edward's feuds, continued with the contested dukeship in Brittany (Charles de Blois versus Joanna's husband, John de Montfort, and then Joanna herself), and dragged on for many years beyond.

When we learn about the conflict in history class, we're mostly introduced to male names. History books refer to Jeanne as "Olivier's widow" or "Sir Walter Bentley's wife," but the truth is that during this conflict—and indeed throughout the Middle Ages—women were also often fighting hard for their families, values, and countries.

Books written for noblewomen encouraged them to learn the art of war. Joanna la Flamme was famous for telling the ladies of Hennebont to cut off their skirts and take up arms. And nobles of all genders saw themselves as

# HISTORICAL ENDNOTE

the warrior class—their role in life to support their kings, rule their lands, battle alongside their dukes, and defend their castles.

Which brings me to an important point—all the powerful warrior women Jeanne mentions throughout the book were real people (though I have changed the names of many, because apparently everyone was named Jeanne). Sybil of Anjou. Empress Matilda. Isabella the She-Wolf. Joanna (Jeanne) la Flamme (also known as Jeanne de Montfort or Jeanne de Flanders). Queen Philippa (the first black queen of England). Juliet (Jeanne) de Penthièvre (Duke Charles' duchess). Joan (also a Jeanne, King Philip's queen), who governed France while her husband rode off to do battle before eventually dying of the Black Plague. Amée is the only significant female character here who is a product entirely of my imagination.

Anytime I needed to write about Jeanne's rage, I thought about how furious it makes me that I never learned about these women in history class, that they were mere footnotes in a story always told through a male lens. This is a work of fiction, but it's also an attempt to remedy a false impression of Medieval Europe. Because *yes, there were warrior women. No, they weren't as rare as we think.* If this is a topic that interests you, Dr. Katrin Sjursen's doctoral thesis on warrior women is a wonderful read.

Speaking of rage, another myth about Medieval Europe that needs to be burned to the ground is that it was an all-white space. Anthropological evidence shows that Black people lived in London at least as far back as Roman times. Cross-continental trade routes were open, and literature and art from the period has plenty of myths, stories, and historical documentation of Black saints, knights, ambassadors, and peasantry.

# HISTORICAL ENDNOTE

Saint Maurice, who Pieter is mistaken for in the book, is an actual Christian saint. One of the Knights of the Round Table (Sir Morien) was Black. Queen Philippa was England's first Black queen and her son, Edward of Woodstock, was known as The Black Prince. And if you pay attention, you'll find plenty of other references, paintings, myths, and stories that tell us that Europe was a more diverse place than we've been taught. If this interests you, one easily digestible source of info is *medievalpoc.tumblr.com*, and the work of Dr. Cord Whitaker—to whom I owe a great debt of gratitude in my own research—is well worth seeking out.

Documenting Jeanne's life in a world where she's a footnote in most history books was no easy task. Where facts are known, I generally tried to stick with them, though I've also made exceptions for good storytelling—for example shortening timelines, dramatizing certain events, taking a firm stance on Olivier's innocence (which is by no means certain), and changing the timing of Charles' sainthood for maximum impact. Where the facts weren't clear or historians seemed to disagree, I've opted for the version of her story that felt most interesting and aligned with the kind of person I imagined her to be.

If you want to try and tease fact from fiction, the most thorough and easy-to-read resource I found on the truth of Jeanne's life is Dr. Katrin Sjursen's article published in *Medieval Elite Women and the Exercise of Power 1100-1400: Moving Beyond the Exceptionalist Debate*.

Untangling truth from myth is near-impossible when it comes to Jeanne de Clisson, so I've very purposefully let the characters in on the joke—having them recognize, laugh about, and harness the power of myth and rumor. I'm sure some of what's made it into this book is just that, and that's part of the point. History is not pure, unadulterated truth.

## HISTORICAL ENDNOTE

It's a collection of perspectives deeply influenced by the person telling the story (nearly always a powerful white man) and the time in which they were written down, painted, or passed along by spoken word.

# ACKNOWLEDGMENTS

Let's start with Gladys Qin—mentor, friend, exceptional writer. After 100+ agent rejections and more than a little fear that this book would never see the light of day, you chose me for mentorship in Pitch Wars and changed my career. Thank you for guiding me through this book's revisions with such incredible skill, thoughtfulness, and kindness. I am forever grateful to you for paving my path into publishing and making this book what it is today.

Next, Lani Frank. Your keen eye for detail, exceptional editorial skill, and friendship all mean so much to me. Thank you for making this book fit for readers. There's no one I'd rather work with.

Additional thanks to early readers, including Dr. Emily Peppers, Barb Benfante, Linda Walker, Kerra Bolton, Elisa and her book club, Daniela Petrova, Jessica Lewis, and Kate Dwyer. To both my agents—who fought for this book for years—Veronica Park and Paige Terlip. To Meara and Ada for sensitivity reads and consults. To Scream Town for the screams. To The No Drama Zone for not living up to its name.

No acknowledgements would be complete without David De la Rosa (my ride-or-die forever) and Andrei (thank you for holding me as tenderly as you hold my words). You both make my writing and my life better every single day.

An *enormous* thank you to Jason Porath and the Rejected

Princesses blog, where I first fell in love with the wild, brutal story of Jeanne de Clisson. You started me down a research rabbit hole of Medieval lady warriors and I am forever grateful.

Another substantial thanks to the incredible historians who shared their work, answered my questions, and pointed me in the direction of other great historians and resources—especially Katie Sjursen, Professor Cord Whitaker, Professor Sharon Farmer, and Professor Michael Bailey. And to accessible online resources like Medieval-POC. Any errors or embellishments in this book are mine and not the fault of these brilliant historians and researchers.

Finally, *no thanks* to the men who tried to write women like Jeanne out of history and to so many men like the king who—still today—continue to kill for the sake of maintaining their power (and think it shall have no consequences). May you have the lives and afterlives you deserve.

# ABOUT THE AUTHOR

GIGI GRIFFIS writes edgy, feminist historical stories for adults and teens, including *The Wicked Unseen, We Are the Beasts,* and *The Empress* (as seen on Netflix). She's a sucker for little-known histories, "unlikable" female characters, and all things Europe.

After almost ten years of seminomadic life, she now lives in Portugal with an opinionated Yorkie mix named Luna and a collection of very nerdy books. While she has never sought vengeance on the English Channel, she did visit the ruins of Jeanne de Clisson's castle and just might have paid her respects to the piratess's ghost.

GIGIGRIFFIS.COM

# ALSO BY GIGI GRIFFIS

FOR ADULTS

*The Empress*

~

FOR YOUNG ADULTS

*The Wicked Unseen*

*We Are the Beasts*

Milton Keynes UK
Ingram Content Group UK Ltd.
UKHW032056231124
451423UK00013B/991